## Books by Cheyenne Meadows

*Wind Warriors*

Tiger's Lily
Loco
Summer's Night
Sky's Lark
Silver Spoon
Blue Blood's Trifecta
Ghost's Treasure

*Sexy Snax*

Triad
Broken Bridges

*Single Titles*

Turbulent Rain
Worth Fighting For
Cowgirl Up

Worth Fighting For

ISBN # 978-1-78651-356-4

©Copyright Cheyenne Meadows 2016

Cover Art by Posh Gosh ©Copyright 2016

Interior text design by Claire Siemaszkiewicz

Totally Bound Publishing

Published in 2016 by Totally Bound Publishing, Newland House, The Point, Weaver Road, Lincoln, LN6 3QN, United Kingdom.

# WORTH FIGHTING FOR

## CHEYENNE MEADOWS

# Dedication

For all those service men and women who return home to start new lives. Thank you for all you've done.

# Chapter One

"Mr. Delaney, I presume?"

Dusty glanced up from his seat on a bale of straw, where he was repairing a halter. Ben, his Belgian Malinois, sat beside him. He told the dog to stay before answering. "Yeah."

A woman stood at the entrance to the stable with the sun at her back, outlining her like a bright angel. As she strode closer the glare receded, allowing him to see details of his visitor.

She wore jeans and a T-shirt, a common enough outfit in this part of the country. Her oval face spoke of curiosity and determination, while her movements snapped with contained energy. Medium-length dark-blonde hair, which had been pulled back into a ponytail, bobbed with each step. Wispy, short bangs that curled slightly at the ends fluttered in the light breeze, adding to her youthful and innocent appearance. Grace defined each movement, as if she were well versed in physical activity. Considering her slender form and the toned arms he glimpsed, she probably spent her fair share of time working out. A runner, most likely, with that lithe yet athletic build.

With a few more steps, she drew closer. He scented a light floral fragrance, noted the feminine curves of her body and felt his cock sit up and take notice. Intelligent blue eyes the color of a morning sky met his gaze.

Grumbling under his breath, he berated himself for reacting so quickly to the fairer sex. As if he hadn't been badly burned by women in the past.

"What can I do for you?"

"I'm looking for a stable to board my horse and I hear you're the best."

He stood, uncomfortable with her standing over him. Primitive instincts made the position unacceptable. He topped her by nearly a full head and probably doubled her in weight, yet she didn't appear nervous or back up an inch.

He ignored the compliment. He enjoyed his job, loved the animals and pampered them like prized pets. Horses were in his blood. The 'best' treaded the line of subjectivity, but he didn't really care what others thought. He did what he'd always dreamed of doing and left it at that. "What do you want to know?"

She glanced around the airy room, where several stalls sat empty. After feeding the horses their morning meal, he'd put them out to pasture for the day. Horses needed room to stretch their legs, grass to graze on and simply to do what nature intended — be a horse.

"Let's start with what you charge."

He placed the halter down on his makeshift chair. "Two hundred per month per head. That includes everything — feed, grooming and farrier service. The only extra expense you might incur is a vet bill. I cover the basic vaccinations, but anything over is yours."

"I see." She glanced around the room before her gaze landed on him once more. Interest and intrigue sparked in her baby-blue eyes. He found the sight somewhat captivating. "Do you offer training?"

"Yeah, but that's extra, depending upon what you're interested in. Anything from basic saddle breaking to specialized advanced training. I can do just about anything with a Western saddle, but draw the line at dressage and jumping. Since I have no experience in such, I don't feel comfortable trying to teach a horse how to do all those fancy maneuvers."

"I'm just looking for trail riding, at most. Nothing fancy."

"That's doable then." He appreciated her professional questions, much preferring to clarify particulars now rather than after the fact. His contracts spelled out everything, but he'd noticed that few boarders ever bothered to read the detailed pages. Not his problem. He put forth the information, so legally he was covered.

She gestured to the stalls. "How much stall time versus pasture?"

"I bring them in at night, unless you want them to be on full-time pasture. They're grained twice a day. Pregnant mares occasionally three times, depending on their needs."

"Oh, I won't be getting one of those. I'm going to adopt from the Humane Society farm. In fact, I'm going there next to choose one."

Her revelation shocked him. Not that she appeared wealthy and uppity, but he rarely ran into anyone who wanted less than a gently raised horse with perfect manners. Though none of his business, curiosity prodded him to pursue her reasoning further. "Why would you want one from there? Hell, there's plenty of well-bred animals around here with rich bloodlines and sound training. With the Humane Society it's a crapshoot."

The woman straightened her spine and pinned Dusty with her gaze. "Some of them have seen the worst the human race has to offer, yet they persevered and triumphed over the odds, able to find trust in the wake of inconceivable torture. To me, those horses are diamonds in the rough and wear badges of courage. I'll take a battle-tested and scarred horse over a paddock raised one any day."

He studied her face for a long moment then nodded slightly. *Give her credit for standing up for the underdog and for a kind heart.* He'd seen too many instances of abuse and neglect in his lifetime and each situation had disgusted him to no end. Sometimes he'd been able to step up and help. Other times his hands had been tied. Yet he commended the little lady for her beliefs and for opening her door to a rescued horse.

The words replayed in his mind, hitting home with power. *'Battle-tested and scarred'.* Not just in relation to her pick of animal, either. Unwilling to dwell further, he drew his attention back to the business proposition. He headed through his office door, grabbed a couple of pages of paper and quickly returned to her. "Here's the contract. Pick out your horse, lady, then have them drop it off here."

"My name is April, not lady." She met his gaze steadily while taking the paperwork.

He inclined his head in acknowledgment.

"Thank you." She smiled victoriously. "I know this will be the most wonderful home a horse could hope for." With those final words, she walked out of the stable and back to her car.

The action, combined with the sassy sway of her hips, sent a sharp jolt straight to his groin. *Don't get your water hot, SEAL. You've learned your lesson about women the hard way.* With one more look, he turned away and went back to work.

* * * *

"Oh my. So many choices." April glanced over at her host, the director of the Humane Society farm, then back to the pasture full of a whole herd of beautiful animals. Horses of all colors grazed peacefully, dotting a vast field. While the sizes varied, their predicaments remained the same. All were homeless and looking for a special person to adopt them and love them for the rest of their lives. Sad but a common enough reality, not only with horses, but with other animals as well these days.

"I'm afraid so. Seems the poor economy hit horses pretty hard. People could no longer afford to keep them. Some were simply dumped to range free on their own, while others were abandoned when their owners moved away."

"So frustrating and irresponsible." April's gut clenched at the woman's words. She, of course, knew such things happened, but to see in person the animals that had been abandoned made everything more real.

"There's worse. We've had several neglect and starvation cases. Those really make you want to cry for the animal and beat the person responsible for such horrible conditions."

"I can imagine." April shuddered. She'd seen pictures of gaunt horses on the Humane Society's website as before pictures. Never did she want to see another animal so starved that they could hardly stand. She respected the workers at the farm even more for their caring and for the emotional toll such cruelty had to take on their souls.

Needing to change the morbid subject, April gestured toward the animals. "Can you give me some recommendations? I'd originally thought about Duke, but now that I've seen other horses, I'm indecisive again."

Lois, the director, nodded. "This is just a few of them. There's another pasture to our left and the stables to the right. Let's go visit some of them and see if anything clicks."

"Great." April followed along.

An hour later, she still teetered on the fence. All the horses had their own attributes, yet none of them stood out from the crowd. She'd heard numerous stories, petted many noses, but couldn't seem to narrow down her choice any more than when she'd stepped out of her SUV earlier.

"Nothing yet, huh?" Lois asked with a knowing look.

"No. I don't know what's wrong with me. All of them are sweet and wonderful."

"Don't worry." Lois patted her arm. "It's always hard to choose the right one. In my experience, the horse chooses you."

"Okay." The words only provided a hair more hope for her quickly sinking spirit. After scrimping and saving for years and finally deciding to take the leap to horse ownership, she couldn't settle on a single one. The potential of leaving empty-handed loomed like a dark cloud of failure over her head.

"Come on. There's a few more horses to see." Lois led the way back toward the stable. "Maybe one of them will catch your eye. If not, you know, we're always getting more in.

Some people visit several times before finding their match."

April nodded, but pressure to choose that day weighed heavily on her shoulders. She'd set up everything, including the stable space. The last thing she wanted to do was call the stable owner and tell him to put her space on hold for another six months or longer. Her heart ached at the thought of waiting weeks more for her lifelong dream to take flight.

As they headed toward the main area, April noticed a round pen to the side. A pure white miniature horse stood in the center. "How adorable."

Lois paused and grinned. "That's Mischief. He's quite the ham and definitely lives up to his name."

April moved toward the round pen, noting another horse in the enclosure. She stepped up to the gate and peered over. Sure enough, Mischief lifted his head and turned toward her as if sizing her up. He whinnied and trotted right to her, a large-boned dapple gray filly at his side. Both snuffled her, Mischief at her waist, the taller horse at her neck. April rubbed both of their heads and giggled when the filly tickled her neck with a *whuff* of air. The three rails allowed plenty of room for the mini to stick his head through and the taller filly to put her head over the top board.

"That's amazing." A new voice carried to April.

She kept stroking the horses, yet turned to find a middle-aged man staring at them in astonishment.

"Yes, it is," Lois answered with a wide grin, and turned her attention back to April. "What do you think of them?"

April couldn't wipe the happiness from her face as both horses begged for her to scratch their heads. "They're wonderful. So pretty. And friendly." Using her short nails, she rubbed under the filly's halter as she leaned into the touch, a signal that she definitely wanted more.

"That's just it. Miracle, the gray filly you're petting, is leery of everyone."

April blinked at the oversized pet. "You're kidding."

Lois approached slowly. "Nope. If you look over her

flanks and rump, you'll see some small white marks."

April squinted, and made out several lines nearly blending in with the pretty colors of Miracle's hide. "Now I see them."

"Whip scars."

April gasped. Miracle lifted her head, stared at her and stretched her neck in order to lip at her hair.

"She was one of the worst abuse cases we've ever seen. Starved nearly to death. Could barely stand. Full of parasites, rain rot. You name it, she had it." Lois leaned on the fence and played with Mischief's forelock. "We thought we were going to lose her a dozen times. Yet each time she rallied, partially in thanks to Mischief here."

"They're bonded?"

"Yep. Came from the same place, actually, only she was in much worse condition. We couldn't separate them without both of them becoming very upset. So they've stayed together all along. Even share the same stall."

Her gaze raked the two horses even as her heart bled at what they had both suffered. Something inside clicked. No way could she turn her back on such needy animals. If the filly truly was as skittish as Lois indicated, she might be Miracle's only hope of finding a suitable and happy home for the rest of her natural life. Decided, April lifted her chin. "I'll take them."

Lois looked at her with a serious expression. "Miracle isn't broken to ride. In fact, the vet says she might not be sound for more than a quick ride around the pasture now and again. The starvation probably left permanent physical issues. Her best option might be as a companion horse or pasture pet, a friend and beautiful creature to crop grass in your pasture."

April swallowed. She'd wanted a horse to ride, but had no plans on showing or jumping. Simply saddling up and hitting a trail or toddling around the pasture. No matter. Miracle had picked her and April wasn't about to turn her back on the gray filly. "That's okay. The most I would do anyway is trail ride. Trotting through the pasture works just as well." She laughed when Miracle nudged her with her head, blatantly asking for more attention. Lightly caressing the horse, she knew no matter what, Miracle would come home with her. She'd never forgive herself if she ignored their cause and walked away.

"You mentioned you're stabling her." Lois rotated to face her.

"Yes."

"There's something you need to know. Miracle isn't just leery of everyone, she's afraid of men. Put her in a corner and she'll bite and kick at a man just for being near. I won't lie, she's put the fear of God into some of the workers around here. Kicked a couple who weren't paying enough attention."

The puzzle pieces snapped together. "A man beat her once." April whispered the words, understanding easily why the filly would act up.

"That's what we think too. But that lends another problem for you. How is she going to tolerate a man at the stable?"

The heavy weight of worry about a nearly impossible issue settled over April. She'd come this close, finding the horses she couldn't leave without. Now a big monkey wrench was jamming her dream from coming to fruition. She frowned and racked her brain. "There's only one man that runs the stable. Maybe she can learn to tolerate him?" Surely someone who worked around horses each and every day would possess the skills needed to deal with a frightened filly?

Idly she considered the other boarders, but quickly dismissed the concerns. Those people would come and go. It' the owner Miracle would see every day. He'd care for her individually when she had to work. Thus, her trust rested on him.

"Which stable, dear?"

"Delaney Stable in Sunset."

Lois glanced back at the man still standing there watching

them, then met April's anxious gaze and nodded. "Dusty Delaney has a reputation."

"I've heard he's the best around with horses."

Lois laughed. "Oh, he's wonderful with horses. It's women he doesn't care for in the least."

April blinked. Not that his personal life interested her. Yet her inquisitive nature pushed her for a clarification. "He's gay?"

"Nah. Just got a hold of a couple of piss-poor women is all. Soured him on the rest. But with horses, he's as good as they come."

"So that means…"

"If you want them both, we'll let you adopt them."

April kissed Miracle's nose in celebration. "Did you hear that? You're coming home with me."

Mischief snorted and rubbed his head against her thigh, as if he'd known that all along.

# Chapter Two

The rumble of a truck pulling into the long, winding, gravel driveway that separated the stable from the country road snared Dusty's attention. Another aspect that had not only drawn him to this place, but had prodded him to purchase, the long distance from the road decreased noise, discouraged unnecessary visitors and gave him the vantage point to see who cared to stop by long before they ever stepped from a vehicle. The stable itself, painted a cheerful light blue, sat on the summit of a sizable hill with the pastures dropping away on all sides. He preferred to occupy the highest ground, a carryover from his SEAL days and time spent on the front lines. Safety and a sense of security came from surrounding himself with familiar landscape, one he could easily defend, if necessary.

Two rows of stalls bracketed a fairly decent-sized aisle with a dirt floor. Not nearly as fancy as cement or even the tile covering many thoroughbred farms used, but functional. Large sliding doors closed off the west end of the stable during cold months, but stayed open all summer long, encouraging cool breezes to lower temperatures for comfort. The stalls were made from wood on all sides, strong steel wire mesh in the door so even the foals could see out, with each door opening to the aisle. Every stall sported a window to the outside, which could be opened or shut depending upon the animal's needs. An open area waited at the east end of the row of stalls, affording him room for feed, hay, straw and all the supplies any reputable stable might possess. Right past the storage area, a door led directly into his kitchen. The house was modest by most standards, but the close proximity to his work, while still providing for his basic needs, suited him.

Behind the stable stood another building, this one a smidgen smaller and shorter, an oversized garage of sorts. He used this space, complete with a cement floor, to store his two horse trailers and his truck when not in use. No sense letting big-ticket items sit outside, encouraging a less moral person to try to whisk them away. A thick chain and padlock served as deterrents.

From the moment he'd stepped on the property, he'd known he wanted to spend the rest of his life here, nestled in the pastures, hills and nearby woods, caring for the animals he knew best — horses. The setup called to him, even though the former owners had let things fall into disrepair. Hours and weeks of hard labor had brought the stable back to a state of glory and pride and he'd never looked back since.

Setting the hayfork aside, he stepped outside to check out who'd disturbed his afternoon. Ben, as always, trotted at his heels. The dog rarely ventured far, certainly never out of sight, another habit born of their time together in the combat zone. He brushed his fingers over Ben's head and watched as a white truck entered the lane, a black stock trailer attached to the hitch.

He'd received a call yesterday from the woman who'd showed up unannounced that morning. She'd picked out a couple of horses at the Humane Society farm and they'd be arriving this afternoon. Curiosity piqued as he wondered about the animals she'd chosen. Two, she said. Nothing more.

He never minded taking in new horses, but something about the woman bugged him. Her tenacity, her smile, the swing of those hips. His mind kept replaying their interaction through the day yesterday, leaving his jeans a bit too tight. Odd, especially since he didn't have much to do with women past a one-night stand these days. No commitment, no expectations, no jerking him around to suit their own needs. He preferred his women fast, hot and as a flyby. The woman, April, didn't fit into the previous category, yet he couldn't quite flush her from his thoughts.

Stepping out into the bright heat of late summer in Colorado, he noticed the stock trailer backing up to the large open door to the stables. Automatically, he waved the man closer before holding up his hand in a signal to stop, allowing plenty of room to unload the animals and lead them directly into the stalls.

A door opened and shut. He glanced around to find April hurrying back toward the trailer, her typical ponytail swishing with each step. Denim jeans were painted onto her lower body, sculpting her flared hips like an artist's graceful touch. The tucked-in T-shirt showed off her modest breasts and outlined the rest of her figure. Together with a bright smile of happiness, she radiated beauty and salvation. The combination caught his interest enough that he chastised himself, recalling what vipers women could be.

"We're here." Her light, cheery voice carried easily to him. Though soft, the tone reminded him of a meadowlark's call. Uplifting and intoxicating.

*Get a grip, SEAL.*

Ben trotted over and sniffed at the woman. Normally cool with strangers, he seemed to take instantly to the newest boarder, judging by the wagging tail and dog smile. She grinned and patted him with affection. "Aren't you a pretty boy?"

Mentally shaking his head, Dusty reached for the latch on the trailer.

"Oh, you better let me." April insinuated herself between Dusty and the gate.

The act set his back teeth to grinding. He'd been raised around horses all his life and had performed the mundane feat of removing horses from a trailer countless times. The fact that she pushed him aside like he didn't have a clue irritated him to no end. "Lady, I can assure you I'm more than capable of unloading stock."

April spun around and blinked up at him, surprise and

regret on her face. "I'm sorry. I didn't mean to imply you couldn't do it. It's just... There's a reason I need to collect them."

He scowled.

She sighed. "I'll explain in a minute. Please just bear with me?"

He read the truth in her blue eyes and gave a brisk nod. Whatever her excuse, he'd hear it soon enough.

She unlatched the gate and swung it open.

He secured the gate to the side and stared into the trailer. His eyes landed on a solid white miniature horse. Totally surprised, he could only gape. He'd seen them now and again, mainly in parades. Didn't think of them as much more than oversized dogs. Certainly, they were made to be pets and had little use outside of possibly pulling a cart. This particular one stood perhaps a little over three and a half feet high at the withers, putting his head right around Dusty's stomach level, and about the size of a runt Shetland pony. He only hoped he didn't trip over the bred-down version of a horse.

Looking farther, he found a dark dappled gray filly, eye-catching with the swirls of color over her body. A white tail brushed the ground while a matching mane hung to the left side of her neck, loose and light as if each lock had been brushed out daily to a glorious shine. If her looks alone garnered attention, her build would keep anyone familiar with horses fixated with awe. Her long legs and fine lines spoke of exceptional breeding, thoroughbred if he didn't miss his guess. With a sturdy confirmation, muscular hindquarters and wide chest, she appeared more than capable of hitting the racetrack and dashing past any and all challengers. He couldn't imagine how such a beautiful and refined animal ended up at the Humane Society rather than living her years at a breeding farm producing the next generation of champions.

April latched onto the filly's halter with equal parts confidence and gentleness, then clicked her tongue. The horse followed her without a single complaint, until she spotted him. Then the animal set her feet and refused to budge, wide eyes locked on Dusty.

"Would you please step back, preferably out of sight?" April's voice came across soft and coaxing as she whispered to her new addition.

Dusty did as bidden, moving to the side of the trailer, shielding himself from the filly's vision.

Tugging on the halter, April managed to get the filly moving once more, stepping out of the trailer together. She paused long enough to call over her shoulder. "Come on, Mischief."

The mini stood at the end and peered down as if judging the distance. He looked up at April, who led the filly deeper into the stable. A loud whinny pierced the air.

April paused and turned around. "Now, Mischief. We went through this earlier. You received your treat when you got in and you'll only get your treat when you get back out." She held out her hand and opened her fingers. Two sugar cubes sat in her palm.

Mischief stretched his neck out, then appeared to figure out the only way to obtain the sugar was to comply. He jumped out on a hop and trotted up to the pair waiting on him, taking his treat from her hand and eating with relish.

Dusty shook his head, amazed and amused at the antics of the mini. He'd give the horse credit for brains and cuteness. Still didn't sell him on the idea of raising them, but his job revolved around caring for her animals, not debating the pros and cons of owning such small horses.

After unhooking the gate, he shut the metal barrier and secured it tightly before turning his attention back to April. "Let's put them in the two end stalls."

"Actually, they need to share the same stall." She grabbed Mischief's lead and absently scratched his head.

Dusty frowned and closed the distance between them, only to come up short when the filly swung his direction, flattened her ears and cocked her rear leg in preparation for delivering a vicious kick. He read the horse's body language instantly and began to speak to her in low soothing tones as April had done before. "You're okay, pretty girl. I'm not going to harm a single hair on that dappled body." He sidestepped slowly and cautiously, staying out of the reach of the agitated horse, making his way around to a larger stall on the far wall. "Put them in here."

Once he opened the stall door and stepped back, April led them both inside. After they were fully inside, he closed the door, cracking it enough to let April back out when she removed the lead ropes from both their halters. He secured the latch before turning on her. "Care to tell me what's up with these two?"

She nodded. "Just a second. Let me get my stuff from the truck so the driver can be on his way." She trotted off, opened the passenger door, collected her purse and a couple of folders, then bade the man thanks and farewell.

Heading back over, she handed him the brightly colored folders. "Here are their records. The contracts are filled out and in there as well."

He opened the red one and sucked in a breath at the pictures staring back at him—the gray filly so thin flesh pulled tightly over bones. His gut erupted in fiery anger even as he immediately forgave her for her earlier aggression. Not aggression. Fear. He recalled the widened eyes and spark of terror that had sent ripples over the filly's body. Scanning the information, he discovered she had every right to act up. "Damn."

April stood at the stall door. The top of the wood partition hit her at shoulder height, allowing her to peek at her horses while giving the animals ample opportunity to check out the entire stable from their individual stalls, all except the miniature horse that lacked the vertical height to do so. He had to peer through the metal holes of the stall door. "Yeah. Breaks your heart."

He shut the folder but couldn't dispel the stark images from his mind. Stepping over, he stood next to April and stared at the newest members of his stable family. "The mini keeps her calm?"

"Yeah. They were at the same horrible place together. Bonded there, I guess. Anyway, the Humane Society said Mischief was the only thing that kept Miracle going some days. She'd have given up except for him. They were inseparable from day one. Always together. Trying to get them apart causes an uproar and a lot of stress for them both."

He studied the animals in the bright daylight streaming through the windows. Both were clean and appeared quite healthy, certainly showing no hint of what they'd been through.

Miracle shifted to her left, checking out the thick straw, sending illumination across her pretty hide and revealing long white lines across her back and hindquarters.

Dusty's rage grew. "Someone beat her."

April nodded sadly. "She carries several scars. I can only image the horrors she faced." Twisting, she faced him. "The Humane Society says you're a magician with horses. The only reason they let me adopt them is because they knew you'd work with Miracle and her issues with skill and great care. She fears men, is hesitant around everyone else. Yet she came right over. Chose me. I couldn't leave her behind." She bit her lip and her gaze dropped. "I know she's going to be a challenge, and I realize I'm asking a lot. But I'll pay whatever in addition for you to work with her, help her learn to trust again." Her blue eyes lifted and met his gaze.

His heart lurched. He'd have to be an absolute bastard to refuse her after she'd asked so kindly, even offering to pay extra for the time he would need to spend with the traumatized filly. Not to mention he felt for the animal after just reading a brief summary of what she'd endured.

Something nagged him as he stared into her face. Her words went deeper than the obvious. Unwilling to open that particular can of worms, he focused his attention back on the unusual pair of horses in the stall and made his decision.

He couldn't turn his back on either of them any more than he could build rain clouds and order a soaking shower.

"She's home now. I can't make any promises, but I'll give her my best shot."

A smile spread on April's face. "Thank you."

April breathed a sigh of relief at Dusty's words. In all honesty, she hadn't been sure he'd be accommodating of her pick of horses. While Mischief might be a handful in his own right, Miracle would take hours of patient work in order to bolster her confidence in the human race. Even then, the outcome teetered in the balance.

She'd asked around and researched nearby stables over the past few weeks. One name kept coming up. Dusty Delaney. Everything she'd found lavished praise on the man and his way with the large beasts. With just a bit over a mile separating her rental house from his property, she'd felt the stars lined up too perfectly to be a coincidence. Meeting the man, she'd found him intriguing and tough, yet he had to have a softer side when horses were involved. She'd just seen the first glimpse.

She'd watched his face when Miracle had flagrantly warned him off and again when he opened her file. The tightening of his lips as he'd looked at the pictures and sharp intake of breath told her he'd been just as affected by the cruel abuse and neglect as she. His mood had remained unchanged in dealing with Miracle's threat—calmness and a soothing tone had emerged. Both instances had impressed her and her confidence in the man had soared.

Out of the corner of her eye, she studied him. Tall and built came to mind. Short black hair topped his head while chocolate-brown eyes sparked with sharpness and intelligence. A dimpled chin promised stubbornness while his dark five o'clock shadow added a certain down-to-earth roughness. He carried himself with confidence and appeared totally comfortable with his body and abilities.

Each motion could be called graceful and easy, as if he expended little energy to accomplish each task, reminding her of a jungle cat, smooth yet predatory. A sturdy frame carried plenty of muscles, judging by the ripped arms displayed by the short-sleeved shirt and the jeans outlining a rear she'd love to squeeze. In all honesty, the man was gorgeous.

*I wonder what he tastes like.* Watching his face, she idly pondered what the stubble on his face would feel like against her skin. Abrasive in a sensual way, or magically stimulating as he rubbed his cheeks against her inner thighs, well on his way to exploring her secret parts?

She blinked at the thought, completely unlike her. She'd pretty much given up on men after three disastrous short-term dating relationships. The first boyfriend had used her as a fill-in until he found someone he desired more. April had thought she loved the man, thrown herself into making him happy, and found herself alone when he'd caught another woman, this one prettier, fancier and obviously a ton more experienced.

The second fell into the category of arrogant and egotistical. He'd seemed charming enough until she'd spent more time with him and learned he viewed the world as if it revolved around him. Everything was his, about him, and pertained to him. He cared little for anyone else and put women down more times than not. His outdated male chauvinist view on a woman's place in life left her offended and angry.

Just when she regained the courage to date once more, she'd stumbled across a devil in disguise. He might have been in the same English class in college, but they truly were worlds apart otherwise. What started out as a promising relationship had soon turned downright ugly. Smiles and laughter had gradually transformed into harsh criticism and yelling. One night he'd slapped her. That marked the end of the road for that particular man and for her interest in dating. After the last debacle, she'd thrown her arms up in surrender and focused on her own life. If she ended up a spinster, so be it. Better than a life saddled to a dipstick, especially one who specialized in domestic violence.

Giving up on the dream of finding a life partner, April had poured herself into work and her dream of horse ownership after becoming a nurse. Who needed a man when she could provide for herself and live out her own life?

Maybe that was why she'd gravitated to Miracle. They had both suffered at the hands of men and carried deeply embedded scars as a result.

"I don't know how to thank you." She whispered the words as she watched Mischief try to groom Miracle. Due to his short stature, he only managed to nibble on her lower shoulder. April couldn't help but smile at the warm gesture.

"No problem." Dusty shrugged.

She noted the muscles contract and nearly licked her lips. Powerful mass rippled under his shirt, snaring her attention and stoking her recently awakened libido.

*My hormones must be in ample supply.* What other reason could there be for her to be suddenly not only aware of the yummy man standing next to her but be more than interested in seeing him naked?

With a shake of her head, she stepped away from the stall. "What time will you be feeding them tonight and in the morning?"

He turned toward her, leaning his back against the wood. "In about three hours for dinner and around seven for breakfast."

"Okay. I can come back at those times."

He arched an eyebrow. "Why?"

"To help you feed my horses. Or did you already forget Miracle thinks you're the next best thing to a hungry mountain lion?"

The corners of his mouth hitched up in a slight grin. "Lady, the day I can't convince a horse that eating is more fun than trying to take a bite out of my hide, it's time to retire."

She found the smile as contagious as his amusing

statement. For some reason, he put her at ease. No warning bells went off in her head each time she stepped into the stable. Even with him a foot away earlier, she felt nothing but attraction. A novel experience for the past four years — a promising sign and a welcome arrival. Although she didn't have a clue how to process her interest in the man. Lois said he didn't care for women, yet he seemed kind enough to her.

*I've been wrong before.* She tamped down the small flicker of hope with reality. If he only took care of her horses like others reported, she'd consider him a hero.

"Fair enough." She couldn't keep the humor out of her voice. "Still, I want to spend a large chunk of time with them. What time can I arrive in the morning?"

"I'm normally up by six," he answered flatly, his eyes raking over the area.

The dog trotted up, his tongue hanging out as he panted. She scratched behind his ears and let her silliness run free for a moment. "I'll try to be around after that time. Don't want to rouse you from bed and risk finding out what you actually wear in the line of pajamas."

He blinked at her as if the statement surprised him. She grinned at his obvious puzzlement. For the first time in forever, she found herself relaxing and actually teasing a man. April reveled in the rare luxury.

With one more pat on the dog's head, she walked out of the doors and into the near-stifling afternoon heat.

"Where are you going?" Dusty's voice stopped her in her tracks.

"Home."

"In what? There's no car here."

She shrugged. "I didn't want to keep the Humane Society worker waiting. Besides, I only live about a mile away. The exercise will do me good."

Dusty muttered under his breath she couldn't quite make out. He shook his head and pulled keys from his jeans pocket as he strode over. "Come on. Ben, *hier bleiben und zusehen.*"

"I don't understand." She tilted her head in question, noting the dog laid down in the shade at the stable's entrance and stared at them with keen yellow eyes.

He paused and met her gaze. "It's boiling out here, for one. Not to mention there's no sidewalk on these country roads. The way idiots fly over these hills, they'll smash you before you know what happened. Personally, I'd prefer to avoid road kill. Dead clients don't pay their stable bill."

She blinked at him, then automatically followed him to the large black truck. Granted, she didn't know this man from Adam, but something inside locked onto his inner goodness. Not every man would see a damsel in distress and offer to drive her home.

The thought comforted her as she hopped into the passenger seat and grinned warmly at the man who stepped up to the plate in more ways than one. "I seem to be thanking you a lot today."

He shoved the key in the ignition, started the engine and pulled out into the road.

Though he remained mute, his actions spoke volumes.

# Chapter Three

Dusty glanced up as April hopped out of her dark blue SUV and headed in his direction. He checked his watch. She'd been gone for a whole hour and a half.

A sigh of resignation escaped his lips. Women weren't his strong suit, and why this one had caught his interest, he would never know. The last one he'd dated had taught him a hard lesson he hadn't thought of testing until now. Something about the cheerful blonde with the pretty body made him toss out past wrongs and want to reconsider his earlier rules about dating. Unfortunately, she seemed intent on sticking to him like a burr to a horse's tail. His plan to avoid women worked much better when they actually stayed away. If he needed a night of thrills, he'd drive to one of the bars famous for hot ladies searching for a man to scratch their itch. A few hours of pumping and dumping typically fulfilled his needs for weeks at a time. That was, until April showed up, stole his attention and proved a heady distraction from a casual daily routine. She already made him question the wisdom of allowing her to hang around, considering how much effect she had on him after such a short time.

She walked into the stable. The gentle sway of her hips drew attention to a backside that drew attention and begged to be patted. Full lips tempted him to seal his mouth over hers to find out if she tasted like a sweet treat, and discover if her lips really were as soft and supple as they appeared. Modest breasts strained against the lightweight shirt, jiggling slightly with each step, sending a spear of desire through him as he pictured how her rosy nipples would pebble with a bit of sucking.

*Damn, SEAL. You really need to get laid.*

Irritated, he shoved the erotic thoughts from his mind. Boarder. And certainly off limits. Too bad his cock had other ideas and didn't care for rational rules.

April headed directly to the far stall containing her horses, quickly waving in his direction without breaking stride in the process. He lifted his chin in greeting, not pausing in his brushstrokes over the back of one of the mares. As he worked, he watched April slide into the stall and dote on the pair, speaking softly to them and slipping them a carrot each as a treat.

He couldn't help but grin. No matter what that filly had been through, she obviously trusted and liked April. She snuffled her, lipped her hair and rubbed her head against the woman's chest. Amazing considering how she acted around him. If carrots and sugar cubes could win this pair over, he'd buy a ton of the tasty snacks. Making a mental note to pick some up at the store later, he changed brushes and went over the mare's gleaming hide with a soft cloth.

His mind turned back to the woman. Something about her snared his curiosity and interest, no matter how many times he lectured himself on the evils of the opposite sex. In truth, he knew little about her, but had picked up on a few things. She didn't wear a wedding ring, proclaiming her single. She adored her horses and had a good heart, judging by the special needs filly she hadn't been able to leave behind. While not a great amount of knowledge, the facts only whetted his desire to learn more.

The small rental house he'd dropped her off at earlier had appeared tidy and well kept. Nothing about the small structure had spoken of luxury or richness, yet he hadn't seen any disrepair, overgrown areas or peeling paint. Either she or the owner had to take pride in the small dwelling. Again, a positive sign about April.

*Why bother? She's just a boarder. Nothing more, nothing less.*

After he finished with the mare, he scratched her neck

then left the stall, while automatically scanning the area for April. Sure enough, she remained with her horses. Grabbing up a couple of brushes, he walked over. "Here. If you're going to be hanging out with them, you might as well put the time to good use."

At the sound of his voice, Miracle spun around to face him. Her ears flipped back and forth, but she didn't appear nearly as anxious as before. Slowly, he handed the items over to April, always cognizant of the filly's body language, in particular the carriage of her ears.

"Thanks." April took the larger, coarser brush in hand and started working on Miracle. The gray horse relaxed by increments, although she kept a wary eye on Dusty. He appreciated April's ability to deal with the traumatized horse.

"She's a beauty. Thoroughbred, right?" He kept his voice low and calming. The filly flicked her ears but didn't move otherwise, obviously enjoying the rubdown way too much to bother with trying to take a chunk out of his hide.

"That's what the Humane Society said. She has a tattoo on the inside of her lip, but they weren't able to make out the numbers." April stepped to the other side, nudging Mischief away for the moment. "Ladies first, buddy." The mini rubbed his head against her hip.

Dusty smiled. "Never thought much about miniature horses before, but that one's pretty cute."

April shot him a grin. "I thought so. The director said he's a total ham."

"Makes sense. Looks like I need to invest in some sugar cubes." He watched April make sweeping strokes over the filly's back and envisioned her doing the same to him. Minus the brush, of course. A bite of need flared.

"The Humane Society trainer recommended them. She's all about rewards, especially for the horses they see. I didn't meet her, but that's what Lois told me. So far, it's worked for the trailer business."

She grasped a hoof pick from her back pocket, grabbed

Miracle's foot, and leaned into her side. "Let me have your hoof, Miracle."

Dusty held his breath the moment April asked and the filly didn't respond. In such a vulnerable position, April could have been knocked down, bitten or kicked. He prepared to dash in if things went to hell in a handbasket.

After a moment of pause, the filly shifted her weight and allowed April to lift her foot and clean. Each foot followed in turn. When finished, April stood up and pushed a few stray hairs out of her face. "Cloth please?"

He handed one over, relieved she'd completed the riskiest part of grooming without a hitch. "For a second, I didn't think she'd allow you to do her feet."

April started gently wiping the filly's face. "She's hesitant. I guess the farrier was an issue at the farm since they only had a man for the job. They managed with the trainer and a couple of the female staff surrounding her and helping to hold her feet." She glanced over the horse's back. "I'll make a point to be here when your farrier comes. Surely we can figure out some way to keep her calm and cooperative."

He nodded briefly. Luckily they had a few weeks before having to cross that particular bridge, because right now he wasn't about to stress the filly out by forcing a shoe change on the first couple of days at her new home, with people she didn't know. Hell, the task would be difficult enough after weeks of settling her in.

Finished with the filly, April grabbed up the brush and started working on Mischief. The little gelding lowered his head, sighed and turned into a puddle of mush under her care.

Dusty shook his head. Mischief's rescuers were right. He was a ham, a dramatic one at that. With a brief grin, he grabbed up a couple of lead ropes, headed out of the stable and made his way to the field to start bringing in horses for dinner time.

After a long while, April finished doting on her new pets. She trailed her fingers over each muzzle once more before slipping from the oversized stall.

Her gaze found his. "Thank you again for taking them in."

"No problem." He used the curry comb over Autumn's back. She'd been rolling in the field, somehow ending up with a bunch of dried mud in her coat. More than likely she'd found a wet spot near the water tank and decided on a cool roll in the resulting damp dirt. He couldn't blame her, considering the blazing temperatures outside. He would consider the same if a shower or creek wasn't readily available.

The bay mare was his best broodmare and thus far had produced fine foals with Rule as a sire. His pride and joy, he pampered her and her offspring as a parent cared for their child. The matching foal with a star on her forehead nipped at his jeans. He tugged lightly on her short forelock, unwilling to dissuade the little filly from her playful interaction. Her mother sighed contentedly and shifted her weight to cock one foot in a pose of blatant relaxation.

Totally in his element, he nearly forgot he had a visitor until April walked across his line of vision, only to plop down on a bale of straw, as if she had all night to do nothing more than kick back and watch him work. Come to think of it, she probably did.

"How will you get Miracle to trust you?" The quiet voice carried easily to him across the expansive room.

"Same as the trainers at the Humane Society. Rewards, praise, patience and food." He tucked the handle of the curry comb in his back pocket and picked up a softer brush he'd left waiting on top of the thick stall door. With practiced ease, he stroked the bristles over the mare's hide, ridding the dark hairs of the last of the mud, leaving her coat shiny and clean.

"Have you worked with special needs animals before?" She tucked a leg under her and watched him with banked interest.

He couldn't decide what about him she was trying to

figure out, but her intense look left no doubt he'd snared her curiosity. Dusty considered her question as he walked around the big-boned mare and started on her other side. "I've handled my fair share of difficult horses, had success with them all. But I'll be honest, I've never worked with one as traumatized as your filly."

She sighed loudly and lowered her chin. "Lois spoke highly of you and your abilities. Even one of the trainers readily agreed you could do wonders."

The hope laced in her voice melted over him like tiny snowflakes in the summer sun. April already loved that horse and had put all her eggs in his basket. The unspoken compliment propped up his ego a smidgen more. "Her previous trainer started her out right. With more time, she'll come around."

"And be calm around everyone?"

He shook his head, then realized her focus and turned to the horse in question. "Highly doubtful. Most likely, she'll pick out a few people she trusts and work for them. Strangers will always be on her bad list." Finished with the mare, he used the soft brush on the three-month-old filly. Not that the baby really needed grooming, but he liked to acclimate the foals to all parts of typical daily care at an early age. The foal snorted, turned her hindquarters in his direction, then ducked her head under her mother for a drink. He grinned and caressed the filly's rump even as her short tail slapped his hand on each upswing.

Once more his gaze found April. Concern was etched across her face as she stared at the stall containing her new pets. He'd bolster her confidence if he could, but she'd see results all in good time.

Rule whinnied, drawing his attention. Dusty considered what type of foals the filly might throw when mated with his stallion. Images of speedy barrel racing horses flashed through his mind. "Are you going to breed her?"

"No. The Humane Society has a strict no breeding policy. Considering there's already an overpopulation problem, the last thing they want to do is add to the abundance."

"Understandable." He recalled the information from the file on Miracle. Come to think of it, if the gray filly couldn't be sound carrying a rider over a pasture, the weight of pregnancy could prove just as concerning. He tossed away the thought as fast as it had come.

Finished with the pair, he left the stall, secured the door behind him and gathered up his lead ropes. Without saying a word, he started out of the stable.

The crunch of tennis shoes on gravel alerted him that April followed hot on his heels. He paused and turned, noted the lead ropes she carried, and waited for her to catch up. "Don't you know running shoes aren't safe around horses? If you're going to hang out here, you need a pair of cowboy boots."

"I know. I know. I've just never found boots comfortable. So I decided to make my feet happy instead. After all, this one pair of feet has to last me the rest of my nursing career."

He snorted and headed to the far pasture. "You'll regret that decision first time you get stepped on." Typically the horses waited for him, eager to get inside and to their supper. Not today. They all stood under the huge shade trees, their tails flicking away flies.

"Been there, done that. No biggie." She followed him through the gate and closed the barricade behind her.

*City girl.* He cringed at the term. He'd learned long ago there was a canyon-sized difference between people raised in the city versus those raised in the country. With vastly opposing backgrounds and environments, he rarely came across anyone raised without dust, hayfields and a rooster alarm clock who he could tolerate for long periods of time.

He surely didn't know much about his newest boarder, but her choice of footwear hinted strongly at a suburban lifestyle. *Strike one.* Dusty snorted to himself. What did it matter? As long as she paid her monthly boarding fees, she could come from outer space for all he cared. Just keep her out of his way and off the potential fuck buddy docket and he could learn to put up with the pretty blonde.

Walking up to a couple of the geldings, he then snapped the lead ropes on their halters and handed the ends to April. She gave him the other leads, then made smooching noises to get the horses moving. They followed docilely. He watched her for a second, realizing she'd done this before. Lots of times, if he didn't miss his guess. He re-evaluated his earlier thought, teetered on the fence before deciding she knew something about horses. The familiarity and confidence in her carriage spoke of many things, including hours spent with the large animals.

By the time he'd gathered up the remaining two geldings in the pasture, she'd walked the first ones through the gate, sidestepped them over with the touch of her hand on their shoulders and closed the barrier behind her.

No matter where that girl had grown up, she stood firmly on the country side of things today. In her pink and white tennis shoes. With a shake of his head, he followed in her tracks.

Thirty minutes later, with all the horses settled into their stalls, he poured out grain into a variety of colorful plastic buckets, one for each horse. One variety for the geldings and his stud, another for the mares and foals. A third type for the two senior horses boarding there that needed special feed. He filled the final bucket and rolled down the top of the bag in order to keep the feed fresh and any opportunistic mice out. Grabbing each container in turn, he delivered the evening meal, saving April's pets for last.

"Hold her for me." He waited for April to slip into the stall and grab the filly by her halter before stepping inside. Miracle at once lifted her head and stepped back, her eyes rolling with fear.

April stroked her neck and whispered to her, keeping a snug hold on the halter. "Why don't you let me?"

He shook his head. "The bucket's heavy. Besides, she has to start getting used to me sometime. Might as well be sooner rather than later." His voice joined hers in a quiet, soothing manner, aimed at quelling the obviously scared filly. "It's okay, pretty girl. I'm not going to hurt you. Just bringing your dinner is all." As he spoke, he inched along the front wall of the stall, keeping a close eye on Miracle while ensuring the feed bucket stayed between him and her. Finally he stopped entirely, holding the container perfectly still. "I know you're hungry. Just give it a try."

Miracle's ears flipped back and forth as she shifted nervously in the confines of the stall. Tension mounted, then eased when he did no more than stand before her. Her skin rippled now and again, but she made no move to lash out with hooves or teeth. Instead she watched him like a wild mare would eye a hungry wolf.

Mischief had no such qualms. He lifted his head and tried to sneak some morsels off the top.

Dusty grinned and glanced down at the mini for a split second. "I should have brought yours first, huh?"

The small gelding whinnied as if in answer.

Ever so slowly, Dusty placed the bigger bucket in the holder, then stepped back to grab the smaller-sized one. He cleared the straw out of the front corner by the entrance and set the container on the ground. Mischief wasted no time digging in.

April praised her filly and spent a few more minutes stroking her pet's side as Miracle sniffed the feed, took a tentative bite, then ate with exuberance.

The click of a door closing announced that April had vacated the stall, allowing her horses to eat in peace. "I'd count that as a small victory."

He looked back, found Miracle eating heartily, and nodded briefly. "It's a start."

"The first step in healing," she whispered with feeling.

He told himself that she was speaking of Miracle's long road back to trusting people again. Yet in reality, her words brushed his very soul. Emotional scars ran deep, some too well ingrained to ever be overcome. He knew that for a fact.

# Chapter Four

Ben whined, waking Dusty in an instant. Sitting up, he scanned the area, looking and listening for what might have alerted the dog. Finding nothing, he lay back down and stroked the dog's coarse fur. Though the animal never missed anything, Dusty wondered if Ben suffered from similar nightmares to his, courtesy of war.

They'd been teammates in Afghanistan and Ben had saved his life and others' more times than he could count. He'd scented out explosives as well as sounded an alarm when the enemy had drawn near. Trained for protection, Ben could rip into a man with a simple command, yet he remained as playful as a puppy these days, running around Dusty's stable.

When Dusty had decided to put in his resignation to the Navy SEALs, his sole regret had been losing Ben. Only his luck held as the Navy had decided, due to Ben's advanced age of eight years and his development of arthritis, which affected his mobility, to retire the service dog. Dusty had immediately stepped forward to adopt Ben, bringing him home.

Home. More like his family's home. He'd tried to live there after returning from war. Then his life had splintered. His longtime girlfriend had opted to find another man in his absence. He couldn't entirely blame her, but she'd left his heart broken and aching. He'd been too busy on the war front to grieve over the words written in a short letter that had taken three months to find him. After he'd returned home, he'd leaped back into the dating pool, eager to find a woman to spend his days with. On the rebound, he'd found Rose. From their first meeting, he'd decided he wanted to keep her, falling instantly head over heels in love at first sight. He should have known better. Turned out she specialized in manipulating men out of their money then walking away, leaving them high and dry. His stubbornness had refused to see the truth even after his oldest brother had hired a PI who'd found plenty of incriminating evidence. Hurt and still trying to adjust to life post-war, he'd lashed out, first verbally, then he'd thrown a few punches at Archer, his oldest brother, who'd presented him with proof of his latest folly when choosing a woman. He'd packed up and left that very night, striking out on his own with Ben at his side.

Traveling for a couple of days, he'd finally decided to do what he'd always wanted to do—own a stable and train horses. Lucking into a rundown business, he'd bought the land for next to nothing and spent the next month repairing fences, mending the stable and advertising his services. Slowly but surely, people had brought him their horses. Some to stable and care for, others to break and train. Word of mouth had spread quickly, allowing him ample work and enough of a financial cushion to feel comfortable.

Now, three years later, white hair coated the tan dog's muzzle and Ben relied on daily medication to control his arthritis pain. Dusty lived in the one-bedroom living area attached to the stable, and he cared for twenty horses at the present time. The animals provided him with more than a source of income, they offered him peace and an outlet for his restlessness, nightmares and loneliness. The only thing the animals couldn't fix was the breach with his family. He'd not seen or spoken to any of his four brothers since the night he and Archer had come to blows. His parents called now and again, but he avoided the tense and uncomfortable conversations whenever he could. While he'd said good riddance back then, he'd come to realize his own lack of judgment in the fiasco. Pride prevented him from calling, from doing more than occasionally thinking about them and wondering what life had brought to each of them in the past several months.

Ben sat up and jumped off the bed, his old joints popping in the process. Dusty threw the sheet aside and pulled on a pair of old, worn-out jeans, complete with holes in the knees. With no air conditioning and only a fan, the nights proved too hot to wear anything to bed. Yet he kept clothing close. On the farm you didn't know what kind of critter might wander in looking for food or something else. He could deal with the occasional possum, but the human variety of thief put him on alert the most. Only once had someone tried to sneak in and steal from him. Between Ben going berserk and Dusty cocking a gun in the man's face, the man wasn't about to return anytime soon. Even if he got released from jail early.

"What is it, Ben?" Grabbing his handgun, Dusty followed his dog, pausing to silently turn the knob on the door that led to the stable. Cracking the door open, he let Ben through first, then snuck out behind him. The dog didn't make a mad dash, bark or growl. Instead he wandered into the middle of the aisle and sat down.

Perplexed, Dusty lowered his gun and flicked on another set of lights. "Well, I'll be damned." He stared in disbelief as Mischief stood to one side, tugging at a bale of hay. While he watched, the mini pulled out a mouthful and lifted his head, chewing happily as he glanced up at Dusty.

"How did you get out?"

Dusty glanced toward the stall, finding the door standing ajar. Luckily, the skittish filly remained inside. Walking over, he shut the stall door and headed over to Mischief. "Let me guess, you needed a midnight snack?"

The horse eyed him haughtily and snatched another bite of hay.

Plopping down on the bale, Dusty took his time sizing up the white horse. "I have a feeling you're going to live up to your name."

The horse snorted, blowing specks of hay all over Dusty.

Not in the least upset, Dusty rubbed the horse's head and grinned. "Yeah, I know. You're a growing boy. Growing outward, that is." He noted the round belly on the small horse. Horses loved to eat. Mischief, despite his size, proved no exception. With a chuckle, Dusty gathered up a section of hay and led the horse back toward his stall. He tossed the food in the center of the stall and nudged Mischief back in. Both horses corralled once more, he re-latched the stall door, called Ben and headed back to bed.

* * * *

Just after the crack of dawn, April strode into the stable through the large gate at the entrance, automatically searching for Dusty. She figured he had to be around since the gate wasn't locked and only a fool would run off without securing valuables. Dusty might be stubborn and built like the fabled Adonis, but he wasn't a fool.

Still finding no sight of him, she headed to the stall containing her horses. The last thing she wanted to do was go banging on his door when the poor man happened to be in the bathroom. That would surely put him in a cranky mood for the morning.

The night before she'd stuck around after grooming the animals, watched him bring in all of the horses, groom most of them, then pour out feed for each. Even with her own, he'd refused to allow her to carry the heavy buckets inside. Instead he'd asked her to hold the filly while he carefully entered the stall and fed them, one bucket in the holder, another on the ground in the corner since he didn't have a second, lower device to hold Mischief's bucket. The entire time he spoke gently to Miracle, holding the feed between them so she realized his intentions. Though a bit anxious, she hadn't made any aggressive moves. A definite plus.

Glancing across the aisle, April looked over the horses with interest. Three of the mares had foals at their sides, all absolutely adorable. Dusty's prize palomino stud occupied the end stall, his gleaming golden color catching the morning rays like a chunk of the rare mineral. A white blaze and four white socks matched his mane and tail, the combination more than flashy.

A door clicked. Ben emerged first, followed by Dusty. The dog made a beeline for her even as Dusty's gaze met hers. Automatically, she reached down to pat Ben's head. "What? No pajamas?"

"I don't wear any during the summer."

Not expecting his blunt answer, she felt her jaw drop open. "Well, ummm…" Tongue-tied, she tried to kick her errant mind into gear.

His dark eyes sparked for a moment before his face fell into a serious expression. "Don't you have to work like everyone else?"

She straightened her back and lifted her chin. Granted, he'd asked a reasonable question, yet the words put her immediately on the defensive. "As a matter of fact, yes. I do work." She sucked in a breath. "If you had actually read my contracts, you'd already know I'm a nurse at Three Points Hospital. I work twelve-hour shifts, three days per week. I'm off the next two weeks on vacation in order to get my horses and make sure they're settled."

Mischief lipped at her fingers. She reached in to scratch around his ears. "If it makes you feel any better, I return to work after that, so I'll be out of your hair soon."

He stared at her for a long minute as a tic began in his jaw. "I was just asking, not criticizing." With that said, he headed to a stack of buckets and started pouring out grain.

A soft, appreciative smile lit her face when the shirt pulled tight over his arms and back as he lifted the fifty-pound feed sacks to pour into each plastic tub. He repeated the action over and over again. The flex and tug gave the shirt a workout, which got her pulse pumping. She licked her lips. There was nothing like a powerful man in his prime. She could stand there all day, watching him work. Then once the task was done, follow him into the shower, run a washcloth over his ripped physique and drag him to bed to ride 'em hard—cowgirl style.

*There go my hormones again.* Shoving the erotic thoughts aside, she opted to actually make herself useful.

She wandered over and grabbed up the first container. "Who does this go to?"

He looked up at her in surprise. "I can get it."

"I know. But instead of standing around like a bump on a pickle, I'd prefer to help out."

He studied her for a moment before gesturing to the closest stall. "That's Bobbie's. The little bay closest to us."

Carrying the feed, April opened the stall, found the holder and set the bucket down. Before she secured the door, she heard crunching sounds from a hungry mare. She hurried back, watched Dusty fill another couple of buckets, and grabbed the next container. "This one?"

"That's Rule's. I'll take his."

She released the handle and moved ahead in the line. "That's your stud, right?"

"Take that one to Hailey. The black filly on your left." Dusty walked over, picked up Rule's feed and headed toward the back stall. "Yeah. He's a grand champion quarter horse. I'm lucky to have gotten him at a decent price."

"You raise your own stock then?" She did as bidden, making her way to yet another horse.

"Very few. Two of the colts are mine. The third belongs to a boarder." He returned, picked up another bucket and headed back down the middle of the lane.

"Why so few? I'd think people would be looking for well-bred horses to buy."

"The economy hit horses hard, leaving an abundance, as you already know. Even those who show horses have cut back. While several pay a stud fee to use Rule, I limit the number of mares I breed to two each year. One day I might want to expand the operation, but right now I'm doing good with small numbers that I can handle." He handed her the next one as she approached. "Turnip, the sorrel gelding that looks like he's asleep all the time."

She grinned. "That's what happens when you're old. Naptime is warranted."

His lips twitched. "I suppose so." He grabbed up a couple of buckets and made his way to her horses. He quietly slid the stall door open and stepped in.

April held her breath, debating hurrying over to assist or giving Dusty a chance on his own. Standing still, she watched Miracle's ears flatten only to lift a hair as he began speaking to her, then gradually flip back and forth as if she couldn't decide what to do in this particular situation. He moved lazily across the front of the stall, holding the bucket of feed out to her the entire time. She stared at him for a couple of minutes as if debating the risk and danger of getting too close to a man, then stretched her neck out just far enough to gather a few oats off the top. After she chewed those she repeated the action, gradually becoming bolder. By the time Dusty settled the bucket in the holder, Miracle had eaten part of her breakfast with him holding the bucket and appeared somewhat comfortable.

"Wow. You do have a touch."

He stepped out of the stall, securing the door behind him. "She just needs time and a reason to believe." Without stopping, he headed straight for the few remaining buckets. "These go to Tulip and Tansy, the bay mare with the star on her forehead and her baby. You'll have to hold the bucket for the foal or Tulip will push her out."

"Okay." Gathering up the items, April walked to the stall, stepped in, gave the big mare her food and held the smaller bucket for the pretty little black foal. Out of the corner of her eye she saw Dusty finishing the morning chore, petting Ben's head as he walked by, then pouring some kibble into a bowl. A tortoiseshell cat trotted out of an empty stall, hurried over and proceeded to chow down. Dusty changed out her water as well as dumped a bigger bucket outside before refilling it, presumably for the dog. Cracking open a can, he emptied the contents into another bowl and added dry food alongside. Ben dove right in.

All around animals crunched and ate. April soaked up the sounds and the feeling of peace and contentment. It reminded her of a slower time when life boiled down to the basics, free of the rat race and full of the small things that made the day a bit brighter. She savored the moment and realized she'd found a special place.

Her eyes landed on Dusty as he plopped down on a bale of straw next to Ben. He rubbed the dog's back and glanced up as if sensing her gaze. They stared at each other before April's attention turned to a still-hungry mare looking for a few more kernels of grain from the baby's breakfast.

Something in his eyes touched her. A flash of pain, a sparkle of hope. The man had suffered in his past. Lois' words came back to her. *'Dusty doesn't care for women.'* A man who looked like he did surely he didn't lack offers or feminine attention. Most likely he'd found himself on the losing end in one or more relationships which shaped his outlook on dating. She could empathize.

Glancing up, she found him still looking straight at her. Her belly flipped in sensual delight as her breathing hitched. His eyes could reach into her very soul while his tempered voice could soothe a raging demon. A heady combination.

Wounded he might be, but she knew he had so much more to give. Anyone who worked with horses like he did couldn't be cruel or mean. No. He'd probably just withdrawn from the dating scene like she'd done years before.

Maybe, like her filly, he needed someone to believe, to trust, and to show him not everyone in this world was out to cause harm. Maybe she needed to step up and be the one.

*Like I have any experience with men.* She snorted to herself. *Make that any good experience.* Perhaps if she showed him they had similar experiences with difficult pasts, they could learn from each other?

*Yeah, right. With my luck?* Pigs had a better chance of growing wings than she did of finding a great man and living happily ever after.

The foal finished eating. She collected both buckets and paused to study Dusty once more as he ran his hands down Ben's back in a gentle caress.

Lonely and hurt. He looked like a man who could use a friend of the two-legged kind. How could she turn her back on him?

*I can't.*

*Friends it is.* Decision made, she left the stall and paused when she heard a latch rattle loudly. Locating the sound, she watched in amazement as the lock on her horses' stall door slid back and the door opened wide. Mischief stepped out and whinnied.

She burst out laughing as the mini found obvious delight in his accomplishment.

Dusty shook his head and chuckled, the humor lighting up his face and eyes, making him all the more handsome.

April's breath caught at the difference in the man. Straight white teeth flashed as amusement washed over him. *Delectable.*

"Why, you little escape artist." As if hearing his name, Mischief trotted over to Dusty and nuzzled him.

What Dusty whispered in the horse's ear, April couldn't hear. Yet the sight moved her. Such a strong man, who so far had showed little happiness, now laughed and whispered to a small horse as if sharing age-old secrets. She felt a bit jealous of her little troublemaker.

# Chapter Five

April gathered up the lead ropes after taking her horses to the pasture and releasing them. They had sniffed around the couple of geldings, then started grazing as if nothing new had happened over the past twenty-four hours. Despite the dry summer so far, grass still remained and huge trees stood along the far fence, broadcasting plenty of shade to ward off the heat of the unrelenting sun. As hot as it was right now, she knew that it would only get worse in a few hours. Temperatures had passed the century mark most days for the past month.

Her stomach growled, reminding her she'd skipped breakfast in order to arrive early at the stable and that the noon meal came on fast. "What sounds good for lunch?"

Dusty turned toward her, his brow furrowed. "It's only ten."

She nodded. "Yep. But I have some errands to run in town. Figured I'd pick up some food and bring it back."

"Thanks for the offer, but no thanks." He turned and started back for the stable.

Perplexed, she hurried after him. "What do you mean no thanks? It's just food."

He stopped and stared down at her. A severe frown marred his handsome face while intense anger snapped in his brown eyes. "Listen, lady, I don't know what your game is, but I'm not playing."

His gruffness hit her like a slap in the face, causing her to bite off each word. "There's no game. I figured since I was going for food, it would be hospitable to bring you some as well."

"I can take care of myself. Have for years." Dusty's back straightened, his hands tightened on the lead rope in his hand. After taking one more second to glare down at her, he strode forward, long steps eating up the distance.

April sputtered, completely bumfuzzled by the moodiness and abruptness. She'd thought they had bonded a little just a couple of hours earlier. Grumbling under her breath, she made her way back to the stable. "Care to tell me what's wrong with lunch?"

He swung around with a scowl. "Don't get any fancy ideas in your head about me, lady. I don't date, don't care to hang out with women at all. In fact, the only way I want a woman these days is on the bed with her legs spread for a couple hours of hot and heavy fucking."

The caustic and crude words shocked her, then fed into her anger. She clung to her patience with steely determination, recognizing his motive of trying to drive her away before she got the wrong idea. *Message received.* Too bad her stubbornness refused to back down. She loaded and fired.

"First of all, I didn't have anything in mind besides actually eating and perhaps learning more about horses from you. Secondly, I don't do one-night stands. As far as I'm concerned, men suck in the relationship department, so why would I want to waste my time?" Hands on hips, she glared back at him, daring him to argue.

For a long moment, he stood silent, but gradually a ghost of a smile crossed his face. "Men suck, huh?"

She narrowed her eyes. "You have no idea."

"Yeah, I do." He spun around and ventured farther into the stable.

She bobbed her head in understanding. "So chicken, fish or beef?"

"I said—" His voice increased in decibels.

She waved her hand dismissively. "I'm bringing food. Eat it or not, I don't care. You might as well choose instead of find something you hate in a bag."

He pinned her with his gaze before puffing out a long

breath. "I'll pay you—"

"No way. My treat. Don't complain, just say thanks." She shot him a quick grin, trying to ease the tension between them.

He paused to look at her for another long moment, then his shoulders lowered and he shook his head. "Chicken and thanks."

With a winning smile, she walked back out the door. "Was that so hard?"

"Yes," the word pried itself from his lips.

She laughed and slid into her vehicle.

* * * *

"You and Ben seem so close." She looked down at the dog resting at his feet.

Dusty bit into his biscuit, chewed and glanced at Ben. "He saved my hide more than once." The statement slipped out. Immediately he wished the words back as April's face lit up with curiosity.

"More than once?" She stared at him intently. "He's a police dog?"

"Military." He wanted to kick himself for answering, knowing she'd run with the topic.

Her lips parted. "You were a soldier. Afghanistan?" She sipped her drink.

He'd grudgingly invited her into his home when she arrived back around noon with their food. For her thoughtfulness, he couldn't take the food and send her on her way. Nor could he relegate them to sitting on rough hay bales for the duration of their meal. Instead he'd led her inside, where they plopped down at his small kitchen table across from each other. Close. Personal. A setup made for conversation. *Damn it.* As much as he preferred to ignore her questions, he found himself answering, although vaguely. "Yeah."

"Wow." Her head tilted this way and that. "Come to think

of it, you do have that soldier look to you."

He bristled at the term. "SEAL."

Her eyes widened all the more. "That explains a lot."

He arched an eyebrow and took a hearty bite of his mashed potatoes.

"The way you move. Graceful. Confident. It's hard to explain. It's like you know everything about yourself and your capabilities and know exactly what's around you at all times."

He understood her meaning. Once a SEAL, always a SEAL. Fear registered way down on the priority list and hadn't cropped up since the war zone. SEALs work through their fear because that's just what they do, for their team, for the mission. Not to mention the worst the world could throw at him now paled in comparison to what he'd already faced.

Growing up, he'd figured out two things fast. First, he'd always idolized the Navy SEALs and more than anything had wanted to become one. Secondly, wealth possessed its own drawbacks. His father, a prominent lawyer, earned more than enough to keep his family in all stages of luxury. A sprawling ranch filled with purebred cattle and the best quarter horses around made up a small part of the yearly budget. Dusty had fallen in love with the country lifestyle, enjoying each day no matter the weather, no matter the hours. He'd felt at home on the farm, especially with the horses.

Unfortunately, due to his family's assets, he and his brothers had quickly become chick magnets. Women flocked to them, threw themselves at them, and did just about anything in a bid for marriage and a chunk of the family's money. Dusty had found the situation humorous until his own particular castle had begun to topple. Women had become an instrument of stress release, until he'd met and fallen in love with Colette. War had taken him away and his relationship had become a casualty by the time he'd returned home. His next conquest had proved the ringer his family warned him about over the years, but he'd been too blind to see.

"Dusty?"

April's voice pulled him from his thoughts. "What were you saying?" He forked another bite of fried chicken.

She looked at him with softness, respect and caring. His gut clenched in reaction.

"I asked if the military lets all handlers keep their dogs."

He shook his head. "The dogs may change handlers through their career, until they become too old, injured or unable to do their job. Then they're returned to the States and made available for adoption. I got lucky. Due to his age and arthritis, Ben became available at the same time I resigned. We came home together."

As if sensing the topic of conversation, Ben looked up from his soft oversized pillow near the table. Dusty picked a hunk of meat off the bone and tossed it to the dog, who caught the food and chewed with gusto.

"Thank you." The soft words pulled his attention back to her.

"For what?"

"Your service. The sacrifices you undoubtedly made. For doing what the great majority of people wouldn't do." Her blue eyes, full of respect and admiration, met his.

The praise and her expression warmed his heart, but sent up a red flag as well. The last thing he needed was some woman deciding she wanted him badly enough to be forever under his feet and conniving ways to trap him in a marriage. If he ignored her, she'd soon get the hint.

*Like she took the damn hint earlier?* He'd purposely spat out phrases he'd never used in the presence of a woman before. If his mother had heard him, she'd have had a bar of soap in one hand and a switch in the other. She'd raised her boys to respect woman and show them kindness with manners. Yet he couldn't think of a better way to throw her off his trail. Unfortunately, instead of sending her dashing off, she now sat across a small table from him, talking about his recent history and bolstering his ego with her easy to read face.

He focused on eating, wanting to hurry up and end this somewhat awkward meal. At least she only pressed a couple of his buttons. Too bad they were his curiosity and his libido.

She cleared her throat and took another drink from her cup. "Have you heard anything about rain?"

He recognized the change of subject for what it was. An olive branch. "Nowhere in the near future. We haven't gotten anything measurable for three months. Add that in with last year's dry weather and we're in a severe drought."

"That's going to make it tough, no pasture. The grain and hay prices will soar."

"They already have." He cringed recalling the total feed bill from the previous month. This coming month would prove worse, whittling away at his margin of profit. Once he began to sink into the hole, he didn't have a clue how to dig himself back out. Sure, he could raise the prices to the boarders, but that step would only help somewhat. He couldn't take on a part-time job as the stable kept him more than busy. Besides, he didn't dare leave the horses unattended for long. If something happened, he'd never forgive himself. No, he had to stay the course and hope things worked out. They always had before.

"I know things are bad all around. Even the hospital is feeling the crunch." She spooned a bite of potatoes. "With the economy and lower reimbursements, the hospital is trimming off any and all fat."

He hadn't realized health care would be affected. "Layoffs?"

She shook her head. "No. Not yet. Administration says it's not going to happen. But at the same time, they aren't replacing those who leave and they're not hiring anyone new. We just have to make do with what we already have."

"Just like everyone else."

"Yeah, I think so."

She ate for a minute before speaking once more. "Times are hard all over. I wonder what the next big blow will be."

"There's always something."

"The strong survive, though."

He shook his head, remembering all his fellow military brothers who'd fallen in the line of duty. "Not always." Finished with his meal, he slurped the soda container empty. "Thanks for lunch." In a flurry, he gathered up the trash and threw everything away.

April followed suit. "You're welcome."

He stopped and eyed her for a long moment. She didn't deserve his brashness, not when she obviously tried so hard to become a friend. "I've got a horse to break. Then, later, I want to handle your filly some more."

She nodded. "I know you're a busy man. So I'll head home, but be back later to help you feed my horses."

"It's not necessary. After all, that's what you're paying me to do."

"I want to. Besides, I've got a ton of treats to bring over. Can't run out of snacks for those two." She met his gaze, turned and showed herself out.

Dusty sighed. Why did she have to be so understanding? So pretty? So accommodating and caring?

He could easily reject a selfish woman. Yet for the life of him, he couldn't keep up the snarky persona to shove April away. Earlier the hurt on her face had cut him way too deep.

*Face it, SEAL. She's got your number.*

With that thought, he left the one-bedroom house attached to the stable and headed for the pasture.

\* \* \* \*

"I still can't believe she's taken to you so quickly." April grabbed up a bucket of feed and headed toward the nearest stall.

She'd returned earlier to not only find Mischief and Miracle already in their stalls, but Dusty actually rubbing the filly's head with soft and tender touches. Amazed, she could have been knocked over by a feather when the filly nuzzled his chest as if asking for more. Her spirit soared seeing the huge step a single day made with Miracle and a man who knew horses like he knew his own body.

"There's a long way to go. But with a bucket of feed, some space and understanding, she'll come around." He carried containers of feed from stall to stall, passing out dinner to the animals.

"You're amazing. I'll have to email Lois to let her know. She'll be thrilled."

Dusty went about his work, not bothering to comment. Obviously praise made him uncomfortable, judging by the way he clammed up each time she complimented him on a deed. The realization bothered her, but she told herself with time he'd learn to accept some well-earned recognition. She wasn't going anywhere, nor were her horses.

"Did you hear about the fires down in Madison County?"

"Yeah. It's a perfect storm. Drought, high winds and plenty of fuel in the form of dried-out pastures and trees." He headed toward her horses, two buckets of feed in hand. Speaking softly, he slid along the front wall, keeping the grain between him and Miracle. Her ears twitched, but she made no attempt at aggression. Instead she lipped a bite, then dove in once he settled her bucket into place.

"Think it will head this way?" She rubbed Tansy's nose and held out the bucket so the little foal could eat without having to compete with her mother.

"No telling."

"Have you ever seen this area burn?"

He shook his head. "I've only been here for three years, so I can't really say."

She blinked. Since everyone she asked knew Dusty, she'd figured he'd lived there all his life. "Oh, I thought you were from around here."

"No."

He didn't elaborate, which meant she'd stumbled into yet another topic he didn't care to pursue. Trying to pry information out of this man was like trying to sneak a giant

747 plane down Main Street. Simply wasn't happening.

"Where did you grow up, then?"

He continued with his chores. "Wyoming."

"Does your family still live there?" she persisted, but then bit her lip as she saw tension envelop the man. His steps became a bit stiffer, his mouth tightened. She'd definitely stumbled across a taboo subject. "I'm sorry. I shouldn't be so nosy."

He carried one more bucket and re-emerged from the far stall, not bothering to look her direction.

Weight settled on her shoulders. *Way to go.* He'd started to act friendly, but her big mouth clammed him right up.

She quickly changed the subject, hoping to coax him into speaking once more. "Do you ride your horses much? I've seen the saddles, but haven't seen you ride."

"Yeah."

*One word answer. Wonderful. Yet, better than nothing.* "I haven't seen any other boarders come in. Do they show up very often?"

He opened a can of dog food and poured the contents out, then mixed in some pieces of dry food. Ben wagged his tail and dug in. "Now and again. When the weather is bad, too hot or too cold, they tend to stay away. Same reason I haven't been riding. Way too hot for the horses to do much more than try to find a cool spot in the shade."

The open and airy stable wasn't bad in temperature, although she imagined the horses preferred standing under the trees, making use of any breeze that came their way, while grazing. A score of windows on either side of the building encouraged a crosswind while several fans had been tacked up near the stalls. She hadn't seen them on before, but knew if one of the animals showed signs of getting too warm, Dusty wouldn't hesitate to flick a button and send air rushing their direction.

The filly lipped up the last bit of grain and nudged the bucket for more. April grinned, rubbed the baby's face and slipped out of the stall. After placing both empty buckets back near the feed sacks, she wandered over to a nearby bale of straw and plopped down.

The orange and black cat headed her direction, hopped on her lap and plopped down like she'd found a comfortable spot for a nap. April stroked the pretty cat's back, noting the loud purr that followed. Her heart cracked and a barely healed wound reopened. She'd had to put her old cat to sleep about a year before due to advanced cancer. Tears had run down her cheeks for days as she mourned gravely. Still to this day, she recalled her favorite pet and her eyes misted. Having another cat contentedly curled up on her lap reminded her of the good times while plucking at those tender heartstrings.

"That's Marmalade."

She glanced over at Dusty. "She's friendly. I always thought barn cats were skittish, especially of strangers."

He shrugged and sat down beside Ben, watching the dog lick his bowl clean. "She showed up here one day, skinny as a rail. I took her in, fed her, got some vet work done. She's been friendly since day one. Probably someone's pet that got lost or dumped as a quick way to rid themselves of their responsibilities."

April sighed and brushed her hand over the cat's head. So much sadness in the lives of these animals. Her gaze once again found Dusty.

He fit right in. Wounded and possibly traumatized from his past, he found peace surrounded by creatures that had lived through their own versions of hell. He didn't just own the stable, he spoke the same language as the occupants. They all needed one another. If something ever happened to this place, he'd be just as lost as they would be.

She thought of the fires to their south and sent up a quick prayer for the destructive flames to stay far away.

"How long have you been working with horses?" She opted to spend the evening learning more about the man who had snared her attention.

"Forever. My family raised quarter horses."

"Showed them?"

He nodded and rubbed Ben's head. "For a while we spent every weekend during the summer at a show."

"Did you like it?"

Dusty shrugged and looked down at his dog. "Yes and no. I enjoyed the horses, but the traveling all the time got old. Then college took most of my time. After I graduated, the military took over my life."

Somewhat surprised he mentioned his military career, she debated questioning him further about the part of his life he bristled about earlier. "Did you apply to be a dog handler in the military? How do they decide who gets to be with dogs and who doesn't?" she softly asked.

Marmalade looked up at her and quietly meowed as if encouraging her to resume her attentions. Lightly, she scratched behind Marmalade's ears and ran her fingers down the plump cat's back.

Silence reigned before Dusty finally answered. "You apply. They choose applicants based on several factors." His short answer discouraged further inquiry.

April took the hint. "Lois said their vet recommended Miracle only be used for light riding due to potential bone and ligament damage from her starvation. Do you think it's worth trying to break her or should I simply consider her a pet?"

He lifted his gaze to meet hers. "I'd say that's up to you." He turned to the large stall containing the unusual pair of horses. "She's made good progress with me, but breaking will take a long time. I can have my vet look her over next time he's here, but I doubt he'll disagree with theirs." Dusty's brown eyes found her once more. "Truth be told, after what she went through, I'm not sure I'd even bother with saddle and rider. Most likely she'd be happier and healthier as a pretty filly to decorate the stable."

She watched Miracle shuffle through the thick straw. "I think you're right. It's not worth the risk to her or the upset." Somewhat disappointed, she focused on the purring kitty in her lap.

"If you want to go riding, just say the word."

Jerking her head up, she blinked at Dusty, surprised by such an offer. "You'd let me ride one of your horses?"

"Yeah. They could use the work. That is, if you know how to ride."

A smile flashed across her face. "Didn't I tell you? I worked at a large horse farm all through high school. We did everything—breeding, training, boarding and riding lessons. Even worked with handicapped kids in riding therapy. All through college, I spent my weekends volunteering at Summerset Thoroughbreds."

Respect replaced amazement on his face. He studied her, then nodded slowly. "You'll do, April. You'll do."

She grinned at the rare praise and felt her spirits lift. *Score one for me.* While Dusty might not care for women in general and didn't always appreciate her hanging around, at least he now saw her as a fellow horse person—Common ground with a genuine love for the animals he adored.

They fell into companionable silence, Dusty showering affection on his former war partner and her stroking the barn cat.

*I could get used to this.*

# Chapter Six

*Grenades exploded, sending men flying. Blood splattered and cries of pain and fear burst out over the desert mountain landscape. With no shelter besides a few armor-plated vehicles, men either stood their ground or dove for cover. Those still capable grabbed up a weapon and fired, defending themselves and their unit. Dusty glanced to the side, finding the fixed eyes of his best friend staring his direction. Sharp shards ripped through him even as fury rushed to the fore. With a battle cry, he grabbed his weapon, rushed ahead and put down a scathing flurry of bullets. The next instant he went airborne as another roadside bomb detonated.*

Sucking in great gulps of air, Dusty opened his eyes and sat up. Ben cuddled close, whining and licking his owner's face. For a long moment, Dusty fought to quell the images still running amok in his mind, their claws buried deep in his memory, stubbornly refusing to budge each time he tried to banish them. His heart still pounding, he wrapped an arm around Ben and buried his face in the coarse fur, finally managing to pull himself from the nightmare and back into the present.

Darkness surrounded them, the only light from his alarm clock. Glancing up, he found the time. Three-fifteen.

"Shit." He sighed heavily and looked into Ben's knowing eyes. "Yeah, another one. I know you have them too."

Ben sat up and leaned his entire body against Dusty, tucking his head under Dusty's chin.

Smiling briefly at the comforting snuggle, Dusty did nothing more than pet his dog. Ben had always been there for him during the war — not only as a protector and detector but also as a friend. Without Ben, Dusty might have lost his humanity and his sanity. Instead they'd worked as a team, supported each other and had finally came home together, although a bit rough and worn for the experience.

White hairs covered Ben's muzzle, signifying his advanced age. Once again, Dusty wondered how much time his friend had left and felt a deep pang in his heart at the thought of losing Ben. The downside to having pets was to lose them in the end. Nature's way. Yet he didn't know what he'd do without his constant companion who understood so much more than most people could.

He ruffled the dog's hair once more. No sense in trying to return to sleep, not when he still suffered the adrenaline charge from his harrowing dream. He could sit in bed and stare at the clock or he could do something useful. "What do you say we get an early start on breakfast?"

Ben woofed softly and jumped off the bed.

Dusty followed.

* * * *

"Good morning." April walked through the main gate with a wide smile on her face.

He blinked and gave her a droll stare, not in the mood for bubbly cheerfulness this morning. After a quick meal of toast, he'd gotten to work—thrown laundry in, scrubbed the kitchen, even cleaned his bathroom until the entire area gleamed with freshness. By the time he'd finished the clock had struck five, close enough for feeding time in his book.

Afterward he'd gone about grooming the horses and was working on the third one when his persistent new boarder strolled in.

Ben trotted over, his tail wagging happily. She stopped to lavish attention on him, speak to him and even slip him a dog treat, which he ate with relish. With a giggle, she approached the stud's stall, where he presently brushed Rule's golden hide.

"Either you're early or I'm late." Her gaze darted to the

empty buckets in the stalls.

"You're neither." He clipped the words, irritated with her already. In his rational mind he knew she wasn't to blame for his surly mood and didn't deserve his harsh tongue, yet, he also didn't feel up to catering to her whims today. Why couldn't she be like the other boarders who came and went sparingly? He much preferred to hang out alone throughout the day, not babysit a yappy blonde lady with nothing better to do on her vacation than shadow him.

Her head jerked up and her blue eyes pinned him with fire and intrigue.

Maybe if he pissed her off, she'd go away for the day and leave him in peace.

"I see. Well, I'll just care for my horses and stay out of your way today." With the quiet but haughty answer, she grabbed up a couple of brushes and headed toward the large end stall containing her animals. First she brought out Mischief and tied him to the door. After a touch up brushing session and quick check of his feet, she returned for the filly. Miracle balked at being tied at first, yanking back against the rope, but soon quieted with April's quiet voice and touch. A carrot split among the two seemed to seal the deal for the moment.

He finished with Rule, grabbed a lead rope and led his stallion from the stall. The stud made a beeline for Miracle and snuffled her before Dusty tugged insistently on his halter. "Not happening, boy."

As if understanding, the palomino snorted, then ambled along all the way to the small pasture.

Dusty released him, noting the colors of dawn spreading across the horizon. Another pretty day if you liked baking under the sun and bathing in your own sweat. With a grumbled curse at the weather, he walked back to the stable.

By the time he entered, he found April finishing up with her horses. Without pausing he walked right up to Miracle, untied her and took control of her halter. Her eyes rolled and showed white. Speaking softly, he soothed the nervous horse. "That's it. Just me again. Nothing to get your water hot about."

For a few minutes he did nothing more than stand there and speak to the animal. Finally, when she quieted, he reached up to lightly scratch her neck. Her ears flicked and she sidled away. He held his ground, continued with his motions, and never stopped speaking to her. She calmed, lowered her head and held still. "That's my girl." He dug a sugar cube from his pocket, placed the treat on his palm and held his hand out to the filly's muzzle. She sniffed for only a second before eagerly accepting the reward.

Mischief nudged him hard in the rear.

Dusty shook his head and turned around. "Feeling left out?" He offered up another bit of sugar, which the gelding gobbled down as if someone might steal his gift if he didn't hurry up and swallow.

"Wow. I still can't believe she's standing there letting you pet her." April's soft voice carried to him.

He didn't answer. Instead, he untied the mini and led both horses to their pasture. By the time he set them loose, she'd brought a couple of the geldings and handed them over.

"This is my job." He took control of the leads, put both animals in the field, then unsnapped the ropes from their halters to set them free for the day.

"I like to help." She waited for him to close the gate and start back toward the stable.

"There's no discount for picking up some of the chores." His voice came out terse and flat.

She stiffened as if insulted. "I didn't expect one." She hurried to keep up with his long strides.

Irritable, he frowned down at her. "When are you going to go back to work again?"

April gasped. "What's with you today? I thought we'd found some sort of truce over the past couple of days. Today you're snapping at me like I'm the Wicked Witch of the West come looking for your boots to wear."

Her wording almost put a grin on his face. Almost. "Maybe I need some alone time." He stopped and turned to face her.

Their gazes met. Neither looked away.

"You haven't slept." The words tumbled out of her mouth like pebbles plinking down a hillside. She studied his face. "You've got dark circles and lines of fatigue."

He ground his back teeth, pulling on his patience. "Nice to know I look like shit this morning."

So he hadn't gotten much sleep. No biggie. He'd gone days without as a SEAL. His mind and body still functioned and he could perform just as well. Besides, he'd suffered more sleepless nights than he could remember, all part of the package when one returns from war.

"I didn't say that. Dang, you're testy." She planted her hands on her hips. "If you must know, you look as gorgeous as ever." Color rushed to her face. He'd bet his bottom dollar she hadn't meant to confess her observation. *Too late.* The words soothed his inner restlessness a smidgen.

"I've heard most war veterans suffer from nightmares. Some from post-traumatic stress disorder with flashbacks and other distressing symptoms."

He scowled and began walking again.

"There's no shame in admitting you have bad dreams," she hollered after him.

He spun around on a dime. "Listen, lady, because I'm only going to say this once. I don't speak about that part of my life. *Ever.* Got it?" He bit off each word and spit them out like rotten peanuts.

She blinked, then slowly nodded. "Yes."

"Good. And for your information, if I feel anything about my service, it's definitely not shame." He turned on his heel and marched back toward the stable.

She ran to keep up. "I never said your service was shameful."

He didn't slow up in the least while wondering what it would take to drive this pesky woman away.

"I said there's no shame in having bad dreams."

He opened the gate and closed it right behind him.

"Damn it. Would you just stop and listen for a second?" She unlatched the gate, let herself through and hurried after him once more.

He stopped, crossed his arms over his chest and glared at her.

She approached, a bit out of breath from her near run from the outside fields. "Your service is to be commended and you have more honor and bravery in your little pinky than most people have in their whole bodies. There are a hundred reasons for you to hold your head high and I applaud your courage in doing things most of us couldn't." She sucked in a breath. "I'm not trying to dig through your personal life or trying to tell you what to do."

"I—"

She raised a hand to his lips. "Please, just hear me out."

When he lifted his chin ever so slightly, she removed her fingers. He found the gesture somewhat soothing. Her words eased some of his turmoil and reminded him some people actually looked up to those who were lucky enough to return from the front lines.

"Dusty, I care for you. That's all. I just care."

The hushed words hit him like a fast-moving thunderstorm. Abrupt and powerful at first, then simmering down to a gentle rain afterward.

Unable to resist, he cupped her chin in his hands. Slowly, allowing her plenty of time to step back, he lowered his lips to hers. Softly, he plied her mouth, then tilted his head, wrapped his arms around her waist and pulled her flush against his body.

His shaft stood up and took notice, not just of the beautiful woman in his arms, but of the brushing of her body against his, the light caresses that set his blood on fire.

April gasped. He took advantage, slipped his tongue inside, tangled with hers and circled for a taste of the spitfire blonde who was too stubborn to take a hint.

Hesitant at first, April gradually began to respond, as if testing out the waters in a novel experience. She met his tongue then licked across his lips, exploring his mouth like he imagined she would the rest of his body, with open curiosity and gentleness.

When she hit her stride, Dusty nearly groaned. She mirrored his actions while resting her arms around his neck. Leaning against him, she gave everything back to him with gusto. He deepened the kiss, sought more of her passion and ratcheted up the affectionate act with enough heat to rival the midday sun. Placing his hand on the back of her head, he steadied her as he changed the angle and pushed her to the point of breathlessness.

Reluctantly, he eased back, letting their lips cling for a moment longer before separating. He drew in a deep breath and read her face. April's blue eyes shone brightly, full of surprise and longing. Her lips were slightly swollen from his attentions and pink stained her cheeks as she panted like she'd just run a mile full out. Pleasure radiated from her face as she stared up him with awe and perhaps recently discovered need.

"Amazing," she whispered.

He rubbed his thumb across her lips. Not entirely comfortable with her praise and the expression on her face, he released her completely, turned around and headed to the nearest stall.

She posed too much of a threat to his hard-won control and challenged his rule of only pursuing women for the purpose of a one-night stand. April wasn't a hot to trot woman who enjoyed man-hopping any more than he was a man who sought commitment and the stability of marriage.

*Oil and water.*

He attached more lead ropes and continued the task of moving horses from stalls to the fields outside, kicking his own ass the entire way.

*What in the hell came over me?* Either he needed to get laid badly or the lack of sleep had severely affected his judgment.

One glance found April still standing as before, staring at him with wonder in her soft eyes.

He cringed and berated himself more. *I'm such a dumbass. Give the woman the totally wrong impression next time.* Sarcasm laced his thoughts as he debated beating his head on a nearby fence post. He snorted and strode quickly back down the worn path.

* * * *

That kiss. That absolutely decadent kiss. For the twentieth time so far that day, April recalled the moment Dusty had sealed his mouth over hers and forever changed her opinion of kissing.

She'd read romance novels that spoke of embraces of pure passion, where a simple kiss sounded nearly as intoxicating as sex. A big time exaggeration and a way to ensnare the reader, drag them in and leave them begging for more. Nice sales tactic, but far from reality. She didn't believe in fairy tales, no matter how unbelievably hot the kiss.

Until today.

Her stomach did another slow, exquisite flip. One of many since Dusty had poured delightful magic over her, infusing her with newfound desire.

*I sound like a lovesick fool.* She frowned. Sure, it happened to be the best kiss ever, but that didn't really mean anything in the long run. Her track record with men could be considered dismal and Dusty didn't say another word after walking away. He'd just left her standing there, mouth gaping open, with a dozen questions running through her mind.

They still did. All with no answers forthcoming.

With a frustrated sigh, she grabbed up a pitchfork and began mucking stalls. No sense standing around batting her eyelashes and looking like a freshman with her first crush on the bad boy senior. She'd long since left her teens—and high school—behind. Besides, college had taught her a few lessons about dating and the opposite sex. Enough for her to tread carefully before leaping into any relationship. Avoiding the whole fiasco sounded more rational than risking her heart once again.

She entered the nearest stall and started cleaning, picking up dirty hay and manure, then tossing it into the nearby wheelbarrow. Dusty walked by leading another pair of horses. He didn't even glance in her direction.

*And there you go.*

He'd obviously reacted on some impulsive instinct and now regretted his actions. As much as she wanted him to march over and treat her to another sampling of his kissing abilities, she knew that once again she dabbled in a dream. A man who'd been hurt so badly that Lois, one hundred miles away, would hear about the unfortunate situation, had to have deep scars and a shield of steel encasing his heart.

*Too bad.* If he ever allowed himself to open up again, the lucky woman would most likely find herself wrapped in a love so wonderful she'd dance in happiness for the rest of her days.

With that sad thought, she attacked her chore with exuberance.

# Chapter Seven

April set the grocery bags on the kitchen counter and methodically went about putting items away. Her mind turned back to Dusty and that glorious kiss, which had rocked her world and put him on the defensive at the same time.

She'd gotten up early and driven to the stable, just like every other morning since her horses arrived. Today she'd focused on them while hoping Dusty had put the temperamental attitude behind him. No such luck. He'd barely glanced at her when she entered the stable and hadn't bothered to speak a single word. Ben had greeted her warmly, and returned to Dusty's side as if needing to be close.

The one time she'd tried to say something Dusty had quickly shut her down, then had led a gelding from his stall and taken him out to the pasture. He acted like a bear with a thorn stuck in his butt all because of one little kiss.

A sinful kiss. Hot, passionate and the best one she'd ever experienced. Too bad Dusty didn't appear to feel the same way.

He'd immediately thrown up a solid barrier between them, one she couldn't break through or find a way around. His actions only solidified her belief that he regretted the impromptu action and now preferred to keep her at arm's distance, lest she get the wrong idea. No problem there. She'd figured that out immediately afterward. The resulting sting of rejection served as a vivid reminder not to get too close or expect anything more along the lines of intimacy from the stubborn man.

Completely frustrated, she'd thrown in the towel. April had cared for her horses, settled them in the pasture for the day and left. No sense standing around when her mere presence irritated the guy. Besides, errands and shopping had been on her day's agenda.

She opened the fridge and unloaded the rest of the goods. The plastic sacks were added to a small collection. Taking her bottle of soda with her, April walked into the small living room next to the kitchen, sat down on the couch then opened her laptop computer.

Ben — she'd noticed his devotion and love for Dusty, his graying muzzle indicating advanced age as did his sometimes stiff movements. The war dog, as amazing and smart as he was, was slowing down. How much longer he had was anyone's guess, but his years were numbered. Sad. Very sad to her, but how would the loss of Ben impact Dusty?

April blew out a worried breath.

Sure, she'd heard about post-traumatic stress — a common occurrence with soldiers and others who have been through horrible experiences. Dogs helped, especially the soldiers, and steps had been made lately to unite war veterans with canines in order to help with their symptoms. Successfully at that.

So what did that mean for Dusty?

Taking a chance, April typed words into the search engine and hit the 'Go' button. Several entries popped up. One appeared more official than the others. She chose it, opened the page and started reading.

Ten minutes later, she sat back and pondered what she'd learned. The military did adopt out their dogs for various reasons. Some of the puppies didn't have enough drive to make them good war dogs. Those that had seen action were retired for one reason or another. Or sometimes a medical problem sidelined a dog with great potential or one that had been working already. Understandably, the handlers were given first choice to adopt the dog, but sometimes that wasn't possible. Then the Army opened the adoption process up to the general public. No charge to adopt the dogs, just fill out the forms, go on a waiting list that could be one to two years long, and see if the powers that be would approve of the person. Those on the list would wait for a call, months or even years down the road. If they were chosen, they had to get to San Antonio and spend at least a couple of days getting to know their new friend while learning about the animal's training, familiarizing themselves with the commands and how to transition a working war dog into a family pet. The visit was mandatory before the Army released the dog to the new owners.

She scrolled through the data again, checked out the dogs available for adoption and read their stories. There weren't many, but every one broke her heart.

After a few tours of duty, the dogs needed rest, understanding and pampering for the rest of their natural lives. The puppies were cute, but something drew her to the canines that had done their duty and now earned retirement.

Just like her horses, she'd prefer one who'd been through hell and had the fortitude to plow through and survive. They reminded her of Ben. Smart, brave, loyal. The love they had to give could be seen in their eyes.

How could anyone turn their back on those deserving animals?

She couldn't.

Issues started cropping up in her mind. She would keep the dog in the house with her, but what about her twelve-hour shifts at work? What about any vacations she might take? Who would step up to take care of the animal when she was away?

A vet clinic or dog hotel might be an option, but she hesitated. Chances were those people never dealt with an animal like a military dog who could easily have its own issues. No. She needed someone well versed in the role. Someone like Dusty.

April clicked on the adoption form, pulled it up and printed it out. Reading it over, she noticed a narrative and reference section where she could explain why she wanted to adopt. What she jotted down would help make or break her as a potential forever home for a dog. But what could she say that would set her application apart from dozens of others the facility was sure to get each month?

*Dusty.*

He might be able to help her out with a sound reference.

Great in theory, not so much in reality. Unfortunately, he wasn't in the helpful mood right now.

*The way to a man's heart is through his stomach.* The old adage rang a bell.

Goodness knows Dusty didn't get hearty, home-cooked food very often. Between the heat, his lack of air conditioning in the house and the fact that he'd just be fixing for himself, it was no wonder Dusty lived on sandwiches.

Time for a change.

April turned off her computer and returned to the kitchen. She opened the fridge door, peered inside and debated what she could throw together that Dusty might enjoy. The chicken caught her eye. She had fresh vegetables as well. The menu started to mentally fill in.

With renewed energy, she went to work on her latest goal—a peace offering in the form of a hot, complete meal.

* * * *

Dusty's phone rang. He palmed the device, checked the caller ID, then answered, "Hey, Sam. What's up?"

He and the county sheriff had gravitated toward each other once he'd moved here. They shared a similar background, combat duty, though Sam had been a regular grunt and Dusty a SEAL.

"Had some downtime this morning. Care to meet me at the firing range? See who gets to pay for this round?"

Dusty grinned. He and Sam had a running bet. Whenever

they got together on the shooting range, the loser paid their usage fee. So far Dusty hadn't picked up the tab and he didn't plan on doing so anytime in the near future. "Sure. Twenty minutes?"

"Sounds good to me." Sam clicked off.

Dusty ended the call and shoved the cell phone back into the holder on his belt as he strode from the stable, into the house, and straight for the bedroom where he kept most of his weapons. Choosing two of his handguns, he strapped on his old ankle holster first. His shoulder harness followed. After placing the weapons in their respective holders, he plucked a couple of boxes of ammunition out of his storage case, stood up, and headed toward the truck.

Ben followed along every step.

Dusty patted his head. "You need to stay here, buddy. Watch over things while I'm gone."

Ben sat down, wagged his tail and panted. His sharp eyes met Dusty's.

With one more pat, Dusty headed to his truck.

Several minutes later, he pulled into the parking lot of the firing range. Dusty parked, grabbed his boxes of shells and entered the building, finding Sam chatting with the owner, Tracy Thomas. The gray-haired guy had seen his fair share of action during his days in the CIA. He'd retired a while back, moved back home and opened a gun shop and firing range. As far as Dusty could tell, the guy had found contentment and peace in his near retirement.

"About time you showed up. Sam was crowing about kicking your ass this time. I told him my money was on you." Tracy offered up a halfhearted grin.

"Thanks. I'd hate to break my perfect streak." Dusty sauntered over to the counter to join the small group.

"What is it now? Ninety straight?" Tracy asked.

Sam snorted. "More like five."

Dusty smiled ruefully. "Seventeen, but who's counting?"

"If you don't get a move on, you'll never get a chance to find out if you can make it eighteen." Sam led the way through a side door to the cement room that was enclosed. Five stations waited, all empty. Each had a table to use for loading and unloading as well as a pair of ear protectors. At the far end of the room, targets hung from wires, clean and intact.

*Not for long.*

"What's the plan this time?" Dusty pulled his gun from his shoulder holster and placed it on the table along with the bullets. He didn't have to bother with loading as his guns were always at the ready.

"Five shot accuracy?"

Dusty nodded. "Works for me." He placed the ear protectors on his head, glimpsing Sam doing the same in the station next to him. Without further hesitation, he raised his semiautomatic, aimed and shot between breaths. Five times he squeezed the trigger and watched the target jump. Done in less than three seconds, he lowered the gun and placed it back on the table. After removing his head gear, he pushed the button which then brought his target to him.

"Well?" Sam walked over, carrying his own paper.

Dusty gestured to his, still hanging right in front of him. A single hole went through the head part of the target, right between the eyes.

"Holy shit." Sam shook his head.

Dusty glanced over at Sam's paper. Sam's bullets had torn a large ragged hole in the area of the target where the heart would be. "Nice."

"Lethal, but not near as fancy." Sam grinned. "Remind me not to get on your bad side."

Dusty smiled. "I'll do that."

Sam's radio went off—a woman's voice rattling off information about a situation.

Dusty listened in carefully. Although he didn't carry a badge, he'd helped out more than once when Sam and his short-handed crew ended up in over their heads.

Sam frowned. "On my way." He eyed Dusty before spinning on his heel and hurrying back the way he'd come, pausing only long enough to drop a bill on the counter for Tracy. "Hostage situation near Smithville. An intruder on the run forced his way into a house. Now he's holding the woman and her kids hostage. Threatening to kill them if the authorities try to move in."

Dusty stayed right on his heels. "My specialty."

Sam stopped at his patrol car. "I won't turn down help."

Dusty nodded, jogged to his truck, pulled out a large black duffel bag which he always carried, then returned to the passenger side and slid in. Old habits were hard to break. Carrying his weapons and always being prepared for anything fell under that same heading. "Consider me Barney Fife."

Sam climbed in, fastened his seat belt, cranked the engine and hit the gas. "You do carry a resemblance to him."

Dusty rolled his eyes. The light bantering reminded him of his SEAL days. On the way to missions, the guys tended to throw out teasing insults in an attempt to loosen up before things got serious. He felt right at home now— except for the fact that he didn't have his war gear, Ben, or the authority to blow people to hell.

They arrived at the scene to find a few other police cars in place. Sam hopped out, strode over to a small group of cops and started asking questions. Dusty lagged behind, his gaze locking on the small house, instinctively searching for weaknesses, ways in and potential escape routes the guy might take.

The white house appeared to be of typical size. Maybe two or three bedrooms. Front door. Presumably a rear one as well. Windows in the front had pulled blinds, not allowing anyone a single glimpse into what occurred inside. Trees surrounded the area. Landscaped in the front, woods in the back. That could prove to their advantage.

"You've made contact?"

"Yes, sir. He's demanding money and a free pass. Anything less, he says he'll start shooting."

"Panicked or just lowdown mean?"

The deputy shrugged. "A little of both would be my opinion. He's not dumb. Doesn't stay on the phone long enough to do more than issue orders." The guy checked his watch. "We've got fifteen minutes before he starts the killing."

Hearing the time limit, Dusty took off. He returned to the vehicle and dug his vest out of his bag along with his rifle. The second he secured the protective gear, he strode over to Sam again. "Try to draw the bastard out. If he doesn't take the bait, then we're screwed. Unless you have a concussion grenade?"

Sam shook his head. "What I'd give for one right now."

Dusty sighed. *Small towns and their limited budgets. Fucking hell.* "Just see if you can lure him out. I'll go in if I have to."

The deputy's mouth fell open.

Sam gave a brief nod. "We'll make it happen." He turned to the other man. "Get that guy on the phone."

Dusty didn't waste another second. He sprinted for the area behind the house, keeping to the tree line in case the tango happened to be looking out. Finding a position on the house's flank, he squatted down in the brush, lifted his rifle and peered through his scope, searching for any sign of movement.

A curtain ruffled, but no face showed.

He held back, unwilling to take chances with innocent lives. Instead he waited. Something would give. Soon.

Time dragged by. Dusty remained unmoving. He watched the side and back of the house, knowing the police monitored the front. If the guy tried to escape into the woods, Dusty had him. Alert and attentive, Dusty knew with a single gunshot he'd storm the back door and force his way in. He'd do so now, but didn't want to give the guy a reason to start cutting people down.

With no radio or communication link, Dusty had no clue what conversations were taking place. They didn't matter. He kept his vigilance. Would do so until told otherwise.

Long minutes passed. Still he watched.

"Stand down, Dusty. The bastard surrendered," Sam hollered at him from the front of the house.

Dusty stood up, stretched the kinks out, and made his way back to gathering of cops. He glanced over at the suspect, noted the unkempt appearance, the too-bright eyes and the sunken cheeks.

"That son of a bitch is high."

"Yeah." Sam shook his head.

Together they watched another deputy shove the guy into the back seat of a police cruiser.

Dusty peered over to find a young mother trying to console her small children, who clung to her with fear written clearly on their faces. His gut clenched in rage. Those were the people who would suffer from today's actions. The meth head didn't have a clue. He'd made his choices, all bad. But the innocent wouldn't forget this experience and the stain of terror would potentially linger for life.

He cussed fluently.

Sam slapped him on the shoulder. "I'm with you."

"War is bad news, but at least could eradicate the bad guys. Here there's too many damn rules and justice is too fucking soft."

"You're preaching to the choir, buddy." Sam shared a look with Dusty before leading him back to the car. "I'll give you a ride back to your truck."

Dusty rubbed his face, drew in a deep breath and forced the remaining anger into his kill box. The old SEAL trick for burying emotions so they wouldn't interfere with missions came second nature to him. He couldn't fix this, couldn't take it all away. So carrying the garbage around only added to his already full load of burdens.

With practiced ease, he stored his rifle, stripped off his vest, zipped up his bag and climbed back into the car, more than eager to get back to his quiet life at the stable. Even if he had to deal with a peppy blonde underfoot.

* * * *

"This is good." Dusty chewed with relish. He watched the smile of appreciation appear on April's face. Blue eyes sparkled as if he'd just offered up a huge compliment instead of simply praising a well-cooked meal.

He'd no sooner returned back home than she'd arrived, toting an entire meal, hot out of the oven. After his morning, the thought of sharing a home-cooked meal with April had bolstered his mood.

"Thanks. It's my mother's recipe." She cut off another bite of her chicken.

"You've never mentioned your parents before." He treaded carefully into the topic of families.

After he'd planted a kiss on her yesterday, he'd called himself twelve kinds of fool. April seemed to have taken the show of affection in stride. She didn't harass him, pressure him or even question him. She simply went about chores quietly and efficiently, though he caught her staring at him more than once, her gaze filled with curiosity and wonder with a hint of interest.

*Way to go, dumbass.*

Yet he couldn't quite bring himself to apologize and explain that the show of affection meant nothing. The simple act had revved his dormant engine and heated his blood enough to match the blistering temperatures outside. For some reason, kissing April had meant something more than a prelude to a quick round of robust sex. Her touch sank deeper, softened his resistance and prodded him to consider possibilities.

"My parents still live in Oregon. I grew up there, started college there before I transferred to the University of Colorado. Ended up falling in love with the area and stayed after graduation."

He heard an unspoken hesitancy in her words, as if she was holding important details back. "That's a long drive home. Why did you transfer?"

She looked down at her plate and played with her macaroni and cheese. "I met a guy I thought I could love.

Turns out he had a dark side. The first time he hit me, I left. Finished up the semester and decided to pursue my schooling elsewhere."

He sucked in a breath, grappling with a sudden rage at the thought of a man raising a hand to any woman, but particularly to April. "How bad?"

Glancing up, she met his gaze before lowering her eyes once more, pain written clearly on her face. "It was just a slap. Nothing horrible, but enough that I knew I needed to get away and fast."

His tension eased only slightly. If he ever found the man, to hell with the law. He would beat him to a pulp just for the audacity of hurting her. Everything he'd seen from April told of goodness and kindness, certainly nothing that qualified as deserving of a single blow. "I'm sorry. Some men are bastards and deserve to be shot."

The corners of her mouth hitched up. "Personally, I'd prefer dropping them in the middle of a snake pit, but shot will work."

He slowly grinned back at her attempt at humor. The revelation told him much more about her. She'd thrown out her opinion on men and relationships once before, but he didn't have a clue how deep the sentiment went or for what reasons. Considering what she'd been through, he was genuinely surprised she didn't show more nervousness or edginess around him, especially after he'd ranted at her for offering lunch the first time. He grimaced at his surliness and regretted his abruptness once more. Yet he hadn't known, and she had stood up to him like a mother hen to a hungry fox.

Respect for her grew. She had no reason to trust men any more than he had to trust women.

*What a pair we make.* He couldn't help but grin to himself.

Forking a piece of meat, he ate for a bit before saying anything more. "What did your parents say?"

"They helped me file a restraining order and launch a formal complaint both at school and legally. With no evidence there was no case, but they wanted the mark to be on his record in case he hit another woman."

"Smart people. Show a chain of behavior that would prove his actions weren't a one-time, heat-of-the-moment thing."

April sipped her soda then tilted her head. "You sound like a lawyer."

"My father was one. So's my older brother." He cringed as the words flowed out. He always strove to avoid speaking about his family. Now he'd stupidly opened the barn door, inviting April to fire away.

"You've never talked about them," she quietly said.

"We…don't get along." He chewed and chewed, suddenly finding the delicious dinner roll to be a bit doughy.

"I'm sorry to hear that. When's the last time you spoke to them?"

He debated how much to offer up before giving an answer. "Three years."

April's mouth fell open as sadness and concern filled her eyes. "Oh. I really am sorry."

He swallowed, took a long drink to wash the lump of food down and nodded.

She studied him for a long moment, then glanced down at Ben. "I've been doing some research on adopting former military dogs. Even printed out an application. I was wondering if I can use you for a reference."

He blinked at the change of subject, both relieved and perplexed. "You want to adopt a war dog?"

She nodded. "I know you and Ben share something special. I just thought about what they've been through, the ones that their handlers or the family of the handlers can't take home. The dogs sit in the kennel and simply wait to be adopted. It's downright sad. They've given so much, yet are relegated to a dog run and wondering if that's their last home."

His gut clenched as he considered Ben in such a situation.

"My only problem is I work twelve-hour shifts. I can't be

home to let one outside to potty. But I want an inside dog." Her mouth turned down in a frown.

He took another bite of his pasta, this time swallowing more easily. "I'll vouch for you. Might be able to move things along a bit faster since I'm already in the system." He watched hope and excitement flash in her eyes, the sight enough to shunt blood directly to his dick. He ignored the sudden ache and found himself offering up a solution to her problem. "I'm sure I can spare a few minutes to go over and let your dog out when you work."

"Oh, thank you." She beamed at him. Excitement and appreciation laced her voice. "I'll pay you for the doggie day care service."

"Don't worry about it. Your helping out is more than enough to make up for a few minutes letting a dog go outside to do his business." He shrugged, felt his heart buoy and stubbornly tamped the surge of desire. He was simply helping her out. *That's what friends do, after all.*

Yeah, except he fought the urge to strip her down, lay her across his bed and drill into her depths until she shouted his name in ecstasy. Too bad friends with benefits wasn't an option. Like her skittish filly, April needed time, devotion and a gentle hand. He'd gladly shower all those on her, except for one small detail.

He had no intention of shackling himself to a woman ever again.

# Chapter Eight

Dusty wiped sweat from his brow, noting that more instantly appeared. He wanted to kick himself for not bringing a sweatband or at least a handkerchief with him. Fixing fences always proved hot work in the summer. Add in temperatures in the triple digits and a clear, sun-filled sky and he'd be lucky to have any dry clothing by the time he finished. He yanked off his leather gloves, unsnapped his lightweight shirt and slid it off. His discarded garment safely wrapped around the fence, he tugged on his gloves, picked up the pliers and returned to work.

The crunch of shoes on moisture-starved grass drew his attention. Glancing up, he found April walking his direction, a large Thermos in hand. Her typical attire of T-shirt and jeans covered a petite body with all the right curves. Her blonde hair had been pulled back into a loose ponytail that swayed with each movement. A light layer of makeup covered her face, adding to the natural beauty and supple skin so soft to the touch. Lavender carried to him on the breeze, the scent nearly as enticing as the woman headed his direction.

She'd headed home after helping him with the early morning chores and had obviously bathed and changed. After the past three days of her hanging out with him from sunup to sundown, he found the time alone almost deafeningly quiet and a bit lonely. They didn't have to speak in order to share companionable silence, simply having her close by made his day a bit brighter. Odd, considering he'd moved there three years ago to escape meddlesome family and enjoy a fairly isolated existence. Never once had he felt the depressing weight of loneliness, not with Ben, the horses and an endless list of chores to do. Not until April showed up and stuck to him like a burr in a horse's tail. Since then, he found himself looking for her every morning, anticipating her presence and chipper attitude.

"I thought you might be thirsty. It's sweet tea." She smiled at him and crossed the remaining distance with a long stride before handing over the container.

He stuffed the tool back in his pocket, took off his gloves and set them on top of the thick wooden post. "Thanks." He flipped the lid open and took a long, cooling drink, the liquid nearly as refreshing as a dip in a chilly creek. Each swallow soothed his dry throat and pepped up his energy.

He lowered the container, only to find April staring at his bare chest. Her gaze reflected appreciation, intrigue and a hint of blatant desire. He could almost see the hamster wheel turning in her mind as she checked him out.

Before he might have reminded her of his solidly single status. Now, after spending some time with her and hearing her background, he didn't have the heart to criticize. Instead he soaked up the silent compliment with relish. Women had looked at him before with all sorts of expressions written on their faces. Yet no one had seemed as interested, as enthralled and sincere as April. She continued to focus on him like a man stuck on a deserted island for months looking at a juicy steak. Hungry.

Desire hit him like a runaway train, sending a wave of absolute need straight to his groin. Insistent and aching, his erection protested the tight quarters in his denim jeans nearly as much as the hardness demanded an outlet. Preferably April naked under him, spread for his taking, her nails biting into his back as she begged him to sink deeper, to carry them both straight to rapture.

He drew in a breath and ignored the sultry temptation of the woman before him. Getting all hot and bothered each time she came around would sentence him to walking with a rigid boner the majority of each day. Not a bit comfortable for work, let alone climbing into a saddle. Chastising himself, he pushed his body's needs far from his mind.

Glancing up, he found a pretty pink blush coloring her cheeks, a telltale sign she'd been caught staring at him. He grinned to himself, enjoying her innocent reaction to his exposed body. His groin tightened incredibly as she continued to rake him with her twinkling gaze.

Time for a distraction before he got another silly idea in his head like kissing her once more, slipping his tongue inside for another heady taste of the woman who proved a contradiction to his beliefs about the fairer sex. "I thought you were going home to catch up on chores there."

"I got most of them done. The advantage of living in a small house, the cleaning takes only a short time." She shrugged. "I figured you'd be out here still working since that was on your to-do list this morning and thought you might need something cold to drink."

"I appreciate it." He considered her generosity and the fact she spent so many hours at his stable. If she had a hobby or a social life, he didn't see how. He'd wager her days were spent alone and devoid of excitement, which would explain why she tagged along with him all the time lately.

A sudden observation came to mind. "You've never mentioned having a pet."

"I don't have one."

His eyebrows arched. "As much as you love animals, I find that strange."

She sighed and reached out to steady herself on the corner post. "I had to put my cat down a few months back. Cancer. After that, I'm still not sure I'm ready for another one. Then I saw the love between you and Ben and decided to take a chance with a dog. A war dog."

"I understand." He could empathize. Bonds formed with animals were as strong as family. In his case, stronger. Looking up, he found Ben still lying in the shade at the entrance to the stable, guarding as Dusty had told him to do. Not that he expected someone to try to break in while he worked in the far pasture, but he preferred Ben stay in the cooler shade rather than lie in the hot sun at his side. The dog's thick coat wasn't made for these extreme conditions. His advanced age didn't help, either.

Once more he replayed April's words. To lose a pet, especially having to make the difficult decision to end their life, took a toll on a person's soul. He knew Ben's day would come and hoped Mother Nature made the decision instead of him.

"I noticed the smoke is getting thicker." She turned her attention to the sky, effectively changing the difficult subject. "The news said the fire is still out of control, pushed by high winds, and heading more this direction now."

Dusty took another drink and replaced the lid. "Yeah. It's getting worse." He pinned her with his gaze. "You need to start packing now."

April blinked at him and her face scrunched in bewilderment. "Packing? The news said the fire is still a hundred miles away."

He raked the horizon, sniffing the breeze. The *whoosh* of chopper blades carried to him. Turning, he spotted the helicopter flying fairly low to the ground.

Images flashed into his mind like pictures in a slideshow before smoothing out into a 3D action movie on a big screen.

*Explosions covered the sound of the Black Hawk as it landed. His team jumped out, rifles at the ready, as a hail of bullets flew their direction. Men dove for cover. He hit the deck, felt sand kick up in his face as a bullet landed too close for comfort. Adrenaline spurted into his blood, giving him the energy to regain his feet and surge ahead, running in a crouch to make less of a target. Thick, acrid smoke filled the air along with the stench of blood, battle and death. Gunshots drowned out the yells of the soldiers and the cries of the wounded. Ahead of him, a Humvee jumped as yet another roadside bomb detonated, throwing the passengers high into the air before they plummeted to the ground and lay crumpled like sacks of potatoes, blood covering their clothes. Body parts flew like projectiles through the dust.*

*His team leader waved them ahead. With a burst of speed, Dusty ran flat out to the line of military vehicles, hit the ditches for cover once again, then lifted his rifle and aimed. Rounds burst from his gun at a furious pace. Over and over he aimed and shot, not keeping count of the numbers of men who went down under the relentless barrage. The barrel of his gun heated to near scorching as he shoved yet another clip in and fired once more, laying a steady stream of deadly bullets in an effort to eradicate the enemy, protect his team members and rescue the ambushed Army personnel before they suffered any more losses.*

*Turning his head to the side, he saw a man dressed in white palm his cell phone. Urgency rushed through him at the realization of the man's brutal intentions. Spinning around, he barely aimed, simply shooting off enough rounds to ensure the man wouldn't sit back up, reclaim his cell phone and set off another deadly bomb.*

*A sharp bite of pain drew a vicious curse from his throat. Looking down, he found his shirt turning red. Rage and months of rigid training took over. Ignoring the wound, he emptied the rest of his clip, not stopping until his gun clicked empty and no other tangos stuck their head over the small hill.*

*Hearing a moan, he twisted to find one of his teammates on the ground, holding his leg – or what was left of it. A medic rushed over and opened his treatment box. Another man spoke into his radio, presumably calling for a medical chopper pickup. Hurrying over, Dusty dropped to his knees and took Blaine's hand in his. "Hang in there, buddy. You're gonna make it."*

*Blaine's brown eyes, filled with pain, met his. "Kill that son of a bitch for me."*

*Dusty nodded. "Gladly."*

*The medical staff shuffled Blaine onto a board and scurried off toward a safe landing zone several yards behind them. He watched them go, his heart in his throat as he wondered if Blaine would even survive.*

"Dusty? Dusty?"

For a moment he thought one of the team called his name. A few seconds later, he realized a woman had spoken.

Blinking, he struggled to pull himself away from the

horrific scene.

"What do you see?" April stepped closer, laying a gentle hand on his biceps.

He flinched at her touch, but managed to pull himself out of the waking nightmare. Sucking in a deep breath, he focused on the concern written on her face, the pretty blue eyes full of sympathy.

"A glimpse into hell." The quiet words came out gravelly and hoarse.

"A flashback." She trailed her fingers down his arm, her touch light and soothing. Finding his hand, she linked her fingers with his.

He tilted his head back, drew in air and willed his pounding heart to slow.

She squeezed his fingers. "It's okay now."

Swiveling, he faced her, finding the caress reassuring and helpful in banishing the memories back into the recesses of his mind. He seized the present reality and held on tight.

"Shit." He ran his free hand through his hair and shook his head. Still a bit rattled, he forced calm and control back to the fore.

*That was fucking awful.* He'd had nightmares countless times. Never before had he experienced a flashback and he sure as hell didn't want to see another one. To have his life taken over in a split second, where he could have sworn he'd returned to the front, unsettled him like nothing else could. He prided himself on a will of steel and supreme control. Having a flashback had nearly demolished his hard-won determination and shaken him to the core.

Gathering up his inner control, he blew out a long breath and looked back to April.

She found the scar on his upper arm with her fingers, then lightly traced the roughened and uneven skin. Her brow furrowed. "You were wounded."

He nodded, her caress and fascination had stolen his ability to speak. Emotions flooded him, namely relief and need. No other woman in recent memory had touched him like April did, with care and tenderness. She dug a little deeper under his skin and planted roots.

*Why her? Why now?*

After months of contentment alone, why did she have to come along and show him how much he longed for the company of a woman—the gentle contact, her listening ear? April's gift of humor kept him off balance, as did her stubbornness and refusal to back down at his surliness. He'd thought he just needed to get laid, to work off some built-up steam. Instead he found himself drawn into the moment, standing in the hot sun with April holding his hand and rubbing his arm in a show of support, soothing the last images from his mind as she eased him back into the present.

"Does it still hurt?"

"No." He dropped her hand in order to reach for another drink. He opened the Thermos and took another long swallow, trying to add moisture to his suddenly dry mouth. Done, he replaced the lid and set the container at his feet. "Thanks again."

"Sure." She studied him for a long moment. "Is the fence stable for now?"

He tilted his head, perplexed by her question. "Yeah, why?"

She smiled shyly. "Why don't you come up to the house? I'll fix us some lunch."

Dusty opened his mouth to protest, but quickly changed his mind. The more he tried to push her away, the stickier she became. Instead of a harsh rejection, he met her gaze and nodded. "I'm about done here. Why don't I finish up first while you go on inside?"

"I'll wait." She shifted the weight on her feet and appeared a bit antsy.

For a second he couldn't see the reason for her behavior change, then the light bulb clicked on in his brain. She'd only been in his house once before. Walking in unattended and scouring through his fridge probably crossed the line into awkward and intrusive. He'd feel the same way if the roles had been reversed. "I'll be done in a couple of minutes."

She glanced up at him and nodded. Relief crossed her face. "Okay." April turned and surveyed the horizon. "I know the fire is still a ways off, but I can't help but be concerned." Worry edged into her tone.

He followed the line of her vision. "Truth be told, so am I." He blew out a breath. "I think we should prepare for an evacuation. Without rain and with these winds, that fire will spread worse than a locust infestation across the land." If only heavy moisture would appear. No such luck. The weatherman droned on each night about the same old forecast with no relief in sight. His gut told him something had to break and soon. Unfortunately, right now the break seemed to be coming in the form of an inferno. "Fires are fickle. They can change on a dime. If that happens, things can go to hell in a handbasket real quick." He looked up once more, noticing the distant plumes of gray smoke, and his gut clenched.

"Where will you take the horses?" She looked over the field at the animals standing idle in the shade, their tails continuously flipping to shoo away flies.

The question had entered his mind more than once. Thus far no answers appeared. "I'll make some calls today." *And hope that someone has room for that many animals for an extended period of time and an extra trailer or two to haul them at a moment's notice.*

April eyed the sky with worry written across her face. As much as he wanted to ease the stark lines, he couldn't. He'd make plans and get everything ready just in case the worst-case scenario became reality. His luck had held thus far, but as he'd learned in the military, eventually everyone's luck ended.

* * * *

"You really need to get to the store sometime." April smiled at Dusty over her grilled cheese sandwich. They'd returned to the house for lunch only for her to find he had little available for a quick meal preparation. She made do with sandwiches and chips, but also made a point to remind herself to bring him something more substantial later. "A man can't live on sandwiches alone."

"I've got stuff in the freezer." He took a long swallow of his ice water.

"I have a feeling you don't cook much. Probably not much point when it's just one person. At least that's my experience."

"I've made do. Better than the MREs in Afghanistan."

She blinked at the mention of his service. He'd never really brought up many details, and the fact he did so now surprised and delighted her. A sign of trust and acceptance, hopefully. "Were they tasty?"

He snorted and bit into his sandwich. "It was food. Some days we were too busy to eat anything."

"You went hungry?" Concern swamped her.

He shrugged.

April took a long drink. Never before had she really thought about the frontline troops getting fed, especially during battle. Now Dusty gave her the impression that, at least in his experience, food became a luxury. Once again her heart clenched at what he must have gone though. "I'm sorry. You did so much, and the thought of you doing without bothers me."

He took another bite and chewed. His gaze met hers briefly before he stared at his plate.

End of discussion about his service, obviously. But she didn't want to let the small glimpse into his past end.

She recalled the event earlier, a flashback, a horrible one at that. Presumably the chopper flying overhead had triggered the images. Understandable, yet she worried. In their short association she knew he'd missed sleep one night due to nightmares, now this.

As a nurse, she saw patients with post-traumatic stress now and again, especially veterans. One had even warned her not to touch him when he was asleep for fear of an instinctive response that could endanger her. She'd taken his word and made sure to knock before entering his room each time to avoid startling him. Yet she'd never seen someone have a flashback, seen them transfixed, staring off into space, unresponsive to their name being called. Dusty had done just that. His jaw had clenched, his eyes set, his lips pulled into a thin line. She'd seen his fists tighten and known his heart had to be racing as he suddenly panted for breath.

Her heart went out to him—living with the memories of horror, dealing with nightmares and flashbacks. How he kept his sanity, she didn't know. Probably sheer guts and stoic control. Unfortunately, she worried his tough determination wouldn't be enough over time. He needed the peace and serenity the animals brought him. He especially needed Ben. But in the long run, she thought he also needed some professional help.

"Can I ask you something personal?" She tiptoed into the topic with hesitation and tentativeness. After all, they'd known each other less than a week—not enough time to develop a strong enough rapport to broach such sensitive subjects.

His gaze met hers as he crunched a chip.

"I know most soldiers suffer from PTSD after returning from war. I've read even the war dogs do." When he said nothing, she plowed ahead. "It's got to be very difficult and unsettling. I just wondered if you'd considered seeing a therapist about it."

Dusty stared at her for a long moment, his face expressionless even as his eyes bored through her. She held her breath and refused to back down. Tension filled the room, so much so Ben trotted over and rested his chin on Dusty's thigh. Dusty petted him and finished the last bite of his meal. "I've got work to do." He wiped his hands on a napkin and stood. "Go home and get packed." With those final words, he strode out the door and back into the stable, Ben right on his heels.

April's hopes and heart sank. She lowered her head in defeat. She'd stepped over the line with Dusty and knew it, but only because she truly cared.

Standing, she gathered up the remnants of their lunch, snapped the clasp over the bag of chips and returned them to where she found them. She turned on the hot water, set the plug in the sink and added detergent. After gathering up the dirty dishes, she placed them in the soapy water then started washing, her thoughts a whirlwind.

*At least he didn't yell.* She found one positive in a whole convoluted mess of negatives. She'd seen his face pinch when he ordered her to leave. Evidently she'd hit a touchy nerve and he didn't feel comfortable discussing his issues with a near stranger.

"I'm such an idiot." She sighed and continued with her task. They had found a balance as friends, yet she'd had to push, had to mess everything up with her big mouth.

Finishing the last plate, she quickly dried everything and returned all of them to the cupboard. She wiped off the kitchen table and the countertops, then let the dirty water out. Hanging her rag over the bridge between the sinks, she surveyed the room and gave a nod of approval. *Clean enough.*

With a heavy heart, she exited the house section and entered the stable, searching hard for Dusty, only to find herself alone. Striding outside, she raked the area with her eyes, finally locating him in the back pasture, collecting the black filly he was in the process of breaking.

Uncertain what to do, she pondered her options. She could wait for him to return and apologize. Or leave as he requested. Or try to find some common middle ground. *Decisions, decisions.* Walking away felt like abandonment, yet she didn't want to press her luck by hanging around if he needed space.

He approached, watching her like a hawk. A tad uncomfortable, she lifted her chin and straightened her back. *Don't let him see you sweat.* She snorted to herself. She'd been perspiring since she'd gotten up that morning. He'd long since seen droplets of moisture bead and trickle down her face. Same with him. His clothes were damp in spots and would continue to be so until the horrendous heat broke.

He led the filly in and tied her to a stall so he could saddle and bridle her. His face gave little indication of his emotions, although his dark eyes didn't appear nearly as cold as before.

April met him as he finished tying the knot. "Look. I probably overstepped my bounds. I'm sorry if I offended you, but I'm not sorry I said something. I hate the thought of you hurting." She bit her lip and looked directly at him. "You deserve to be happy and free."

He stared at her for a long moment. "Who says I'm not?" The words came out clipped, full of annoyance.

She went with her gut. "I think anyone with bad dreams compliments of their years of service wouldn't consider themselves happy. Not until they found a way to cope and hopefully control the side effects of being a hero."

"I'm no one's hero."

April refused to look away. "You're my hero."

His mouth opened, but shut once more. Before he could answer, her cell phone rang. Plucking the device from her pocket, she checked the caller ID and immediately answered. "Hello?"

"April? It's Mary from work." Her nurse manager's voice came across loud and clear. "I'm sorry to bother you on vacation, but we have an emergency."

"What's wrong?" April's heart climbed into her throat.

"We're under mandatory evacuation orders due to the fire." The hospital lay approximately twenty miles south of the stable. If the fire threatened them enough to have to move every patient out, things had to be getting much worse. "We need everyone to come in and help transport patients. All the equipment has to be packed and moved as well."

"I'll change clothes and be on my way."

"Thanks, and I'm sorry to interrupt your vacation," Mary replied contritely.

"No problem." April clicked off.

Glancing up, she found Dusty staring at her with curiosity and a bit of concern. "The hospital is under a mandatory evacuation order. I've got to go in and help get patients transported out and pack up supplies and equipment to be stored elsewhere until the threat has passed."

"That's too damn close for comfort." He puffed out a deep breath.

"I'm sure they're closing the hospital early because of the length of time it would take to move everything. Although that's not much consolation." She worried her bottom lip.

His eyes sparked before he lifted his gaze to look around the stalls. "Packing's definitely in order."

She nodded. "I'll be back to help as soon as I finish at the hospital."

Dusty shook his head. "I'll take care of everything. Just take care of yourself."

The firm words didn't surprise her in the least. Dusty had probably never asked for help in his life. *Stubborn cuss.* Just another part of him that both flustered and thrilled her.

On impulse, she threw her arms around him and hugged him tight. He returned the embrace, squeezing her snug. Resting his cheek against hers, he simply held her for the longest time, unmoving except for the puffs of air tickling her shoulder. His actions soothed her, speaking loud and clear where words remained unspoken. He felt something for her. Friendship. Companionship. Perhaps something more. The level didn't matter as much as the basic principle that he cared.

With renewed hope, she savored the moment, soaked in his strength and dug deep to find her own courage. As much as she wanted to spend the day just like this, she couldn't. The hospital awaited.

He slowly released her, setting her a step away. His gaze locked on her face.

She gave him a sad smile. "You can't get rid of me that easily. I'll be back before you know it."

His lips hitched up only slightly, the emotion not carrying to his dark eyes. "Be careful."

Lifting on tiptoe, she brushed her lips across his cheek. "Promise." She took one last look before turning and heading for her vehicle.

# Chapter Nine

Dusty turned on the radio then opened a plastic carrier sitting on his desk. Ben tilted his head as if wondering why he was moving files from the heavy metal cabinet into the smaller tote. Pausing, Dusty plopped down in the old wooden chair, the seat squeaking under his weight, and petted the dog's head. Ben looked up at him as his tail brushed the floor.

"Looks like our luck might run out, buddy. The fire is drawing closer and no one I've called has trailers or men available to haul stock. Even if there was someone, I haven't found a place to take them. With the vast amount of acreage affected, no one nearby has anything left." He ran his hand through his hair and stared at Ben. "I didn't need anyone, was happier alone. Now, when the chips are down, I'm out on a ledge by myself."

He sighed. Except for April. She'd worked her ass off at the stable, volunteering her time and energy to help care for the animals. Even more, she added a bit of humor into his life. Idly, he realized she'd brought a renewed attitude that perhaps all women weren't made from the same mold, and made for an overall good friend. Friend? *Bullshit.* He'd wanted more from the day she'd strode through his doors full of excitement and determination. Only her reservations and his hard lessons had prevented him from throwing out a pick-up line or three.

Then he'd kissed her — the best and worst thing he'd ever done. She'd tasted like ambrosia and had set a flood of desire streaming through his blood that had yet to dissipate. More than that, she'd reached something deeper, tenderer inside, twisted him in knots as he discovered places he didn't know existed with her name written on each and every one. She'd grown on him in their few days together, turning a once awkward silence into familiarity as they worked side-by-side day in and day out.

Now she'd run off toward the inferno to help rescue her small hospital and all those inside.

His gut clenched with worry, even as he reminded himself she spoke the truth. The authorities would clear hospitals and institutions first due to the number of people and time needed to evacuate the essentials to safe ground. However, just the fact they'd made such a declaration stirred up worry and fear, something he hadn't felt in forever.

*"The fire still rages out of control. Latest information claims eight percent contained as the continued dry conditions and high winds push the flames northeast,"* the radio announcer droned on.

Dusty sighed, his shoulders pushed down in defeat. For three years, he'd wanted nothing more than to be alone with his animals, to live in peace and tranquility without the spiky thorn of dealing with too many people. Ironically, here he sat, packing up his office, waiting for Mother Nature's fury to play out, and with the realization of his huge error slapping him directly in the face. With his world going to shit, no one had his back.

He thought of his brothers, the terrible fistfight between him and Archer that had ended any association between them for the past three years. Before he'd acted like an arrogant imbecile and turned on them for pointing out what he refused to see—they'd always stood beside him. He would never have to even ask, they would come running if they thought he had bitten off more than he could chew.

Plucking the phone from his pocket, he pulled up his contact list and eyed Archer's number. His finger hovered over the button.

Despite their anger and hurt feelings, more than likely his brothers would come save his ass. Yet his pride stopped his hand. Slowly, he set the phone on his desk, then released a breath. *I can deal with this.* All he needed was a bit more time and luck.

The thought didn't bolster his spirits in the least. Instead he felt more morose than ever. Scratching behind Ben's ear, he took comfort in his best friend while worries ate away at his gut, leaving his stomach churning. Always before he'd known things would simply work out. After spending four years as a SEAL, he didn't fear much, including death. The trivial matters were just that — trivial — and most things fell into that particular category.

Unfortunately a pending natural disaster fell outside the limits of basic issues he no longer fretted over. His animals and livelihood were in potential peril and the one woman who actually cared had raced off toward the wildfire to save others.

With those unsettling thoughts, he stood and resumed packing, still racking his brain for answers.

\* \* \* \*

The familiar rumble of a car engine slowly entering the drive alerted Dusty to his visitor. He paused in his task of organizing horse feed in order to peek out the stable door to see who had decided to pay him a visit. Instantly he recognized April's large SUV.

Relief and a jolt of excitement hit him directly in the chest. She'd been gone for nearly two days and he hadn't heard a word. Not that he'd actually expected her to call, but deep down, he'd needed to hear her voice, to ensure she arrived in one piece and that the fire didn't threaten her life before she could bolt for home. He'd chastised himself for the reaction, understanding what the sentiment meant deep down, but not anywhere near ready to deal with such profound questions.

She pulled up and parked, then jumped out. "Hi."

"Hi yourself."

Leaning into her vehicle, she wrestled for some items. The position stretched her jeans snug over her curvy backside. He appreciated the view, which only caused him to envision rubbing his hands over her delectable body, testing each hill and valley for suppleness and softness.

With a full plastic bag in hand, she shut the driver's side door. "How are the horses? Did they give you any problem?"

"They're fine and no problems at all. Miracle is coming along slowly but surely." He studied April like a book. She appeared clean and healthy, dressed in her typical attire of jeans and a T-shirt. Pink tennis shoes covered her feet. Yet her face told the story. Lines of fatigue and dark circles under her eyes spoke of missed sleep and stress. Concern cascaded over him. "You look ready to drop."

She frowned and he wanted to kick himself for his less than tactful greeting. Lowering his head, he ran his hand through his short hair and watched her with avid interest. "I'm glad you're back." The words carried truth.

Tension eased from her face as her blue eyes lit up. "Thanks. It was crazy, but we managed to get everyone and everything not cemented down sent to safer ground." She stepped forward to stop in front of him. "I brought lunch."

Guilt pressed his shoulders down. She worked her ass off for the hospital, brought him food, and all he could say was how tired she looked. Whatever happened to his manners? His charm? Hell, he used to be able to pick up a woman with a grin and a line. Now he couldn't even show basic kindness to the woman who had given so much of her time to help him with daily chores. *Stop being a damn prick and wake up*, he chided himself and blew out a breath. "You didn't have to, but thanks."

She beamed, which put a little smile on his own face. "It's meatloaf from the small diner. I hope you like it."

He blinked at her. "Carry-out from Nelly's?"

"Yep."

"My favorite." He wrapped an arm around her and

nudged her toward the house portion of the stable. "Let's go eat."

Ben bounded over, sniffed April and wagged his tail in happy welcome. She paused for a second to pet him. "Don't worry. I brought you some goodies too."

He barked as if understanding every word.

She paused to allow him to open the gate, tripping over a rock. "Umph."

Dusty caught her to steady her. "You okay?"

"Yeah. Just tripped." She glanced down. "What's in the small box?"

"Spare key."

"Smart."

Holding the gate open for her, he waited until she passed through before closing the barrier and striding to open the entrance to the house, not stopping until he reached the kitchen. He started pulling out necessary utensils and glasses.

He poured them each a glass of iced tea while she unloaded the food. Both plopped down after she left an oversized dog cookie on Ben's bed. The radio played softly from across the room where he'd left it on earlier.

"Where did you find those?" He nodded toward the bag she'd pulled the dog treat from.

"A gourmet dog shop on the way back. I never noticed them before, but they have tons of things. Food, toys, even clothing." Her gaze landed on Ben, who lay on his bed, eating with obvious delight. "Looks like I need to swing by there more often."

Dusty watched his companion animal for a long moment. "I'd say you did well." He opened his Styrofoam container, found a full meal still steaming hot, and hungrily dug in. The first bite nearly made him groan with the delicious taste. "Nelly is the best cook around."

April sampled her potatoes and nodded. "I think so too. Didn't know she did take-out until today, though. I wanted something more than fast food, but didn't want to take the time to sit and eat at the restaurant. When I asked, she told me she'd happily fix up a couple of plates."

Not for the first time, he noticed the subtle signs of her fatigue. Her normally bright eyes appeared dull and she only picked at her food. The previous lines grew more prevalent as time went by.

He'd learned how to determine how close a man stood at the end of his rope with the SEALs. God knew the supervisors had pushed him and the other recruits to the brink over and over again. He'd always managed to find a little more buried inside that served him well then, on the war front and even now when nightmares limited his sleep dramatically.

"You could use a nap."

She glanced up at him. "Maybe later."

She ran close to her body's limits, though not quite at the end of her rope. Dusty didn't want to push her to see how much more she could take. His protective instincts leaped to the fore, demanding he care for her, provide a comfortable place for her to rest until she caught up on much-needed sleep. He hadn't felt the urge to look after a woman since, well, quite a while ago. Realization of how deeply April had dug under his skin should have shocked or concerned him. Instead he felt comfortable warmth spread through him. He might only have known her for a few days, but her inner self remained transparent and rang true. *Just admit it, SEAL, she's grown on you. Big time.* Oddly enough, the thought didn't send him into defensive mode.

"You can use my bed. For a nap, that is." He gauged her reaction closely.

Her eyes widened in surprise before her face softened. The corners of her mouth curled up as she met his gaze with genuine appreciation. "Be careful. I just might take you up on the offer."

Her lighthearted teasing prodded his sense of humor. "It's all yours. Unless you prefer Ben's oversized pillow." He looked down at the canine finishing his snack. "But I should tell you he snores."

She giggled, the sound rivaling a happy meadowlark in the spring. "Does Ben's owner snore as well?" She peered up at him through her lashes.

"Now that would be telling." He jumped into the humorous bantering with both feet and a teasing smile.

April grinned and dug into her food. He matched her in pace and soon both sat with empty containers as he polished off the last of his tea. "The sheets are clean, if you're ready to lie down."

She tilted her head as if seriously considering his offer or trying to figure out a particularly complex puzzle. "What will you be doing while I sleep in your bed?"

Images of a naked April snuggling into his sheets sent a spear of desire through him. She would curl up, her long hair spilling over the pillows. He'd crawl in beside her, find her nape with his lips and commencing kissing her until her need grew to such a fevered pitch she begged him to cover her, to make her his.

His cock reacted to the erotic image, causing a definite discomfort in his jeans. Dusty sucked in a breath and tried to cool his overheated body.

The radio squealed blaringly, followed quickly by the disc jockey's voice, now serious and excited. "This is an emergency warning for residents north of Jackson Station, east of Boulder City, west of Union and south of Fairway. The wildfire has turned. Strong winds are driving the fire rapidly northwest. If you are in these areas, evacuate immediately."

Dusty's gaze met April's widened eyes. He stood and tossed away the empty container of his meal. "Go on home. You've got to pack so you can get out of here."

She shook her head, followed his lead, and walked quickly through the office door to the stable. "No way. I'm not leaving you like this. You can't get everything here boxed up and the horses loaded in time by yourself." She paused to look at him. "Besides, my bags are already packed."

He tilted his head toward her, surprised both by the fact she refused to leave and that she'd actually done as he'd advised.

A small smile crossed her lips. "Yeah, sometimes I actually do listen to you."

"You're already tired." He knew she was ready to drop but also saw a spark of energy, compliments of the dire situation. "I can't ask more of you."

She lifted her chin haughtily. "You're not asking. I'm offering. Now what do you need me to do first?"

He would have grinned at her sassy reply except the alarm screamed once more, propelling him into action. Surveying the stable, he made a quick decision. "I need the office computer and the files. I put them in the plastic carrier to make them easier to handle than in the big file cabinet."

With the wildfire raging for days with little progress by the thousands of firefighters in the area, he'd begun making preparations for the worst-case scenario days ago. Everything possible had been sorted and stored in portable containers already, making for a timely and easy load. Except for the horses and the lack of trailers. As much as he stewed, he couldn't figure out a way to get them all moved with the two trailers he owned. He'd called about renting more, but all to no avail. Besides, he had no one to drive a third vehicle to pull another horse trailer. Now his lack of success was sure to cost him everything he valued.

No. He wasn't ready to throw in the towel yet. Striding outside, he headed for his truck, stopping when a highway patrol vehicle pulled up. A uniformed man got out and nodded in greeting. "You heard about the fire and mandatory evacuation?"

Dusty nodded. "Yeah. We're working on packing the last things right now."

The middle aged man's brow furrowed as he surveyed the place. "Better hurry. Forest Service's best guess is that fire will come like hell on earth."

"How long?"

The officer shrugged. "Best estimates right now for this particular area, four to six hours."

Dusty's heart seized. He might have some things ready, but that didn't leave any time to spare, not when he had twenty horses to get loaded and moved. Not to mention he had nowhere to take the animals. They couldn't stand in their trailers for days on end. He needed to find pasture, a stable, somewhere with room to absorb them without issue.

April emerged from the stable, carrying the box of files with the computer on top. She beeped open the back door of the vehicle, then slid the items inside. Spinning around, she hurried back for another load.

The policeman returned to his car and drove off, presumably to alert others.

*Damn. I can't make it. Not in that time frame.* With his back against the wall, desperate and totally out of ideas, he sighed wearily and pulled out his phone. He'd sworn he'd never do this, but if he was to save the animals and April, he had no other choice.

"Hello?"

"Archer?"

"Dusty?"

"Yeah. I..." He sucked in a breath and ran his hand through his hair, his gaze automatically searching the pasture, finding his prize mares with their foals grazing contentedly. He steeled his resolve. "I need a favor. A big one."

"What is it?"

"There's a wildfire coming. I have two horse trailers, but it's not enough. The highway patrol say I've got four hours before the fire barrels in and destroys everything. I've got to —" His voice broke.

"No problem, bro." Archer's voice came through with confidence.

"But you're three hours away. It's going to be close. I don't have anywhere to take them, either." Defeat sat upon his shoulders as he rattled off the many problems he faced.

"Actually, we're more like five minutes away, just turning off the highway."

Dusty blinked at his oldest brother's words. "We?"

"The news started talking about the fire turning this morning. We got together, hitched up the trailers and started your way."

"God bless you." Hope returned on an angel's wings.

"That's what brothers are for." Archer chuckled. "Now get to packing, bro. We're on a tight schedule and not about to leave anything behind."

"Thank you." Dusty clicked off and jogged back into the stable. "April. My brothers are bringing in more trailers."

She paused as she carried another armload of stuff toward her car. "Thank goodness." She stared at him for a moment. "I know it cost you a lot to call them, but I'm proud of you."

He nodded slightly. "With their help, we're going to make it." Dusty gestured toward her vehicle. "You've got a hitch. I'll need you to pull my extra trailer, if you don't mind."

"Sure. I don't mind in the least."

"Thanks. That'll answer one problem."

April shot him a quick smile. "We'll get to them all. No worries."

He saw her enthusiasm and optimism and wished he felt as upbeat. Yet things were indeed looking up.

As he thought those words, three trucks pulled into the driveway, each towing an empty trailer. Relief eased his tension just the slightest. Striding over, he met Archer as he stepped out of the lead vehicle. "Thanks." He reached out a hand. Archer ignored it and pulled him into a big bear hug.

"No thanks needed."

The trucks parked and his other three brothers jumped out. They all carried smiles and warm greetings, each one giving him a hug. Old resentments seemed downright petty now as he faced the people his ego had forced from his life. Now they came to his rescue. "I can't repay you enough."

Colt slapped him on the back. "Seeing your ugly mug again is payment enough."

Dusty chuckled.

"No time for a family reunion, boys. There's work to do." Archer gestured toward the stable. "What do you need packed?"

"April is working on the office stuff at the moment since she has an SUV to keep things from blowing away."

"April?"

Four men shot him cheesy grins. He shrugged, but couldn't help but smile back. "She's...one of my boarders."

"Uh-huh." Evan waggled his eyebrows. "Must be easy on the eyes too." He offered up a lopsided devilish smile to Dusty. "Never knew you to gravitate to ugly women."

"Who said anything about her looks?" The corners of Dusty's mouth hitched up as he fell into the old habit of sparring with his brothers. *Damn, I missed this and them. Too much.*

Archer nodded slowly. "Your poker face isn't working, Dusty. You've been checking out that girl and sizing her up for keeping."

Not willing to admit anything to his brothers when he hadn't already decided for himself, Dusty forced himself to focus on the issue at hand. "Let me show you where things are." Dusty stepped back into the stable.

"Nice place," Brand said.

"Thanks. Damn shame that blaze will demolish it very soon." The potential reality threw a damper on Dusty's spirits. "We need to take the feed. With the price of hay this year, I don't want to lose it. We can start filling the back of my truck. See how much fits and go from there."

"On it," Evan replied.

Dusty tossed him the keys. "It's parked in front of the shop. Hook up one of the trailers. We'll use April's vehicle for the other one."

April stepped out of the office, suitcases in hand, and smiled. "Hello. You must be Dusty's brothers."

"Yes, ma'am." Archer tipped his hat toward her.

"April this is Archer, Brand, Colt, and the one walking

toward my truck is Evan."

"Nice to meet you," they said in unison.

"The same. Sorry it's under these circumstances." She looked at Dusty. "The office is cleaned out, but you might want to double-check. I've shut Marmalade and Ben in there for now. Don't want them to get upset and hide where we can't catch them."

"Good thinking." He watched his unattached brothers eye April with avid interest. Protectiveness rushed to the fore as well as a healthy dose of selfishness. He might not have made any overt moves on April, but that didn't mean he would stand by and let one of his brothers snatch her out from under his nose. His sudden annoyance quelled as April looked to him with admiration and approval in her eyes. She made him feel special and singled out with the brief glance. Clinging to the warm feeling, he began rattling off tasks to be done.

Dusty pointed toward a large rectangular wooden box. The blue color set off the elaborate design on top which announced the stable's name and emblem. "Let's see how much that can hold of halters and grooming supplies." He looked around. "The saddles need to go as well. Buckets too." He spat out orders and everyone scurried to do his bidding. In less than an hour, they had all the side items loaded up, the trucks' beds full.

He sighed with relief as they managed to stuff the essentials in every nook and cranny of the trucks and the areas of the trailers made for storage and equipment. April's vehicle now sported a trailer just like every other vehicle. Dusty looked around then made the decision. "Let's go get the horses." Grabbing a pile of lead ropes he'd sat aside, he passed two out to each person.

"Any particular order?" Archer asked.

Dusty shook his head. "I'll get the stud. April will collect the mini and the gray filly. Feel free to fetch any of the rest."

"A mini?" Evan arched an eyebrow. "You're raising novelties these days?"

Dusty snorted.

"The mini is mine. Came with the filly." April clutched the soft ropes and started for the pasture.

The heavy scent of smoke carried through the air. A stout wind blew harshly across the area, hastening in dry air, heat and devastation. Dusty noticed the plumes in the distance and swore under his breath. He wouldn't bank on the short four hours they were promised.

The horses sensed the tension and the fire—not far away, judging by their nervousness and reluctance to be caught in a couple of instances. Those were left for last as the brothers rounded up those they could, led them to a trailer and encouraged the animals inside. Dusty supervised the loading, choosing carefully who he placed together. The stud went in first with a group of geldings. The mares with foals were given ample room with another mare in the same trailer. Miracle and Mischief loaded just fine, as did most of the horses. The final two stragglers didn't want to be left behind, as they stood at the gate for easy catching.

With all the horses loaded, Dusty breathed a sigh of relief. Thick smoke grew in intensity, a sure sign the fire was still building and engulfing acres in its path. He didn't hold out much hope for his stable and home for the past three years. Yet with his brothers' and April's help, they were going to make it.

*Speaking of April…*

She darted back in the office and emerged with a cat carrier and Ben on a leash. Archer helped her load the pets, their food and supplies. Dusty took the opportunity to look around, searching for anything he might have missed. They still had to stop by April's rental house to pick up her luggage, and the vehicles were full, but he needed to look one more time.

Striding through the living area, he did a quick yet thorough scan. His bags had been taken already along with the laundry basket of shoes to April's SUV. The few pieces of furniture remained, waiting for Mother Nature's wrath, as did his bed. Heading to the kitchen, he plucked a twelve pack of bottled water out, setting it on the table. They would get thirsty on the three-hour trip back to the ranch and they might as well utilize what he had.

Sadness weighed his shoulders down as he realized he was probably walking through his home for the final time. The belongings didn't matter so much as the living creatures, yet he couldn't help but grapple with grief over the situation. Everything he'd worked so hard to achieve was soon to burn to the ground. He sucked in an unsteady breath, put the morose thoughts from his head and focused on salvaging anything and everything he might possibly need. Finding nothing else in the house, he carried the water to his office, placed it on the desk, then quickly went through drawers. April had wiped the place clean of the necessities. What remained was too big to take or negligible in the scheme of things.

Picking up the water once more, he made his way to the stable. Everyone stood around watching him, April holding onto Ben's leash as he stood panting, his head cocked in canine bewilderment. Evan stepped forward and took the water from him.

"Thanks." Dusty walked the length of the aisle from stall to stall, checking every nook and cranny, ensuring nothing would be left behind. Satisfied, Dusty faced the others. "Okay. I think that's it." His heart clenched at the deep sorrow he felt.

Archer slapped him on the back and hooked a hand over Dusty's shoulder. "Then let's get going."

No sooner had they stepped from the stable than Ben barked, jerked the leash from April's hands and darted off. "Ben!" April sped after him.

Dusty followed suit, his heart in his throat. Great black clouds pushed closer, reminding him of the short time left before they would be overtaken. He couldn't leave Ben, but he didn't have much time to waste either. "Ben! Come back here!" His dog rarely disobeyed, and always for a good reason.

By the time he'd run through the paddock and into the back field, Ben was trotting back, dragging his leash and herding a goat.

April turned to blink at Dusty. He shrugged, having absolutely no clue where the animal came from. Since the goat wore a collar, he decided it must be someone's pet that was lost or perhaps had been left behind. The thought turned his stomach.

The goat bleated and hurried right up to April. She grabbed its collar. Ben rushed to Dusty, leaping into his arms. "You did good, boy. Took a decade off my life, but you did good." He patted the dog and walked back to the others waiting beside the trailers. "I suppose we have room for one more."

They shook their heads but collectively grinned. "Can't leave such a cute thing behind." Brand took the goat from April, lifted her up in his arms and deposited her in the back of the nearest trailer.

"Anything else?" Brand shut the trailer and secured the door.

"That's it. We just need to swing by April's house for a minute to pick up her bags."

"Okay."

They divided up the water, each taking a couple of bottles.

"I don't mind pulling your spare horse trailer, Dusty, but I've never driven with such a thing before." April looked at her SUV then back to him. "Do you mind to drive? I'm afraid of taking turns too sharp, and the thought of backing up gives me heart palpitations." The corners of her mouth hitched up.

He shared her smile. "Sure. Evan can drive my truck." He dug through his pocket and frowned.

"Still have the keys, bro." Evan shook them in the air and jogged to the large black dually.

Dusty opened the door of the SUV, placed Ben inside, then slid into the driver's seat. April settled beside him and closed the door securely. Both sat for a moment in stillness, looking at the place.

"It's in God's hands." Dusty shoved the key in the ignition and turned the engine. With ease of long practice, he maneuvered the vehicle around, complete with trailer, and hit the road.

# Chapter Ten

"Where do you want them, Dusty?" Archer strode over to the gathering group of people. "There's stable space, but not enough stalls for each of them. The front paddocks are empty right now. It's close and there's enough room with the divided areas to separate them into groups."

Dusty sighed as he looked over the ranch. Three long years since he'd seen not only his brothers, but the house and land they'd been raised on. *Home.* When he pulled into the driveway the word popped into his mind and stuck. He'd come home.

He looked over the trailers and people, noticing someone was missing. "Where's Brand?"

"Brand called just as we started back. A highway patrol officer noticed his empty trailer, stopped him and sent him on a rescue mission to help out a lady with her animals not far from your place. He was delayed but should be here soon," Archer answered.

"Okay."

"I imagine you want the stud by himself?" Colt asked.

The question jolted Dusty back into the conversation. "Yeah. As much as he would enjoy hanging out with the girls, I'm not sure they'd be as thrilled." He glanced over the area once more. Lush green grass spread across the acres for as far as he could see. Envious at the obvious abundance of rain in the area, Dusty knew the horses would be thrilled with this temporary home. "Let's put him in the east section. It's smaller, but still roomy enough for him. The mares and foals… Let's go with the westernmost paddock. We'll put April's filly and the geldings in the center area."

"On it." Archer walked to the nearest trailer, unlatched the back gate and swung it open.

"I'll get them." April hurried over, Dusty on her heels.

She stepped into the trailer, spoke softly to the filly and attached the lead rope before doing the same with the mini. Clucking, she led the pair out. Until Mischief dug in his feet and refused to exit the trailer.

Dusty shook his head. "Stubborn cuss."

April shushed him with a frown. "Now, Mischief. We've had this discussion before." She tugged on his halter. Miracle, already out, turned around and stared at her friend. Mischief didn't budge.

"I'll give him a shove." Before Dusty could take two steps, April held up her hand.

"Okay, Mischief. I have one carrot left." She pulled the treat from her pocket. "If you don't get out of that trailer this instant, I'm giving it all to Miracle."

The mini stretched as far as he could without actually moving his feet.

She pulled the carrot back farther. "No way, buddy. If you want it, you have to come and get it."

He squealed, then jumped down with excitement.

Dusty chuckled at the horse's antics, joining in with the rest of his brothers.

"Pretty damn cute." Archer slapped him on the back.

Dusty grinned. Whether his brother spoke about the horse or the woman he wasn't sure, but in his mind they both fit the description. "Yeah."

April moved closer, leading her two horses. As Miracle came abreast of Archer, she stopped, flattened her ears and reached out as if to bite.

"Nasty tempered beast." Archer quickly moved out of range.

The gray filly bumped into April, then sidestepped as she walked forward at her owner's bidding, yet kept an eye on Dusty's oldest brother at the same time.

"Don't care how pretty that filly is, that attitude isn't

something I'd deal with," Archer grumped, his eyes on the horses.

"You'd have the same attitude if you went through what that filly did." Dusty sobered in remembrance of the pictures of Miracle the Humane Society had sent with her records.

"What happened?" Colt paused with one of the geldings in hand.

"Somehow she ended up in the hands of a bastard who not only beat her, but starved her. By the time the neighbors called and the sheriff stepped in, several horses were dead on the property. The few who survived were in horrible shape. Parasites, long hooves, so thin you could see through their bodies. Miracle had to be assisted to even stand. They didn't think she'd make it as she'd lost half her body weight. The Humane Society worked for a year to get her back to the condition she's in now." He sucked in a breath, rage boiling in his gut at the thought of such cruelty. "She still carries whip scars."

"Shit." Archer looked at him. "Did they arrest the bastard?"

Dusty nodded. "From what I understand, he hired a big-time lawyer and managed to get the charges dropped."

"Get me the information." Archer's lips thinned.

Dusty arched an eyebrow.

"What? I'm just going to look into the case."

"Uh-huh. I don't think you have jurisdiction." Though Archer happened to be a district attorney, Dusty doubted he could do much about a case in another state.

"Doesn't matter. When it comes to a bastard that would not only beat an animal, but starve it to death, I'll find someone who can prosecute him."

"Thanks." Dusty tilted his head. "April will adore you forever."

Colt looked across the pasture, then back to Dusty. "How'd she end up with that filly and the mini?"

"Mischief and Miracle bonded at the place they were

rescued. The rescue couldn't separate them without them getting very upset. Mischief was in better shape, from what I understand, and the staff believed the only reason Miracle survived is because of Mischief. They refused to adopt them separately. When April went to the farm to pick out a horse, she fell in love with the filly and ended up bringing them both home."

"Can you even work with her?" Colt asked.

"Yeah. She's gradually settling down. She's not mean, just scared of men. With April she's an angel."

Dusty watched as April released her horses, fed them the carrot, gathered up the lead ropes then closed the gate.

"Do you have a chain or rope for that gate?"

"Yeah, why?" Archer shut the trailer door.

"That mini is a little Houdini."

"Lives up to his name, huh?" Colt chuckled and walked toward the pasture April just vacated.

"You have no idea." Dusty shook his head, grinned, then strode toward the next trailer to collect his stud.

Ten minutes later all the horses had been unloaded, leaving Colt holding the collar on the small goat. "Where do you want her?"

Archer shrugged and looked to Dusty. "Brand said he was bringing in a herd of llamas or some such. Seems to me those might be a bit more goat-sized than the horses."

Dusty looked over the land. "How about let's put her in the foaling area? Everything else is filled, it's close, and I imagine about the right size for smaller stock."

"Sounds good to me." Colt tugged on the collar. The little brown animal balked so he ended up gathering her in his arms and carrying her.

Dusty grinned as the little goat nipped at his brother's hair, clamped her teeth on a mouthful, then gave a sharp tug.

"Ow!"

"I think she likes you." Evan laughed as Colt managed to juggle his load enough to flip him off.

The sound of a vehicle pulled Dusty's attention back toward the long driveway. He found Brand's black truck, complete with stock trailer, slowly navigating the gravel drive and a white SUV in his wake. He drove by them, heading straight for the small foaling shed with a downsized pasture. By the time he'd backed the trailer up to the gate, a woman had parked her vehicle and hurried over.

Dusty and his brothers walked over to meet them.

"I thought you were picking up animals, not a pretty little lady." Archer grinned and tipped his hat at the woman.

She smiled up at him. "I'm Tess, by the way."

Evan opened the gate while Brand and Tess took care of the trailer exit. Colt waved in greeting, standing to the side of the pasture, still holding his newest friend. "We didn't think your animals would mind one lonely goat."

"I think she'll fit right in." Tess eyed Colt's armful for a minute, then stepped around the gate.

"You've got quite the menagerie." Dusty blinked at the smorgasbord of animals in the trailer.

"They're my pets." She cooed to the animals, trying to get them to exit the trailer. None of them bothered to move.

Tess climbed in, untied the tallest occupant and led him out. The llama stopped at the end of the trailer, turned toward Brand, and spit.

"Bogart!"

"Damn llama." Brand wiped his face with a handkerchief he pulled from his pocket.

"I'm so sorry." She shot him an apologetic look and tugged hard on the lead rope. "Come on, you ornery cuss, before Brand spits back." The long-legged pack animal jumped out of the trailer. The alpacas bolted after him.

Evan shut the gate behind them. Dusty smirked at Brand, noting the flashing eyes of anger toward the ill-tempered llama. Yet he didn't miss the softening expression as his brother watched the redhead. They might have just met, but his brother liked what he saw in the woman, mean pet or not.

A brunette trotted over and threw herself into his arms. Dusty caught her and hugged her tight. "I was wondering if you remembered me."

Carrie smacked lightly at his chest. "Remember? How could I forget you?"

Out of the corner of his eye he spied April with confusion plastered on her face. He released Carrie and turned to face April. "April, this is Carrie, Archer's wife. Carrie, this is April."

A true smile replaced curious concern on April's face. "It's good to meet you. I can't thank you guys enough."

Carrie looked at Dusty, then back to April. "No thanks necessary." She waved her hand dismissively. "I better get to cooking. These men are bound to be hungry soon, and boy howdy, can they put away the food."

"I'll be glad to help. Besides, I need to grab Marmalade and find somewhere for her to stay for the duration." Hurrying back to her vehicle, April pulled out the cat carrier and a large shopping bag filled with cat supplies. April met Dusty's gaze for a split second before hustling to catch up with the other woman, Marmalade meowing pitifully all the way.

Colt elbowed him in the ribs. "You decide to move on to greener pastures, let me know. I'll be glad to take a shot with that pretty blonde."

Dusty shook his head, too relieved and happy to see his brothers again to get the least bit upset. After the hurt feelings between them, he couldn't have scripted a better reunion. They'd stepped up to save his ass and he wouldn't forget it. "She's like her filly, bro. A bit skittish around men."

Colt only grinned. "I'm charming."

Archer snorted. Evan coughed.

Colt frowned. "I am."

"Uh-huh. You remember something about having too many girlfriends and getting their names mixed up?" Evan nudged Colt in the back.

"He didn't!" Dusty's mouth fell open.

"Oh, yeah, he did. Hilarious!"

Again Dusty truly realized how much he'd missed in the long months of separation. Evan, his youngest brother, had grown up and filled out, a dramatic change from the gangly teen he'd been when Dusty left. He didn't have a clue about any of the happenings in his family's life over that period of time.

Well, he had nothing but time on his hands waiting to see if the fire engulfed his place or not. Until then, he could catch up with his brothers and see if they were still the troublemakers he remembered.

"I'll just find a local motel." A woman's sweet voice, laced with determination, cut through the air.

Dusty turned to find Brand and Tess leaving the small pen, arguing as they walked side by side.

"No way. There's plenty of room in the ranch house. Hell, there's six bedrooms. I'm sure we've got more than enough space for someone your size."

She tilted her head to stare up at him. "My size? Are you calling me short?"

Brand scowled. "No, if I wanted to call you short, I would have said short. I was saying you won't take up much space, so you're going to stay here, close to your livestock."

"I refuse to be a burden." Her tone grew haughty.

He threw up his arms in frustration. "You aren't a damn burden, all right?" He sucked in a breath. "Why don't you go in and meet April? You girls can share a bedroom."

She opened her mouth but closed it again. A long moment passed before she nodded. "Okay. I'll stay. Just for a short time though."

"Whatever you want."

Tess started toward the house, then stopped. "Thank you, Brand. For coming to my rescue." With a small smile, she continued toward the large brick house.

"Shit, Brand. She likes you," Evan whispered loudly to his older brother.

Brand narrowed his eyes at the youngest in the group. "She's just beholden is all."

"Uh-huh." Archer nudged Brand in the ribs. "Been there, done that. Ended up tying the knot."

Dusty grinned at the slightly nauseated look on Brand's face. None of them cared to strap on the ball and chain. Archer had taken the leap a few years back, but he'd found the most wonderful woman in Carrie. With such high expectations set by the little brunette, the others spent their free time chasing women, engaging in one-night stands and enjoying playboy lifestyles. No lady had lassoed them yet, as hard as they'd tried.

For a moment Dusty recalled Rose, the woman who'd tried to corner him into marriage even as she'd demanded expensive gifts and slowly sunk her claws into his bank account. He hadn't been able to see past her luscious curves, fantastic blow jobs and the hot, kinky sex to the real woman underneath. Thankfully his brothers had. Archer had hired a private investigator who'd found solid evidence of Rose's man-hopping. She used her body and skills to catch a wealthy man, take him for everything he had, then ride off into the sunset to find another victim.

At the time, he hadn't appreciated Archer's interference. Now he needed to suck up his pride and admit his error. "Archer?"

The man swung around to face him.

"Thank you. For pointing out what kind of person Rose was." Dusty swallowed and ran his hand through his hair. Apologizing was still hard. "If not for you..."

Archer smiled and wrapped an arm around Dusty's shoulders. "You're welcome."

"I was an ass."

"Aren't we all from time to time?" Archer squeezed Dusty's shoulder.

Relief washed over Dusty. After all the tension that had passed, the wedge between them seemed to dissipate with those simple words. Wanting to kick himself in the rear for not saying something sooner, Dusty instead reveled in the moment. He'd missed his brothers, their teasing and gouging, their constant rowdiness. For the next few days he intended to get to know them again.

# Chapter Eleven

"I'm Tess, by the way. I don't think we've been formally introduced."

April looked over at the woman — an inch or so shorter — with the vivid, naturally curly red hair, the ends tickling her collar. A handful of freckles dotted the woman's face, reminding April of a pixie. "I'm April, and this is Carrie."

"Nice to meet you," Carrie and Tess chimed in unison.

Marmalade meowed once more.

"Let's put her in Archer's office. It's smallish and receives little traffic." Carrie led the way.

"Let me help." Tess took the oversized bag of cat supplies from April and brought up the rear of the line.

Stopping halfway down a short hall, Carrie opened the door and ushered the others in before shutting it behind her. Tess started pulling items from the bag, found the litter box and set the plastic pan on the floor. Carrie plucked the kitty litter from the container then promptly filled the box about halfway full. April wrestled with the food and water dishes as Tess emptied the rest of the stuff, setting a few toys on the floor along with a rope-covered scratching post. Carrie dashed off with a bowl and quickly returned with fresh water.

Glancing around, April nodded. "I think this will work just fine." Her gaze landed on the large wooden desk complete with office chair and she frowned. "I hope she doesn't decide to start scratching on the furniture. As far as I know she's always been an outside cat."

"No worries. Both are old and run-of-the-mill. Besides, I doubt she'll do much more than hide for a while, then find a cozy place to curl up and sleep."

April opened the front of the carrier and whispered to the occupant. "Marmalade, we're in your temporary home."

The cat looked up at her but made no motion to leave the small carrier.

"Maybe you should just leave it open. She might consider it a place of refuge," Tess advised.

"Good idea. I'll give her some time to adjust and check on her later." April started to the door, finding Carrie and Tess leading the way back out into the hall. Spying a wiggling nose at the opening of the box, April grinned, then slipped out before the cat could get any ideas about escaping from her appointed room.

"I need to get cooking if we're going to have more than a sandwich tonight." Carrie's long strides carried her back through the living room.

"I'll be more than happy to help," Tess said.

"Me too. It's the least I can do." April realized she spoke the absolute truth. Dusty's family had taken her in without question and, so far, asked nothing in return. Not a commonplace situation these days as charitable acts and human kindness oftentimes folded under the strain of scam artists, criminals and downright evil in the world.

Following her host straight into a kitchen made for a professional chef, April blinked and gaped. She'd never seen the likes of such. Appliances of every sort appeared new and shiny, their metal doors gleaming in the afternoon sunlight. Granite countertops in earthen browns ran in a near square around the room, covering tons of cabinet space while allowing plenty of room to work. A separate island stood in the middle, the matching surface absolutely clean. Smaller devices sat against the matching tile wall, a chopper, blender, coffee maker, mixer, even a couple of items she'd never seen before all stood waiting for use.

"Wow. This is gorgeous."

Tess concurred. "Downright amazing. Makes my kitchen at home look like a cave."

Carrie smiled warmly. "The only luxury I ever asked for."

Carrie headed to a doorway in the corner of the expansive kitchen, opened the door and slipped inside. "The brothers still live here. Evan is in college. Brand runs the cattle operation, so he's always around. Colt owns a regional oil company. He splits his time between here and an apartment across the state."

April noted the absence of Dusty's name and understood why. He'd moved out a few years back full of hurt pride, bitterness and animosity toward his family. Thankfully, due to the poignant shove by Mother Nature, he'd returned and seemed to be quickly making amends, judging by the easygoing smiles and lighthearted bickering she'd heard as they'd worked together as a team to load up his belongings and stock earlier in the day.

The brunette waved from inside the large pantry. "Pot pie? Roast? Turkey?"

"Are you asking or telling?" Tess inquired.

"Asking."

Tess glanced out the window before sticking her head inside the panty. "Considering the size of them, I'd say all of the above."

Carrie tittered. April grinned. Tess certainly had some spunk. "What do you do for a living, Tess?"

"I'm an ophthalmologist."

April's eyes widened. "Wow. A doctor."

Tess waved her hand. "Please don't make a big deal of it. I still put my pants on the same as everyone else."

"Impressive." Carrie emerged from the small room, her arms laden with cans and boxes. "April, what do you do?"

"I'm a nurse." She stepped forward to take some of the items from her host. "I've been afraid to ask, but Dusty never mentioned his parents, except to say his father was a lawyer. Are they still living?"

"Yep. They retired a couple years ago and bought a fancy RV. Now they travel full-time. Come home now and again to bother their children, then take off on another adventure."

April smiled, cheered by the thought.

"They sound like they're happy," Tess observed.

"Very. I think they're on their fifth or sixth honeymoon." Carrie grinned widely, set some items on the counter, then returned to the pantry for more.

April stuck her head inside and blinked in surprise at the shelves laden with every kind of foodstuff imaginable. "How much food are we cooking again?"

"Enough to make up for the past three holidays that Dusty's not joined us."

"Oh, boy." Tess glanced at the growing pile, then up at the cat clock, the tail swinging in beat to every second. "No time for a full turkey, though."

"No worries. I have turkey breasts in the freezer. We'll make do."

April looked at Carrie. "Why do I get the feeling you've done this before?"

"That's because I owned the local diner before I married Archer."

That explained so much.

"Let me guess, the way to a man's heart *is* through his stomach?" Tess pulled a couple of pots out from under the stove.

"Not necessarily, but it sure doesn't hurt," Carrie answered. "Speaking of, what's up with you and Dusty?"

Placing the vegetables on the cutting board, April glanced over at Carrie. "Nothing." She'd figured the inevitable questions would come sooner rather than later.

"I hate to admit it, but I was surprised to see you with him. He's been badly burned by a woman before."

"I know. He's never said anything, but I've been told that fact by others." April opened a box of stuffing mix and poured it in a large bowl Tess handed her.

"How long have you two been dating?" Tess asked.

The term made April ponder for a moment. "I can't say we've ever dated. I adopted my horses, brought them to his stable. That was Monday. Since then, I've been hanging out with the horses and him most of the day. We've shared a meal or three, but that's about it."

Carrie turned to stare at her in puzzlement. "He hasn't asked you out? Not even for dinner?"

April shook her head. "No."

"Have you even kissed?" Tess pulled out another larger pan and stood back up.

"Once."

"Once?" Carrie scrunched her face as if trying to decipher a complicated recipe.

"How was it?" Tess whispered as she organized the cookware.

April smiled at the memory. "Sinful."

"The best kind." Carrie chuckled. "You might not be following the traditional steps in a relationship, but Dusty adores you. Otherwise he'd have kicked you out of his stable long ago. Certainly he wouldn't have packed you up and brought you here if he didn't really care for you."

He cared, April knew that. How much, she didn't have a clue. If not for the one kiss, she would have claimed they were friends and nothing more. "He needs help with Miracle. My filly is afraid of men. She's still nervous around him. I don't know that he could handle her in such circumstances by himself."

"A convenient excuse."

April blinked at Carrie.

"Listen to me, girl. If I know Dusty, and believe me I do, that man can work wonders around horses. He'd have found a way to deal with your filly. Easy-peasy. By letting you think he needs help with her, he gets to see you again, spend time with you."

"I don't know. He's not said anything or made any overtures."

"All in good time." Carrie dug out a cookbook.

Tess nodded in agreement. "Men are fickle creatures, but the good ones come around eventually."

April couldn't help but turn the tables on her new friend.

"Good men like Brand?"

Tess shrugged. "Just met him. Besides, he hates my llama."

Carrie laughed. "You should have seen the expression on his face."

"Mentally sizing up Bogart for the roasting rack?"

"Nope. Checking out Bogart's owner's hiney." She waggled her eyebrows. "He liked what he saw. Big time."

Tess sighed, but her green eyes sparked. "He's stubborn and probably has a dozen women lined up in a harem."

"Stubborn, yes. Harem, no. Most women don't speak their own mind around him, wanting to please him. He hates that. Runs this ranch like a tiptop ship and he's the captain, but he doesn't care for people who can't think for themselves."

Tess tapped her lips. "I don't know…"

Carrie handed Tess a bag of potatoes. "Peel while you think. It helps."

Tess grinned. "Helps me think or helps the cook?"

"Both."

* * * *

"That was fantastic." Archer tossed down his napkin and smiled at his wife. "Outdid yourself this time."

Carrie smiled. "I had lots of good help."

"I'd forgotten how wonderful Carrie can cook." Dusty sipped his tea. He'd forgotten so much. Dinners together at the oversized dining table, the good-natured ribbing he and his brothers threw out constantly. The laughter. The tasty food. So many small details he'd shoved aside because of his hurt pride.

Archer kicked at him under the table. "Stop staring at my wife like that. She's already taken."

Dusty grinned and shifted to protect his shins from Archer's bony feet. Carrie made everyone shed their shoes as soon as they entered the house. She'd made the rule one day after cleaning up mud and muck from the hardwood floors, left behind by their work boots. He couldn't blame her and didn't dare disobey. Not when she threatened to make them clean it up. Important lesson learned.

"Besides, you have your own woman," Evan tossed out from across the table.

Dusty glanced to his left, noting April suddenly found her plate enthralling. He didn't miss the pink blush, either.

He liked her, had enjoyed working with her this week at the stable. Never once had she complained about the heat, the endless chores, the fact she volunteered and didn't receive any pay for all her hard efforts. He couldn't recall many women like her, giving and kind as the day was long. They had developed an easy rapport, and even after only a few days, he found her growing on him like moss on the north side of a boulder. He cared for her, preferred his brothers didn't hit on her, but more than that, he couldn't say — way too early to be considering such profound decisions.

"Which reminds me, why isn't Colt dating? Last I heard he proclaimed himself God's gift to women." Dusty purposely shunted the conversation away from him and April.

Colt rolled his eyes. "Even the world's greatest man has to have a day or two of rest in between."

Archer chuckled. "More like running the oil business is keeping him hopping from sunup to sundown."

Colt snorted. "Trust me. I have plenty of time for the ladies."

"All fifteen of them." Evan snickered, then yelped when Colt whapped him hard on the arm.

"Just wait until you head off to college, whelp. You better keep your head in the books and off the rears of women," Colt cautioned.

Evan flashed him a cocky grin. "I can do both."

"What are you studying?" April asked.

"I'm pre-vet right now. I should start vet school next fall if I get off my lazy rump and start applying."

"Wow." She noted that all the Delaney brothers were

smart, motivated and not afraid of hard work. "What specialty?"

"Large animal, of course. While dogs and cats aren't too bad, I have to draw the line at birds and snakes." He shuddered dramatically. "So not my thing."

"I don't blame you," Tess said. "Birds bite and snakes are just eww."

Evan nodded. "Agreed. So, let's hope I do well at large animals and can avoid moving to Miami and caring for the exotic pet population there."

"You'll do just fine," Brand replied. "Hell, you've been helping run this ranch since you could walk. If there's something you haven't seen yet when it comes to horses and cows, it can't be much."

"There's always something new. Especially in the ladies' department." Evan peered over at April and waggled his eyebrows.

"Horn dog central. Were we ever that young, boys?" Archer asked.

"Nope," Brand answered right away.

"Well…" Cole grinned wickedly.

"Some of us haven't left that stage yet," Brand offered, his focus on Cole.

Dusty shook his head before checking his watch. "I better get a move on. The horses will expect their dinner soon." He emptied his glass in one gulp.

"Do you need help?" April glanced up at him.

He debated on how to answer. In all fairness, he could see to the horses himself, even in a pasture situation. Hell, his brothers could help him if they would get off their lazy rumps and do so. On the other hand, he enjoyed her company, but didn't want her trying to deal with a half dozen hungry horses running free in a pasture. If one of them even accidentally stepped on her, he'd feel worse than a steer with a belly ache.

Archer pushed his chair back and stood. "Come on, boys. We've got stock to tend to."

"I haven't eaten my cherry pie, yet," Evan protested.

"Eat it when you get back." Archer bumped his chair. "Let's go. It's going to take a few of us to keep those horses out of one another's grain buckets."

Dusty inclined his head toward Archer, then met April's gaze. "Don't worry. I'll take care of your babies personally." With a small grin, he followed his brothers outside, almost relieved by Archer's timely intervention.

* * * *

With the three of them working on clearing the table and cleaning dishes, the women finished in record time. Carrie excused herself to jump in the shower. Tess wandered out to check on her pets. April, alone and a bit lost, plopped down on the front porch swing to watch everyone at work.

As promised, Dusty carried feed to both Miracle and Mischief, even stayed with them while they ate, ensuring the geldings in the same pasture didn't pressure them to give up their food. Ben sat at his side, raking the horizon, constantly searching for a threat.

*What am I going to do about him?* Not for the first time since arriving at the huge ranch, April questioned herself and Dusty. The women had lifted her spirits and confidence earlier only for Dusty to shoot her down when he refused to answer Evan's comment about being Dusty's woman. He probably didn't want to discuss his personal life in front of the large group in attendance. Understandable. Yet his silence sliced into her.

*Nice pickle you've gotten yourself in, April.* What to do? She'd succeeded in becoming friends with the quiet and sometimes surly cowboy. That had been her goal after all. But she wanted more. She wanted Dusty to look at her as Archer looked at Carrie. To tease, to kiss, to be unable to keep their hands off each other even after five years of marriage. She wanted sheer happiness covering both their faces. She wanted Dusty and love all rolled into a neat little package.

Unfortunately, he didn't seem to be in the same frame of mind.

Yes, he'd been burned. Horribly so, to leave him so leery of women. She'd experienced her fair share of hard knocks in the relationship department, too. Still, she couldn't help thinking as nicely as she and Dusty clicked, there had to be more there.

*It's only been a week, you ninny.* She sighed sadly. Patience. The one virtue she didn't possess a lick of. Miracle wouldn't get over her fears in a week, and Dusty wouldn't move past his issues in the same time frame. Perhaps, down the road, she'd wake up to find her dream come true.

"Penny for your thoughts."

Startled, April snapped her head up. She found Dusty staring down at her with an inquisitive expression on his face. "Oh, just thinking." She gathered her wits.

"I got that much." He sat down on the swing next to her, sending the seat into a gentle rocking motion. The Belgium Malinois flopped down on the porch, his tongue lolling out as he panted. "What about?"

She didn't want to push, to appear clingy, yet she couldn't lie to him. Taking a moment to consider her words carefully, she finally answered. "So much has happened in a week's time. I became a horse owner, a dream since childhood finally fulfilled." She met his gaze. "I met you and found a man with a special talent, a good heart, and one that knew how to work hard."

He remained mute, but didn't look away.

"I've learned so much from you. About horses, about life, about carrying on when the chips are down." She sucked in a breath. "I don't know where the road of life will lead, but I hope I'm not near done with this pit stop anytime soon."

The corner of his mouth hitched upward. He intertwined his fingers with hers and brought her hand up for a gentle kiss. "You know what they say about pit stops?"

She shook her head.

"Gives people time to look around and decide if they like the scenery well enough to stay."

The softly spoken words soothed her soul. No declaration of love or even a mention of a future date. Just a philosophical statement that renewed her hope. She couldn't have been happier.

Maybe, just maybe dreams could come true.

# Chapter Twelve

Carrying her suitcase, April followed Carrie down a hallway with doorways on either side. Tess pulled up the rear with her belongings. "Wow. How many bedrooms did you say there were?"

"Six, according to Brand," Tess replied.

"Yep. One for each brother, then one for their parents. Although how they knew they were having five children when they built this place eons ago, I don't have a clue."

"Maybe they always planned on five?" April peeked into a room, found a large bed, a dresser and what appeared to be a bathroom along the front wall.

"I'm not sure. I do know there's nearly ten years between Dusty and Evan. So either Evan was an oopsie or they tried and weren't successful for quite a while." Carrie paused in the middle of the hallway, her light footballs on the hardwood floor ceasing. "This first bedroom belongs to his parents. We keep it tidy and prepared in case they drop by without notice." Walking backward like a museum tour guide, she pointed first to her left. "This is Archer's room, where we sleep now. Directly across the hall is Brand's room."

Tess stepped forward and into the room. "Interesting."

Carrie and April shared a knowing grin.

"Who are we going to kick out?" Tess asked, still eyeing the place where the next-to-oldest brother spent his nights.

"Colt and Evan both offered up their rooms."

April frowned, wondering why Dusty hadn't done the same. Then she recalled his bad dreams and realized that waking up in a strange place might make those nightmares worse, and thus he'd need more time to recover once he did wake up. Status quo sounded like the best bet for a man like Dusty, troubled with brutal memories of his time spent in the service.

"Colt's room is on your left. Evan's is one door down."

"Which one is Dusty's?" April hated to ask, but curiosity drove her to catch a glimpse of where the serious former SEAL grew up.

"This one." Carrie gestured to her left.

April unashamedly looked in, found blue walls, a large bed with a bright quilt, a dresser and a small desk complete with an old wooden chair. Neat and well-arranged, the room seemed spacious despite being smaller than the front two bedrooms. She could imagine Dusty sitting at the desk, doing his homework, or perhaps lying across his bed, pondering the meaning of life.

Immediately she compared this room with his house back in Colorado. She hadn't seen past the kitchen and main bathroom, but didn't believe his bedroom now could stand up against his old one, not in organization, belongings or interior design. This had been his place of sleeping in his youth. Now, as a grown man, a retired warrior, he most likely preferred everything much more simple and plain. Maybe he just didn't want to take the time to paint or spend his energy trying to fancy up the place. Or, deep down, he'd spent so many nights curled up on the ground that a ritzy room no longer felt comfortable.

"What's wrong?" Tess asked as she halted beside April.

"I was just thinking."

"About?" Carrie asked.

"How much Dusty's changed since he left home."

A pregnant pause filled the air before Carrie broke the silence. "So, Colt's room or Evan's?"

April frowned. "I hate to boot them out of their beds. Can't I just sleep on the couch?"

Tess nodded. "Me too. You all are so kind to take April and me in, I can't bear to be any more of a burden."

Carrie waved her hand dismissively. "The guys volunteered. Besides, they'd no more let you girls sleep on the couch than they'd let a cow go without food during a snowstorm. Their mother raised them right, and years of her lectures actually stuck."

"But—" April started to protest, only for her hostess to cut her off.

"If you try to sleep on the couch, don't be surprised if one of the men comes along, scoops you up and delivers you to a bedroom."

April's heart fluttered. The thought of Dusty cradling her against his chest, nuzzling her cheek as he carried her up the stairs to his bedroom, then placing her in his bed sped her heart and made her stomach flip-flop. He would tuck her in and climb in beside her, spooning together with her under the covers as they drifted off to sleep.

A woman's laughter broke through her thoughts. April blinked as Carrie chuckled.

"Oh, my. You've got it bad. Both of you."

April looked at Tess, then they both grinned.

"Can't help it if my imagination took a bunny path." Tess cleared her throat and shrugged.

April concurred.

Carrie shook her head. "Okay. Just in case that plan fails, let's consider where to stash your belongings."

Both women strode forward, not stopping until they stepped into the last room. "Where will Evan sleep?"

"With one of his brothers or on the couch if he snores too loud. Knowing him and his playboy nature, I wouldn't be surprised to find him trying to sneak in to sleep between you two." Carrie grinned with genuine humor.

"I wouldn't mind," April replied honestly. "It's his bed. Besides, it's not like we're going to do more than just sleep."

"You might not mind, but I bet Dusty and Brand might not be as accommodating." Carrie winked at them and started to retrace her last few steps. "The bathroom is directly across the hall. There's another downstairs if you need it, as well as one in the master bedroom," she rattled on, completing the tour in quick fashion.

Tess plopped her suitcase down inside their designated bedroom. "Do you want to shower first or second?"

April shrugged.

"You can both go at the same time. Tess, why don't you use the hallway bathroom? April, follow me and I'll take you to the master bath. That way you won't have to wait."

Twenty minutes later, April brushed out her hair, having already slipped on shorts and a T-shirt, the sleeping attire she normally wore in the summertime. The pink shorts were loose and comfortable along with the white shirt. Her hair dampened the top where tendrils dripped droplets onto the cotton material, but she didn't care. The loose strands would dry soon enough and besides, who would actually see her travel from the bathroom to the end bedroom?

With one more stroke with the brush, she packed up her small bag, folded her dirty clothes into a neat pile and headed back to the bedroom. No sooner had she stepped from the doorway than she collided with a hard, unmoving body.

"Oh, I'm sorry."

Strong arms reached out and steadied her.

She looked up to find Dusty staring at her as if she'd grown wings since the last time he'd seen her. His eyes raked her from head to toe before lingering on her wet shirt a second longer.

"Ummm. Hi."

Dark brown eyes met hers. "Hi, yourself."

The corners of his lips curled up in either amusement or quirkiness, she wasn't sure which. Either way, her mouth went dry and her heart picked up the pace as he stared at her with a look rife with interest, longing and something resembling hot desire. Not that she had much experience in reading lust in a man's eyes, but the appreciation she noted couldn't be ignored.

"We're sleeping in Evan's room. Although I still think I

should sleep on the couch so he can have his own bed." The words slipped out as she tried to deal with a surge of heat owing nothing to the temperatures outside and everything to do with his proximity and the sparks in his eyes as he studied her.

"Evan won't mind. He'll bunk with Colt." Dusty's low baritone voice carried no farther than her ears, sending a thrill over her entire body.

They had spent hours together before, but in the process of chores or simply sharing a meal. Standing face to face in a hallway seemed definitely more intimate than they'd been before—barring that one kiss that still prompted her dreams, both during the day and at night. "You have a nice room." She nearly groaned at the lame compliment. Her mind ceased to function normally as long as he stood there, arms hanging relaxed at his side, his short black hair ruffled from the breeze. Jeans covered his lower half while a button-down Western shirt covered the top. Tan arms stood out against the brightness of his clothing. She knew the color reached at least his waist from working outside without a shirt. Just another tidbit that added to the overall yumminess that made up Dusty.

"Thanks. I wouldn't have minded you taking my bed."

The offer didn't surprise her as much as the exquisite tightening in her stomach. For a second she wondered if the sheets still carried his scent, but quickly decided that after so long and a few washings, they would smell like detergent instead of musk and horses, Dusty's everyday cologne. "I wouldn't kick you out of your bed. Heck, I still feel bad about burdening Evan to move." She sighed. "Carrie wouldn't hear of Tess and me taking the couches, but I might just do it anyway."

He cupped her chin and lifted until her gaze met his. "My mother would jump on a plane, dash home and take a switch to my rear and the rest of my brothers if we let you ladies spend the night on the couch." His grin was rife with promise. "Sleep where you like, but you'll end up in a bed before the night is done."

Butterflies took flight in her stomach. "Whose bed?"

Dusty's smile widened to show teeth even as his eyes twinkled down at her. "Whose bed, indeed?" He traced his finger along her jaw line.

She swallowed and found herself sinking into the charm of a man she'd only known for a week. If he carried her off to his castle and kept her, she wouldn't utter a single protest at that moment. She soaked up the rapt attention to the fullest before kicking her floundering brain into gear.

Footfalls announced someone trotting up the stairs. Dusty released her but didn't move. April's feet refused to budge as well.

Evan stepped into the hallway, spied her and grinned. "Hey, April. I hear you girls are stealing my bed for the night."

"Yes. I'm sorry." The words came out a bit more breathless than she'd intended. Dusty glanced down at her but remained mute.

"Don't worry about it. I'll share with Colt." He approached her, leaned down and whispered in her ear. "Besides, I'll have the privilege of knowing two beautiful ladies not only slept in my bed, but dreamed of me too." He waggled his eyebrows.

Dusty rolled his eyes and snorted, but his lips twitched just enough to give him away. He found his little brother entertaining, just wouldn't own up to such a fact.

April jumped on board. "Oh, I'm sure Tess and I will have all kinds of dreams. Wonderful dreams. Filled with handsome men."

"Naked men and women?" Evan asked excitedly.

Her face heated, yet she continued, unwilling to let the humor end. "Maybe…"

Dusty's eyebrows shot up. "Erotic dreams?"

"You know about erotic dreams?" She turned the tables on Dusty.

His grin could only be called sinfully wicked.

Evan coughed loudly. "I think that's my cue to leave." Without another word, he turned and headed back down the stairs.

The mood faded quickly with Evan's departure. Dusty shook his head and shifted his weight. "I better jump in the shower before Evan uses up all the hot water."

"Okay." She blew out a breath. "I know it's late and everyone has an early morning."

"Yeah." He looked at her. "You should sleep in. I know you were already worn out from work when you came over earlier today. I'll take care of the animals. Just use the opportunity to catch up on your sleep."

"I needed to be there, to do what I could…"

His mouth opened and shut again.

Waiting patiently, April finally decided whatever Dusty intended to say would be forever a secret. "Thanks again. For bringing me along."

"You bet." He didn't budge an inch.

Neither did she. "I guess I should go on to bed."

"Okay." Still he stayed put, staring at her as if trying to work out some unique puzzle.

"Goodnight, Dusty."

"Goodnight, April."

They remained in place for a bit longer before April forced her leaden feet to move. Brushing past Dusty, she went directly into Evan's room, shut the door behind her and flopped down on the bed.

Tess blinked at her from a small recliner. "Problem?"

"Men." April threw her arms over her head. "I don't understand them."

"Welcome to the club." Tess walked over and sat next to her.

April propped herself up in a sitting position, tucking one leg under her. "Don't you have to take a class in medical school about men and relationships or such?"

Tess chuckled. "I wish. The closest I ever got was sex ed back in high school."

"I thought doctors knew everything," April teased her roommate.

"Not even close." Tess eyed her. "So, what's up between you and Dusty?"

"I don't have a clue. One kiss and that's it. Since then he's backed off, treated me like a stable hand or even a friend. Then tonight I run into him in the hallway and he looks at me like I'm a medium-rare steak and he's a hungry wolf." She picked at the quilt.

"Sounds like he runs hot and cold."

"Yeah."

"Probably still trying to decide what he wants. Maybe even fighting his feelings too."

April considered Tess' words and found them sound. Considering what Lois had told her about Dusty having no use for women besides carnal activities, April could see how he might be as confused as she was. "True. So, tell me about Brand."

"Nothing to tell." Tess focused on the window as if the world outside proved enthralling.

"Uh-huh. I've seen the way he looks at you. Carrie noticed it too. He's definitely interested."

"Then he opens his mouth, grates on my nerves, and we bicker." Tess sighed sadly. "I don't know why we can't get along. He's really very sweet. Saved my small herd and insisted I stay here free of charge."

"Foreplay."

Tess turned and blinked. "What did you say?"

For the first time that evening, April truly smiled. "Foreplay. Seems to me he'd rather kiss you, but he's not sure, so he ends up with ruffled feathers. You both do. Next time you start to berate him, kiss him instead."

"That could be dangerous." Tess tapped her lips.

"Like gasoline on a raging wildfire?"

"Oh yeah." A slow grin appeared on Tess' face. "I have a feeling that hunk of a man might carry enough explosives for the both of us."

"Just let me know, and I'll be sure to stand clear." April giggled. She genuinely liked the eye doctor and couldn't wait to see if love panned out between her and the tall, brown-haired brother who ran the ranch. "When you kiss him, I'll bet sparks will fly all the way from here to the Colorado line."

Tess chuckled. "We'll see."

They each slipped under the covers. April glanced out of the window and thought of her bedroom at home. Worry ate at her. "What will you do if your home is burned to the ground?" She quietly voiced the question.

Her roommate sighed. "The clinic I work for closed a couple of days ago, being much closer to the fire. I worry about it most." She paused for a long minute. "I suppose if I lost everything, I'd search for a place to start over. Since I'm an employee of the clinic and not an owner, I have options. There'll be other offices and even different homes." Tess turned toward April. "Same as you, most likely. If your hospital takes a hit, you'll find another place to work and live. Probably move, at least in the near future, then decide where you want to settle down once more and piece together your life."

April didn't want to move or piece her life back together. She'd finally found a quiet pool among churning white-peaked rapids and hoped to enjoy the relative tranquility for a long time to come. Dusty's words came back to her. 'It's in God's hands.' With that sobering speck of hope, she drifted off to sleep.

\* \* \* \*

"Never seen the like. A fuzzy animal on stilts spitting in Brand's face and all he does is cuss." Colt lurched to the side, avoiding Brand's attempt to smack his arm.

"Nasty tempered beast, I'll agree. Glad he's not mine." Getting comfortable once more on the wide leather couch, Brand crossed one leg over the other.

136

Dusty stood at the entrance to the living room, listening. His lips curled up at the corners as the brothers continued to give Brand a hard time.

He'd just said goodnight to April upstairs — and stumbled over every word. He mentally shook his head as he recalled the memory. All he could say for himself was that her wet T-shirt and loose shorts had distracted him. Big time. He'd always seen her in jeans and summer shirts, never in such casual attire. The dampness had emphasized her modest breasts, minus a bra, and hinted at rose-colored nipples that had tempted him to taste. He'd been so close to kissing her again. Probably would have if Evan hadn't come along.

Good thing he had, though.

As much as he enjoyed the sight of April, he couldn't put all his eggs in her basket. Too many wounds from the past still hadn't healed. To saddle her with those would be completely unfair.

Overall, his day had ended up pretty good despite the mad dash away from the quickly spreading flames. Worry still sat on his shoulders, but he didn't lament. After all, he couldn't do a damned thing about the wildfire. At least his brothers had opened their arms and home, taking him in and treating him as if nothing had happened. A blessing in all respects. That part shone brighter than the noonday sun. So spending the evening with some downtime, hanging out in the man cave, made for a perfect ending.

"Beaten by a llama. What's the world coming to?" Evan asked.

"Llama stew, probably. Except he doesn't want to get on the bad side of that perky little redhead." Archer reclined back in his chair.

"She's got some nice curves," Colt offered up.

"And she's a doctor too. Talk about a catch," Evan replied.

Brand rolled his eyes. "I don't care about her money."

"Maybe not, but I saw how you looked at her today. It's a miracle she didn't go up in smoke from spontaneous combustion." Archer grinned wickedly.

"I'm just doing her a favor. Besides, she's a prickly little thing." Brand took a drink of his beer.

"Uh-huh." Dusty walked in, headed for the smaller love seat and plopped down. "I think she's caught your eye, bro."

"Just like that little blonde caught yours?" Evan asked.

Dusty kept his features carefully schooled. "April is just a boarder. Nothing more, nothing less."

Four sets of eyes stared at him. He glared right back.

"That's good to know. I'm thinking about asking her out." Evan nodded slowly. "Nice body, pretty hair. Sweet-tempered. Yeah, I could get used to her sleeping in my bed."

Possessiveness and protectiveness jumped to the fore. Dusty opened his mouth, then shut it again promptly. The gut reaction confused him. April wasn't his girlfriend. A friend, yes. They'd found an easy companionship working at the stable. Still, that didn't mean he'd set sights on her as a future bride. They had shared one kiss, a reckless impulsive act that he couldn't quite understand and refused to dwell on. That didn't a relationship make. Nor did that explain why he didn't care for the idea of his younger brother asking her out. All he knew from the knee-jerk reaction was that he didn't want another man to snatch her away. His rational mind argued he couldn't have it both ways.

Maybe not, but that didn't mean he would encourage his single brothers to sniff around April. She could make her own choices, certainly, but he didn't have to like them.

"If I wasn't married, I'd certainly consider April. That girl has a brain and isn't afraid to get dirty." Archer crossed his legs at the ankles.

"You'd never have to worry about her wandering off, unless it's for another animal in need," Colt added.

"Exactly." Evan sipped his beer and nodded. "I'm definitely going to ask her out."

Studying Evan, Dusty couldn't decide if his younger brother was simply trying to yank his chain, prod him into opening up more about April, or if his interest proved sincere. Try as he might, he couldn't picture Evan and April as a couple. Not with vet school right around the corner, the physical distance between their homes and a few years separating them in age. Certainly some obstacles, but that didn't always ensure a quick end to any blossoming relationship.

The thought of April as a sister-in-law struck a sour chord.

Dusty bit his lip, sipped his beer and remained mute. As much as he reminded himself how many times he'd been screwed over in the past by the fairer sex, the flimsy excuse sounded weak to his own mind.

He'd been sitting on the fence for a while when it came to April. Now, he saw what he could lose if another man swept her away. A wave of possessiveness rushed over him.

April might have walked into his life unbidden, but she'd set down roots along the way. He wanted her, plain and simple. Despite all the past hard lessons in dealing with women.

Maybe April could be the exception to the rule.

*The question is, am I willing to take that bet?*

# Chapter Thirteen

April finished loading the dishwasher with the dirty breakfast dishes before washing her hands and drying them on a nearby kitchen towel. Carrie returned items to the fridge while Tess placed the clean china back into its respective places.

Sleep had come off and on the night before. Tess hadn't woken her with snoring or tossing around. Instead, her mind had refused to pipe down for the night.

"Tess?" Brand's voice carried to them from the mudroom.

With a perplexed glance to April and Carrie, Tess hurried out into the living area in order to see him.

April and Carrie followed in her wake.

"Yes?"

His eyes locked on her as a ghost of a smile teased his lips. "I thought you might want to come check out your critters with me."

Tess frowned, worry causing her eyebrows to furrow. "What's wrong?"

"Nothing's wrong." He smiled at her. "Just counted an extra alpaca this morning. A little white baby that wasn't there yesterday."

Tess beamed. "A baby? Really?" She hurried over and started tugging on her shoes. "I didn't know any of the females were expecting."

"Well, I'm not an expert on alpacas, but I can tell you it's not a calf, a lamb, or a baby goat. Guess that makes it an alpaca." His slow drawl carried a healthy dose of teasing.

Tess rolled her eyes. "You, sir, are pulling my leg." She stood on tiptoe and brushed her lips across his cheek. "And

I thank you for doing so." With one more glance, she pushed on the door handle. "Now let's go see the new addition. I can't wait." She grabbed his hand and tugged hard.

Brand followed her out, a wide smile covering his face.

April watched them with a smile. *They're made for one another.*

"Fate works in mysterious ways," Carrie said as she watched them hurry across the yard.

April concurred. "Yep. If the wildfires hadn't struck, endangering us, they'd have never met."

"And you'd still be back at the stable shoveling horse manure all day." The corners of Carrie's lips curled up slightly.

"Probably."

For a long moment, neither woman said another word. Carrie finally broke the silence. "I need to go grocery shopping. Would you care to ride along?"

"Sure." April didn't mind pitching in, even financially, for her stay. She wasn't a princess and didn't expect to be treated as one during her visit, however long that might be.

"Great. Let me get my purse and we'll get started."

Fifteen minutes later, Carrie pulled her big SUV onto the highway.

April, belted into the passenger seat, watched out the windows, taking in the pretty rural scenery along the way.

"I noticed the way you and Dusty look at one another."

*Uh-oh.* April blew out a breath. She really liked Carrie. That didn't mean she wanted to open up her greatest secrets to the woman. "He's a good man and great with the horses. He worries about those he cares for." Darn it, that was the truth. The problem wasn't with his protective instincts in bringing her along. Instead, it resided with his ability to give her a chance to see if they could match up stronger than simply friends with his general distrust of women.

"All of us were surprised to see Dusty brought you along. Granted, we haven't talked to him in a while, but considering his past with us, that says something big."

This was the second time Carrie had mentioned her shock. April shrugged it off. "He was just worried that I had nowhere to go."

"Bull crap. He could have sent you off elsewhere, left you to your own devices, like the rest of the boarders. If you haven't noticed, he didn't pack them up and bring them along as well. Yet he brought you with him to stay with his family, even though he probably wasn't certain about the reception he'd receive after all this time of hurt feelings."

The facts bolstered April's spirit a bit. "He never said what happened. Never spoke of you guys at all." She folded her hands in her lap and treaded carefully into the personal lives of Dusty and his family. "I got the impression that it was a sore spot with him."

Carrie peered over at her before turning her attention back to the road. "Maybe if I filled you in, you might see what the rest of us do."

*Please do.* April craved insight into Dusty while also understanding the need to keep personal information to herself. No problem. She'd never been one to participate in gossip anyway. "Okay."

"It all started back on his last tour of duty. He'd been assigned to the Middle East for months. SEALS are wrapped in secrets and cloaked in darkness. We never knew anything. Just received a phone call once in a blue moon from Dusty telling us he was okay."

That lined up with what little April knew about military life in a war zone.

"He was engaged at the time he left. Her name is Collette."

"Engaged?" April blinked. She'd never considered that Dusty might have been that serious with a woman before.

"Yeah. Engaged. To a worthless woman whose only fine points revolved around a drop-dead gorgeous body. The rest of her made for a pretty useless human. None of us cared much for her, but Dusty claimed to love her. We stayed out of it and waited to see what would happen." Carrie spared April a glance. "Anyway, seems Collette didn't care for her man being thousands of miles away with very little communication. She wanted him at home to take care of her. Hard to do when the Navy owns your ass and you're fighting just to survive day in and day out for months at a time."

"I imagine. That's so...selfish." April couldn't believe that another woman would be like that. Certainly life as a military spouse had to be difficult. That was a no-brainer. Yet those serving needed all the support and understanding they could get.

"She sent him a Dear John letter in the middle of his deployment, calling off the engagement. A couple of weeks later she hooked up with another guy, ran off and got married."

"Whoa." Several scenarios rushed through April's mind, none of them portraying Collette in a good light.

"Yeah. Dusty didn't receive the letter for a few weeks. He was devastated."

"A hell of a time to break that kind of news to a person. Right in the middle of a war. What was she thinking?" Anger added a bite to April's words. That kind of distraction could get a guy killed. He'd had enough on his plate without a narcissistic bimbo throwing a big monkey wrench into his life.

Carrie pulled into the lot of a large grocery store, found an empty space and parked. She cut the engine and turned to April. "It gets worse. When he came home, discharged from the Navy, he took up with another woman. Rose." Carrie's lips thinned. "She clung to him, flirted outrageously and insisted on only the finest things for her. She would have milked him dry and left him penniless if Archer and the other boys hadn't stepped in. They hired a private detective who dug up her background. She was a gold-digger. Period. Had taken three other men for their life savings then ran off, leaving them destitute."

"She should be locked up."

"I thought horsewhipped, but locked up would work

too." Carrie sighed. "When Archer dropped the evidence in front of Dusty, Dusty became furious. He yelled, cursed and started throwing punches. After a tussle with Archer, he cussed out all of the brothers, vowed to never return, and drove away."

"His pride was hurt," April whispered. He might have had a clue about Rose, but for his brothers to shove the evidence in his face must have made him feel like an idiot. So he'd turned his anger on them as well as himself.

"Yeah. We haven't heard from him since that time, three years to be exact, until he made the SOS call to pick up his horses. We'd kept tabs on him, knew where he settled down, and purposely didn't change any phone numbers, waiting on the day he might relent."

"It took a natural disaster for it to happen." April shared a sorrowful look with Carrie. "I'm sorry. Stubbornness isn't always a great quality to have."

A soft smile creased Carrie's face. "True, but that's the Delaney men. They come by it honestly."

"They seem to love one another. All that ribbing."

"That's their way of showing affection." Carrie tilted her head. "Let's get to shopping or we'll get a heatstroke sitting out here in this hot truck."

April collected her purse, climbed out of the passenger side and clicked her door locked before shutting it. She hurried around the vehicle, met up with Carrie and walked into the store. A refreshing blast of cool air conditioning hit her as she entered.

Glancing around, April found the store to be like most others—aisles and aisles of goods just waiting to be chosen and placed in baskets for purchase.

April's thoughts returned to the previous conversation. "Okay. I can see now why you were stunned when Dusty not only called for help, but brought me along for the ride."

Carrie grabbed a grocery cart, dropped her purse inside and started toward the produce section. "He'd sworn off women as far as we could tell."

"Probably decided they weren't worth the effort," April added.

"Yet here you are." Carrie met April's gaze.

"Here I am," April repeated. "Going with the motions, not pushing for fear of running him off. Wanting more than he might ever be able to provide." She slouched with the truth.

Carrie paused at the fresh vegetables. "Good things come to those who wait." She grinned ruefully, snagged a plastic bag and started loading it up.

"I'll be old and gray with saggy boobs," April lamented with a small groan.

Carrie laughed. "Dusty's smart. He won't wait quite *that* long."

"Promise?"

"Nope."

"Oh." April's moment of optimism faded fast.

"What I can say is this. You're ahead of the game. You're here. That's first base. There will be at least a few days of hanging around Dusty at the farm. Granted, it's not one-on-one like you're used to, but with his brothers underfoot, Dusty will be busy beating them away so he can have you all to himself. That's second base."

April took the full bag from Carrie and placed it carefully in the cart. "What's third base?"

"That, my dear, is up to you." Carrie smiled. "Men are simple at times, complex at others. The foundation is set. You just have to decide where to go from there."

April pursed her lips in thought. Carrie had a valid point. With Dusty's brothers around, they might nudge him in the right direction. Or turn him completely against her. If the quiet time on the back porch swing the previous night meant anything, Dusty hadn't rejected her at all. He'd embraced her in a sweet, subtle, tentative way. A start. A good one at that. "What if I get thrown out sliding into third base?"

Carrie glanced her direction. "Then you know where you stand."

"True." April sighed. "Why does this have to be so complicated?"

"They're men. They don't come with a user's manual or a guide book. I'd say most of their wants revolve around sex, but Dusty is the exception to the rule. Break his code and you'll be the most protected and adored woman around."

April shook her head. "How did you get to be so smart?"

Carrie shrugged. "I've been around the block a time or two." Her smile reached her eyes. "Had to do some convincing and basically sit on top of Archer to get him to settle down, but it was all worth it. I'm a very lucky woman."

April noted the loving expression painted on Carrie's face. A spark of envy clicked. "I want what you have." The admission slipped out.

Carrie stared at her a long moment. "Then fight for your man. Give him time, patience, understanding and love. If all that fails, be prepared to fight."

"Just call me Annie Oakley."

Carrie laughed. "You'll do, April. You'll do."

Together they walked down every aisle, loading up the cart as they went. April delved in, paid for part, against Carrie's objection, and took her advice to heart.

If she wanted Dusty, she needed to stay the course and batten down the hatches. It might be a bumpy ride.

For taming a wild stallion had never been easy.

He'd already thawed considerably toward her. Maybe, just maybe, the shield around his heart would dissipate, leaving an opening for her.

Only time would tell.

# Chapter Fourteen

Finished with lunch and clean-up, Tess, Carrie and April joined the men hanging out in the living room, enjoying a bit of downtime while they digested their meal. The temperature outside remained warm, yet nothing like the over the century marks Colorado had seen throughout the past month or so.

Finding an empty spot on the love seat, April plopped down. Tess sat down next to her while Carrie squished between her husband and Colt on the couch. This must be nice, simply hanging out with the family after lunch. *Nothing special, just another day to strengthen the cohesive bonds among siblings.* With one notable exception—Dusty. He'd left after cleaning up from his morning chores to run some errands alone, declining the offers from his brothers and April to tag along. He probably needed to be by himself. After three years of basically living with only his animals, sharing a house with seven other people probably chafed on his sanity.

"When did Dusty say he'd be back?" She voiced the question that had been at the front of her mind all morning, since Dusty had pulled out with Ben.

"He didn't." Archer offered her an encouraging smile. "Don't worry. He's probably off at the nature trails. That's where he used to run off to when he needed some time to think. He'll be back before you know it."

April read the confidence in Archer's face and blew out a breath. She could easily see Dusty wandering through the wilderness, just communing with nature. After what he must have seen overseas, he probably needed time away.

Peace and quiet well apart from the rat race and civilization. If that helped him deal with the horrific memories, awful nightmares and terrorizing flashbacks, more power to him. Though it had been three years, she understood inner scars don't just go away.

"I'm surprised you guys are home today," Tess threw out. "Considering your very important jobs."

Archer shrugged. "Decided to take a few days off, not only to help Dusty out, but to spend time with this ragtag crew."

Colt agreed. "I can work from here as easily as the office. Might as well hang out for a few days."

To get to know their younger brother again. April drew in a deep breath and quickly changed the topic. "Tell me more about this ranch. From what I've seen, it looks huge."

Brand smiled proudly. "Eight hundred seventy-five acres total. At any moment, around four to five hundred head of beef cattle. We also raise hay, corn, wheat and silage. A self-sufficient operation and profitable as long as we stick to our budget and don't screw up."

"Wow. That's amazing. You definitely need a full-time rancher and a couple of helpers." April blinked in awe at the size of their family farm. No wonder the men knew how to work and work hard. They had probably been busting their rears their whole lives to keep this place afloat while their father worked in the court system.

"It's a big investment, I'll say that. Brand keeps this place going like a well-oiled machine though." Carrie smiled. "The others step up, as well. Just because they've been at work all day doesn't mean they come home and sit on their rumps."

"Got to work off all this wonderful food you feed me." Archer smiled, wrapped an arm around his wife and pulled her in for a quick kiss.

Brand's gaze settled on Tess. "What does a person do with alpacas besides keep them as pets?"

"Shear them and sell the hair, of course. It's similar to

wool, without the lanolin, hypoallergenic and soft. It's a specialty market in the US but there's a demand." Tess warmed to her subject. "They're easy to work with and don't eat as much as you think, mostly grass with a little grain, and they're pretty cute."

"Looks like they'd make an easy dinner for a hungry coyote," Brand pointed out.

Tess nodded. "That's the big problem. A lot of people who raise alpacas keep stock guard dogs with them all the time to ward off predators. I went a different direction and purchased Bogart. Llamas are instinctively very protective and make a suitable guard for the herd."

"At least that spitting monster has a use," Brand grumbled under his breath.

Tess chuckled. "Yeah, he does. Poor Bogart had too much interaction with people at a young age, so he tends to treat people like he would another llama. Blame the people who raised him. But he's really sweet." Her eyes twinkled. "He's gelded, if that makes you feel any better."

The dark-haired man shrugged. "Maybe."

"I have the alpacas sheared in the spring, so they're a bit ragged right now. Not sure I could make a living off the wool they produce, but they definitely pay for themselves. And for Bogart too."

"How much room do they need?" Brand sat forward, clasping his hands together.

"Oh, the literature says about ten animals per acre. If you rotate pastures, I suppose that can work. As a bonus, they all eliminate in the same place, so you have a fairly clean walk through their enclosure."

"I can see the wheels turning." Evan shook his head at Brand. "Don't tell me you're thinking of adding alpacas to the herd?"

Brand grinned. "Maybe." He stood, walked over to the loveseat and held out an arm to Tess. "I'd like to visit your pets again and learn more about your program."

Tess stood and linked her arm in his. "Of course. I love

educating people about my babies."

Together they strode to the front door and slipped out in the early afternoon sun.

"Oh my." Carrie fanned her face. "Talk about a smoldering look he gave her."

"I guess I should consider her off the market?" Colt asked.

Archer bobbed his head. "Probably a smart idea. Brand can be a bit temperamental when it comes to his woman."

April grinned, thrilled Tess had finally found common ground with Brand. The little redhead had settled in for what hopefully proved a romantic and long-lasting relationship with the tall man who reminded her of Dusty. Heck, all of the brothers enjoyed common features, a testimony to shared genetics.

As long as she hung around them, she couldn't quite push Dusty from her mind, not with the constant reminders in physical appearance — smiles, gestures, and even the way they walked.

"That leaves you, little lady."

She blinked at Colt. "What about me?"

"Looks like you're still on the market for a man lucky enough to corral you."

Her face heated. "Ummm." What could she say to such a blatant proposition?

Evan came to her rescue. "No way, bro. She's sleeping in my bed. That gives me first dibs."

"And you're sleeping in my bed, so what does that mean?" Colt fired back.

"You're cuddly as a teddy bear?" Evan smirked and jumped out of the reach of one large paw headed his direction.

"I'll show you a bear." Standing up, Colt began stalking his younger brother.

Evan waggled his eyebrows. "Bear, huh? I always thought so with that thick mat of hair on your back."

"I don't have hair on my back."

"How would you know? You can't see your back."

"You're cruising for a bruising."

"Gotta catch me first."

April's gaze flicked back and forth between the bickering brothers. She giggled as Evan winked at her, then made a mad dash out the front door, Colt hot on his heels.

"It's like working in a day care some days, I swear." Archer shook his head, but the grin gave him away. He enjoyed the bantering just as much as everyone else.

She sighed as a wave of sadness cascaded over her. In the two short days she'd spent with Dusty's family, they'd grown on her. Too bad she might not ever see them again once she returned home.

With that depressing thought, she stood. "I better go spend some time with Marmalade so she doesn't think we've totally forgotten her." Ambling down the hall, she headed toward Archer's office.

* * * *

"Umm...April?"

She glanced up from pulling on her tennis shoes to find Tess staring out the front door.

Marmalade had tolerated the fussing for a bit before jumping into Archer's office chair, curling up and drifting off to sleep. That left April back to her own devices for the next couple of hours until she could start to round up dinner for the horses. Too antsy to plop down on the couch, she'd opted to go grab a horse and do some grooming to pass the time.

"Yeah?"

"Your white miniature horse is on the front porch."

April's heart stuttered. She quickly tied the shoestrings and rushed over. Sure enough, Mischief stared back at her through the screen door. "Oh, no. How did you get out?" She opened the door, caught his halter and raked her gaze over the nearby pastures, praying he hadn't unlocked all the gates, setting the rest of the menagerie of animals free.

Tess closed the screen door behind her as she stepped out with them.

Brand walked up the steps of the porch, stared at Mischief and shook his head. "I wouldn't have believed it if I hadn't seen it with my own eyes."

April shared in his amusement, rubbing her pet's face. "He's a troublemaker, all right. I know he can unlatch doors, but the gate is supposed to be chained."

"He's a little guy. Seems to reason he could either crawl under the gate or sneak out between the bars."

"True." She tugged on Mischief's halter. "Come on. Time to go back to your temporary home."

Mischief walked as far as the edge of the steps, then planted his feet. No amount of coaxing would get him to move.

"He's too heavy to lift and I'm afraid giving him a shove might send him toppling. Better to avoid that if at all possible," Brand pointed out while rubbing his chin.

"I have an idea." Tess disappeared and returned with a carrot. "Here. Try this."

April shot her an appreciative smile and held out the treat to Mischief. He stretched out his neck, but she kept it out of reach as she trotted down the stairs and stood on flat ground. "You got up the steps, you can get back down."

Mischief whinnied.

Miracle answered from the pasture.

April turned in time to see the gray filly rush to the gate and start pacing, obviously concerned her best friend wasn't closer.

"Why's she getting all worked up?" Brand eyed Miracle before turning his attention back to Mischief.

She recalled Brand had been absent when they'd first arrived and explanations were given. "They bonded at their previous home, a horrendous place where the owner not only starved his horses, but beat them as well."

Brand frowned as his jaw ticked. "The bastard."

"Yeah. By the time something was done, several of the

horses were dead. The Humane Society came in, rescued the rest and started the long road to recovery. Miracle was nothing but skin and bones, nearly dead from neglect. Mischief kept her going through the whole ordeal." She glanced over at Miracle, who still crowded the fence, whinnying now and again in summons to her buddy. "Miracle survived but carries scars, both physical and mental. She's afraid of men, doesn't care for strangers and will lash out if cornered."

"Damn." Brand shook his head as he watched Miracle. "Guess that means we better get this little guy back to her before she has a total meltdown."

"Yep." April waved the carrot in front of Mischief. "Come on, you stinker. Come and get it."

Mischief took the first step, then the second before jumping straight to the ground, nearly running over April in his bid for the treat.

"What am I going to do with you?" He crunched happily as April lightly scolded him.

She tugged him along, heading for the pasture where Miracle waited anxiously.

Brand and Tess followed along.

"You said that gate is supposed to be chained?" Tess asked.

"He's a little Houdini. Normal latches won't keep him in. Everything has to be chained or tied." April ruffled his forelock. "He's too smart for his own good."

Almost to his pasture, Mischief took a hard right, nearly dragging her over to the smaller enclosure containing Tess' pets. He stuck his head through the gate and sniffed at a couple of the alpacas that had come over to check him out.

"Aww. They like him." Tess chuckled as the rest of the small herd came over and snuffled Mischief, each trying to push closer to the little guy. Even the llama stopped by, lowered his head and nuzzled Mischief. "Even Bogart."

Brand snorted. "Of course that fuzzball on stilts would like him. He's not a man."

April grinned at Brand's put-upon tone.

Tess *tsked* him. "He might be a bad llama, but I still love him all the same."

Brand sighed and rolled his eyes.

April read between the lines, knowing Brand tolerated the beast because of Tess, the woman he found attractive and intriguing right now. The sparks were there, if they would just mosey on down the path of romance together.

A sliver of envy took foothold before April shoved it aside. No sense wallowing in self-pity when she should be happy for her new friends.

"Okay, Mischief. Meet and greet time is over." She nudged him back to the entrance to his pasture. Miracle met them there and immediately pinned her ears when Brand moved to open the gate.

"Whoa." He stepped back slowly and lowered his voice. "It's okay, little lady. I'm not going to do anything but return this hardheaded, sawed-off horse to you."

"Here. If you hold him, I'll get Miracle in hand." April stepped through, took Miracle by the halter, then nodded toward Tess, who grasped Mischief's halter. "You'll be fine. Women don't bother her."

Tess led Mischief into the field and released him. Miracle lowered her head and sniffed Mischief, seemingly content that her best friend had indeed returned. Immediately, she settled down.

April released her and followed Tess back out the gate, making sure to fasten both the latch and the chain behind her.

"Are those whip scars on her rump?" Brand asked.

"Yes."

Brand cussed under his breath. "No wonder she gets all bent out of shape around men. How can Dusty deal with her?"

"With gentleness, patience and food. He's slowly gaining her trust. Any other stable, the Humane Society wouldn't let me have them, but his reputation with horses gave me their approval." April swallowed the lump forming in her throat. "He's got a touch. A magical touch." The soft words faded.

"With horses. Lousy taste in women," Brand said.

April's mouth fell open.

"Until now." Brand strode closer. "He's a changed man because of you. I don't think he would have bothered to call us for help if you hadn't been there."

"He wouldn't have endangered the horses."

Brand shook his head. "Of course not. I'm just saying he would have found another way. You've made an impression on him, little lady. A damn good one."

Heat radiated across April's face, and not from the warm temperatures either. "I'm being a friend."

"Good place to start." Brand winked at April before turning his gaze to Tess.

"I agree." Tess moved abreast of Brand. She peered up at him with a softness that couldn't be mistaken. "Does that mean we're friends?"

"Well, yeah." He blinked down at her. "What did you think we were?"

Tess shrugged. "Just clarifying things."

Brand blew out a long breath. "Woman, you tie me in knots."

"Is that bad?" Tess smiled innocently up at him.

Brand's lips curled up. "You might drive me insane, but God knows I keep coming back for more."

April, feeling like a third wheel, started back for the house. The sparks off those two fired hotter than the summer sun. They didn't need her sticking around and butting in. Besides, she needed to get started on caring for the herd. Dusty was bound to show up sooner rather than later. When he did, she wanted to have made a big dent in the chores.

# Chapter Fifteen

Dusty pulled into the gravel driveway, drove over to the old barn and parked his truck. After sliding out of his seat, he collected Ben, sat him on the ground, then shut the door. Automatically checking out his surroundings, he made his way to the front porch and plopped down on the top step. Ben trotted over and sat between his legs.

He looked out over the land, noted the horses grazing contentedly, the blue skies, the light breeze. The pristine ranch spoke of a caring hand and oversight attentive to detail. The same as he remembered growing up. Unlike then, the family farm didn't offer contentment.

Needing to get away for a while, he'd spent most of the day hiking the trails of the local nature reserve in an effort to dispel the restlessness he'd woken up with that morning. The forest surroundings had offered up a few answers, though nothing groundbreaking. He'd missed his brothers and intended to take the opportunity to grow close once again, to catch up and be part of the family once more. Never again would he let simple pride cause a chasm between them. Yet at the same time, he'd realized he could never return to the ranch and live full-time. No way. Too many things had changed. He'd changed. And this was no longer his home.

Nightmares plagued him from time to time. Those wouldn't go away any time soon, if ever. He found comfort in his somewhat isolated stable and surrounding land. People rarely visited and those who did didn't stay long. His animals provided an income as well as companionship. They would be part of his days come hell or high water.

Ben whined as if sensing his owner's inner turmoil.

Dusty reached down to scratch the dog's head as he stared at his longtime companion. The gray hairs on Ben's muzzle told the story. Time had passed and he was no longer a pup anymore.

Looking up, his gaze landed on April, still working with the horses in the center pasture. Her dark blonde ponytail swayed with each step as she moved around the large animals with easy familiarity, brushing and petting each one, even taking the time to check their hooves for stones or mud. She didn't have any makeup on and, quite honestly, didn't need any. A healthy glow and natural radiance showed on her supple skin while those big blue eyes completed the pretty package. As he watched, she wiped a trickle of sweat from her forehead using the pulled up hem of her white T-shirt. Dampness showed through the upper section, a testament to perspiration in the summer heat.

His stomach flip-flopped as his libido sat up and took interest.

The squeak of the front door snared his attention. Dusty didn't bother to turn around, figuring whomever stepped onto the porch would make themselves known soon enough. The strong footfalls of boots clued him in at least to the gender of his visitor.

Archer started down the steps, stopped, then sat down next to Dusty, his legs stretched out in front of him. For a few beats he mirrored Dusty, just raking the horizon with his eyes. "Got something on your mind?"

Dusty bent one leg up. No sense in lying or avoiding answering. Archer had inherited their father's penchant for making people talk. He'd needle someone until they finally grew frustrated enough to blurt out the answers. That quality made him a top-notch lawyer and a pretty decent brother. "Not particularly. Just restless."

"Have anything to do with your three a.m. walk around the property?" Archer arched an eyebrow.

A little surprised at being caught, Dusty met Archer's

gaze. "Hell, you should have been a SEAL. Got the instincts and sharpened senses of one."

"How do you think I snuck out so many times and never got caught as a teen?" A ghost of a grin appeared on Archer's lips.

Dusty grunted in answer.

Archer locked his fingers together and rested them on his lap. "I didn't expect you to come home from hell and not carry more than a few scars."

Dusty tensed. He couldn't help it. Those secrets remained too personal, even for his brother. "Yeah."

"No need to hide all that from those who care about you." When Dusty remained mute, Archer studied him for a moment before turning his attention back to the field. "She's a damn hard worker. Carrie said April even insisted on footing the bill for part of the groceries today."

That fact didn't surprise Dusty in the least. April never seemed to expect or want handouts. She pulled her own weight and then some. Dusty considered her past. "She's had a hard time. A former boyfriend hit her. She's leery of men."

Archer's jaw ticked before he blew out a long breath. "She's like her filly. A survivor. I bet she'd respond to a man's gentle touch just like that filly responds to yours."

*I'm afraid to find out.* Dusty bit back the truth. After his last fiascos, he hesitated in setting his future on another woman. The last two situations had been bad enough. A third might break him for all time. *Hell of a time for a SEAL to hesitate due to fear.* He snorted at himself. "I've got issues."

"We all do, bro," Archer affirmed softly. "From what I've seen that girl means something to you or you wouldn't have brought her along. If she gives you peace and happiness then don't let her slip through your fingers. God knows you've had little enough of those things recently."

April brought him companionship. But happiness? Peace? He couldn't quite say. The world appeared a bit brighter and less gray with her around. She didn't gab all the time, make demands or get in the way. Instead she simply shared his space, easing a little of his burdens in doing so. Her curves and sweet smile lashed his arousal while her upbeat personality had put a smile on his face more times than he could count. Yes, he cared for her or she wouldn't be here now. Was caring enough to take that chance and place all his bets on April? "I'm not sure."

As if sensing the topic of conversation, April chose that moment to glance up. She met Dusty's eyes and smiled.

His breath caught.

She tossed the brush into a bucket, patted the chestnut gelding on the rump, then picked up the bucket and started his way.

"Don't take too long figuring it out. The brothers have already put their bids in," Archer cautioned.

Dusty frowned. "They'll have to get in line."

"That's what I'd hoped you'd say." He turned his focus to April. "There's a barn dance Friday night. You might consider asking her to it." Archer stood up and smiled at April. "Seems to me all that work polishing their hides will be for naught when they start rolling in the dirt again in a couple of hours."

April grinned back. "Probably. At least they were shiny and pretty for a little bit."

"True." Archer inclined his head. "If you'll excuse me, I'm going to see if there's any of Carrie's cherry pie left." He disappeared back inside the house, leaving the two of them alone.

"Hi."

"Hi." Dusty watched as April fussed with a stray strand of hair that had fallen out of the ponytail and blew across her face. "Thanks for taking the time to groom them."

"No problem. It helps fill in the hours and keeps me busy. You know what they say about idle hands." She shifted her weight from one foot to the other, drawing his attention to her feet still encased in those damn running shoes.

*No time like the present.* "Want to go out for ice cream?"

April's eyes widened. "Won't we get in trouble for ruining our supper?"

Dusty smirked. "I won't tell if you don't. Besides, Archer is pigging out on dessert as we speak. If he can do it, we can too."

"Ice cream sounds heavenly."

Dusty stood up and brushed off the seat of his pants. "Then let's go." He took the bucket from April's hands, placed it on the front porch and gestured for Ben to follow.

April glanced from the dog back to Dusty.

He shrugged. "Ben loves vanilla."

April chuckled. "Then, by all means, he should get his treat as well."

Dusty stopped at the truck, loaded Ben inside, waited for April to get settled, shut her door then went around to the driver's side. He snapped his seatbelt and took a second to peer over at April. Despite being windblown and sweaty, she'd never looked more beautiful.

Maybe Archer had a point after all.

With that thought, Dusty cranked the engine and drove down the driveway.

* * * *

"You're dripping." Dusty watched as a line of vanilla ice cream made its way over the edge and continued on a path straight to her hand.

"Ack!" April licked at the leak in an attempt to stem the tide. She was only marginally successful.

At their feet, Ben licked up the last bit of vanilla ice cream from the Styrofoam bowl. He hadn't waited for his to melt. Instead he'd dove into it and eaten with gusto.

Dusty lifted another spoonful of his sundae and placed it into his mouth while focusing on April. The way she lapped at her treat made his cock sit up and take notice. He could almost picture her doing the same to him. Sliding those full, rosy lips over his tip, then flicking that cute pink tongue all

160

over his aching dick.

He bit back a groan and shoveled in another bite in an attempt to cool off his quickly heating blood. As tasty as the frozen dessert was, it did nothing to quell his rapidly developing hard-on.

*Ice cream might have been a bad idea.*

His libido disagreed as he watched her attack the cone with enthusiasm.

The shaded patio offered protection from the sun as well as more moderate temperatures. It was still hot enough to melt their treats, but not totally uncomfortable. With Ben along, they'd had two options — either take up temporary residence on the patio or eat in the truck. The decision had been unanimous in favor of keeping his truck fairly clean and the interior free of sticky residue. Ben had even participated in the vote with a quick bark.

"This really hits the spot. Thank you." April collected a couple more napkins and wrapped them around the cone portion.

"You're welcome. It seemed like a good day for ice cream."

"Any day is a good day for ice cream." April grinned happily.

He smiled softly in return. He couldn't recall the last time he'd sat outside an ice cream shop, eating and chatting with a woman. Most of the women he'd dated wouldn't have come within a mile of this place, citing the need to stay on a strict diet in order to keep their perfect figures. He found April refreshingly different. "How's your stay so far?"

She glanced his direction. "Wonderful. It's like a vacation with the Waltons."

He snorted and took another mouthful.

"Really, your family is so sweet, taking Tess and me in. They've been nothing but gracious."

He heard the respect in her voice. "I'm glad."

"The question is, are you enjoying being back?" She met his gaze.

"Yeah. For the most part." He debated how much to add.

"It's just odd going from being alone for so long to being dropped into the middle of a busy household. Takes some getting used to."

"I can see that. With four ornery brothers, I'm sure that takes a bit of adjustment. Not to mention the lack of privacy."

He arched an eyebrow. "Privacy? What's that?"

April laughed. "That's about right." She swallowed another bite of her treat. "Must have been a bit challenging growing up. Not like you could hole up in the bathroom for some alone time."

Dusty grinned. *Talk about an understatement.*

She tilted her head as mischief sparked in her eyes. "Bet you were popular in school. Girls chasing after you all the time…"

He shrugged. "I had my fair share."

"*Had?*" She blinked at him.

Continuing to eat, he playfully peered up at her now and again before flashing a wide grin.

April rolled her eyes. "I don't even want to go there. Details might send me into hiding for a day or three."

"Or, at the very least, turn your cute cheeks scarlet." As he spoke the words, a bright pink blush appeared on her face. "Just like that." He found the coloring added to her beauty.

"Oh, good grief." April peeked down at the ground. "Ben? Think you could help a girl out?"

The dog stared up at her, eyed her cone and wagged his tail.

April shook her head. "Can he have the rest?"

Dusty nodded.

"Here you go then." She fed him the last bit.

Dusty heard Ben crunch a couple of times then lick his chops. Not a bad day for the old guy.

His phone binged. Plucking it from his belt, he scanned the text message. "Well, hell."

"What is it?" April's face conveyed worry and restrained

162

fear.

He wanted to kick himself for causing such fright, especially knowing they both waited eagerly for word about their homes. "Brand just sent me a message. Severe storms are moving in fast. We need to get home and get the horses inside before they arrive."

"Oh." April gathered up their trash, dropping it into a nearby wastebasket. "We better hurry then."

After digging out his keys, he called to Ben and strode quickly to the truck. Lifting Ben with ease, he deposited the dog inside then slid into the driver's seat. Plans quickly clicked into place, lining up tasks that needed to be done before the storms hit. He cranked the engine and started off.

"The old barn will have to do. There's not enough stalls for all the horses, but if we leave a couple of the geldings to roam inside, we'll make it."

"What about the alpacas?"

Dusty turned on the highway and hit the gas. "Brand will see to them. They're small enough to fit comfortably in the foaling shed in their paddock." He ran details through his mind. "We'll have to put straw down in the stalls. Right now it's just dirt. The feed is in the feed room. There's a gate that can be shut to keep the geldings out of the hay that's stored at the back of the barn."

"Okay. So what's the plan? Straw first, then gather horses?"

Dusty checked the horizon, noting the darkening skies to the north. "If time allows. If it doesn't, we'll focus on the horses first. Last thing we need is for one of them to get struck by lightning."

He glimpsed April pale out of the corner of his eye. He understood completely. With any chance of storms, he made sure the horses were inside and under cover. His family had lost a few head of cattle over the years due to lightning. Never a good situation.

Reaching over, he took her hand in his. "Don't worry.

We'll make it."

Twenty minutes later, he wasn't so sure.

Wind whipped dust, leaves and plants around like tumbleweeds. One look at the sky made up his mind— bring in the horses first. Straw could wait.

They'd pulled in the driveway to find the brothers and Tess corralling the small stock into the foaling barn. Dusty knew as soon as that task was done they'd chip in with the horses. Until then, he had to gather up lead ropes and catch the nervous animals.

April hurried to the barn alongside him, grabbed a handful of lead ropes, then trotted to the nearest pasture. He made a quick pit stop in order to put Ben in the house to keep him out of the way. Never would he take a chance of Ben being kicked or trampled by scared horses. The dog might not appreciate the separation, but it was for his own good.

Horses whinnied loudly. Some stood at the gate, more than ready to come in. Others sprinted across the pasture as if trying to outrun the threat.

"Get Miracle and Mischief. I'll grab the stud. Mares and foals to follow." He had to yell to make sure she'd hear him over the deafening wind.

She waved at him, made a beeline for the middle pasture, collected her two pets and led them through the gate. Another gelding stuck so close to Miracle that she couldn't separate the two. Dusty watched her take out another lead, snap it onto Turnip's halter, and take him along with them.

With a nod of approval, he whistled for Rule. The stallion galloped from the far end of his pasture and slid to a halt right in front of him. "Good boy." Dusty attached the lead, opened the gate and jogged in with the stallion.

By the time he had Rule in a back stall, April had gone out again. He hurried to catch up, noting his brothers in the paddock with the mares. Frightened foals stuck close to their mothers, especially when a booming roll of thunder shook the earth.

"Shit."

Dusty dashed through the gate Evan held open. He tossed a couple of leads over to his brothers. "Mares with foals first." He didn't have to tell them as they already had the right idea. Still, he needed to make sure the foals didn't panic and bolt away from their mothers.

He didn't wait to see if they heard, too busy trying to catch his black filly, Hailey. Her eyes showed white as another rumble of thunder rocked the land. "Come on, sweetheart. The sooner you let me catch you, the sooner you're safe in the barn." A couple of near catches had her dancing away. Finally he managed to snag her as she crowded in with another of the mares.

He turned to find Archer leading Bobbie in. "Here. Take this one too. I'll start on the geldings."

Archer nodded, snagged the rope and tugged. Dusty had to give Hailey a firm shove to get her going. As soon as they cleared the gate, Dusty turned his attention to the final pasture.

Brand and Tess left the foaling area and started his way. He waved them off. They only had a handful of horses left to go and fat raindrops had started to fall. Cole passed him by with two of the geldings, leaving three remaining.

Evan manned the gate.

April had managed to catch the three horses in the pasture. She waited for Dusty to approach and handed the first two off. "Take them. I'll follow with Dodger. He's wound to the hilt."

Dusty started to protest but a bolt of lightning across the sky startled him into motion. As quickly as possible, he moved the horses out of the pasture. He paused a second at the gate. "Go on inside, Evan. We've got the rest. Take Archer and Cole with you."

"You sure?"

"Yeah. Just go."

Dusty watched Evan sprint to the house, getting only marginally wet with the sprinkles, then entered the barn.

With all the stalls filled, he settled for tying the geldings to the gate at the back of the barn until he could get Dodger in, shut the door, and set them free to roam. The last thing he wanted to do was take a chance on one of them panicking, dashing back outside and leading them on a merry chase through the nasty forces of nature.

Double-checking the ties on each of the horses, he nodded in satisfaction. They would hold. For now. He swung around, expecting to see April. She wasn't there.

Worry crept up his spine. He ran to the entrance and came to a stop at the sight before him. April had managed to get just outside the gate with Dodger before the horse balked. She tugged, then scrambled to tighten the lead, forcing the horse to run in a circle around her instead of dash off to who knew where. A couple of seconds later she grasped his halter with her right hand, the lead still in her left.

Rain began to pour in earnest.

Another bolt of lightning raced through the dark sky, this time hitting the ground a distance away.

Dodger reared.

April held on tight, was lifted off her feet for a second.

A lump lodged in Dusty's throat. He battled with the need to race to her side, knowing that sudden movements would send Dodger right over the edge. Instead he moved stealthily, quickly, with as little excess motion as possible, speaking soothingly to the frightened animal. "Easy, Dodger. We're almost there. If you'll just chill long enough to give us a chance."

The horse's ears flickered his direction before Dodger pinned them against his head once again.

Dusty moved closer, slowly reaching for the halter on the opposite side of April. "That's it."

Dodger threw himself into reverse. Dusty snagged the halter and dug in. He caught April doing the same thing out of the corner of his eye.

With one strong tug, Dusty encouraged the horse to move forward. "Let's go already."

Thunder boomed. Dodger darted ahead, nearly dragging them along in his effort to get inside.

The second they were in the clear, Dusty shut the large barn doors. "Let him go." He walked over to the other two geldings and released them from the lead ropes, leaving their halters on for easy catching.

With that small chore done, he turned his full attention on April. "Are you okay? I was sure he'd tear your arm out of socket when he reared like that."

April waved her hand. "I'm fine." She sounded out of breath. Understandable considering what she'd just been through. "I knew I couldn't let him go. He'd take off to parts unknown. The only option was to hang on."

Dusty approached her, reached out and touched her shoulder. She was soaked and water dripped from her hair. They'd both been drenched before they could get Dodger inside.

He prodded her arm and moved it in a circular motion. If the movement hurt, she didn't let on. *Thank God.* He blew out the breath he hadn't known he'd been holding. "You'll be sore tomorrow."

She shrugged. "I'll be fine." A gust of rain-cooled air blew in from the windows.

April shivered.

He cussed to himself, spun around, strode to the stack of hay in the back and returned with an old stable blanket. "It's not much, but it'll ward off the cold until we can get you to the house."

April smiled softly as he wrapped it around her shoulders. "Thank you."

"Come on." He tossed a bale of straw onto the floor. "Have a seat for a minute."

She walked over and settled down on the makeshift bench. He turned her so she faced the window and climbed on behind her. Wrapping her in his arms, he pulled her snugly against his chest. Being just as wet as she, he didn't have as much body heat to share. Still, he couldn't resist the urge to try.

She sighed and leaned into him. "This is nice."

He nuzzled her nape and chuckled. "Sitting on a hard block of straw, dripping wet, while the heavens unload?"

She twisted to peer at him. "Yep. Because you're here."

He stared at her for a long moment. Gradually he leaned in, brushing his lips over hers.

The second he made contact she responded. Sweetly. Beautifully.

Dusty opened his mouth, licked the seam, then darted his tongue inside on her gasp. She tasted of vanilla and sunshine—an addictive combination. Over and over again he sampled her unique flavor.

Just as she turned to meet him head on, his phone rang. The sound startled April, as she jumped.

Dusty answered gruffly, "Yeah?"

"Just wondering if you two are coming in." Archer's amused voice carried to his ear easily despite the storm raging outside.

"When the rain slacks. Probably after evening chores, too." Dusty kept one arm around April, smiling as she snuggled into his chest.

"Need some help?"

"Nope."

"Thought so." Archer chuckled. "Guess we'll see you two later." He clicked off.

Dusty lowered his phone to the bale of straw and enveloped April with that arm.

"Let me guess. They're checking on us."

"Oh yeah." He nuzzled her nape, noting the silky skin starting to warm. "Will you go with me to the barn dance on Friday?" He hadn't been sure he wanted to attend. Now the idea sounded promising.

"I'd like that." She smiled up at him.

He grinned in return. "Good."

April looked out the window again. "Think it's raining like this at home?"

168

"It's coming out of the north, so no. At least not yet." He inhaled the scent of lavender from her hair.

"Too bad. We could use this." She rubbed her cheek against his. "But I wouldn't have missed this for anything."

"Me either."

He kissed her again, in no hurry to finish the chores and return to the house. She felt too damn good in his arms to let her go now.

A horse nudged him in the back. Hard.

Dusty groaned.

April giggled. "I think he's trying to tell you something."

"Probably." Dusty shoved at the muzzle only for it to immediately return. "No rest for the weary, I guess." He released April and helped her to her feet.

"I thought that was no rest for the wicked. At least in your case." She grinned slyly at him.

"You haven't seen wicked yet, lady." He caught her before she sprinted off, lifted her, then lowered her enough to seal his lips over hers. Dusty plundered, not letting her down until they both needed to come up for air.

"Wow."

"Yeah." He drew in a deep breath and ignored the aching in his groin. The barn wasn't the place to start stripping down. Not with three nosy horses ready to not only witness, but nip if they didn't get their supper soon.

April shed her blanket, leaving him with a clear view of clothing plastered to her body. Curves caught his eye as did her small, perky breasts with pebbled nipples.

*Damn.*

Later. Much later. He'd pick up where he'd left off. Come hell or high water.

# Chapter Sixteen

Dusty spun April around, instinctively catching her when she stumbled.

She chuckled and beamed. "You've got good reflexes or I'd be on my butt right now."

He smiled down at her. "I'd never let you fall."

"I know you won't."

The lights in the three-sided barn shone brightly enough to see details and avoided the spotlight effect at the same time. He clearly saw her face and all the people around him as well. Chairs lined one side, allowing attendees to take a load off. A couple of tables held plenty of food and drink. The dance floor remained in the center. A disk jockey kept the country songs playing while people came and went, dividing their time between dancing and wandering out to peer up at the stars. A couple of tiki torches burned outside the entrance in an attempt to deter bugs. Barring that, an old-fashioned blue fly zapper did the trick.

Dusty scanned the area. Nearby, he glimpsed Tess and Brand dancing close in each other's arms. They radiated happiness and perfect chemistry by the warm expressions they both wore. Completely enamored with each other. *About time Brand found a girl.*

Cole, on the other hand, entertained a handful of ladies near the seating area. Not surprising that the playboy of the family would garner the attention of several of the single women. A gift, to hear Cole tell the tale.

Archer and Carrie caught his eye next. They were on the other side of the dance floor caught up in each other. Evan hung back in one of the corners, talking with a couple of his buddies. No doubt Evan bided his time, even if he might appear to be a little shy. That wouldn't last long. Evan carried Delaney genes. He'd enter the fray soon enough and would end the night with a girl on his arm. No other scenario seemed likely.

"I think I can. I think I can."

Dusty couldn't help but smile at April's words. "Does that work?"

"I'm not sure, but it's worth a try." She sighed then tried the steps of the dance once again. "I don't think I'll ever get the hang of this."

She'd proclaimed herself a poor dancer with two left feet as soon as they'd arrived at the barn dance. He wasn't much of a dancer himself, but had figured between the two of them they could manage to stay upright for the duration of the night. So far his prediction had proven true.

He led her into another turn, slower this time. She glided across the floor, steady and sure at this more sedate pace. "Looks to me like you've got it now."

Her eyes met his. "That's because you're such a great lead. I start to go the wrong way, you literally pluck me off the floor and put me where I'm supposed to be."

"Hardly." He couldn't help but absorb her compliment like a thirsty man gulped water. They'd been at the dance less than an hour and April already made him feel special. Dozens of other people attended, some on the dance floor, some along the periphery, enjoying refreshments or simply chatting. Yet even with the abundance of potential dance partners, she seemed to be totally focused on him.

The past three days had flown by as they'd fallen into a routine. Chores kept them all busy, April doubly so, as she helped out around the house as well as the ranch. Carrie commented with praise—and quite often—how much her houseguests did, from cooking, to cleaning, to laundry. Still, he caught her gazing at him from time to time, curiosity and interest sparking in her pretty blue eyes. She offered sunshine into the dreary times along with humor.

The couple of kisses they'd shared had seared his soul. So good they had nearly unbalanced him completely. For a guy who reveled in controlling things with an iron will, he found April an enigma. She compelled him in many ways. Enough to break the bonds of the past? That he couldn't say.

"Looking good." Archer and Carrie two-stepped next to them.

"Thanks. It's all Dusty though," April pointed out.

Archer snorted. "Momma's dance lessons rubbed off the least on him."

April lifted her chin and pinned Archer with a hard stare. "He's a great dancer. Light on his feet. Keeping me on mine. He could give anyone here a run for their money."

Dusty's ego grew. He squeezed April slightly in thanks.

"Yeah, she's got it bad. Can't see the forest for one tree," Archer muttered, grinned, and moved away.

"A little biased?" Dusty asked when the others had moved out of hearing range.

April shrugged and peered up at him. "Nah."

He smiled down at her as the song ended. "Need a break to catch your breath?"

"Definitely." She wiped a lock of dark blonde hair out of her eyes. Tonight she'd left her ponytail holder at home, wearing her hair down for the first time since he'd met her. The long, soft strands hung nearly to the middle of her back. The light breeze played with her hair, only adding to the allure.

The long white dress hung below her knees, lightweight and airy. He knew she'd borrowed the dress from Carrie, as April hadn't packed anything more than the basics to bring with her. Still, the garment fit wonderfully, hinting at curves while remaining demure and innocent. The combination matched April's personality to a T.

"I'm going to get a drink. Do you want one?"

Dusty shook his head. "No thanks. I saw Trevor Wallace on the other side of the room. I'm going to catch up with him for a bit."

"Okay." She strode over to the refreshment table, plucked a bottle of water from an ice-laden cooler, opened it and took a long drink.

Dusty turned his attention to one of his friends from school who he hadn't seen in ages. Trevor had always been a hard-working farm kid with a bright future. A good guy, he'd come along for more than his fair share of adventures with the Delaney boys.

Trevor dressed like the rest of the men in attendance. Fairly new jeans, a nice Western shirt and cowboy boots polished for the occasion. Nothing really fancy. It was a barn dance after all, not the prom.

Stopping in front of the man, Dusty held out his hand. "Trevor. Good to see you again."

Trevor stared at him for a couple of beats before recognition lit up his features. "Dusty Delaney. What the hell have you been up to?"

"Been around. And you?"

"Still here. Doing the same thing that I've always done." He gestured across the room. "Married Tammy. Remember her from school?"

Dusty followed the other man's gaze only to land on a lady dressed in an emerald green maternity dress that emphasized her basketball-sized baby bump. "Looks like she's ready to pop."

Trevor lifted his head proudly. "A boy. Our first. Her due date is next week. Not sure if she's going to make it that long, though."

"Congratulations." Dusty studied Trevor's face. He'd seem the same expression before on other men. Pride. Happiness. Contentment. Something about impending fatherhood made a man strut around and want to show off his lady to the masses. Dusty knew those traits would only strengthen when the baby arrived.

"I better go check on her. She's looking a bit tired." Trevor nodded to Dusty. "Good seeing you again. If you're around these parts again soon, stop by and pay us a visit."

"Will do." Dusty watched Trevor make a beeline for his wife, wrap an arm around her and lead her to a group of chairs waiting nearby.

He shook his head in amusement. Trevor might have been a wild hare in school, but he'd obviously tamed down as of late.

*How things have changed.*

Dusty picked up a glass of punch off a nearby table and sipped. He tasted a slight bite of alcohol and grinned. *Apparently some things haven't changed.* Someone always managed to spike the punch bowl.

For a moment he considered fatherhood. He might have something to offer and pass on to his kids. However, that meant settling down with the right woman — something he'd pretty much given up on.

His gaze scanned the room until he found April, standing with a small group of both men and women. She held her water, sipped now and again while listening to the others talk. Relaxed and with a small smile on her face, she paid rapt attention to the speaker. As if unable to hear, she leaned closer. The guy bent over and whispered in her ear. April laughed. She turned her head and met Dusty's gaze.

Memories flooded his mind. Not of war this time, but of another barn dance a few years back. Rose, dressed in a flowing red dress with a low-cut bodice had stood just as April did now, surrounded by others, presumably the life of the party. Men had brought her drinks, chatted her up and stuck to her like glue. She'd soaked up the attention, giggled and flirted outrageously. Dusty had stood in the wings, as he did now, watching Rose flaunt her charms, jealousy raging inside. She'd shyly peered his way now and again, making sure he took notice of her princess status complete with court.

As much as he'd wanted to pick her up and carry her away, he'd held back. She'd teased him mercilessly in public. Later, she'd invoked another sort of torment, that one sexual. She'd played him like a tightly strung guitar, enlisting rewards for her favors.

Like a lovesick idiot, he'd obliged. Over and over again. Watched her play her manipulation games in order to extract high-priced gifts later.

His gut clenched. Tension yanked his shoulders higher. His breath picked up as a trickle of sweat moistened his lower back.

*I was such a fucking fool.*

April left the others and sashayed over to him. She peeked up at him coyly from under her eyelashes. The action reminded him so much of Rose that his stomach churned. "This is so much fun. I'm glad you brought me along." She stopped right in front of him. "I was thinking, maybe we could do this again sometime. Drive back for some of the activities."

His breath caught at her words. The admission caught him totally off guard and left him reeling as the present and past merged. He narrowed his eyes. "What?"

She wrapped her hand around his forearm. "I think we make a good team. Now and in the future." April sucked in a deep breath. "Not to be forward, but I guess now is as good a time as any." She paused. "I really like you, Dusty. I was hoping we could discuss dating. Maybe more. Take our relationship up a step. Become an official couple. A committed couple." She stared up at him with expectation written clearly on her face.

*She's fishing for a fucking ring.*

His heart chilled. Pressured, pushed and cornered didn't begin to describe the feelings flaring through his mind. Just like before. Rose had used games to get what she wanted. April simply tossed her wants right out there. Either way, he froze at the implications of commitment. *How in the fucking hell did I get into this predicament again?*

Old wounds reopened, allowing pain and bitterness to slip out.

He glared down at April, watched her lips turn down, her

eyes widen and eyebrows furrow.

Tears would come next. They always had with Rose.

He didn't want to be around for that particular scene.

Dusty removed her hand from him, dropped it like a hot knife, turned on his heel and strode out. He jumped in his truck, cranked the engine and drove off.

Well away from his past and the unsettling present. Away from women and their marriage-minded ways. Away from society and all the matchmaking pain in the asses that were his family.

*I was damn happy on my own. Why now? Why me? Fucking wildfires and fate.*

He shoved the truck into another gear and headed off the beaten path. Alone with only his memories for company. For good or bad.

\* \* \* \*

April watched Dusty leave, confused, ashamed and angered. She'd thought after what they'd shared so far that tonight might be a good time to discuss formally dating. *Obviously, I was wrong.*

With a stiff upper lip, she stared at the retreating lights of Dusty's truck until they blinked out of view.

"What happened?" Archer drew up beside her along with Carrie.

April sucked in air and grasped her composure with an iron fist. "I mentioned that I wanted to talk about taking our relationship to the next level. Dating. Other things. He looked at me like I'd just told him I'd cut his fences and stolen his cattle." April spun around to face them.

"Did he say anything?" Carrie asked.

"Not a word. Just dusted my hand off his arm, glared at me then stormed off." April found her bottle of water enthralling. "I don't know what I did. Pushed too hard, too fast, I guess."

Archer patted her shoulder. "It's not you. It's him."

April lifted her gaze. "I know about his past. I should have given it more consideration. I just figured we were getting along so well this week…"

Carrie wrapped an arm around her shoulders and gave her a squeeze. "Dusty is a hard nut to crack."

"I'd like to take a shot," Archer growled.

April shook her head. "It's okay. Please. You guys are just back to getting along. Don't jeopardize it because of me." She pinned him firmly. "I might be a blip in his life, but he *needs* his family. Someone has to have his back." As much as Dusty had been through, he deserved an anchor. A solid one that wouldn't crack. His family was that for him. Never would she want to be the cause of another rift that might not be repairable, ever.

Archer bobbed his head once. "I'll stay out of it."

April released the breath she'd been holding. "Thank you. I know you want to throttle him at times. It's human nature. We just have to remember that he's haunted by memories. Those don't go away. I don't think ever."

Archer looked away. "When he first came home, he blew hot and cold. None of us ever knew what would set him off. He'd just gotten a handle on things and started to settle in when that witch Rose screwed him over." Leashed fury resounded in Archer's tone.

"He's been through some really bad stuff. I can't blame him if he doesn't want to spend his life with a woman after that. Most importantly, he needs to find an outlet and something to ease his demons. Even if I'm not that person for him."

"If anyone can, it's you." Carrie sighed wearily. "A girl can't wait forever, though."

Archer glanced toward his wife before focusing back on April. "Want to catch a ride home with us?"

"Please. No hurry, though. I'll hang out until you're ready." April hated to mess up their date night.

"It's okay. We were about ready to take off anyway," Carrie said. "Tomorrow is another early morning and we're getting too old to be up all night long then pull our weight the next day."

"Ain't that the truth?" Archer grinned.

"Well, if you're sure?" April hesitated. The family probably rarely got time to just have fun. Leaving so soon after arriving slashed their date night into an exceptionally brief time frame.

"I'm sure. Besides, I have a hankering for some of Carrie's pie. If we get home first, there's liable to be some left. It's first come, first served, you know." Archer waggled his eyebrows playfully.

April smiled at his antics. "There's that."

"Then, ladies, your chariot awaits." Archer led them through the barn, pausing only to whisper to Brand before escorting them to his truck.

April watched all the couples dance under the lights and slumped. Tonight had held so much promise.

*Why did I have to push?* She chastised herself for her lack of patience that had led to the rejection. Concern for him swamped her as well. Dusty preferred to be by himself, which wasn't always the best way to be. While some people might thrive being always alone, she didn't think Dusty fit into that category. The affection between him and his brothers told the truth. He'd missed them and would do anything for them. They might have had a huge canyon between them at one time, but after they bridged the gap, anyone could see how they felt about one another. Dusty needed people. Family. Love. He was just too stubborn and blind to see it. Which led her right back to the same place she'd started. She'd made her feelings known, thrown in her bid and heard nothing in response. His body language and actions spoke volumes. No declaration of love. No offers for dates. No comments about careful steps and taking plenty of time to follow that particular path. Nothing. Just an endless blind alley filled with hopelessness. *Could I change his mind? Who knows?* Even if she could, how long would it take? Months? Years? Never? She wasn't getting any younger and the thought of waiting for the next decade for Dusty to come around left a bitter taste in her mouth. Spending the rest of her life alone sounded better than chasing after a man for the next several years all for naught.

*At least I have my answer. Time to pick up the pieces and move on. Alone.*

# Chapter Seventeen

Sleep barely came to her that night. The girls as well as the rest of the family had rallied around her the night before, offering up condolences, encouragement and promises to kick Dusty's butt. She thanked them all, waved off the threats and prodded them to lean toward understanding when it came to their brother. He'd been through enough, after all. Besides, she had the feeling a SEAL — either current or retired — tended to make his own path in the world, against the grain if he had to. Whatever Dusty felt was best was the direction he'd travel. No matter what anyone said.

Tess had sat with her at bedtime, chatting amicably and trying to boost her spirits. April appreciated the effort and had told her friend so. She'd laid down with one ear tuned to the front door, hoping to hear when Dusty returned home. She never heard it.

By five the next morning, April had given up, gotten dressed and walked to the paddocks, intent upon feeding the horses before she left for home. After a week of filling buckets with grain twice a day, she could do the task in her sleep.

Starting with the stud, she gathered up his bucket, filled it with his feed and lugged the heavy container to his pasture. Not bothering to open the gate, she simply sat the bucket against a corner post just inside, waited for him to start eating, then headed back to the barn.

Archer met her there with a stern look. "What are you doing?"

She strode right past him, aiming for the next section of buckets. "Feeding the horses."

He followed right on her heels. "Dusty's job."

Grabbing another sack of feed, she poured out generous amounts into several buckets. "I was up anyway. Might as well feed the herd before I head on home."

Archer grumbled under his breath. "If it helps any, Dusty is an asshole."

She couldn't help but grin at the identical phrase she'd overheard used a couple of times before retiring for the night. Picking up two handles, she started the long trek back to the pasture. "He's not ready for romance, Archer. Maybe he'll never be. Maybe I'm not the right gal. Either way, I can sit around and pine away for him or move on."

"You'll pine anyway."

She shrugged. He wasn't telling her anything she didn't already know. Brave words fell flat when she admitted the truth to herself. "I just need to get home, check things out and find a way to get my horses back home."

Archer picked up a couple of buckets and followed along. "He'll come around."

She managed to shrug despite the heavy load. "I'm not holding my breath." After setting her load down, she spun around to gather more buckets before entering the pasture with the mares and their foals. Once she put the buckets down, there would be a squabble over the food unless there were adequate buckets for each animal spread all around.

Archer's long strides carried him to her side. "I'll speak to him. Set him straight."

April stopped in her tracks. "No."

"Why not?" He stared down at her with furrowed brows.

"Because I'll not be the cause of another split in your family. Dusty is a grown man, he's seen more than most people will ever see, the horrors of war and the worst humanity has to offer. Whether anyone knows it or not, he struggles with nightmares and flashbacks now and again, courtesy of serving his country." She puffed out a breath. "If anyone deserves happiness, it's him. No matter who he chooses, it's his life, his heart, his future. Don't stand in his way." Finished with the lecture, she grabbed up more buckets and retraced her steps.

"You'd make a great attorney." He grinned over at her as he collected more breakfast for the horses.

She snorted. "That's a scary thought. The first time I declared 'off with their head' I'd probably be dismantled."

"You mean disbarred."

"That too." She lifted another bucket. "I think I'd better stick to nursing."

"And stable hand." He opened the gate, set his buckets along the far fence then hurried back for the rest as she carefully placed hers on the ground.

"I used to think so." With those words, she left him to watch over the foals to make sure their mommas didn't get greedy and returned to the stable. Her horses and the nine geldings were left. The sooner they were fed, the sooner she could leave the ranch in her rearview mirror.

* * * *

Dusty stepped out on the front porch, dressed and prepared for the morning chores. Ben darted off the porch, sniffed around the front yard, and found a place to do his business.

The sun scraped past the horizon, casting light and colors across the land in a rainbow of pinks, oranges and blues. Beautiful and breathtaking.

Yet he couldn't raise the effort to enjoy the gift of morning, too consumed by his thoughts about the prior evening.

He'd allowed the past to color his present, sending him running scared. Not one of his prouder moments. Sure, she'd shocked the hell out of him, but that was no excuse. He cringed as he recalled what an ass he'd been. To April of all people. She'd done nothing but voice her feelings. For that, he'd outright rejected her, driven off leaving her at the mercy of others and probably left her sour, hurt and with an irreparable breach of trust.

*I'm such a fucking idiot.*

Archer walked across the yard, coming to a stop at the bottom of the front porch steps. "I see you're up and at 'em this morning." He stared at Dusty's face. "Bright-eyed and bushy-tailed after dragging home in the wee hours of the morning?"

Dusty saw the jab for what it was, an expression of displeasure in Dusty's choices. He bit back the urge to blast Archer for his uppity attitude and reminded himself he'd been in a similar situation in the past. His volatile temper had caused a lot of hurt feelings that day. He wouldn't make the same error twice. Besides, it wasn't like he'd had a hot rendezvous to attend. Instead, he'd spent most of the time at a nearby lake, trying to make sense of a muddled situation. "Actually, yeah. I needed some time to think."

"And?"

"I was an ass. Seem to have a habit of that lately." Dusty rubbed at his forehead. "I'm going to try to fix that today."

"I always knew you had brains."

Dusty grinned at the backhanded compliment. "Is April up yet?"

Archer nodded. "Up, fed all the horses and gone."

"Gone?" Dusty tilted his head. *Where would she go before dawn?*

"Home. They lifted the evacuation order. She took care of the horses then took off like a hound sprayed by a skunk. Said she needed to get back, check out everything, make sure things are sound, then figure out a way to get her horses back."

Dusty frowned as guilt settled heavily on his shoulders. She was running. Because of him. Headed to Colorado on her own because he couldn't see the gift right before his eyes.

He felt lower than a worm.

Instinct and desperation made him dig his keys from his pocket and march toward his waiting truck.

"Where are you going?" Archer called after him.

"Home. To see if I can patch things up April." He opened his truck door and looked back at Archer. "I'll be back for the horses later today. With any luck, she'll be by my side."

"For just today?"

Dusty considered the question. He didn't have to think long. "For as long as she'll have me."

Archer smiled widely enough to show even white teeth. "Good luck, bro. You've got a touch with horses, let's hope you have the same skills with that particular woman." With a wave, he entered the house.

Dusty whistled for Ben, lifted him into the truck, then settled in himself. He shoved the key in the ignition and started the engine. His seat belt in place, he put the truck in gear and headed down the long driveway.

One way or another, he'd explain everything to April. Show her how he felt.

*'Help her learn to trust again.'*

The words she'd spoken the day Miracle and Mischief arrived at his stable replayed through his mind. She hadn't just been talking about her filly.

Motivated and determined, he hit the highway and headed home.

* * * *

After stopping by her house, finding the area untouched by flames and everything accounted for, April couldn't repress the urge to jump in the SUV once more and drive down the road. Besides, she still carried his office equipment and files in her vehicle. Not wanting to wake the whole crew to unload the boxes, she'd simply decided to bring them back with her, borrow Dusty's hidden spare key and replace his belongings as if they'd never left.

As much as she tried to deny the fact, she needed to see the stables, assure herself they stood as they had before, untouched by the flames of nature's wrath. Her horses' future depended upon this stable, for she didn't think she could find a better person to work with Miracle's issues than Dusty.

*Dusty.*

A deep pain throbbed in her heart. *That's what happens when you're reading into things that aren't there.* Sexy men with nice incomes didn't single out ordinary women for a lifetime together. Even if she rushed out to purchase glass slippers, her lot in life wouldn't change one iota. Fairy tales simply didn't happen to girls like her.

Cutting the engine once she pulled up the driveway, she grabbed the spare key and headed to unlock the chain on the large doors. *It's not breaking and entering if you use a key. Besides, I'm returning items, not stealing them.* After tugging with all her might, she finally got one stubborn door to budge open far enough to allow her ample room. Noting everything seemed in order and no black charred earth stood as far as she could see, April returned to her vehicle and began unloading the office's contents.

Twenty minutes later, she bent over, plugged in the laptop and sighed. The clear container sat on Dusty's large wooden desk, awaiting his return. She would start transferring files to the cabinet, but didn't know his system. Better to wait and let him sort things than spend twice as much time fixing them later.

Glancing across the office, she decided she'd done all she could. She stepped from the room and locked the door behind her. Ambling down the lane, she noted the undamaged walls and felt another sprinkle of relief. They'd gotten lucky. She sent up a quick prayer in thanks. If the fire had engulfed the stable, she couldn't imagine what Dusty would have done. This place provided him with much more than a simple business opportunity. The animals offered therapy and solace, companionship and unconditional love. He obviously felt deeply about his family, but this was his home now.

One she'd hoped to get to know much better with time. Now, she wasn't so sure.

The depressing thought pressed her shoulders down farther.

The clang of a gate startled her. Looking up, she found Dusty standing just inside the stable's front entrance. Dressed in his jeans and a snug blue T-shirt, he made her heart speed and mouth water. She'd never seen a more handsome man and probably never would again.

Ben bounded over as if thrilled to see her again. She just wished his owner would feel the same. Greeting the dog sincerely, she stroked his head as she watched Dusty walk toward her, his face blank, leaving her no clue as to his mood.

She steeled her resolve and decided on a quick explanation before making a hasty exit. The longer she stayed in his proximity, the larger the hole in her heart. With no hope for any future, she preferred to limit the pain and mourn in private. "I put everything back in your office that I could. If you'll let me know when you plan on bringing back the horses, I'll help with Miracle."

For a long moment, he remained mute.

Dejected, she brushed past him only for him to gently grab onto her upper arm, stopping her retreat and spinning her to face him.

"I handled last night completely wrong. I'm sorry."

She blinked, surprised by his apology. However, in the long run, his words didn't change a thing. She remained way out of his league and he had a difficult past too powerful to overcome when it came to women. "You're forgiven." Her feet refused to budge even though he released her.

"I'd like to talk. Would you ride back with me to the ranch? I intend to load up the horses and bring them home."

Irritation rushed over her. "I'm not sure what there's left to talk about. I've got eyes and a brain after all."

He blew out a breath. "Please. It's important."

She studied his face, finding concern and hope. Her

marshmallow heart gave in. The rational voice in her mind reminded her that he needed help with her horses regardless of anything else. With no excuse to bow out, and curious about his intentions, she slowly bobbed her head. "Okay."

Lines disappeared and his lips curled up ever so slightly at the corners as tension eased in his face. His stance relaxed as if in relief. "Let's put your SUV in the shop for safekeeping, then hit the road."

"Works for me. Can we swing by Tess' place? I promised her I would check out her house."

"Sure."

Ten minutes later they drove down a gravel road with charred areas spanning both sides. Though only about five miles from the stable, Tess' house hadn't survived the inferno.

April looked over the ash-covered area and ruins of the house and her heart sank for her friend. "Oh my God. She's going to be devastated." She couldn't imagine what Tess would go through once she found out she was now homeless. With nothing more than what she'd packed up and hauled with her, the woman had a tough road ahead, one no one would envy.

Dusty pulled into the driveway, shut down the engine and simply stared. Concern and sadness covered his face. She knew he thought of his stable and realized this could have easily been his fate.

Ben pushed up onto the console and whined as if feeling the pain from both of them. Dusty patted his head.

Unsure what to do, she scanned the area, wondering if there happened to be anything salvageable in the blackened mess. "Should we walk through things, see if anything is left?" Even as she offered up the suggestion, she knew the idea wouldn't hold merit. Not with such total destruction.

"No use. Nothing would have survived."

"Maybe I should take a picture to show Tess. So she can see how bad things are before driving all this way."

"Good idea."

April hopped out and took several pictures with her cell phone, showing the property from all angles. After carefully saving them, she returned to the vehicle, sadder than ever.

"How are we going to tell Tess? She'll be crushed."

Dusty palmed his phone, scrolled and punched a button. "Brand? Yeah. Is Tess still there?"

He waited a moment. "You need to be there when we get back. She lost it all."

Silence reigned.

"April has pictures to show her. Just be with her when we return."

"Will do."

Disconnecting the call, Dusty placed his phone on the console. "Brand's going to stay close to her, be there with her when we tell her."

"Good. She's going to need support. Big time."

"That's one thing I can guarantee. She'll have support. From the entire family." Dusty sighed and stared at the devastation once more. "You don't know how lucky you are some days." He cranked the truck back on, backed out and headed toward the highway.

A short time later, he turned on the interstate and headed north. Ben settled back onto the second row seat, curled up and closed his eyes. April stared out of the passenger side window, her heart in her throat. Her thoughts wandered between the images of Tess' destroyed home and the man sitting beside her. Dusty had said he wanted to talk, but not about what. Tension filled the air as her mind ran wild with possible topics, none of them listing in her favor. With her patience growing thin and her stomach beginning to churn, she struck up the conversation. "You said you wanted to talk?"

He glanced over at her before turning his attention back to the road. "Yeah. I wanted to explain why I did what I did. It revolves around a couple of poor choices that I made in my life regarding women. The first was my fiancée. I thought she was the one for me. Beautiful. Sweet. I really thought we had something going. Until she sent me a letter during my deployment, breaking up. I didn't receive it for weeks after she sent it. She'd already moved on to another man by the time I read it at base in Afghanistan."

April already knew most of the stories of both women thanks to Carrie. Still, she wasn't about to break Carrie's trust, so she kept her mouth shut and let Dusty tell his versions.

"I'm sorry. That had to have been devastating."

Dusty stared at the road ahead of them. "Yeah. Made for a bad day. When I got back, I had problems adjusting. I wasn't the same man that had left. War left wounds. In my fumbling attempts to get back to what I thought was normal, I fell for another woman, Rose. She was a professional flirt who knew who to wrap a man around her finger and get exactly what she wanted."

"Money? Status?"

"Yeah." He glanced in her direction before focusing on driving again.

"Anyone could have fallen for that. Especially since you were already unsettled from just getting back and finding your world had changed. There's no shame in the need to find love and acceptance and making an error in judgment along the way."

"She cost me my family until recently." He paused then shook his head. "*I* cost me my family. Archer figured out her game and hired a private detective to get evidence. When he showed it to me, I lost control of my temper. Even swung at him." He sighed. "I was a fucking fool."

April reached over to rest her hand on his upper arm. "You're human, Dusty. A man who'd been through a rough time and had lost his place in the world. Your family doesn't hold that against you. Heck, I'd say they understand more than others why you did what you did. That didn't stop them from keeping track of you and coming to the rescue. Maybe both sides had too much pride to make the first move, but the important part is that you did. Now things are so much better. You have them back again."

He placed his hand over hers. "Yes. Then I screwed up again. At the dance. You told me your feelings and I walked out."

The sting in her heart renewed at the reminder. "Yes."

"I couldn't help but remember another barn dance at the same place a few years ago. I'd taken Rose. She spent the evening flirting with other men to make me jealous. It was all part of her game to get what she wanted. When I saw you talking to that group, laughing, having fun, then looking over at me, it was like a déjà vu moment."

April gasped at the admission. "I wasn't flirting and I only had eyes for you. That's what I was trying to tell you. As far as I was concerned you were the man for me…" Her words trailed off as she realized she was wasting her breath trying to make Dusty understand. He obviously saw her as comparable to a less than flattering woman in his past. She stared out the side window as new pain rolled through her.

"April?"

April pulled on her waning inner strength and turned to face him.

"I know. You see, I got a bit mixed up and a little panicked when you started talking commitment. The past came back and bit me in the ass. Caught off guard, I didn't handle the situation well and I hurt you. I'm really sorry."

She nodded. "It's okay."

"No, it's not."

"Dusty, you don't have to sugarcoat things for me. I'm not what you want. It is what it is. There are other women that would be more suited. Wealthy, beautiful, charismatic."

She sighed as her shoulders weighed down with downtrodden misery. Pride forced her chin up and built a quick wall around her heart. She'd put a smile on her face and pretend happiness. Later, when she crawled into bed, would be the time for tears and heartbreak.

"Is that what you think I'm looking for in a woman?"

She blinked over at him and shrugged. "Isn't that what all men want? A trophy wife to make other men drool with envy? A woman who keeps herself up, with a body that won't quit?"

He shook his head. "Maybe some men do, but I certainly don't."

His words slowly sank in. Hope reignited from a single remaining ember. Before she latched on tight, she needed to be certain. "Meaning?"

"Meaning I need a real woman. One with inner substance and fortitude. Sweet, kind, gentle. Hardworking. Someone who isn't afraid to get dirty." His gaze met hers briefly.

"Oh." He hadn't said beautiful, but April knew it had to be an accidental omission from the list.

He shot her a curious expression. "Why aren't you angry with me?"

At least this question she could answer truthfully. Sort of. Deep down she carried anger, but her mind constantly pointed out reality. "I didn't have a right to be angry. You took in my horses, and have spent extra time with Miracle. You've tolerated me being underfoot for days on end. Even brought me along to your family home when the mandatory evacuation order came down. After all that, I couldn't be mad that you don't want to date me. People love who they love. Sometimes that feeling doesn't go both ways." She watched his face carefully. "Whether you believe me or not, I really do want you to find happiness. You've done so much, sacrificed yourself time and again. Now it's your turn. No matter who it's with."

His eyes grew darker as his expression softened. "Will you give me another chance?" Dusty's voice lowered in decibels, yet became fuller at the same time, as if emotion dripped off each word.

Her heart stuttered. "I don't understand. Chance at what?"

"A chance to live up to your high regard and praise. A chance to see if we can click again. A chance to see if something might come of this. A chance to see if you can learn to trust me." His voice strummed her heartstrings.

*I already do.* She recalled the words she'd spoken to him when Miracle had arrived at the stable. She hadn't been just talking about the nervous filly. She'd been hurt by men before, but her gut demanded she take this chance — a second chance that could pay off in dividends. Still shy after her previous train wreck relationships, she warned herself to tread carefully.

"I don't want you to just say that out of pity or guilt." She held on to hope and waited.

"First of all, I would never do that." He glanced over at her. "I'm sincere in this. Thinking clearly now. Yes, I was stupid. Blind. I can't take that back. But I can say truthfully that I see what's right in front of my eyes now. I like you, appreciate you, and want to see if we mesh together."

"No strings attached?" She worried her lip. What-if questions ran through her mind.

"No strings attached. Just two friends getting to know one another better. Go out with me a couple of times. No pressure, just one day at a time."

"Just one day at a time?" she echoed.

He nodded.

Her soul lightened as her spirit soared. That was exactly what she'd been asking for the night before. Refreshed and relieved, she smiled. "Yes."

He grinned back. "Thanks."

She forced another moment of reality into their conversation. "I have to warn you, I've not had very good luck with men in the past. I've kissed toads and they remained toads."

"That's what happens when you start with a toad." His lips twitched. "Starting a bit farther up the evolutionary scale helps."

"Really? How far up do I need to go?"

"At least to Neanderthal. Maybe a bit higher."

She couldn't quite keep the amusement from her face.

"Hmm. Where exactly on the scale do you fall?"

He chuckled, the deep sound soothing to her senses, contagious and warm. "I'm a bit behind, but working hard to catch up fast."

"Don't worry. I'll slow down and wait." She met his gaze and sighed happily.

Reaching out, he found her hand with his, intertwined their fingers and gently squeezed.

April smiled a bit as she settled in for the ride back, never once tempted to move her hand. He'd handed her an olive branch and a genuine reason to believe. Only time would tell, but they had a darn good start.

# Chapter Eighteen

Just under four hours later, Dusty pulled into the driveway of the ranch, feeling much better about life in general than he had when he'd left that very morning. April had seemed to understand and accept his apology and, if she had any animosity over the ordeal, she hid her emotions well. His military career had taught him to read people flawlessly, thus he believed her words and actions. Probably good-hearted to a fault, April meant to give him a second chance.

No way in hell would he blow it.

"I don't know how to tell her." April glanced his way, her voice full of worry and regret.

He stopped just in front of the large house, turned off the engine and put his full attention on the pretty blonde at his side. Her eyes, normally bright and sparkling with excitement, happiness or mischief, now appeared flat, matching the expression of concern written all over her face. "There's no easy way. We'll just come right out and say it." While he could certainly sympathize with what Tess would be going through, he'd thanked his lucky stars a dozen times his home had survived.

"You're right." April blew out a deep breath and climbed out of the truck.

Dusty followed suit, then opened up the second door, picked up Ben and set him on the ground to run. He spied Tess and Brand leaning against the paddock fence watching her alpacas, and strode their direction.

Brand looked up, met Dusty's gaze, and returned a grim acknowledgement. He steadfastly stood next to Tess, ready to bear the bad news at her side.

April walked over, giving a wan smile when Tess turned around.

"Oh, you're back." The redhead grinned in welcome. "I take it things are better?"

Dusty's shoulders weighed down. "For us, yes. For you, not so good."

Tess' face fell. "The fire?"

"Destroyed everything." April's calm voice barely carried across the space. She pulled out her cell phone and moved close. "I'll show you."

Seconds later, tears trickled down Tess' cheeks and deep pain and forlornness appeared on her normally cheerful face. "It's gone. Everything." Her voice cracked.

"I'm sorry." Dusty spoke the words knowing full well they didn't help a single iota. Guilt washed over him seeing how the loss affected her while all his belongings remained untouched by devastation. Life's unfairness never flashed brighter.

"I'm so sorry." April laid a hand on Tess' shoulder.

Brand wrapped Tess in his arms, holding her tight as she wept. He felt her upset as much as she did, judging by his frown and how close he cradled the small doctor. Easily reading between the lines, Dusty knew his older brother would stand behind Tess, care for her and ensure a bright future either here or back in Colorado. The man's reaction spoke of possession, protection and devotion. They might have just met a few days before, but Dusty would bet his large trust fund that Brand had fallen head over heels and wasn't about to turn his back on this special lady.

Sniffing, Tess stepped back, her eyes locked on Brand's face. "Thank you."

His brows furrowed in confusion. "For what?"

"For my animals. If you hadn't come along and hauled them away, they might not have survived at all." She wiped at a stray tear. "I might have lost the house, but I still have my pets and my life. All considered, I'm a pretty lucky woman, thanks to you." She reached up, wrapped her arms around Brand's neck and hugged him.

Dusty met April's eyes, reached out his hand and led her toward the house. Tess and Brand needed some time alone to digest the news and start the process of planning and healing. He and April would only be in the way.

Opening the front door, Dusty gestured April in first with Ben at her side, then stepped into the living room, finding four sets of eyes staring in his direction. Most likely Brand had quietly passed the word around about Tess' loss and the rest of the family had prepared to step up to the plate. Though that didn't explain why they looked at him like he'd just returned from Oz minus the ruby red slippers and Toto.

Carrie broke the silence. "Poor Tess."

April nodded. "You should see her place. There's barely a wall still standing. Just charred remains and a few embers still smoking. Here, I'll show you the pictures."

Everyone closed in to see the visual evidence of the destruction.

"What's she going to do?" Evan asked the question at the top of Dusty's mind.

"We spoke briefly of this very scenario the first night here. She said if she lost her home and her clinic burned down, she'd pick up the pieces, probably somewhere else." April reached down to pat Ben's head as he leaned against her legs as if trying to provide comfort.

"She can pick up the pieces right here," Carrie said.

The rest of the room's occupants nodded in agreement.

"Brand's with her now." Dusty glanced at Archer. "I know the timing sucks, but I was hoping to load up the horses this afternoon and take them home."

"You won't consider staying longer?" Colt rubbed his forehead.

A spear of indecision hit Dusty in the chest. He'd found happiness and forgiveness on this visit. Truly, he'd enjoyed his stay. He'd mended old wounds with all his brothers, realized his love for them and vowed to never stay away

196

again.

Yet Colorado was home. Always would be. The sooner he returned, the sooner he could resume a normal schedule and relax into the comfortable existence he'd worked hard to carve out for himself for the last three years.

"I need to get home." He turned to meet Archer's gaze. "It's been just like old times. You welcomed me with open arms, and I appreciate that to my very marrow. I found what I'd been missing too. So it's time to leave before I screw everything up again." He grinned in mild amusement.

Archer cracked a smile. "If you weren't such a stubborn cuss…"

"Then I wouldn't be your brother." Dusty's lips twitched.

"Now that's calling the kettle black." Colt snorted. "If we get a move on, we can be on the road by lunchtime."

"I'll pack lunches for everyone." Carrie hurried to the kitchen.

"Thanks." Dusty slapped Colt on the back. "Brand's needed here." He turned to Evan. "Care to drive this time?"

"Sure."

Feeling someone staring at him, Dusty twisted around. April stood with a knowing expression painted on her face. Pride and happiness flashed through her eyes. Stepping forward, she brushed a kiss across his cheek. "You're a good man, Dusty."

Evan whistled. "That explains a lot."

"He's in a hurry to get home because he wants April all to himself," Colt noted.

"Yeah. Far away from me. Damn it." The youngest brother mock frowned. "Here I was going to ask pretty April out tonight."

Dusty watched a splash of color blast across April's face and grinned mischievously.

"Sorry, bro. I might be as dumb as a box of rocks from time to time, but I've decided to keep this one."

"Time to time?" Evan snorted. "I'd say most of every day." He leaped toward the front door as Dusty pounced his direction.

Archer laughed. "I guess we should get to work before you and Evan end up in a spat, rolling in the dirt."

"You were always the smart one." Colt chuckled, walking toward the front door.

* * * *

Since they hadn't unloaded any of the items they'd brought except the animals and food for the dog and cat, packing to leave proved quick and fairly easy. Colt and Archer hooked up their trailers as Dusty did the same. Just as Dusty pondered who would drive the fourth vehicle and pull his second trailer, Brand walked up, Tess at his side.

"We'll go with you."

Dusty searched Tess' face. "You don't have to." After the shock he'd delivered earlier, he didn't expect she wanted to do more than spend time with her small herd and Brand.

"I want to see for myself." Her words came across strong if a bit sad.

"I'd appreciate it." He collected the lead ropes and handed them out. "Like before. April will get her horses. I'll grab the stud. The rest are free game."

With ease, they gathered up the moderate-sized herd, loading each animal into a specific trailer at Dusty's direction.

April struggled a moment with Mischief as he set his feet and refused to step up into the trailer.

Tess hurried over, holding out her hand. "I remembered what someone said about treats."

April grinned at the other woman, took the sugar cubes and urged Miracle into the front of the trailer before turning back to the solid white miniature horse.

"Here you go, buddy. Sugar just for you."

Dusty grinned as Mischief extended his neck but didn't budge. They'd been through this before. When the mini decided to get in for his treat, he'd do so. Until then, patience ruled the day.

"Come on, Mischief." April made a big show of feeding Miracle her reward.

The gelding whinnied. Finally, with a snort of resignation, he hopped into the trailer and made a beeline for April. She praised the little troublemaker, gave him his treat and shut the section gate in order for the guys to load some geldings behind.

"I'll go get Marmalade." April stepped out of the trailer and headed for the house.

"Okay." Dusty instructed his brothers on how he wanted the rest of the horses loaded, then looked across the vast pastures. Buckets had already been stashed in the storage areas of the trailers, as well as everything else related to the big animals.

Within minutes, April strode his direction, a cat carrier in one hand, a large bag of supplies in the other. Carrie followed in her wake, carrying brown bag lunches and bottled water. Tess brought up the rear, lugging a plastic sack and a large bag of dog food. Ben's supplies.

Opening the back door of his cab-and-a-half truck, he took the cat carrier and placed Marmalade in a secure position behind his seat. The food and bowls he placed in the floorboard, then he picked up Ben and set him on the seat so the dog wouldn't try to jump, which was too hard on arthritic hips.

"Lunch for everyone." Carrie passed out bags with a bottle of water to each person.

"Thanks." Dusty set his on the console of the truck before looking to his brothers. "We ready to go?"

"Yeah," they answered in unison.

He climbed in the vehicle, buckled himself in and waited for April to do the same. She glanced over at him, an expression of anticipation on her face.

"Let's go home."

"I'm ready."

She smiled and his heart kicked against his ribs.

* * * *

"Don't be a stranger." Archer reached out his hand.

"I won't." Dusty ignored the handshake offer and enveloped his oldest brother in a big hug. "Thanks. I owe you. Big time."

"That's what brothers are for." Archer stepped back, allowing Colt, Evan and Brand to take their turns saying goodbye.

Dusty hugged each in turn. "Take care of Tess."

Brand nodded. "I will. Believe me. You do the same with that pretty little filly of yours."

"Will do." Dusty shared a grin with his older brother.

"Call if you need anything." Colt tilted his head, then led the parade of brothers and Tess back to their waiting vehicles. They each climbed in, cranked their engines and drove away.

He watched them leave with a stab of melancholy. At least they had mended their fences. The fact warmed his soul and put a grin back on his face. While he might not want to move back to the ranch, he knew he'd visit. Often. Not to mention they were a quick call or text away.

Waving once more, Dusty glimpsed dark clouds on the horizon and got in gear, putting the rest of the big equipment in the shop, safe from hail. The horses had been unloaded into their stalls, Ben and Marmalade were stowed in the office for the moment and April waited for him inside.

The first splashes of rain started no sooner than Dusty had hopped out of his truck and stepped to the entrance. Hurriedly shutting the large door, he trotted back to the stable, shutting the gate behind him just as the first rumble of thunder pierced the early evening. Relief and a resurgence of hope cascaded over him as fat drops pelted the roof. He'd never heard a more musical sound in his life. Unless it was April's laughter.

*Speaking of…* He glanced around, found April setting out feed buckets and hurried over to help. The horses had been unloaded directly to their stalls first. Supplies and feed had followed. Now the animals waited on their supper and there were water buckets to be filled before they would be content for the night. Then the smaller animals needed care. The chores lined up as he jumped in with both feet, for once eager to finish so he could spend some quality time with his newest boarder.

By the time everyone had been cared for night had long since fallen. Thunder rolled and bright shards of lightning split the air, cracking loudly as they struck the ground nearby. The horses shuffled nervously in their stalls, but at least were out of the elements. As soon as the rain started pelting inside, Dusty shut the large end doors and secured them for the night. A stiff breeze still came in through the stall windows, more than enough to allow everyone inside to enjoy the drastically cooler air. Rain and a moderation in temperature were desperately needed reprieves from the scorching drought.

His stomach growled, reminding him they had missed supper while settling the stock back into their home. April had eaten only the sandwich Carrie sent with them for lunch and he would bet nothing else for the entire day. Yet never once had she uttered a single complaint as she worked alongside him through the afternoon and evening hours.

Glancing up, he found April sitting on a bale of straw, tiredly stroking Marmalade, who'd been released from the office a while back, once all the horses had been cared for. She and Ben had received their meals before Dusty and April had started on the boxes of supplies, which were thankfully finally all put away. Sure, they could have waited until the morning to finish, but he didn't know how to leave a job undone.

Taking a moment to study April, he noticed the lines of fatigue had returned, as well as the dullness of exhaustion in her eyes. She'd beaten him up this morning by a long shot, which meant she'd climbed out of bed way before dawn. Now, nearing ten, she'd just about hit her physical limit.

Once more the sky bellowed, shaking the building, reminding him of Mother Nature's fury expressed outside. No way could he send her home in such weather. Not after everything she'd done for him over the past several days. Besides, her SUV sat in the shop behind one of the trailers, preventing her from simply jumping in and driving out. He could drive her home, but preferred she simply stayed the night. Under his care. At least for one night.

"Why don't you stay here tonight? It's too nasty to be driving."

April looked up as she continued to pet the cat, her brow furrowing in contemplation. "Are you sure?"

"Yeah. I'd worry if you tried to make it home." It was the truth after all.

"Okay. My bags are still in my vehicle. I can go get them so I'll have some clothes and stuff." She made as if to stand.

"I'll get them." He strode closer. "Keys?"

She dug them out of her pocket and handed them over, appreciation covering her face. "Thanks."

"No problem." He took the side door nearest the shop, sprinted through the downpour then shoved a key in the smaller entrance door to the shop. Once inside, he went directly to her car, collected her suitcases and backtracked, making sure to lock everything behind him. Five minutes later he returned to her side, a bit damper for his efforts.

"Come on. Let's go inside the house." He led the way, glimpsing April gently returning Marmalade to her feet, standing, then following in his wake. No sooner had he turned the knob than Ben nosed the door wide open, eager to get inside to his comfortable bed.

Dusty stopped at the living room and set her bags down. "If you want a shower, go ahead. You already know where the bathroom is. While you're doing that, I'll change the sheets on the bed, so you can sleep better."

"I'll take the couch." She stepped forward and met his

gaze. "I refuse to kick you out of your bed. I feel guilty enough over Evan and he had a backup plan."

"I can't take the bed and let you sleep on the couch. It's short and lumpy." He frowned as she shot him a quirky grin.

"Good thing I'm tough, soft and short." Opening the nearest bag, she pulled out a change of clothes and a smaller container the size of an average purse. "All I need is a blanket and a pillow, if you have spares."

He nodded, totally unbalanced at the sheer glow about April along with her stubborn teasing. Though worn out, she still had the energy to stand up for what she wanted. His respect for her grew even more. Most women would expect him to offer up his bed, never consider anything less. April insisted on the couch, putting his comfort before hers. *'You can sleep where you like, but I guarantee you'll wake up in a bed.'* His own words came back to him. The corners of his mouth curled up as she walked to the bathroom. She might start on the couch, but that didn't mean she'd stay there all night.

His heart lifted at his good fortune. His home and stable had been saved. He'd made amends with his brothers. The rains had returned with a vengeance, the heat wave broken, and pretty little April would spend the night in his bed. *Things are damn well looking up.*

Chuckling to himself, he ran his fingers over Ben's head before walking into his bedroom. He had a bed to prepare and wet clothes to shed, all before his guest stepped from the shower. Not to mention he had to throw some laundry in and find something to fix for a late dinner.

Twenty minutes later the door to the bathroom clicked, opened, and April stepped out. Dusty glanced up and found her shoulder-length damp blonde hair hanging loose and full of natural waviness. Moisture soaked the top of her gray T-shirt, turning the damp area much darker. Matching shorts and white socks completed the package. Devoid of makeup, she still outshone the sun. In that instant, he realized he'd made the right decision not only in asking her to give him a second chance, but in offering her shelter for the night. Her presence felt right. Natural.

Blue eyes landed on him and a soft smile crossed her face. "Your turn."

"After we eat." He flipped the grilled cheese sandwiches once more before he began gathering plates and glasses.

April stepped forward and quickly set the small table. "What do you want to drink?"

"I wouldn't trust the milk or juice. We probably should stick with water or soda."

She nodded, filled the glasses with ice then moved to the sink and turned on the faucet. A low rumble of thunder heralded another flash of lightning. She jumped, splashing some of the water from the glass back into the sink. "That was close."

He grinned at her, plated their meals and set them on the table. "Scared of storms?"

"Not really, but this sounds intense." She carried their drinks to the table and sat down.

Raindrops pelted the roof, the clinking sound moderately loud inside. He wouldn't be surprised if small chunks of hail were mixed in, as hard as the wind blew. "A good thing you decided to stay."

"Storms are better shared?" The corners of her mouth hitched up.

"Interesting idea. I guess we'll find out tonight." He sank his teeth into the sandwich, watching as April did the same. Pleasure appeared on her face. "This is good." She blinked at him as if surprised he could actually whip up a small meal.

His ego buoyed with the knowledge that he'd provided food she actually enjoyed. Granted, a grilled cheese ranked far below Thanksgiving dinner, but he would eagerly take any and all victories, no matter how small. Pleased, he tilted his head.

"Didn't think I could cook, huh?"

"It's not that. It's just…" Her voice faded.

"Just what?" Curiosity prodded him.

"I don't think any of the men I ever dated would have taken the time or energy to cook for me. It's refreshing." She smiled brightly and nibbled once again.

His heart thudded even as his erection made itself known. The tightening began immediately as he absently considered her straight white teeth nipping lightly at his chest, his belly, his bottom lip before he moved to cover her, find her innermost secrets and send them flying into blazing rapture.

Sucking in a deep breath, he ignored his body's reaction, determined to pursue April with baby steps, allowing her to not only grow confident in their relationship, but to learn to crave him as many women craved chocolate. Skittish fillies couldn't be won over in a single day and April wouldn't fall all over him less than twenty-four hours after he left her standing alone at the dance. Despite what she'd told him earlier, he knew his behavior had hurt her. How could it not have? He'd seen the softness in her eyes, the avid interest, the wonder after he'd kissed her the once.

She smiled at him now, but he recognized the difference. While not unhappy, she needed solid evidence to put her trust in him again. Wise woman. He knew without a doubt he was up to the task. April would find out in time. Until then, he intended to court her and protect her like the rare treasure she was.

After he finished his sandwich, he washed the final bite down with water.

She only ate half before passing the remainder over to him with an apologetic look. "I hate to waste food and it's very good. I'm just full right now."

Studying her face, he decided she probably couldn't finish due to tiredness more than not liking the sandwich. She looked ready to crash. Understandably so.

He ate the rest of her meal in two large bites, then stood and started clearing the table. She followed suit until he shook his head. "I'll get this. Why don't you go on to bed before you drop?"

April blinked at him and sighed wearily. "I'll just brush my teeth then head to the couch."

"I thought you were taking the bed?" He put the dishes in the sink, turned and collected the rest.

She snorted. "You said bed. I insisted on couch."

"Uh-huh."

"That's what happens in your old age. You get forgetful."

His lips twitched. "Old, huh?"

"Definitely. At least as old as dirt." She grinned teasingly.

He shook his head. "I'll show you old…" He lunged for her.

She squealed and dashed off toward the bathroom, her giggles carrying to his ears. He smiled and met Ben's inquiring gaze. "We're not old, are we, boy?"

Dusty stepped over and petted the dog's head. "Between you and me, what do you think about keeping her?"

The dog's mouth opened in a smile as his tongue hung out the side. Ben's tail thumped against his oversized pillow. A definite affirmative in dog terms.

* * * *

Dusty stepped from the shower, still towel drying his hair. His chest bare, he'd pulled on a pair of shorts in order to shelter her from embarrassment should she wake before he did, turn over and find him not only entirely naked, but fully aroused as well. As much as he would love to greet her in the morning with burning kisses leading to fiery caresses and finally a joining of their bodies so profound, so addictive she'd never get enough, he chided himself to go slow and easy with the little blonde.

Automatically, his gaze raked the room, searching for his houseguest. Ben sat up and wagged his tail from his position right beside the couch. Sure enough a human-sized lump lay under a blanket, curled up in a ball.

He grinned, remembering the challenge she'd put forth earlier. She'd taken the couch as promised. Now he simply had to carry her to the bed as he'd also pledged. Turning, he tossed the towel in the bathroom hamper and strode straight for the couch, taking a moment to stare down at the angel come to earth. April rested on her side, her hands curled against her chest as if chilly in the storm-cooled night. Her hair remained loose while her soft breathing spoke of fatigue from physical labor, too many hours awake and an emotional roller coaster over the past few days.

With equal parts gentleness and care, he slid an arm under her knees and another around her shoulders, tenderly cradling her in his arms as he stood, while trying to avoid waking her. She whimpered and shifted slightly as she rested her head against his chest before remaining still.

A splash of warmth engulfed his soul.

Walking across the room, Ben hot on his heels, he headed straight for his bedroom, not stopping until he stood next to the large bed. Just as easily as he'd picked her up, he laid her down, reluctantly slipping his arms from her body. She sighed but remained asleep as far as he could tell. Tugging the sheet and blanket up, he covered her. Moving to the other side of the bed, he slid in with finesse, keeping the jostling mattress movement to a minimum. Once in, he drew the blankets up, scooched over to April and wrapped her in his embrace. With a light kiss to her crown, he settled in for the rest of the night, holding onto his prize with contentment.

# Chapter Nineteen

April woke slowly, the warmth of a cocoon nearly tugging her back into dreamland until her senses nagged her into opening her eyes. Sure enough, her short couch had indeed been replaced by an oversized bed. *'You can sleep wherever you like, but you'll wake up in a bed.'* The words replayed through her mind. A tiny smile followed. Overbearing men and their penchant for chivalry. The fact only endeared Dusty to her more.

Speaking of, she felt the light *whoosh* of breath on the back of her neck. A weight around her middle told her he'd not only carried her to bed, but then wrapped her in his embrace for the rest of the night. Protected. Comfortable. Safe and secure.

Twisting slightly, she found him still dozing, sharing her pillow with his face pressed against her neck. No shirt covered his upper body and the covers shielded the rest of him from her questing gaze. Surely he wouldn't come to bed naked? The image of Dusty in all his nude glory sent her stomach into a slow, exquisite somersault and released a handful of butterflies at the same time.

To sleep like this every night. Wake up in his arms. Roll him over, explore his body, then climb on board for a delicious gallop. Speaking of, an intriguing bump pressed against her bottom. *Oh, my.* Idly, she considered his shaft. Big feet. Big hands. Big…all over.

"What are you thinking so hard about?"

His quiet voice whispered across her ear, the puff of air a tempting caress.

Her libido jumped tenfold as her thoughts centered on

Dusty's endowment. "Does size really matter?"

He chuckled, and the rich sound sent a cascade of tingling over her quickly heating body. April's distracted mind took an extra beat to realize she'd just inadvertently spoken the thought out loud. A blast furnace crossed her cheeks.

"I can assure you size does matter. Good thing I was always an overachiever in everything." He lightly nibbled on her earlobe. "I'm pretty damned good in the sack, babe, if I do say so myself."

His ego also crossed the line into the overachiever status. She nearly snorted, but gasped instead as one of his hands cupped her breast, the cotton material a thin barrier between his skin and hers. For a second she remained absolutely still, trying to decipher the blaring messages from her body. Ever so gently, he pinched her nipple, sending a spear of pleasure straight to the junction of her thighs. His lips kissed a trail across her nape before he nuzzled her cheek.

"You'll just have to wait a little longer to sample my talents." He rose to a sitting position.

She turned and looked up at him, confused and more than disappointed at the sudden stoppage of what had been the perfect morning. "What? Why?"

He grinned down at her, reached out and drew his fingers across her lips. His eyes sparkled with desire laced with mischief. "Because I intend to savor you, inch by delectable inch."

*Sign me up right now.* Her mouth opened but nothing emerged.

Once more he laughed, then threw back the covers and stood at the side of the bed.

She scanned his body, noting not only the wide, muscular chest she'd taken in before, but matching thighs, promising stamina and power. Her mouth dried up as she blatantly stared at the most perfect male specimen she'd ever seen alive, in magazines, on television or anywhere else. Scars dotted the tanned skin here and there, not detracting from his gorgeous looks in the least. Instead they provided a roughness, a hint at the warrior inside, which only added to the overall beauty of the entire man.

Dusty walked to the dresser, pulled out a pair of jeans and slipped them on, giving her a primo view of his perfectly sculpted backside. *If I only had a quarter.* "Wow."

When he glanced back, his gaze met hers. His brown eyes danced as a wicked smile crossed his face. After buttoning his jeans he headed toward the closet, opened the door, and pulled out a short-sleeved Western shirt. He slipped the garment on without bothering to button up the front, giving her another splendid view of his chest and six-pack abs. If the man carried an ounce of fat, she couldn't see it.

"I'm going to get started on the chores. Sleep some more. You've earned it."

He called to Ben and strode out of the bedroom. A moment later she heard the door to the stable open, then click shut once more.

Rolling to her back, she released a pent-up sigh. Sleep some more? No way. Daydream about being covered by Dusty and finding out for herself if size did matter? *Bring it on.*

Mentally, she kicked herself. No sense in lying around being lazy. She would save the images for her dreams at night. Until then, she needed to pull herself together, quit sizing Dusty up for a romp or three hundred in the hay, and get busy. After all, he needed food to keep his strength up for a good, savory round of bliss.

Crawling out, she quickly made the bed then headed toward the kitchen, determined to throw something together for breakfast before driving into town for some much-needed grocery shopping.

* * * *

Dusty couldn't wipe the smile off his face as he traversed the length of the stable, heading directly for the feed sacks and waiting buckets. *Damn, I feel good. Except for my jeans presently chafing the hard-on from hell.* He shook his head and pulled the door open to allow Ben outside to do his business.

In all honesty, he'd been granted a renewal on life. The fire, as horrible and devastating as it had been, had had a silver lining. He'd made up with his family, reforged the bond that held them together through thick and thin. His stable had been spared, his assets all were intact, the rains had finally arrived and April had spent the night in his arms.

Talk about being damn lucky.

He'd felt the tension encompassing her body at his intimate touch. While she quickly softened, he'd dared not press her further. Patience proved the key to winning over skittish fillies and women. Besides, taking the time to tame the little blonde would prove pleasurable and intoxicating for both of them. He'd make sure of it.

A steady beat of raindrops met him as he stepped out into the morning. In a single night, everything appeared to not only have soaked in the much-needed moisture like a man lost in the desert gulped down an entire gallon of fluid, everything looked greener. The once lackluster pastures had perked up a smidgen, the leaves glistened with beads of rain and even the dreary sky couldn't put a damper on such a wonderful morning.

*Shit, when did I become so sappy?* He snorted to himself, drew in the smell of rain and went back to work, heralded by the whinnies of hungry horses. With practiced ease, he poured out grain into waiting buckets, his mind returning to the woman still inside. April. He'd expected her to at least grumble about their sleeping arrangements. Instead she'd snuggled up against him like a cold kitten in a warm blanket. If that hadn't surprised him, her muttered comment about whether size mattered would have shocked the boxers right off his body, if he could have stopped laughing. She'd thrown him for a loop and proceeded to stare at him with a look of downright appreciation, enjoyment and sensual longing. In all his experience with women, he'd never had a single one look at him like the sun rose and set on his shoulders. He carried too many scars and remained rough around the edges, compliments of his time as a SEAL. Never would he fit into a pretty boy mold, but then, April didn't seem to care. Judging by her expression, she liked him just fine and already wondered what lay hidden under his shorts.

She'll find out. *Soon,* he promised himself as he gathered up feed buckets and started handing them out. His earlier words were true. He meant to savor her. Lick her. Kiss her. Make love to her until they were too exhausted to do more than exchange oxygen and carbon dioxide. Only, after he gave her ample time to acclimate to him, come to terms with intimacy in their relationship and make sure she wanted him as much as he wanted her. Because one thing was certain, once he had her, come hell or high water, he wasn't letting go.

* * * *

"April? How would you like to go out? For lunch. Today?" He nearly stumbled through the offer, a bit unsure if he pushed too quickly. Sure, she'd slept in his arms the previous night and they had found a truce as well, but that didn't mean she was ready to take a leap of faith and start dating.

He'd tossed the idea around all morning as they worked side by side, debated, then decided to just go for it. *Nothing ventured, nothing gained.*

She glanced up from her seat on the straw bale, petting Marmalade. A slow smile appeared. "I'd like that."

Relief and a small sense of victory flashed through him. He grinned in return. "The Corner Cafe has excellent food. We could go there." The small restaurant had kept the locals coming in for decades for the delicious offerings while providing a hangout for the retirement club, drinking their coffee and sharing the latest gossip.

"Okay." She lightly petted the cat. "Looks like I need to get up, girl." She picked the cat up and set her down on the floor. "Since it's close to lunchtime, I probably should get cleaned up."

"Go ahead. I'll be in shortly."

Dusty stretched his legs out from his seated position on another bale and watched her walk back into the house. Absently, he reached out and scratched behind Ben's ears. "Wish me luck, boy."

Ben wagged his tail and licked Dusty's hand.

"Thanks, buddy." Standing up, Dusty headed inside as well, the dog on his heels.

Thirty minutes later, they sat at a corner table in the small restaurant. The middle-aged waitress had dropped off glasses of water along with menus earlier. After looking over the available options, Dusty quickly selected. April did the same. The waitress gathered up the unneeded pieces of cardboard and trotted away.

April glanced around the room, interest written all over her face. "I've never been here before."

Dusty sipped his water. "Really? I thought everyone in a twenty-mile radius ate here at least now and again."

She shook her head. "I rarely eat out, to be honest. It's easier to make something at home, even if it's just a sandwich."

He easily read between the lines. She'd been saving her money for so long to afford her dream of horse ownership. Probably had long since gotten into the habit of pinching pennies and wouldn't be dropping a small fortune on designer shoes any time soon. Just another difference between her and the other women who had sought him out simply for his money. Scratch that. Not his money, his family's money.

Rain pelted the window next to them, much lighter than the rough storms of a few hours before, yet more than welcome. The land, water levels and pastures would recover if the moisture continued to fall in a consistent fashion. He prayed that would be the case.

"Well, look what the cat dragged in." A man's voice carried over to him. Glancing up, Dusty spied Sam, the county sheriff, standing just inside the door. Making a beeline over, the tall, brown-haired man smiled wide. "Dusty, how the hell are ya?"

Standing, Dusty held out his hand and shook Sam's with strength. "Better now that it's raining. How's your day? Handing out speeding tickets right and left?" Dusty smirked. Every time he saw Sam, he couldn't resist teasing him about one of the many stereotypes about cops.

Sam snorted. "You're thinking of the city police. I'm the one out beating the bushes for bad guys."

Dusty's gaze flickered to April. "Where are my manners? April, this is Sam. Sam, this is April."

They shook hands. Sam smiled at her brightly. "My pleasure." The words tumbled easily off his tongue.

She grinned and a pink tinge colored her cheeks when Sam kissed the back of her hand.

Biting back a small wave of jealousy, Dusty refrained from kicking his friend in the butt. "She's my girlfriend, you ox."

Sam spared him a glance that said it all. He'd gratefully take his chance at April if she were free, but not now. Friends never poached from other friends. "My rotten luck."

April chuckled. "You're very kind."

Dusty snorted. "That's not what the criminals say."

"That's for damn sure." Sam smiled wolfishly.

"Did you want to join us?" Dusty offered, silently hoping his friend would decline. He liked Sam, considered him as close a friend as he had, yet he didn't want any distractions from his time with April.

"Can't. Sorry. Just stopped by to pick up lunch on the go." Sam met his gaze knowingly. "Give me a call sometime and we'll go to the shooting range. I still owe you from last time." With a quick nod, Sam headed to the register, collected his bag of food, paid and left with a wave.

April watched him go. "Something about the way he moves. Not the carriage you have, the absolute confidence, but yet, more than an average man."

Dusty admired her observation skills. "He's a former Iraq war vet. Moved up the ranks in the regular Army."

Her blue eyes met his. "That makes sense. I imagine Special Forces carry themselves differently because of their training. Something inside, pride, command. I don't know. Just something that shouts alpha."

He smiled in amusement. Everyone in Special Forces could pick out a SEAL just by the way they walked. He never thought much about it, but if around another SEAL, present or former, he could single them out in a heartbeat. *Alpha.* The term fit as well as any, he supposed.

"Sam's a good guy. He's been there and always has your back." He couldn't give much higher praise than that.

She nodded. "Sounds like you two have bonded over the years."

"Yeah. We're friends. Spend time together now and again."

"At the shooting range?" Her eyes lit with mischief.

He chuckled. "Usually."

April's head tilted. "What does he owe you?"

"The losing shooter pays the usage fee for the next session."

She took a drink. "Let me guess. You've never paid a fee yet."

He grinned widely. "Nope."

The waitress brought their lunch, setting a plate full of food in front of each of them. After asking if they needed anything else, she hurried on her way, leaving them alone once more.

"This looks wonderful." April eyed the oversized hamburger.

Dusty grabbed the ketchup bottle and poured some on his burger. "They're the best in the county. Why else do you think Sam stops by here for lunch?"

They dug in hungrily, eating in quiet for a while before April spoke. "I have to return to work tomorrow. As much as I hate to."

Dusty recalled she'd mentioned once before this marked the last day of freedom for her for a while. He would miss her, but knew she had to get back to work. Short of winning a huge lottery, they both had to carry their own weight. Besides, she might need a breather from him now and again. *Absence makes the heart grow fonder and all that.*

"I thought you liked your job."

She stuffed a French fry in her mouth. "Most of the time." She blew out a breath. "But I've gotten spoiled these past couple of weeks. Had a ball hanging around the stable, and I don't want that to end."

"Just think, you don't have to muck stalls tomorrow."

She laughed. "I'll be cleaning up poop of another kind, probably."

"Possibly." Staring at her for a long moment, he lowered his voice and threw out the question screaming in his head. "Gonna miss me?"

April's face softened before a flash of troublemaking appeared. "I think I'll miss you more than horse manure."

Her teasing proved contagious. He joined her with a genuine chuckle. "Hell, I hope so."

She rested her hand on top of his, then squeezed. With only the gesture and her expression, she warmed his soul.

He'd be a fool to let her slip through his fingers. He might be dumb from time to time, but he wasn't a fool.

* * * *

"Feel up to riding today?"

Brushing her hands off on her jeans, April glanced across the aisle at Dusty. When she'd first boarded her horses, the near boiling temperatures outside had stunted any interest in horseback riding, though he'd mentioned the idea once before. In all honesty, she'd nearly forgotten his offer to let her ride some of his horses in the rapid-fire happenings in the stable's daily life. The idea sounded wonderful, especially when evening rains cooled the day to a moderate, comfortable level. "Sure."

She'd worked the past three days, one long shift after another. Now she had a couple of days off to recover before having to return for another one. Almost in habit, she found herself up before dawn, hurriedly dressing and driving to the stable in time to help pass out breakfast to the horses and start the list of daily chores. Staying home had been an option, but simply hadn't appealed. Not when Dusty and her pets waited just a mile down the road.

"Great. There's a neat trail a few miles away that carries into the national forest." He picked up a couple of lead ropes.

"Sounds nice."

"I'll bring up a couple of horses. We'll trailer them to the place."

An idea popped into her head. Checking her watch, she made a quick decision. "Is there a pretty spot we can stop and have a picnic?"

Dusty paused, glancing at her with a look filled with interest and appreciation. "I suppose so."

She smiled. "Then I'll see about gathering up some food while you ready the horses."

"Works for me." He matched her grin. Happiness lit up his face, making him all the more handsome, stealing her breath.

*Dang, April. You've got it bad.*

Ever since the night they'd returned, their relationship had crept along at a snail's pace. She didn't complain, simply understanding and needing them to move slowly. Dusty could use some time to gradually enter into something more than plain old friendship. Both bore their own scars and rushing into intimacy could derail the train. Slow and methodical made much more sense. Even if her body clamored for more touches, caresses, kisses. Anything and everything.

*All in good time.*

Two hours later, they stopped under a huge oak tree, the limbs spreading far and wide, creating shade for everything underneath. Dusty had chosen to leave Ben behind at the stable, citing that the steep slopes and a few miles of trotting to keep up would be too much for Ben's advanced age. The dog had seemed to take the decision in stride, flopping down in the shade of the stable as he watched them leave.

Sliding down, April handed over the reins to her bay gelding, Latte, to Dusty. He led Latte and the black filly, Hailey, he'd been working on breaking to saddle for the past few weeks, under the tree and wrapped the leather leads around a low-hanging branch.

Looking over the view, April found the trees, hills and meadows stunning in their natural state. The recent rains had turned all the vegetation green once more, allowing grass to grow and bushes to bloom. A myriad of colors greeted her, making for a feast on the senses, including the delicious scent of mock orange from a nearby shrub. "It's beautiful."

Dusty walked to her side, carrying an old tablecloth and two insulated containers filled with their meal. He raked the area with his eyes. "I've always thought so. When I first moved here, I spent quite of bit of time in this spot."

His words touched her deeply – along with the fact that he'd chosen to share this special place with her. A man lost and trying to find himself after leaving unending training sessions followed by war would need such a place. To ponder the new meaning of life, to consider options, to work toward new dreams and desires. She could understand what had attracted him to the top of this particular rise, where you could see for miles and find no other human in sight. No houses. No roads. No businesses. Only pristine forest, which felt little change due to man's hand. One of the few places still around. Wild and free, the scenery fit

Dusty like a pair of his Levi's jeans. Comfortable.

"I can see why. It's serene. Tranquil. Like we're the only people for miles around."

"Yeah." He grinned and spread out the material. "That's always how I felt too." Reaching for her hand, he tugged her to his side then sat down.

She promptly followed, automatically clutching one of the lunch containers and opening it up. Peeking in, she found his goodies. "This is yours. Trade me." They swapped and each started unloading their meal. She bit into her sandwich and studied the man next to her. The roughness of his five o'clock shadow only added to his edgy appearance, making him all the more appealing.

He belonged here. Heck, he could have lived in this very area one hundred fifty years ago and still fit in. She had no doubt he could and would fight for everything he earned, work harder than most and still respect Mother Nature along the way. She grinned at the image of him with a Colt .45 strapped on his hip.

"What's so funny?"

She glanced over at him. "Just picturing you here generations ago. Complete with chaps and gun belt. Walking around, ready to draw on the bad guys and rid the tiny towns of varmints."

An odd expression covered his face before the corner of his mouth curled up. "SEALs live in the shadows and have more smarts than to walk down the street in broad daylight staring down a man in preparation for a quick draw, winner-takes-all shootout. Hell, one of the villain's friends could do you in while you're counting paces and waiting to draw your gun." He chuckled. "The intent is the same, I guess, just a different approach."

"I can't imagine how big a change that must have been for you. From the military to a stable owner." She sipped her bottled water.

He took a healthy bite of his sandwich and gazed across the horizon. "Yeah. I was lost for a while. I'd changed and nothing seemed to fit anymore." He turned back to her. "It took a while for me to realize you can't go back. You can only move forward, baggage and all. Find a new normal."

"Sounds like a good motto for us all." She appreciated the intimate glimpse into Dusty's life, a tiny portion that made up a complex and sometimes puzzling man. He had so many stories to tell, but she knew he'd hardly reach the tip of the iceberg due to promised secrets he'd take to the grave. Too bad. But then again, maybe all for the better. Who wanted to remember the horrors of war when there were other, much brighter and more pleasant memories to share?

"So is this a modern oracle? The place to come for answers?" She grinned over at him.

He shrugged and smiled slightly. "Not answers per se. More like simply clearing my head in order to see things more clearly."

"Ah-ha. Too bad." She kept her face carefully schooled, though the mischief rushed to slip out.

"Why's that?"

"I could ask the oracle a few things myself."

"Such as?" His head tilted in open curiosity.

Waiting a few beats, she finally answered. "Oh, I'd like to know some lottery numbers, maybe some good investments. Whether I might happen to be growing on a certain former SEAL." Her words faded as she watched his face.

The corner of his lips slowly hitched up into a full-blown smile. Setting his sandwich aside, he leaned in, capturing her lips with his. Gently, he coaxed her, treated her to a soft merging of their mouths with a string attached to her heart.

All too quickly he pulled back, his eyes sparkling with sultry longing. "Like mold."

Her distracted brain took an instant to catch up. "Mold?"

"Yep. You're growing on me like mold on the north side of a barn."

She furrowed her brows. "Is that good?"

A wolfish smile appeared on his chiseled face. "I'd say really good."

With a happy laugh, she took the initiative this time, kissing him with the same reverence, though more heat than before, pouring all her unspoken words into the act. He gave back for a little bit before breaking contact once more. Perplexed, she stared at him. With no clue to his actions on his face, she decided to ask. "Don't you like kissing me?"

Her face heated at the awkward question, but she couldn't bear not knowing why he cut the affection short when she so readily wanted to continue.

Dusty took another bite of his sandwich and chewed, his focus on her the entire time. "Yeah, but it's damn uncomfortable riding a horse with a hard-on."

"Oh." She blinked, surprised by his candidness but appreciative of the honesty. "Umm. Okay. I can understand. After all, well…"

He shook his head and brushed his lips over her nose. "You go to my head like potent whiskey, babe."

After his less than stellar record with women, she wondered if that admission proved foretelling. "Is that bad?"

"Only when I have to climb into the saddle for a long ride back." He licked her bottom lip, sucked it for a split second then returned to his previous position with a long sigh. His eyes sparked.

She picked up her water and drank deeply even as her heart sang. This date had already stacked up as one of the best in her life. Dusty had shared his special place with her, opening himself up section by section. Judging by his body language, he wanted her, but the timing wasn't right. He wasn't pushing her, either. Another point in his favor. Add in his confession that she was growing on him and she felt pretty darn good about her lot in life.

Her gaze raked over him, noting the sexy, muscular body wrapped in typical Western wear. The clothing and rugged land fit him like a glove, adding to his overall aura of primal male in his natural habitat, the top predator in this area. She had no doubt he could handle just about anything, including her enthusiastic advances.

The thought of opening his shirt and nibbling on his tanned flesh flashed through her mind. *Or, better yet, Dusty with a light coating of chocolate syrup. Talk about a tasty treat.*

Confident and relaxed, she watched Dusty eat and wondered what he'd say if he could read her mind. She bit back a chuckle.

*He'd smile as bright as the heavens and tell me to bring it on.*

Storing the idea for later, she looked across the land and knew this day would live in her memory for a long time to come.

# Chapter Twenty

He wiped Miracle's hide with a finishing cloth, pleased to see her dark gray dappled coat shine with health and cleanliness. With April at the hospital today, he'd decided to work with the skittish filly some more, even taking her to the bathing area and washing her down. To his amazement, she'd not only tolerated the bath, but had seemed to enjoy every minute. Not once did she fuss about the hose, the water, or even the sponge and soap. Mischief, on the other hand, had decided that trying to bite the water proved fun, sending a shower spraying over them all. The little imp definitely lived up to his name.

With both horses dry, he stood with Miracle, her lead rope tied to a support beam, while Mischief wandered around inside the stable, pausing now and again to snare a bite from a bale of alfalfa. She stood quietly as he groomed her, no longer the edgy, antsy horse who'd first entered his life nearly six weeks ago. Proud of her progress, he continued to dote on her, praise her and slip her food rewards at every turn.

Nearly a month had passed since he'd returned home from taking shelter with his family—a glorious time that had found April back to work and practicing as his shadow on her days off. Officially dating, they had moved their relationship along at a comfortable, if not slow, pace. He didn't complain. After all, each day he found April more relaxed, more attentive, could see the last of her fears and concerns falling away. Thrilled at their progression, he kept the steady course, taking her out now and again, otherwise sharing their time whenever possible.

On the days she had to work, she normally drove straight home. With twelve-hour shifts, she didn't have much downtime before she had to be up and ready the next morning. He looked forward to her nightly calls on those days, having fallen quickly into a habit of talking to her before she crawled into bed for the night. In all reality, they didn't chatter away for too long, but he drew comfort from the knowledge she'd made it in for the night without any problems. He didn't want to smother her or make her feel less than capable, but his protective instincts couldn't be denied. For now, he'd be content with the phone calls. Down the road that might change.

April fit in well. She stepped up as a team player, provided humor and solace and never once asked for anything more than a simple request here and there. She was so far removed from the other women he'd been around, he found himself shaking his head in disbelief at times. Yet he found her humble honesty just as compelling as the rest of her, making for a tempting package perfectly suited to him.

She'd grown on him. Big time. He wanted her more each day. Not just for a sexual romp, but for something bigger. He cared for her, wanted to keep her safe, comfort her, love her.

*Love?* The word rarely crossed his mind, but he couldn't discard the emotion fast and easily. *No.* While not at that point yet he didn't doubt, given time, his feelings for the little blonde might encompass that level.

Ben loped down the center aisle, barking, interrupting his train of thought.

Dusty jerked his head up to see what was bothering the dog.

The clang of the gate latch drew his attention. Mischief whinnied and dashed over like a door greeter as an older couple walked in, but quickly paused to close the barrier behind them. Ben followed behind Mischief. Dusty glanced at the people, blinked, then stared. His parents. Here. He hadn't seen them in over three years and in their travels, never once had they stopped by to see his place. Shock and a bit of concern ate at his gut.

Obviously deciding the people posed no threat, Ben trotted back to Dusty's side, staying a step ahead of Miracle's hooves as she danced around, though his focus never ventured far from the new arrivals.

Miracle shifted restlessly, her eyes whitening as the people drew near. Jerking against the rope holding her, she fought the tie. Immediately Dusty yanked on the end of the lead, undoing the half knot and setting her free. Grasping her halter, he steadied her as she nervously eyed the strangers, shoving against Dusty now and again in an effort to keep as much distance between her and the approaching people.

"It's okay, Miracle. They won't hurt you." He spoke soothingly to the filly, watching her ears stand up to listen for a fleeting second, then flatten on her head once more. Good thing he didn't have many visitors or she'd be a bundle of nerves all the time.

"Mom. Dad." He kept his tone low and calm. "You might want to stop there for a second until I can put her back in the stall."

A glimpse told him not only that his parents had taken his advice, standing in the middle of the row, but also that Mischief had discovered them and presently snuffled each for any sign of treats. He shook his head and grinned. The little mini didn't have a shy bone in his body. "Come on, Miracle. Let's get you back inside. You'll feel more comfortable there." Backing her up to allow her a chance to keep her attention on his visitors, he softly stroked her neck, patiently easing her fears as he led her through the open stall door. Once there, he dug out a baby carrot from his pocket. He'd loaded up that morning in preparation for the day's activities with the pair. Hell, he'd started using them on all the horses with resounding success.

Unsnapping the lead, he waited for Miracle to take the carrot from his palm, then slipped out, shutting the door behind him. She stepped to the front of the stall, put her head over the top and whinnied loudly, an obvious summons for her friend.

Mischief ignored her, too intent upon checking out the newcomers for potential goodies while soaking up attention.

Dusty hurried their direction, curious and concerned why they were there. "What brings you two here?"

His mother looked up at him, still petting Mischief. "We wanted to see you, dear. And your stable."

"Archer told us all about it, so we had to see it for ourselves," his father echoed, running his hand down Mischief's back and grinning. "Found a new mascot?"

Surprised yet pleased, Dusty shrugged and smiled. "Something like that." Reaching their side, he met his mother with a big hug. She kissed his cheek and he realized exactly how much he'd missed them. He stuck out a hand for his father, only to be pulled into a big bear hug complete with a thump on the back.

"Damn, it's good to see you."

"We would have come earlier, but weren't sure we'd have been welcome," his mother said a bit hesitantly.

"I was a complete jackass, but know better now. Besides, you're both a sight for sore eyes."

Growing up, he'd loved his parents, but possessed an independent streak a mile wide. By the time he'd hit his teens, his parents had cramped his style and served as overseers and rule-makers, something he rebelled against any chance he got. Only when he'd walked completely away from the family then returned did he actually realize how much his parents really did mean to him and how deeply he missed them. Learning humility and surviving the wrenching agony of war had done wonders for his insight.

Mischief nudged his hip hard. He glanced down at the gelding. "Okay. Okay. I've got your carrot too." He dug the final piece from his pocket and held it out. The little guy lipped it up and crunched loudly.

His mother giggled. "He's cute."

"Yeah, he is." Grabbing Mischief's halter, he inclined his head. "Come on in. I'll show you around."

Leading the miniature horse back to the stall, he opened the door and gave him a light shove. "In you go. Miracle is having a small meltdown without you." As soon as he closed the door, he noticed the two horses nuzzling each other as if reassuring each other they were indeed all right and back together again.

"This must be the filly your brothers told me about. The abused one who's afraid of men." His father came closer, but still maintained a healthy distance from the gray horse.

Dusty nodded. His father had spent many hours with horses, knew stock and how to read their body language pretty well. He also knew a well-bred horse when he saw one. "She's slowly coming around with me, but yeah, as you saw, a strange man appears and she's totally on the defensive."

His father's practiced eye raked over the animals. "Too bad. She's got some bloodlines behind her."

"At least she clicked with April, so now she has a good home for the rest of her days. Along with her best friend, of course."

"Where is this April? I was hoping to meet the woman your brothers spoke so highly of," his mother said.

"Working today. She's a nurse at the hospital. Twelve-hour shifts, so I doubt she'll come by after work."

"Oh." Disappointment clearly covered his mother's face.

*Well, hell.* He knew a matchmaker when he saw one. Good thing he'd already set his sights on April or he might have gotten a bit nervous himself.

"So what's between the two of you? I couldn't believe when Archer told me you brought her along with the horses to stay at the ranch while the fires burned nearby," she persisted.

"Her filly does much better with her around."

She snorted. "Dusty, I might not know much, but I know

this—you can work your way around any horse on this planet without a helper. So what's the real reason you brought her along?"

*Busted.* He could never get anything by his parents.

"Isn't it obvious, Delia? The boy's smitten." His father grinned wickedly.

Dusty sighed. His father had spent years grilling witnesses. Judging by the look on his face, he intended to drag every morsel of truth about Dusty's blossoming relationship with April—along with other personal details—from his lips. He straightened his spine and lifted his chin. Once a SEAL, always a SEAL. No one ever pushed a SEAL to do anything he didn't want to do. Besides, he came by his stubbornness naturally. With a sly smile, he arched an eyebrow at his father. *Bring it on.*

Ben stepped between Dusty and his father, keeping a close watch on the pair as he took up a protective position. Automatically, Dusty reached down to scratch behind his ears. "It's okay, buddy. They're my parents."

The dog looked up at him, his dark eyes full of sympathy.

Dusty chuckled and continued to run his hands through Ben's thick fur. "By the way, you remember Ben."

His parents looked at the dog with interest. "Your war dog?" His father reached out a hand slowly, allowing the Belgian Malinois to sniff. "He's an old guy now."

"Yeah. He saved my ass so many times I couldn't leave him behind before, and I'll stick with him all the way to the end." Memories flashed through his mind of nights spent on patrol or catnapping, snuggled together for warmth and security.

Respect and something akin to sadness and concern flashed across his father's face.

Dusty stiffened. If his father dared to offer commiseration or condolences, he'd frankly lose his temper. His time with the SEALs hadn't been easy, but had proved a life changer. He wouldn't trade the experience for anything in the world. In fact, he considered returning to the ranks now and again, before always changing his mind. No, he and Ben had retired together for good. In the time since he'd resigned, he'd lost a step or three. While getting back in shape might be fairly easy, he'd also lost the drive. Not to mention, the scourge of war had followed him home in the form of nightmares and flashbacks. Returning would most likely worsen the situation.

Dusty shook his head, immediately discouraging any conversation. "Don't ask." He refused to talk about his military career, even if he could. National security and a SEAL's oath kept his mouth shut then and now.

His father's lips thinned.

"Dusty? Why don't you show us around? I'd love to see the rest of the horses and find out how one runs a stable." His mother smiled cheerfully.

He nodded, relieved with the change of topic. "Since you've already met these two" — he gestured toward the stall with April's horses — "let's move on to the end."

By the time he finished the tour, his father's expression had changed to one of respect and appreciation. "This is a first-class operation."

Dusty nodded, the praise stroking his ego. His father didn't offer compliments willy-nilly, so when he did, they definitely meant something. "Thanks. It's been a lot of hard work, but well worth it."

"I can see that. Between that great stud and this upscale stable, I think you're well on your way."

His mother bobbed her head. "It's impressive. Not that we ever doubted your abilities." She grinned at him.

"I know. I know. It was touch and go there for a while." He smiled, remembering all the trouble he'd given his parents during his rebellious stage. More than once they'd moaned over the gray hairs he was giving them.

"Just remember one day, when you have kids, you'll be paying for your raising." Her brown eyes twinkled with mischief.

Dusty rolled his eyes.

"Speaking of kids, maybe you should sit down and tell us all about April."

His cell rang, interrupting at a perfect time. Checking his caller ID, he answered. "Hey, Evan."

"Dusty. What are you up to today?"

"Talking to the parents, actually."

"Ouch." Evan chuckled. "They were here for the past couple of days breathing down our necks. About time you had your fair share."

"Gee, thanks. Now, what did you need?" Dusty met his father's knowing gaze and shrugged. They all loved Evan, but he could certainly be a thorn in everyone's side from time to time.

"Just wondering if you've moved on yet, so I can have my shot with April."

"Not happening, bro." Dusty sighed. Evan called seemingly every other day to ask the same question. He truly doubted Evan was that infatuated with April and knew that he most likely inquired just to either yank his chain or to be nosy on the status of his relationship with the little nurse. Neither option earned him any brownie points.

"Well, hell."

"Go sniff elsewhere."

Evan blew out a breath. "So are you bringing her for Thanksgiving?"

"Maybe. I haven't thought much about it yet." He hadn't considered the traditional get-together at all. Hell, he'd just gotten back into a routine after the worst fire in forty years. Three months away sounded like forever at this stage.

"Okay. If you decide you don't want her, I get first dibs." Evan sounded like he could barely keep the humor from his voice.

Dusty shook his head. "Go find your own woman, pest." With that, he clicked off.

Turning, he found his parents staring at him, each of them smiling like a Cheshire cat. He smelled a setup. "What?"

"Did you hear that, John?"

"I sure did. Dusty's not willing to share, not even hand-me-downs." His father shot him a knowing look.

Dusty groaned. *Just great. Why me?* More importantly, why weren't his parents back at the ranch bugging the rest of his brothers about their social lives? He had enough issues of his own without two strong-willed matchmakers right on his heels. Come to think of it, when did his tough, no-nonsense attorney father turn into Cupid? Must be his mother's romantic notions rubbing off from being together night and day for the past few years.

"Think he's twitterpated?" his mother asked.

"Oh, definitely."

*Twitterpated? Well, shit.* "I don't think you've seen the house part yet." Dusty strode through the door, more than eager to change scenery as well as topics.

Life was so much simpler alone.

*But a hell of a lot more mundane too.*

"This is nice." His mother turned a full circle, taking in the small home attached to the stable. A far cry from the mansion they'd built and still lived in from time to time.

"Smart design. Keeps you close to the horses so if anything is awry, you'd know about it quick," his father pointed out.

"It works for me." Dusty observed their reactions carefully. No grimaces, no frowns. Simply curiosity and earnest attention.

He'd worried what they'd think about his living accommodations, considering the way they'd raised him. Wealth had bought them luxury, which they'd passed down to their sons. However, Dusty had ventured down a different path, learned basic necessities were sometimes a blessing, and preferred to leave the showcases of the rich and famous. Contentment radiated from his stable and he had no intention of returning to his previous, misspent life. Sure, the gap between him and his family had been sealed, a definite positive in the recent weeks. However, he'd figured out exactly how much the land, his land, called to him during his days away.

He opened the door to the stable and ushered his parents through. "What would you like to see next?"

"I—"

His cell phone chimed, and at the same time the radio announcer interrupted in the middle of a song. "We have breaking news. There's been a shooting at a convenience store in Jackson Station. The school is on lockdown. The suspect was last seen running into Three Points Hospital across the street. He's considered armed and dangerous. Please call police if you have any information."

The text alert basically said the same thing. Dusty blew out a breath. "Three Points Hospital. April." His gut clenched in worry and fear. He shut them both down. Running hot on emotions got people killed.

Jackson Station was still a small town, fairly rural as well, compared to bigger places like Boulder City. With a miniscule budget, the police couldn't afford more than a chief and a handful of part-time cops, with nothing to spare for luxuries like a SWAT team or even a police dog. They'd have already called for backup and a dog, but with everyone traveling from the nearest base location of Boulder City, forty minutes away, the hostage could be long dead before they arrived. Hell, the tango could be long gone as well. Or have killed dozens of people in a bid for freedom—or just out of pure hatred.

*April*. Protective instincts welled up. He had to get to her. *Now*. Nothing else mattered.

Dusty spun on his heel and re-entered his home. Opening his closet, he pulled out a long bag, unzipped it, and quickly checked that all the parts of the rifle were intact. He had his usual bag in the truck, but decided to grab additional firepower just in case. Satisfied, he pulled a small handgun from under his pillow, tugged up his pant leg, then shoved the gun in the holster just above his ankle.

He yanked his Kevlar vest from the closet and slipped the protective device on, feeling a sense of nostalgia and security with his torso covered. His SIG remained, as always, in his shoulder holster. He never stepped outside without the weapon. Not that he imagined using the gun much in the normally quiet town, but he honestly felt vulnerable and naked without it.

His mother's gasp carried across the room.

He finished gathering his weapons, then stood to meet his parents' curious and worried expressions.

"What are you going to do?"

He met his father's eyes. "Go hunting. Stay here. I should be back soon."

"But..."

"Come on, Ben. We've got a job to do." The dog, almost as if sensing the seriousness, trotted at his side. Partners to the marrow.

Without another word, he strode toward his truck.

# Chapter Twenty-One

Driving up to a police blockade, Dusty pulled off slightly to the side, waiting for the sheriff to notice him. Sam turned from the first vehicle in line, glanced in Dusty's direction, then strode over.

Grim worry covered Sam's face. "I was hoping you'd show up."

"What's up?"

"Shooter tried to rob the convenience store. One of my off-duty officers was inside at the time. He drew on the guy, but took a hit before he could do any damage. The manager was also shot. Perp ran into the hospital. Security chased him out the back door, but not before he grabbed a hostage and ran. We haven't seen or heard anything from him since."

"Who's the hostage?" Dusty's breath caught as he waited for the answer.

"From what I know, he left the hospital, found a young woman getting out of her car in the visitor's lot and took her hostage." Sam met his gaze steadily. "Clarice Livens. She'd just showed up for her volunteer shift at the front desk."

"Shit." Dusty forced himself to breathe. He read the same anger and concern on Sam's face.

"We'll get her back." Sam's words carried more optimism than Dusty presently felt.

Dusty studied the nearly chaotic scene in front of him as people gathered around, media pulled in and the few local cops tried to keep everyone at bay while presumably also searching for the man responsible. A challenging task for a force three times the size of Jackson Station.

"With all the houses around here, and the woods, he could be anywhere. From what Tom said, the guy's armed to the teeth and has a death wish."

"The wounded?"

"Manager is critical. Tom will survive but be out of commission for a while." Sam scowled. "If the perp gets into a business or house, he'll make a big splash just to show he can."

"Then I'd better get on it."

"Consider yourself deputized. Whatever you can do, go for it. I've got your back. I want this guy before he takes out half the town, or, worse, finds a way into a place with a lot of innocent people. Trent will say the same. He mentioned giving you a call, but you beat us both to it." Trent held the police chief position in the small town of Jackson Station. Another former Army member, he'd spent his fair share of time overseas as well. Dusty counted him as one of the few friends he'd made since moving to town.

Sam met Dusty's gaze. "I called for the tracking dog, but the K9 unit is two counties over. It'll be a while before they can arrive."

"Got anything that smells like the guy for Ben to sniff?"

"Not really. But, you're more than welcome to begin at the store. Jerry's guarding it. I'll radio ahead and let him know you'll start there."

"Keep your men away. I work best alone."

"I'm coming with you."

Dusty frowned, but shrugged. Sam's county, his responsibility. He much preferred to work with just Ben, or at most, with a special ops team covering his six. Sam had spent some time in the Army, which boosted him above an average cop. Too bad he didn't reach the highly trained top ranks.

At least with the sheriff along, he'd be spared a dozen questions afterward. "Don't slow me down."

"Not a bit." Sam patted the top of Dusty's door. "I'll meet

you at the store in a minute."

Dusty parked his truck farther down a small gravel side road, lifted Ben out, and quickly put together his sniper rifle. Within a couple of minutes, he'd jogged the short distance to the corner, located Jerry and stepped into the store. "Ben. *Duft.*" The commands were issued in German, the language Ben had learned to listen for and obey as a pup. Anytime he heard the language he turned intensely serious, as if he realized the game of find and seek had deadly implications.

The Belgian Malinois sniffed around the area, nose to the floor. Dusty pointed out a trail to the door, then out. Sam stepped forward, his gun still in the holster at his waist. Dusty spared him a glance before focusing back on Ben. "*Verfolgen.*"

Ben lifted his nose and started loping, his head up but dipping now and again to double-check the trail. Just like Ben had done in Afghanistan, he followed the culprit with intense focus. He didn't bark. He didn't look around. Instead, he stuck with a winding path first to the hospital, then the parking lot and through yards, around outbuildings, and finally into the wooded section.

Suddenly Ben picked up speed, his tail straight out like a rudder.

Their tango was close. Too close for the sniper rifle. Dusty pulled out his SIG nine millimeter and pointed the barrel at the sky. He noted Sam followed suit, his weapon at the ready, staying right behind him every step of the way. Anything within fifty yards would fall into his range. Over that, he'd shift back to the rifle.

Dusty collected the dog and slowed his pace. Dashing in without visual contact bordered on stupidity. He needed to scope out the situation and formulate a plan of action. The hostage's life depended on it. Ben's life depended on it. The dog would obey his every command, even die in an attempt to bring down the tango. Dusty wasn't about to let that happen.

Grass squished under his boots, but he didn't make a

single sound as he worked his way from bush to tree to rock, always searching, always considering his next move to a protective position.

A woman's cry blasted across the area. Dusty moved steadily closer, Ben right at his side, his ears pricked. Finally he caught a glimpse of movement, and circled around for a better angle. Gesturing to the east, he pointed out their target. Sam nodded.

Approximately twenty meters away a grubby man dressed in jeans and a hoodie held the short, dark-haired woman with a tight grip on her upper arm—definitely more than hard enough to leave bruises. The tango turned this way and that, constantly looking over his shoulder as he growled orders to the nearly hysterical woman.

"Shut up. One more sound from you and I'll kill you on the spot." He waved his handgun in her face before aiming back at the way they had come.

A nervous man with a weapon made for a dangerous man with a weapon. Most likely he'd pull the trigger at a moment's notice, just from excitement. Dusty watched for an instant more, then fell into old habits.

Calm and cool determination washed over him. He'd been in this same sort of situation more than once. It always ended the same way when the SEALs were involved. Carefully, he laid his rifle on the ground, needing only his handgun for this particular task.

For an instant, he debated giving the guy a chance. On military missions SEALs moved in, killed with precision and disappeared under the cover of darkness, few the wiser. However, this wasn't a military mission and the local cops tended to be a bit softer in their dealings with criminals. Thus, he'd let the man make his own choice, already knowing what it would be.

He nodded toward Sam. "Go ahead and warn him."

"Police. Drop the gun. Release the woman. Get on the ground. Now. Or I'll send the dog in." Sam poured authority and command into his words.

The tango swung around, drawing a whimper from his hostage as he yanked hard on her, nearly sending her nearly stumbling. "I'll kill her. I swear I will." He used her body as a shield, but their differences in height left his head an easy target.

"Drop. The. Gun. Now," Dusty barked out. *"Angreifen."*

Ben surged out of the cover, barking wildly as he sped toward the couple.

Dusty stepped out as well, his gun sighted on the man. Purposely, he put himself in a vulnerable position, giving the man an opportunity to take his shot and to divert attention from a charging Ben.

Everything happened in a blur. The man fired at him, then shoved the gun against the woman's head and screamed at the fast approaching dog. The bullet slammed into a nearby tree. Dusty pulled the trigger. Once.

The man collapsed just as Ben arrived, sinking his teeth in the man's leg and shaking with all his strength. The woman screamed and hurried out of the line of fire, only to stop and stare at the unmoving body. Her hand covered her mouth as a flood of tears began to fall in earnest.

*"Ben freilessen. Kommen."* He called Ben back as he walked closer. He didn't doubt the man had breathed his last, but he needed to check. A single glance told him the answer. No one could survive such a traumatic head wound.

Sam approached and shared a look with Dusty. Awe flashed through his eyes.

Dusty turned his attention to the woman. She appeared fairly unhurt, though quite shaken. "Miss? Are you all right?"

Her gaze lifted from the dead man to him, then to the sheriff. Panic mixed with astounded relief covered her face. "I... Thank you."

"If you'll come with me, ma'am, we'll get you back." Sam held out his hand.

She wrapped her arms around her middle and began walking. Dusty followed, pausing long enough to pet and praise Ben and to collect his rifle, letting Sam run the show from there on out.

They had barely covered one hundred meters when a couple of deputies hurried over. Their stares took in first Dusty then the woman.

Sam tilted his head in indication of their back trail. "Suspect down just over the small rise. Call the coroner and get a cleanup crew. And, Tyler, please take Miss Clarice. She'll need to get checked out. I think a cup of coffee might be in order as well."

"Yes, sir." Tyler held out his arm and spoke softly to the woman, leading her away.

Sam blew out a long breath. "Damn."

Dusty watched her go, knowing her nightmare wasn't nearly over yet. Emotional scars ran far too deep to ever forget.

"Why did you step out in the open? Shocked the shit out of me." Sam turned toward him, having long since holstered his weapon.

"He would've shot the hostage and my dog. He was nervous, in a corner. I figured his shot would miss due to the adrenaline surge and wasn't about to take a chance on that bastard killing them both."

"So you put yourself in his sights as a distraction?" Sam's voice rose with disbelief.

"Yeah." Ben leaned against Dusty's legs. Reaching down, he rubbed the dog's head, as proud of him as he'd always been. Despite Ben's advanced age, he still performed at a high level, more than up to the task for today's crisis.

Sam looked at Ben, then lifted his gaze. "You *sure* I can't talk you into working for me?"

Dusty shook his head with a grim smile. "No thanks. Now and again in a pinch, I don't mind helping out. But the stable keeps me too busy." Not to mention he'd retired from active duty for a reason. The last thing he wanted to do now was sit in a patrol car all day, chase down speeders and watch all his hard work catching real criminals fly out the window as they received a slap on the hand and were released back into the community. *Too little reward, too much red tape. No way.*

"Understood." Yet another cop appeared, spoke to Sam, then dashed off. Sam sighed wearily. "I hate press conferences."

"Don't blame you a bit."

Sam shook Dusty's hand and pinned his gaze. "I'm putting you in for a medal."

"No."

"You deserve something, Dusty. Shit, you did what a dozen cops couldn't do in record time. Think of the lives that you potentially saved."

"*No.*" Dusty added emphasis to the adamant rejection. SEALs didn't like public attention and never truly felt comfortable with a big fuss after doing their jobs, much preferring to remain in the shadows and slip away unheralded.

"You SEALs are all the same."

For the first time since the radio had announced the event, Dusty grinned with humor. "Once a SEAL, always a SEAL." With that said, he picked up Ben, loaded him into the truck and climbed in.

Sam shook his head. "You guys saved my ass in Iraq. Now today. I can never thank you enough."

"You just did." Dusty slipped the key in the ignition, cranked the motor and pulled onto the street, heading for the nearby hospital.

He needed to check on April, assure himself she was fit and fine and bring her home. His home. Maybe for good.

\* \* \* \*

"Thirsty, huh? Well, you've earned it and more." Dusty watched Ben drink from the bowl he kept in the truck. He'd poured a full bottle of cool water into the container earlier, only for the dog to suck the bowl nearly empty. Refilling,

Dusty patted Ben's head and sighed.

He sat in the parking lot of the hospital. While probably still on lockdown, they would receive word soon enough that the danger had passed. In the meantime, due to the overnight rains and heavy cloud cover, the temperature wasn't awful while sitting with the windows down. A light breeze stirred now and again, adding to the more temperate day.

His thoughts turned to April. If the suspect had run into the hospital, started firing, or even chosen her for a hostage… His gut constricted at the thought of April injured, scared or in the slightest bit of danger. Protective instincts surged to the fore, pushing other minor issues to the bottom of the totem pole. *I'll kill any man who dares hurt her.*

The truthful words stuck like Super Glue.

*Why April? Why now?* The questions brushed through his mind even as his soul warmed contentedly. His track record with women left much to be desired. Yet April remained, maybe not quite as flashy or outgoing as some of the others, but she possessed an inner goodness and toughness that put the rest of the women to shame. In essence, she'd stumbled into his life, made the sun shine brighter, soothed his inner turmoil and stepped up not only with the workload, but in understanding. He could spend a decade or three searching for someone like her and still end up empty-handed.

Checking his watch, he found April still had a bit over four more hours in her shift. As much as he needed to see her, reassure himself she was fine despite the scare, he found the timing sucked. He could venture inside and spend a couple minutes with her, but she wouldn't be able to leave for some time yet. For a moment he considered his options but he simply knew he couldn't drive away without setting eyes on her.

His phone rang. Checking the number, he immediately answered. "April? Is everything all right?" Concern speared him in the chest. She never called while at work, since cell phone use was forbidden except during lunch or when off the clock.

"Yep. Well, it is now, I guess. We were on lockdown for a while due to a shooter at large, but they say the threat is over."

Dusty reached out to scratch behind Ben's ear. "Good thing."

"Anyway, I wasn't really calling about that, I was calling to let you know that I'm getting off work early since our census has dropped."

He perked right up. "When do you get off?"

"Right now. I just finished giving report. I'm gathering my stuff and getting ready to walk out."

"I'll be right outside waiting for you."

Silence reigned for a long moment. "You're in town today?" There was bewilderment in her voice.

"Yeah. I stopped by to see about you and was just about to walk in the front doors, but this is better. I'll wait here for you."

"Okay."

She walked out, searching the parking lot, spied him and headed directly toward him, clicking off the phone in the process. A few more strides brought her right up to his driver's side window. "Hi."

"Hi." Dusty studied her face, saw the genuine smile appear and felt his heart thump against his ribs. He found no sign of fear or anxiety, only happy welcome in her pretty blue eyes.

Her gaze flickered over to Ben, who climbed on Dusty's lap to get closer to her. Dusty flinched as a large paw landed directly on his groin. The dog's weight immediately followed. Quickly, he grabbed Ben's foot and moved the appendage to a more comfortable position, unwilling to risk being unmanned at this stage in the game.

"Hello there, superstar. How's my favorite war dog today?" April scratched the dog's scruff then tilted her head. "You came to town and brought Ben with you?"

He could almost see the wheels turning inside her head.

"At this time of day..." Her eyes widened in realization. "You were part of the manhunt."

Way too perceptive by far. He shrugged but didn't say more. Besides, he much preferred to turn the conversation to a lighter topic, such as getting her home and kissing her senseless.

Except his parents were there. He groaned audibly.

Her face clouded. "What's wrong?"

"I almost forgot. My parents dropped by today for a visit. They're still at the stable."

Her lips languidly curled up at the corners. "How long are they going to stay?"

"I don't know."

She reached up and cupped his cheek, then laughed. "It's hard when your family craves your attention."

Dusty rolled his eyes. "I liked my life just fine for the past three years." He couldn't resist brushing his lips across her palm.

"Maybe so, but you have to admit it's kind of nice to have them around to hug you, love you and call you George." Mischief twinkled in her eyes.

He snorted in amusement. "Not quite sure about that."

"But you wouldn't have it any other way."

"No, I wouldn't." The words soaked into his very soul.

# Chapter Twenty-Two

Thirty minutes later, they stood before his parents, who eyed them with equal parts curiosity and interest. "Mom. Dad. This is April. April. My parents, Delia and John."

John's build reminded her so much of Dusty and his other brothers. Tall and strong. He might have spent much of his career at a desk, but he hadn't grown fat because of it. Silver hair at his temples provided a nice contrast with the otherwise dark-brown color, the short length not quite meeting his collar.

Delia, several inches shorter, had black hair presently cut in a fairly short — but trendy — style. A smile had sat on her lips since she'd spied April, as if she were pleased with what she saw. April sure hoped so. Both were dressed in slacks with nice shirts. John wore cowboy boots while Delia had chosen matching flats.

"It's nice to meet you." April held her hand out, nervous to finally meet Dusty's parents. She'd heard quite a bit about them during her short stay at the ranch. Now that they met her gaze, she felt like a child at her first piano recital, nervous and excited.

"Ditto." John reached out and shook her hand gently.

Delia smiled at her as if sizing her up for a wedding dress.

April cleared her throat and wracked her brain for something to say. "You must be very proud of Dusty."

"We are. For lots of reasons." Delia smiled at Dusty.

John stared at his son for a long moment. "The radio said the suspect had been tracked down and eliminated, the hostage saved."

April understood John's train of thought, for she'd

considered the same thing all the way home. As usual, Dusty had been as tight-lipped as a clam, but she knew he'd had a big part in today's events.

"Yeah. Excuse me a minute. I need to get some stuff from my truck."

Ben stayed by her side, even as his eyes followed Dusty the short trip back to his truck. April watched as he pulled out a black vest and a rifle carrier.

Dusty shut the door and strode back toward them, his steps filled with confidence. He was in full SEAL mode, April realized. Intense and brimming with power and determination. She'd seen the strut before but never connected the dots. Until now. Understanding hit her like a heavy sack of flour. Dusty hadn't just worked as a SEAL for a few years. He still *was* a SEAL. The qualities, skills and internal fortitude inside each man who'd achieved such a high military status didn't simply fade away once they retired. Instead every piece sank deep, becoming part of the man. You could take Dusty out of the SEALs, but you couldn't take the SEAL out of the man. The fact only endeared him to her all the more, if that was even possible. Since the first day they'd met, he'd touched something deep inside her.

"Dusty? I don't suppose you had anything to do with capturing that man?" Delia voiced the obvious question.

Dusty shrugged and brushed past them, still carrying his gear.

Leaning forward, April whispered, "I don't know what you think about your son, but he's a hero in anyone's book."

"Yes. Yes, he is." John's voice filled with certainty and a bit of awe, as if he was just realizing the extent of Dusty's abilities.

"He's a great man," April added.

"He was a good kid. I always knew he'd do something incredible with his life," Delia said.

"He did and still is." April's heart buoyed at the love she read on their faces. Whether Dusty knew it or not, he had the support of his whole family, not just his brothers. The realization touched her, so she knew Dusty felt it too.

* * * *

"More cherry pie, anyone?" Delia asked.

"No thanks." Everyone shook their head.

She liked his parents. John, much quieter, had a tough demeanor, but possessed a softer inside, especially when it came to his family. Easily, she could see why he made such a fierce prosecuting attorney, as he'd intimidated her from the first moment with a simple, blank expression and a stare that bored into her very soul. Only after spending some time with him and seeing him tease his wife mercilessly did April begin to feel more comfortable around the man.

On the other hand, Delia proved likeable from the get-go. An obvious extrovert, Delia jumped right in to help cook, talking the entire time. In truth, Dusty's mother reminded April of the leader of the church social activities back at home. The woman didn't know a stranger and couldn't sit back and watch anyone work without chipping in to help.

"How's Tess?" April had thought about the petite redhead often during the past few days. More than once she'd picked up her phone to call, but thus far only succeeded in speaking to her new friend once.

"Holding up as far as we can tell. She's been getting her ducks in a row from our home and searching for a new job. Poor girl. She apologizes every day for being a burden."

"She's no such thing." John shoved a bite of dessert in his mouth. "Besides, Brand has his eyes set on her."

"I thought interest existed on both their parts before I left. I'd hoped he would be by her side every step of the way." April patted her mouth with a napkin.

"Oh, he is." Delia sipped her tea. "The brothers have a running bet on how soon until they make an announcement."

"Really?" April arched an eyebrow and stared at Dusty. "No one said anything about a wager to me."

Dusty shrugged and sipped his drink. "Perhaps they didn't want you to tip the scales by telling Tess."

April rolled her eyes. "What other wagers do you guys have?"

John and Dusty shared a look that could have meant anything.

"Nothing important," Dusty answered.

"Uh-huh." April stood and began clearing the small dining table in Dusty's kitchen. She didn't buy his evasive words for a minute, but honestly didn't care to pursue the subject.

Ever since he'd met her in the parking lot of the hospital, she hadn't been able to rid herself of the excited jitters, and more than anything she wanted to crawl into bed, feel Dusty curl protectively around her, and savor the sensation of safety and care. Nothing could mean more to her at that moment. If a little hanky-panky ensued prior, she'd jump in with both feet.

Delia followed April's example, gathering up dishes and dropping them off at the sink. The men snapped lids on food and stored the leftovers in the fridge for another time. By the time April had loaded the dishwasher, Delia had wiped down the table and Dusty and John had disappeared back into the stable, presumably to care for the horses.

"You're good for him." Delia washed out the dishrag before draping it across the middle section of the sink.

April blinked. "I'm not sure what you mean."

"Dusty was lost, isolated from his family, stubborn pride making him hold his head high even as his soul cried out in loneliness. Then you came along. Now look at him. He's content, happy and banters with his brothers just like nothing ever happened."

"The fire is responsible for their reunited status. Not me. He had no one else to call for help."

"Hogwash." Delia waved her hand dismissively. "He didn't have to bond with his brothers again. Didn't have to become part of the family again. Didn't have to open his door in welcome to us. Yet he did. What's changed? You're not only in his life, but showing him some wonderful things. Reminding him what love is."

"Dusty doesn't love me." April spoke the truth, though her heart protested what her mind already knew.

"Are you so sure about that?" Delia gestured toward the dining room chairs. She took a seat and waited for April to sit down.

"He's never said anything—"

"He won't. Not until he's sure. Look at the trail of women who've taken strips off his hide. All because he fell for the wrong ones." Reaching out, Delia laid her hand on April's forearm. "His feelings show in his actions."

April sighed. "We started off fairly rocky, but I think we've made decent progress lately, considering the bumps in the road and our dismal failures in our romantic pasts." She looked up and met the older woman's gaze. "But that's a far cry from love."

"You know what Dusty did when the radio announced the hostage situation?"

"Gathered up Ben and rushed to the rescue. He's a former SEAL. From what I understand, that's just who he is then and now."

"Yes, but there's something else you should know."

Intrigued, April waited impatiently for Delia to continue.

"He whispered your name. Said the name of the hospital, then your name." Delia waited a beat. "I'm sure he didn't mean to speak aloud, and he only whispered, but I heard. You were not only his first thought, but you should have seen his face. He turned deadly serious and went into a zone, as if preparing to face the devil himself in order to battle his way to your side."

Stunned, April soaked up the words, her mind whirling. "I'm sure he understood the hostage's life depended upon him rushing to the scene."

"Maybe. But that still doesn't explain why he followed you back here and hasn't let you out of his sight until just now."

"I don't know."

"The question, dear, is do you want him?" Delia leveled a steady look at her.

"Yes." The answer slipped out unbidden.

A wide grin appeared on Delia's face. "Then by all means, tell my son how you feel."

"What if he doesn't want me in return?"

Delia patted her arm. "I might not be as young and spry as I used to be, but I'm not blind or dense. I know my sons very well, all of them, and I know love when I see it."

April stared for a long moment, her mouth hanging open. Gradually, she shut her mouth and stood. "I hope you're right."

"Have a little faith, April. Have a little faith."

Standing, Delia started toward the stable, opened the door and waited for April to follow. They entered the area and stopped, watching as the men finished carrying buckets of grain to the horses and topping off the water at the same time.

"My, oh my. Isn't he handsome when he bends over?"

"Umm. Which one are you talking about exactly?" April's lips twitched.

"Why, John, of course. My son is perfect, but I'm not about to ogle his butt." Delia grinned wickedly. "My husband, on the other hand…" She fanned herself.

April couldn't help but laugh. "Good to see the romance doesn't fade away over the years."

"Fade? Oh, goodness no. That man is like a sex machine."

*I really didn't need to know that.* Heat blasted across April's face at the other woman's candid remarks. *Like father, like son.* The thought kicked her dormant libido into full gear.

Dusty stepped out of Rule's stall and turned off the hose. His father added his empty bucket to the growing pile and stood with his hands at his sides, his gaze directed toward his wife.

"Oh, goody. The come-hither look," Delia whispered,

then walked closer to the object of her attention. "Thank you for your hospitality, Dusty, but I think your father and I need to retire early."

John arched an eyebrow. "We do?"

"Definitely. I believe you intended to explain the laws of possession to me tonight."

John's eyes sparkled as a slow smile appeared on his face. "Why, yes. I think you're right." He strode over to Dusty and held out his hand. "I know I don't say this often enough, but I'm proud of you."

Dusty blinked at his father and accepted the handshake, only to be pulled into a big hug. "I love you, son."

"I love you too, Dad." Dusty hugged him tight in return.

Delia winked at April, who remained quiet, unwilling to interfere in the touching moment.

Stepping back, John held out his arm, collected Delia and led her out the entrance gate and straight into their fancy RV.

"Now that's something I never expected." Dusty watched them go.

"What's that?"

"My dad getting all sentimental."

April grinned. "He's proud of you and obviously thought you should know." Slipping her fingers between his, she turned him around to face her. "Although the thought of him giving her lessons on legal possession in their RV makes me need some serious mind soap."

He pulled her into his embrace with a warm chuckle. "Yeah, there is that."

# Chapter Twenty-Three

April stepped out of the bathroom wearing only Dusty's shirt. The tails reached her upper thighs, but each step fluttered the hem just enough to glimpse white panties underneath. Still damp, her long locks hung straight down her back, swaying with each step and drawing attention to her slender neck, pretty face and perky breasts. Daylight from the evening sun streaming through the bedroom window silhouetted April in a golden aura, like an angel.

Dusty licked his lips and couldn't tear his eyes off the blonde beauty walking toward him. His dick hardened instantly and he knew he couldn't wait any longer to touch her, savor her — to make her his.

The scare earlier today had reminded him life could be short. Sure, he'd always known the simple fact, but he hadn't pondered the vulnerable side of life since retiring from the military. Now he recalled how every moment became important when you saw yourself and others as mere mortals. The thought of what could have happened to April solidified his resolve. She was his. Now and forever.

"You take my breath away."

Blue eyes lifted to meet his. "I don't know what to say." Curiosity and a modicum of nervousness flashed across her face, only to be replaced by a healthy dose of longing.

He opened his arms. "Say you want me. Say you'll stay with me. Say you'll spend the night with me."

A pregnant pause followed before April slowly smiled. "Yes, I want you, more than you can know. Yes, I'll spend the night with you, stay with you, for however long you want me." She stopped right in front of him, coyly looking up through her lashes, a mischievous smile on her face.

He enveloped her like a rare treasure, pulling her snug against his body while leaning down and sealing his lips over hers. When she didn't immediately open her lips, he licked the seam then nibbled on the bottom one, earning a gasp. Taking advantage, he slipped his tongue inside, found hers and tapped.

She wrapped her arms around his neck, angled her head and met his exploration with a welcoming passion that surprised him in its intensity. His heart buoyed even as his cock tightened to a near painful level. Deepening the kiss, he tasted her, searching for her unique blend of sugar and spice, an intoxicating elixir he'd craved since their first toe-curling kiss. Drinking from her lips, he poured emotion into the caress, showing her how he felt in the absence of words.

April broke away, her breathing ragged, her blue gaze locked on his. Taking advantage of the space, he started unbuttoning his own shirt off her body. He grinned wickedly.

"What is it?" she asked in a whisper.

"I've never removed my own shirt from a bedmate before." He finished in quick fashion and pushed the edges apart, revealing April's modest yet perky breasts. Unable to resist, he cupped one in his hand, then leaned forward to suck the other.

April gasped and shivered.

He lifted just enough to peer down at her face. "Do you like that?"

Her wide eyes found his. "Yes. Definitely, yes."

He chuckled and resumed his attentions, licking until the raspberry nipple drew taut. Only then did he switch to the other side, serving up delicious sensations intended to get her fire burning until he could get down to more serious business.

When the nipple popped out of his mouth, he took a moment to savor the results of his work. Both breasts were damp, topped with tight peaks. Sensual heat covered

April's face as her eyes sparked with need. A need he was fully prepared to fulfill.

Pushing his shirt off her, he let the garment fall to the floor, leaving her bare except for her cotton bikini panties.

She grasped his shirt and started tugging, finally releasing it from the waistband of his jeans enough to slip her hands underneath. Lightly, she traced the contours of his abdomen, then higher to his chest. He unbuttoned the material with practiced ease, just in time for her hands to brush over his pecs, discover his nipples and tweak them. He bit back a groan as he tossed the unwanted clothing aside. April nuzzled the area then flicked her tongue over it, mirroring his actions from moments before.

His erection throbbed.

She slid her hands down his body, latched onto his waistband, then slipped the button from the hole. Languidly, she lowered the zipper and nipped his chest as his jeans sagged.

"You're going commando."

Her softly spoken words were filled with awe. Boldly, she wrapped her fingers around his shaft, testing his hardness while learning his overheated flesh.

A spear of fire hit him square, causing him to swell impossibly more.

She moved her thumb over his tip, found a bead of moisture then rubbed the proof of his arousal all around. Her breath hitched as she glanced up to meet his gaze.

He grappled for control. Between the look of avid appreciation and her hand lightly exploring his cock, Dusty ground his teeth, determined not to rush. Yet he couldn't help his body's response.

April made him feel special, like he carried the power of the sun. At the same time, her almost tentative caresses nearly brought him to his knees.

Swooping down, he covered her mouth once more, aggressively treating her to a precursor of what was to come. His tongue wrapped around hers as he ran his hands down her torso, not stopping until he cupped the junction between her legs.

She froze on a quick intake of air.

Feeling the dampness beneath his fingers, he didn't lift his hand. Instead he poured everything he could into the kiss, luring her back under his spell, ramping up her arousal to, hopefully, match his. After only a moment she leaned into him, widened her stance a smidgen and allowed him ample room to investigate.

He didn't waste a single second, first rubbing her through the soft material then dipping under, to touch the softest skin he'd ever encountered.

April mewled and pressed into his caress, blatantly asking for more. Frustrated with the limited space, he grabbed the crotch of the material and tugged downward until her panties puddled at her feet. As she stepped out of the garment, he replaced his hand, slid a finger between her folds, felt the abundant moisture. Still kissing her senseless, he levered one finger against her entrance, then slowly pressed inward a hair in a teasing manner.

Heat and tightness met him, along with unmistakable dampness.

His patience at an end, Dusty pulled away, smiling when April whimpered in disappointment.

"Don't worry, honey. There's plenty more to come. After I put you in bed." He nuzzled her ear and teased one earlobe before scooping her up. Turning, he placed her in the center of the mattress. She lay flat on her back, her hair spread out like a halo. Her blue eyes raked his body, easily seen in the still-bright light of early evening. He paused for a second, letting her look her fill, then turned to the bedside table. He opened the drawer, found a condom and palmed the foil wrapper. With quick movements he opened the package before rolling the condom into place.

"Did anyone ever tell you, you have the best rear in the county?"

Spinning around, he found April on her side. She'd

propped her head on her hand and boldly stared at him. He didn't mind in the least.

"Just my ass? Nothing else?" He grinned and waited, the unabashed prompt for compliments helping him regain his control before the erotic dance began.

She smiled teasingly as her gaze traveled his body once more then locked on his erection. Her baby blues darkened to midnight as she ran her tongue over her lips.

He groaned softly, thoroughly enjoying her appraisal. In her eyes, he felt like an immortal god.

"Well, since you already have a big head..." Her words faded as a blush flashed across her face.

He laughed, climbing on the bed, not stopping until he covered her. Settling over her, he kissed her nose then lightly met her lips. "You go straight to my head."

She snorted. "I'd say a place a bit lower."

The grin remained as he sat back on his heels. Reaching out with one hand, he traced a path up the inside of her leg, all the way to the junction of her thighs. Watching her face, he caressed her with one digit, gradually sliding between her labia.

April arched, her mouth opened and more natural moisture released. She squirmed. He moved his thumb into play, brushing across her small bundle of nerves.

April whimpered. "Please. Please don't stop."

He set his back teeth and strummed her again. Her hips bucked, shoving his fingers into her opening and against a silky barrier.

Dusty stilled immediately as he felt the membrane barrier blocking him from her depths. *Surely not.* Very gently he prodded, reinforcing his first thought. *Virgin.* Though he'd expected her to have limited sexual experience due to her rough dating history, he'd never considered she might be an innocent.

"You're a virgin." He didn't realize he'd spoken out loud until she answered.

"Yes."

He stared down at her. Never before had she let a man touch her like this, enter her. Yet she lay nude before him, stretched on a rack of pleasure, asking for him to take her.

He would be the first to touch her, to teach her, to show her how wonderful sex could be.

A mighty wave of possessiveness hit him. *Mine.*

"Dusty?"

He focused on her face, his digits still locked inside her core.

"I need you. I want you. Please."

In all honesty, he should get up and walk away, wait until they were both level-headed and cool in order to make such an important decision. But nothing short of Armageddon could tear him away and probably not even that. He'd never wanted anything more in his life than to join his body with hers, push her to the crest and discover the depths of passion they possessed for each other.

For a fleeting second he considered breaching her with his fingers, then immediately discarded the idea. This situation called for sensitivity and intimacy. Besides, he wanted to watch her face as he took her for the first time.

To reach that moment, she needed as much pleasure as possible before his entry.

"You've remained a virgin this long. Are you sure you want to do this now?" He offered up one more chance to change her mind. His body protested the idea, but his only concern lay with April. The last thing he wanted was her to regret a spontaneous decision that would change her life forever.

"Yes."

He stared down at her, studying her expressions.

"I never found the right man to be with. Until you. Now, I finally understand. All that time I was simply biding my time until we met." She ran her fingers up and down his forearms, the only part of his body she could presently reach. "I couldn't ask for a better man than you." Truth and sincerity carried in her words. The corner of her mouth hitched up. "Besides, I think I love you."

The words formed in his mind, but he couldn't verbalize them. Refusing to analyze his feelings at the moment, he simply smiled and brushed his lips over hers. A promise of things to come.

Unable to turn away from such an admission, he sat back up and focused his attention on the woman spread out before him. Come hell or high water, he'd ensure she reached the moon in his arms.

Steeling his resolve, he bumped her clit once more, earning a loud moan and reflexive jerk. He played her skillfully, nudging her higher and higher, not stopping until she fisted the sheets with a desperate strength, her body taut with need. Only then did he move to cover her once more. "Bend your legs, April. Give me room."

She immediately complied. He lowered his weight to his forearms, lined up their bodies by feel, and nibbled on her lips. "Slowly now," he reminded himself and her at the same time.

With steady pressure, he entered her channel, finding initial resistance and a snugness he could quickly learn to crave.

"Hang on." He pressed forward, trying to push through.

April flinched, her hands flying to his sides. Her eyes closed as she braced herself.

"Look at me." Remaining absolutely still, he waited for her to comply. "Stay with me, honey. Don't look away. I'll be as gentle as I can."

She nodded and locked her gaze with his.

He saw the discomfort written clearly on her face and couldn't bear to put her through more pain than was inevitable. While proud he would be her first and only lover, he hated knowing he would also bring her pain this first time. With a muttered curse, he steeled himself for the inevitable. He pulled back slightly and surged forward with power, breaking through.

She hissed, her body jerked and tightened in an instinctive

effort to withdraw from the pain. Her eyebrows furrowed as a tiny yelp escaped her lips. Every muscle in her body tensed.

Her inner walls gripped him so tightly he couldn't have moved if he wanted to. Instead he focused on her face, peppering kisses over her cheeks, her lips, nuzzling as he whispered sweet nothings. Arching his back, he focused on her breasts, sucking until she wiggled with renewed hunger, her breath coming out in short pants. Gradually, by increments, her body began to relax and respond to his caring caresses again. Only when her pretty eyes were no longer clouded in pain and her core eased did he retreat marginally and ever so slowly return. Watching her face the entire time, he found no signs of discomfort, only the return of pleasure. Still, he needed to be sure. "Hurt?" He repeated the motion.

She shook her head, her hands hot lashes across his back and flanks. Each touch threw yet another cherry bomb on his already raging inferno.

For the longest time he did nothing more than test the waters with short, tender jabs, stoking her fire to match his. Each sigh, each sexy cry from her lips, ramped up his own pleasure tenfold as he showered her with burning pleasure, pouring his emotions out through actions.

When she lifted to meet his thrusts, he boldly drew back farther, lengthening his strokes yet keeping the pace languid and gentle. Hard and fast had no place in this first loving. Instead he drew on every skill he possessed to march her steadily toward the pinnacle, needing her to reach the top and crash over. He needed her to experience a bright, earth-shattering climax under his tender care as much as he needed air to fill his lungs.

He changed his angle slightly and found a raspberry nipple, drawing the treat into his mouth and laving the tip. She whimpered and squirmed. Lifting up, he looked down at her body, saw her head thrown back on the pillows, her blonde hair spilled all around her. April's mouth fell open as she closed her eyes. Sensual pleasure covered her face.

Adjusting his position slightly, he shifted his weight to his right arm, freeing up his left. Searching between their bodies, he once more found her bundle of nerves, now taut and begging for attention. With exquisite care, he caressed the nub, felt her jerk under him, and repeated the motion.

April's body began to tense. He easily read the heightened level of arousal and blatantly pushed her for more, intent upon drawing out every morsel of passion from her body then rewarding her with hot rapture. "That's it, sweetheart. You're almost there. Wrap your legs around my hips." When she complied, he sank even deeper. "Yeah, just like that. Fuck that's good."

A grunt emerged from her throat, followed by a sharp cry of frustration. She tossed her head. "I…" Licking her lips, she tried again. "I can't…"

"Shhh. Look at me, April."

Her eyes fluttered open and her gaze locked on his. He surged in and out of her moist center, short, exceptionally deep penetrations that rocked them together as one. "Don't look away. Stay with me." He arched his back in order to lean down for a quick kiss to a juicy nipple. "Take what you need from me."

He plumped her clit with the gentlest of touches. She lurched and cried out, the motion squeezing his already granite-hard member in a velvet glove, sending sharp shards of ecstasy straight to his groin. "Come on, baby. Just. Let. Go." He pressed the bundle once more then began to strum quickly.

April curled her back, sucked in a breath and yelped out as rapid-fire contractions squeezed his cock so tight he saw stars. Her clipped nails dug into his back, the slight sting only adding another element to his overflowing arousal. Determinedly, he rode out her first orgasm, intent upon seeing every flicker of pleasure wash across her face, feeling her body's every reaction and savoring every second.

The base of his spine began to tingle as her continued

milking action pushed all his buttons, driving him to the very edge, and finally shoving him over with gusto. A hoarse shout tore from his throat as he shoved deep inside her depths and stilled, locking them together as one.

* * * *

"Tired?" Dusty pulled her into his embrace.

April leaned into him, soaking up his warmth and solid strength as she rested her head against his upper chest. After her first taste of passion, she'd excused herself to the bathroom to get cleaned up. Dusty's eyes had followed her every step of the way. Only after she'd tossed the used washcloth into the hamper and collected her wits had she returned to bed. One glance told her he'd done the same as she, since he'd laid stretched out, condom-free and cleansed. Unable to resist and craving comfort, she'd slipped into his arms. "Yeah. Today was crazy enough without going on lockdown."

He rubbed her back with long, light strokes. "If you had been taken hostage, I would've lost my mind."

Surprised, she leaned back in order to look up into Dusty's face. She found concern and something more. Something deeper. Her heart sang. "You would have done the same thing you did today. Shared your skills with the rest of us and saved the day."

While he'd never indicated one way or another, April knew Dusty had most likely not only participated in the manhunt, but been the one to track the man. Why else would he have had Ben with him, a Kevlar vest and a long rifle she'd never seen before in his truck? Dusty had gone hunting just like he'd done countless times before.

"I'm so proud of you." She whispered the words against his throat, then lifted high enough to seal her lips over his.

He responded immediately, seized control of the kiss and quickly showered her with a healthy dose of passion. She gasped as his tongue entered her mouth, searching out every nook and cranny, tasting her as if she possessed ambrosia and he'd been thirsty for a long time. Wrapping her arms around his neck, April threw herself into the affection, giving back with everything inside, showing him what she couldn't say out loud, at least not yet. She'd hinted before, but now knew without a doubt she loved the former Navy SEAL turned stable owner. He hadn't spoken the words back to her earlier, leaving a small sting in her heart, so she hesitated to say them again. Not yet. But soon. No sense denying the truth.

Before she could get carried away, Dusty pulled back. Disappointed, she whimpered with a sigh before meeting his knowing gaze.

He grinned down at her with a new softness. "You're going to be sore if we continue."

"I want you too much to care."

"Then why don't you climb on top? Ride me. You can control the pace."

The offer made April's stomach flip-flop with slow, delicious motions. *Ride him. Just like the stud he is.* She giggled at the naughty thought, so unlike her.

"What's so funny?"

Sitting up, April straddled his hips. "Oh, I was just thinking how appropriate it is for me to climb aboard and ride you. Like a big, beautiful stallion." Her face heated but seeing the reaction on Dusty's face next made the small admission worth it.

His expression grew taut and filled with sexual longing. He cupped the back of her head and brought her down for a kiss of the ages, a deep plundering that left her breathless while promising a passionate discovery to rival no other.

The pole light outside allowed enough of a glow from the window for her to see him in fairly decent clarity. As she sat up, she once more appreciated his physique, running her hands over his chest, stomach, then lower. Scars riddled his otherwise perfect body, adding to the handsomeness rather than detracting. *A warrior to his marrow.* She saw the old marks as badges of courage and sexy as hell. Tracing each one, she marveled over his ability to take such punishment and return for more. Courage and bravery in spades, to be sure. "You're gorgeous."

"Too beat up for that, but thanks." He lifted one hand to cup her breast, gently brushing his thumb over the tip.

She sighed and pressed closer. "To me, you're the sexiest man alive. Forget movie stars, you bypass every one of them hands down." With a knowing grin, she wrapped her fingers lightly around his erection. "I'd rather have a horse that's been through hell and fought back than a paddock-raised one any day. The same goes for a man."

He smiled up at her, the act softening the lines of his face, adding to his already captivating appearance.

Lightly, she stroked his impressive cock, learning both the feel and texture, experimenting with different grips and motions to discover which he liked best. Her finger found a bead of moisture resting on the slit. Boldly, she spread the moisture all around the mushroom head.

He groaned and jerked under her.

"Like that?" The whisper carried easily across the silent room.

"Way too much." A foil package appeared in his hand. He ripped it open with his teeth then rolled it on. "I can't wait for you to take me, baby. Slide down on me. Show me how a cowgirl rides her man."

The words ratcheted up her arousal and motivated her to lift up and move a few inches, enough to align their bodies.

Dusty, his cock in hand, rubbed the tip against her hungry core. "You're wet. So wet." He ran a finger between her folds before centering the head of his erection once more. "Open for me, April. Take me deep."

Gradually, she pressed downward, aided by Dusty's grip on her hip. Her body protested at first, then finally relented, allowing him to enter marginally. She sucked in a breath, gyrated her hips and came down farther. Overused muscles complained, but she ignored them, choosing instead to focus on Dusty's face, watching as she joined their bodies.

Finally she rested on his body, his shaft snugly lodged deep inside her. Not quite comfortable, she rocked slowly back and forth, feeling him rub against secret nerve endings, all of which fired hotly. She gasped.

"You okay?" His voice carried concern.

Peering down at him, she smiled. "Yeah. It's just—"

"Tender?"

She nodded her head. "A little, but nothing to fret about. It's just amazing. I feel full. Complete. Like I'd been made just for you." Her body eased, allowing her to move with more enthusiasm. Dusty guided her motions, keeping her close and at a leisurely speed. Over and over she moved, savoring his presence deep inside her. Unhurriedly, she tried different angles, alternated motions and put them both through their paces in a gentle loving which seemed to go on forever, yet not last nearly long enough as bright rapture flickered in temptation just ahead.

He bit his lip and bucked to meet her next downward stroke, sending a shockwave of sensual pleasure cascading over her.

"That's it, baby. Take what you need from me. Anything. Everything." He used his free hand to tunnel through her folds where they joined. A second later, bright stars burst in front of her eyes as she ground her hips against his. His touch, his skill on that particular body part, made her crazy. Suddenly she couldn't get enough. Enough of him, his glorious cock, enough of his fingers working her sensitive button. A whimper escaped her as she latched onto the greedy hunger and shot higher.

Again he feverishly yet lightly worked her nub. Every muscle in her body tightened as she braced herself.

"Let go, sweetheart. I want to watch you come."

His words, complete with another exquisite lash of her clit, shoved her right up to the peak then toppled her over. With a ragged cry, she wiggled and squirmed, keeping his pleasure-producing cock as deep as possible.

He shouted out, both hands bracketing her pelvis as he held her in place so tightly she couldn't have moved if she'd tried. Dusty's face scrunched up as he drew in great gulps of air. His shaft twitched deep inside her as strong peaks crested through her before slowing as the brilliant orgasm abated.

April crumpled on his chest, panting and worn out. Though the ride hadn't lasted as long as she would have liked, she'd poured every ounce of energy into the experience. All more than worth the effort, but now she wasn't sure she could move another inch.

"Damn," Dusty whispered in her ear as he nuzzled her cheek. "You can ride me anytime."

Adjusting her position, she rested her head against his chest, closing her eyes in total relaxation. "That sounds like fun." She blew out a breath and started to drift off.

Dusty chuckled, wrapped his arms around her, then rolled them over. The comfortable mattress now at her back, she relaxed into the cushiony pliability. While she might have liked to fall asleep on him, this new position made more sense for his ability to breathe and move for the rest of the night.

He pulled back, his now semi-erect cock slipping from her body with one final caress to the previously untried and now slightly raw tissues. She flinched on a gasp.

"Sorry." Dusty brushed his lips over hers, then exited the bed.

Half asleep, April didn't realize he'd returned until she felt moist warmth and terry cloth between her legs. Embarrassed, she clamped her legs together and met Dusty's gaze.

He rested his hand on her upper thigh. "Let me wash you. You'll sleep better without all the stickiness."

Giving in to the realities of sex, she let Dusty cleanse her, appreciative of his kindness. She doubted any of her previous boyfriends would have bothered to even consider her comfort, let alone bathe her. "Thank you."

The cloth pressed against her core twice more before he slid off the bed and headed to the bathroom, only to return a second later. The bed dipped as he slid under the covers and pulled her up against his body.

Content, she snuggled in.

He kissed her nape. "I take care of my own."

With those words ringing in her ears, she fell asleep.

# Chapter Twenty-Four

*Dusty found himself in the middle of the desert, bullets flying like a strong hailstorm all around. Men shouted as the roar of helicopters drowned out everything but the loudest cry. His rifle spat out ammo like a furious dragon breathing fire. Every minute movement in the rocky trenches, he'd aim for, hoping to eradicate the tango threat long enough to secure the area and rescue the small Army regiment presently under direct fire. He shoved clip after clip into his rifle, then scurried for higher ground. No sooner had he left his position than a grenade exploded, sending him flying through the air. Pain lanced his side as a fiery trail creased his upper arm.*

Jerking awake, he raked the room with his gaze and drew in gulps of air. Ben whined and licked his face. He instinctively reached out and ran his hands through the dog's fur. The familiar activity soothing him by great measures. A movement to his left caught his attention. April scooched closer in a sitting position, watching him with a concentrated expression full of concern.

"Are you okay?"

He rubbed a hand over his face. "Just a bad dream." One of hundreds he'd had since the war. Nothing new.

"About the war?"

Her baby blues reflected worry and gentle caring. At least he didn't find pity in their depths. That was one thing he refused to accept. "Yeah."

"Not surprising, considering what you did yesterday." She reached out and laid a hand on his shoulder, her fingers lightly caressing the flesh.

Ben, obviously deciding the worst had passed, hopped

off the bed and flopped down on his fluffy pillow nearby.

She trailed her fingers over his bare chest, the action both soothing and stimulating.

"I'm sorry. I wish I could make them go away."

"Me too. But it's all part of the package." He shrugged, reaching out to plant his hands on her thighs, noticing how her nipples pebbled in the chill of pre-dawn. He recalled their taste and licked his lips. *Slow down, SEAL.* Remembering her nearly untried state, he doused his morning libido with good, old-fashioned common sense. After all, she would be sore this morning and penetration would only add to her discomfort. Best to wait a day or two, when she could accept him in her body again comfortably.

"How are you feeling?"

She smiled contentedly.

He recognized the expression of a woman well-pleased with her man. His heart thumped.

"Good. Very good." The words dripped like honey.

Dusty grinned in return. "No aches and pains?"

April shrugged. "Nothing to worry about." Leaning over, she flicked her tongue over his nipple, giggling when he jumped.

Happy beyond measure, he shook his finger at her. "None of that, now. I'm trying to be good."

Her head tilted. "Why?"

"Because I refuse to give you a moment's more pain," he answered seriously, truth filling his voice. "Never again do I want to hurt you."

She sat quiet for a long moment, water collecting in her eyes. A tear slid free.

He collected the drop on his finger. Worry broke into his morning bliss. "What's this?"

"I'd given up hope of ever finding a man who could care for me more than he cared for himself. You can't imagine how special you are." She sniffed and a ghost of a smile appeared on her lips despite the emotional response.

His heart broke. Sitting up beside her, he pulled her up

against him, holding her tight. "You're the special one, April. Kind. Generous. So beautiful." He nuzzled her cheek, baring his very soul for the first time. "You gave me a second chance when anyone else would have turned their back and stormed away. Always giving, you've shown me what love can be between a man and a woman."

She pulled back to look into his eyes. Another drop fell. "I love you, Dusty. I know it's soon, but you've been a blessing."

Humbled and proud, he brushed his lips over her cheek, supping away the trickling tear. "No more than I love you, baby."

She sucked in a breath. "But I have baggage."

He grinned. "Baby, as you've already seen, I have more than enough baggage for the both of us. Yet I don't see you running for the door."

"And I never will. That's a promise." She leaned down and pressed her lips against his. "You're a keeper, Dusty Delaney." Lifting just enough to meet his gaze, she grinned at him. "Besides, we've already decided you've grown on me."

"Like algae."

"Or fungus. One of the two."

He groaned then chuckled. Reaching out, he wrapped her tight in his arms, cherishing her like a rare treasure. Sharing a kiss rife with promise, he proceeded to put their words into action by taking her mouth as he wished to take her body. Slowly. Thoroughly. Leaving no part untouched. Meshing their mouths as they joined their souls.

Love made everything better and brighter—a lesson Dusty couldn't wait to explore further.

Unfortunately, duty called in the form of hungry animals waiting impatiently for their breakfast, and April's body needed time to recover. Reluctantly, he broke their lip-lock. "As much as I'd like to spend the day in bed with you, I think the horses might object."

She grinned. "Probably so. They tend to be needy

creatures."

"Uh-huh." He brushed his lips over hers once more. "I'd better go tend to them."

"I'll help." April climbed out of bed and started pulling on clothes.

Dusty took the opportunity to watch, his arousal increasing when she bent over to retrieve her pants, giving him a perfect view of her heart-shaped ass. Images of her maintaining that position while he sank balls-deep flashed through his mind. His randy dick jumped in reaction. Later. Work first, play later, he promised himself, then, ignoring his morning wood, he pulled on comfortable jeans and a shirt. By the time he had dressed, April had disappeared and he smelled coffee brewing.

Fortunately his parents slept in, not emerging from their RV until well after breakfast had been eaten, the stock cared for and put out to pasture for the day. That allowed ample time for his erection to subside, more from the awkward concept of his parents noting his tented jeans than from anything else. If they weren't present, he'd probably have walked around with a boner most of the day until he could cajole April back into his bed for another round of hot, gritty sex.

Ben barked excitedly, announcing their visitors. Dusty glanced up to find his parents emerging from their house on wheels.

"Good morning, Dusty." His mother hurried over to hug him. Her shorts and T-shirt combo was bright, although reasonable for the summer season.

His father followed at a more sedate pace, his gaze flickering to Delia's rear now and again. Dusty ignored the obvious gesture, unwilling to tread into the waters of his parents' personal relationship.

April walked up, two lead ropes in hand, returning from taking Miracle and Mischief to the pasture. "Oh, hello." She smiled at their guests.

John stared at her for a long moment, then turned his eyes

on Dusty. He arched an eyebrow as if in need of verification of what he saw.

Dusty remained mute on the topic, but hitched a small smile and shrugged in response to the unspoken question.

"How are you this morning, dear?" Delia strode over to meet April, then walked her in.

"I'm doing fine. Thank you." April appraised the older woman. "If you're hungry, I can throw something together for an early lunch."

"Actually, we're going to town today. Do some sightseeing. Get a few more groceries," John announced.

Delia turned and pinned him with a curious expression. "We are?"

"Yep. About time we toured the sights of Hollow, don't you think?" He waggled his eyebrows.

Without missing a beat, Delia beamed. "Oh, yes. That's right. Drove all this way just to visit Holman—"

"Hollow," Dusty supplied, biting back a grin.

"Yes, that's right. Hollow." Delia patted April's arm. "We'll be back later."

"Actually, I think we'll spend the night there. Heard the café has the best flapjacks around." John wrapped an arm around his wife's waist. "Let's get a move on before it gets too hot."

April stood there blinking, but waved when they started up the engine on the large vehicle, then pulled out of the drive. "Is it just me or did it seem like they couldn't get out of here fast enough?"

Dusty took a cue from his father. Lightly placing a hand at her back, he nudged her toward the stable. "I think you're right."

"Wonder why? They seemed happy enough with the visit last night." April frowned as he took the lead ropes from her hands and replaced them on a waiting peg.

"They probably needed some alone time." *Just like we do.* He didn't want to confess his theory for fear of embarrassing her, but he could easily discern the reason. His father's look had said it all. He had read between the lines, noted the changes in April this morning and put two and two together. Dusty would thank him later for his discretion and fast thinking to afford him and April the day together. Alone.

"What's to see in Hollow?"

He bit back a laugh. "A post office and lots of dirt roads between there and the interstate."

"Oh, boy. Guess they did need some alone time. Lots of it."

"Yeah, I think so." He blew out a breath. "I'm hungry. Let's go inside."

"I'll fix you something. What sounds good?" April walked through the stable and toward the house section.

Opening the door to the house, he ushered Ben then April in before shutting and locking it behind him. Only then did he spin April to face him and answer. "You."

She blinked.

He cupped her cheek and leaned in to brush his lips over hers. "I crave you."

A softness appeared on her face along with a spark in her eyes. "I think I like you hungry." The resulting smile lit up her face, stealing his breath. "Goodness knows I can't seem to get enough of you."

With a groan, he swung her up in his arms, sealed his lips over hers and strode to the bedroom. Once there, he set her on her feet, reluctantly ending the kiss for a moment in order to allow them a much-needed breath of air.

Seizing the hem of her shirt, he tugged it over her head to toss to the floor. She returned the favor, adding his shirt to the pile, then started working on his jeans, unbuttoning them with trembling fingers that only ramped up his desire all the more. He gritted his teeth and bore the small torture, letting April take the lead for once. Her enthusiasm amused him while her brief touches left burning pleasure in her wake.

He assisted her by toeing off his boots, stepping out of

his jeans and boxers, and finally standing nude for her appraisal.

"You're gorgeous." April slowly circled him, trailing her hands over his chest, shoulders and back. She pressed kisses to his nape and squeezed his ass as if checking for resiliency before finishing the short tour.

Her heavy-lidded eyes and increased respiration told the story. His heart thudded against his ribs even as his cock surged to greater hardness.

Unable to wait a moment longer, he ran his hands down her sides, caught her waistband and shoved the material down, snagging her panties along the way. She stepped out of the puddle and bent over to untie and remove her shoes, giving him a heady glimpse of her soft pink folds. He found the clasp on her bra, undid it, then pushed the garment aside in order to mold one breast in his hand while he leaned down to suck the tip of the other.

April's breath hitched as she grabbed the back of his head, holding him in place. He worried the tip until it tautened under his ministrations before switching to the other side.

"Oh, Dusty." Her whispered voice spurred him for more.

Dropping his free hand, he traced up her inner thigh, delved through her labia, discovered her ample dampness and inserted a finger into her channel. The muscles gripped him like a vise.

She gasped.

He lifted his head and peered down at her. "Sore?"

April shook her head, then clarified. "Just a bit tender. Nothing to fuss about."

She'd gifted him with her virginity less than twenty-four hours before. The fact drew in his raging needs to a decidedly calmer level. As much as he'd love to bend her over the bed and fuck her like there was no tomorrow, such rowdiness would have to wait. Because, by damn, he'd never hurt her again during sex. Quickly, he switched to Plan B.

"Can you take me comfortably?" He doubled his presence

inside her and widened his fingers to ease the tension and pave the way for his cock.

Her grin could only be called playful and mischievous. "Oh, yeah. Besides, I expect you to finish what you started."

He chuckled. "You think I'd leave you hanging?"

Her features morphed into a halfhearted frown. "You do and I'll have to take matters into my own hands."

The image that statement brought forth set his libido into overdrive.

A moan left his lips as he stared down at the woman who had captured his heart.

She wrapped her hand around his bobbing dick and began to stroke. "So big. I still can't believe we fit together."

The sweet torture became too much to bear. He shackled her wrist and backed her up against the bed. "Lay down, April. Let me show you again how well we fit."

She complied, flattening out on her back, her head on the pillows at the top of his bed.

He paused a moment to savor the sight of her naked, aroused and waiting for him to sink his aching cock into her core, sending them both to heaven in the process. As he watched, a blush appeared on her cheeks. She lifted a leg to try to shield her femininity from his view.

*Not happening.*

After quickly digging a condom out of the bedside table, he rolled it on with practiced ease, his gaze still glued to April.

He climbed on the end of the bed, encouraging her thighs to part with a firm, guiding hand. "Open for me, baby. Let me see."

Her face brightened all the more. He smiled at the reminder of her innocence. "Feeling shy?"

"Yes."

His gaze locked on hers. "You're beautiful, April. Just perfect." He nudged her thighs once more. "Give me room, sweetheart."

When she did, he stretched out in the open space, his face

against her swollen folds.

"Dusty…" Uncertainty carried heavily in her voice.

"Shhhh. It's okay. Relax. Feel." He intertwined his fingers with hers, hoping to provide a reassuring force as he introduced her to another aspect of sex. He dipped two fingers of his other hand back into her slit, and ran his tongue along the seam between her folds.

She jumped.

He repeated the motion, lapped up some of the copious, tasty moisture, then centered his attention on her clit. "Delicious. Addictive." He blew on the small nub. "I'm going to love watching you come as I eat you out."

Her grip tightened on his hand. He flicked his tongue around her clit and licked directly over it in a slow, sensual rub. She lifted her hips as if pleading for more.

He gave it to her. Clamping his teeth ever so carefully around the sensitive area, he suckled gently, then worried her clit with a few tender lashes before sucking once more.

She cried out and bucked, her body tensing tighter with each additional caress.

Over and over he worked the area, pushing her level of arousal constantly upward while savoring every sweet cry along the way. After her initial hesitation she responded openly, her body showering his fingers as he drew out every ounce of passion she could give.

Dusty feasted, strummed and licked, all the time denying the pounding need in his cock, the tightening of his balls and the urge to take her before she reached her climax. Intent upon giving her pleasure, he refused to stop short. April deserved this and so much more.

He lipped her clit and groaned as he felt the resulting tremor zip through her. Persistently, he pressed her further.

Her body tightened more, the muscles of her inner core clinging to his fingers as if they were a buoy in the vast ocean. Adding more vacuum, he gave her everything he had, needing to send her over the edge more than he needed his next breath.

She cried out his name and lurched before the first rhythmic contractions clamped down on his fingers. Still he continued, not about to withdraw until the very last ripple left her body. He moved with her near-frantic gyrations, determined to stay the course.

After a minute her body relaxed, sinking back into the mattress as if in exhaustion. Her breath still came in near-desperate gasps, but began to slow, and her core eased, releasing his digits held captive during her moments of ecstasy.

Withdrawing, he sat up, noting the flush to her skin, the scrunched-up expression on her face, the look of hot passion plundered and released. He lifted up and crawled over her in order to kiss her swollen lips.

April met him after the first brush, pouring sweetness into the affection. Her receptiveness right after climax turned him on all the more.

"April?"

Her eyes opened, revealing a banked fire rife for the taking. He'd pleased her, but she was up for another round. The look on her face combined with the way she rubbed her hands over his back told him she had just gotten warmed up.

Good thing, since he couldn't wait another minute to join their bodies.

Instinctively, he knew she needed intimacy provided by him covering her. That was okay by him since he preferred the top position, which allowed him to take command and run the show. Not that he didn't care for trading off. Just the opposite. He'd take April any way he could. Just at this moment, he needed to make love to her, not just settle for a quick fuck. The difference didn't go unnoticed by him.

Too distracted and overcome with hunger, he pushed the thoughts to the backburner. Right now he had more important things to attend to. Like making April go crazy under him.

He settled into the vee of her thighs, lowered his body

and slid his arms under hers. Unable to wait a second more, he lined up the angle and began a slow, determined penetration.

Her eyes widened as he sank home.

"Okay?"

"Oh, Dusty…" She bit his shoulder and tilted her pelvis. "More. I need more."

He chuckled, pleased with her immediate response. "Wrap your legs around me, baby. Hold on tight. We're going on one hell of a ride."

As she did so, he edged deeper.

Her whimper went straight to his cock. Languidly he rocked, a slow, easy motion meant to touch every inch of her snug core and wring every drop of erotic rapture from her once more. Taking advantage of their closeness, he rained kisses on her neck, licked up to her earlobe and nibbled the delicate feature.

She lifted to meet his thrusts, digging her heels into his back along with her short nails. He might carry marks tomorrow, but he didn't care. Not when she writhed under him in pure bliss.

"That's it. Take me. Deep. Just like that." He groaned as he reached the very depths of her channel, lightly bumping into her cervix.

She jumped and mewled, but didn't appear to suffer any discomfort from his actions. Going with the flow, he kept up the leisurely pace, let their chests rub together and soaked up the thrill of one intense round. The closeness felt right, as did the way she wrapped herself around him and clung as if he were the rock in a steadily shattering world. The electrical current between them seared him so deeply he knew he'd never be the same.

Still he stroked in and out. Over and over again. Building the fire between them to a white-hot, raging level.

Her back arched as she latched onto him in a near desperate hold. A yelp followed.

He peered down at her, read the expression on her face and

kept up the tempo with steely determination. Tingling and tightening warned of his impending climax. Stubbornly, he pushed himself further, needing her to topple before shooting his load. "You have me ready to come, baby. So fucking hot I can't last." He growled and nipped at her collarbone. "Let go, already. Fly with me." The last words came out on a low, drawn-out moan as he slammed into the peak of rapture and began a freefall.

Absently, he realized she hit the same pinnacle, as her core clamped down so tight when he plunged balls-deep he couldn't have moved another inch if he'd tried. The hard contractions milked his cock, demanding every drop from his balls and then some. Eagerly, he complied.

A soft roar was lost between her lips as she kissed him with authority. He aggressively took control, shoved his tongue inside and played with hers as wave after hard wave washed over him. His dick pulsed in a sharp rhythm that then began to fade as he glided back to earth on a cloud of sexual satisfaction.

April blew out a breath and lightened her hold on his body, her fierce grip lessening to tender touches. "Wow."

He lifted up enough to stare down at her, pride coursing through him at the happiness he saw clearly written across her face. "Liked that?"

"Uh-huh." She licked his chin with the tip of her tongue.

He felt good. *Damn good.* Tired. Sated. And very satisfied too. Not just physically, but somewhere down deep as well.

Never would he have believed the first day she'd walked into his stable that she would steal his heart and offer hers in return. Despite their ups and downs, she'd stayed the course and stood by his side, her belief in him intact.

That meant a lot.

He locked their lips once more, softly, thoroughly, before breaking them apart again. "You taste so good."

"I have a confession to make." She stared up at him with a mischievous grin.

"What's that?" Curious, he kissed her chest and waited.

"I used your toothpaste. But not your toothbrush. I just used my finger instead."

He chuckled. "You're welcome to use my toothbrush and toothpaste any time you like."

"Good thing you love me. I have a feeling if anyone else stole your toothpaste, you might shoot them in the foot."

He laughed. "I just might." He sobered and kissed her gently. "Come to think of it, you should bring a few clothes over too. You probably don't care to run around in the same scrubs day after day. Or the buff. As much as I might like it."

Her mouth fell open. "You mean it?"

"Yeah. I think I can spare some closet space." He nuzzled her cheek.

"Does that mean you're gonna keep me?"

He met her gaze steadily, saw the hope, and grinned. "Yeah. I'm going to keep you." *For now and always*. The words lodged in his throat, but he knew she got the gist by the beaming smile that lit up her face.

"I love you, Dusty. You make my life full and happy."

He matched her joyful expression. "I love you too, April." He smiled ruefully. "I'll try to keep you...full." Pulling back, he thrust lazily forward.

Her eyes flashed with burning desire. "I'll hold you to your word."

"You do that, because I'll always keep my promises to you." He sealed his lips over hers, meshing them together as one as he started up with the sweet lovemaking again. Promises were never taken lightly. This one especially. April provided comfort, acceptance and a balm to his raw moods and nightmares. More than that, she showed him how wonderful love could be.

Dusty intended to hang on to the best thing in his life, for he understood one thing well—he couldn't live without a soul and April shared his.

# Epilogue

*Three months later*

"You outdid yourself, Carrie." Delia looked around the large kitchen, her face full of appreciation and awe.

The woman in question smiled. "I had lots of help."

April finished smashing potatoes and set the pan aside. "We couldn't let you do all the work."

"Especially when you're feeding this many." Tess clicked the burner off.

"I appreciate all the help. Every bit of it. Including the dish washing afterward." Carrie winked at the other women.

A collective moan carried across the room followed by chuckles.

"Ladies, let's get this meal on the table. Then we'll lasso the men into doing the dishes." Delia picked up the pan of stuffing and headed out of the door.

"Sounds like a plan to me." Tess followed, holding the handles of two more side items.

April lugged the heavy dish of mashed potatoes out, holding the door open for Carrie, who brought the oversized turkey.

After a couple more quick dashes for the remaining items, the whole family sat down at the long dining room table, eyeing the feast.

"Wow. This looks delicious." Archer grinned at his wife.

The other men agreed.

Finally taking her seat next to Dusty, April felt a cold nose press against her jean-clad leg. Glancing down, she found Holly, the latest acquisition to the family, laying her head against her leg. "Aww. Do you need some attention?" She patted the dog with affection.

"When doesn't she?" Dusty stroked the German shepherd's back. Ben wedged himself between them, nearly stepping on Holly in the process. "Jealous, huh?" He scratched behind Ben's ears.

A little over a month ago, April had received the call from the military dog adoption office. Her turn had finally come, but she'd had to drive to San Antonio and spend a couple of days learning about the animal and what commands she had been taught. Thankfully, Brand and Tess had volunteered to watch over the stable for the weekend and Miracle had accepted Tess without a single ear pin or ripple of nervousness. With everything covered, Dusty had loaded up Ben and they had all headed to Texas to meet and greet.

The short trip had proved enlightening in numerous ways. Dusty had showed her the sights and stayed right by her side, attentive and caring as they spent the day visiting the base, learning about the dogs and preparing to adopt another. The nights sizzled as they came together in heated passion, love and such deep emotion, she knew she would never forget his touch, his caresses, the sultry grin he gave her before he launched her into yet another entirely new realm. Her stomach flip-flopped at just the memory of the look that turned her to pudding each and every time.

Another tidbit had revolved around Dusty's entering an Army base for the first time in several years. He'd held his head high and moved with such striking grace all the military personnel had paused to stare. While Dusty wore civilian clothes, April knew they saw much more than an ordinary man. They saw a SEAL, a man due respect, one with pride, courage and sheer guts. The trainers had treated him with supreme reverence and camaraderie, greeted Ben with enthusiasm, and offered them their choice of dogs. Though he'd never once mentioned his former ranking, he didn't have to. Everyone had known from the first glance.

She could still see Holly, sitting in the back of her pen,

shaking with fear. Although they'd had five dogs to choose from, a couple of them puppies who simply had lacked the high drive to succeed, she'd gravitated toward Holly. Dusty had as well. Still unsure, they'd brought Ben over and what happened next had sealed the deal. Ben had stood at the gate to the kennel, staring intently inside. Holly had perked up, her ears had pricked and she'd stood. Gradually, she'd approached them, her tail had begun to move and after a minute, she'd tried to lick Ben through the wire. Her fate had been sealed at that moment. The two dogs had been inseparable since.

Like most of the other animals, Holly had her own story. After three tours of Afghanistan with the SEALs, she'd developed such severe post-traumatic stress she would curl up in a ball and quake in terror. She'd lost one handler along the way, which seemed to have scarred her toward other missions, and she hadn't bonded with other men like she had the one who had sacrificed everything. The military had sent her back to training, to no avail. She'd refused any reward, her eyes dulled and she'd become depressed. Nothing had seemed to bring her out, so they'd decided she would be better off adopted out to a caring family rather than trying to force her back into action, despite her younger age of four.

A few weeks after adoption, she'd blossomed. Entirely comfortable now, she'd found a steady companion in Ben, who showed her the ropes, played with her and snuggled up with her at night. A pair if April ever saw one.

Speaking of pairs, she studied the man sitting beside her. While starting out fairly rough, they'd found common ground and discovered love. He made her feel special, happy, and fulfilled all her dreams. Four years ago, she'd given up on men entirely. Now she sat at a huge family gathering, beside the man who'd stolen her heart.

As if sensing her gaze, Dusty turned. He smiled warmly, his brown eyes lighting up with softness and affection. Never would she tire of that particular look.

"Hello, lovebirds. Are you going to eat or just sit there and stare at one another all day?" Evan nudged Dusty in the ribs, still holding a pan of food.

Dusty rolled his eyes, accepted the food and spooned out a few bites. "You'll be there one day, little brother. Just wait and see."

"Uh-huh. Until then, I'm starving, so get a move on with the food."

Laughter followed.

Tess leaned over and whispered in her ear. "Looks like you two patched things up."

April nodded. "I couldn't help but notice your big shadow." She grinned as she whispered.

Tess shrugged, but the smile on her face told the story. *Definitely smitten.*

Before long, everyone had full plates and dug in, commenting on the rich taste of the large meal. Idle conversation popped up now and again as hungry people ate with relish.

"Oh, I almost forgot." Archer spoke over the chatter, garnering everyone's attention. "Remember that bastard who owned your filly before she was rescued?"

April paused in mid-chew. "Yes."

"Well, I looked into the case."

Dusty sipped his drink. "It's out of your jurisdiction."

"True. But I have a buddy in Colorado who was all too happy to check it out. Seems he tracked down the man, found him with horses on his property once more."

April gasped, fearing what would come next.

Archer waved his hand. "They weren't in such desperate shape this time and have been rescued by the Humane Society already. But, more importantly, that breaks his agreement to keep him out of court. The bastard is in jail, waiting for the whole book to be thrown at him. Not just this instance, but all previous ones as well. He's looking at ten to fifteen and, as angry as Luke was, I'd bet he'll make sure the judge collars him for every single day of the term."

The lawyer grinned wolfishly.

His father smacked him on the back. "Well done, son. I couldn't have done it better."

"Thank you, Archer. From the bottom of my heart. That's the best news I could wish for." April smiled brightly at him before turning to Dusty. "At least he won't be able to hurt other horses again."

Reaching under the table, Dusty took her hand and gave it a squeeze. "And your horses are safe and more than spoiled, thanks to you." He leaned over and kissed her cheek. "Sometimes families come in handy."

"You better believe it." Evan leaned around Dusty to see April. "You getting tired of this baboon yet?"

She chuckled, her gaze taking in Dusty's face. "Nope. Not even close."

"Well damn." Evan went back to eating.

* * * *

An hour and a half later, leftovers had been put away, the men had chipped in to help wash dishes and the kitchen and dining room gleamed with cleanliness. Full and lazy, everyone had retired to the living room to digest and rest before time forced them to get moving once again.

Dusty stood in the doorway, watching everyone else find a seat. In no hurry, he simply leaned against the wall, Ben at his side. Automatically, his eyes locked on April as she chatted with Tess. Her sheer beauty and genuine goodness had stolen his heart. Months back, to be exact. Yet he'd waited for this moment patiently. First of all, to give her plenty of time to solidify her feelings and for their relationship to grow. Secondly, he'd envisioned the perfect scenario over and over again. In front of his family. After all, it only seemed fitting, since they'd had a small part in getting him and April together.

Pulling a small, red, pint-sized bag out of his pocket, he stood the handles up and gave the object to Ben. Without hesitation, the dog gripped the lightweight object in his mouth. Leaning down, Dusty whispered in his ear. "Take it to April. Go."

Dusty watched as Ben obediently trotted over to April and sat in front of her.

"What's this?" She took the small sack, praising Ben and patting him for the delivery service. After peeking in, she plucked a square velvet box out. Her eyes widened. Slowly, she opened the lid, looked inside, then blinked up at Dusty in stunned surprise.

He strode over, bent down on one knee and took the box from her hand.

"April? Will you marry me?"

The whole room fell silent.

His heart thudded as if he'd run a mile sprint. Yet he only had eyes for April. Joy radiated across her face as tears welled up in her eyes. He could hardly breathe waiting on her answer.

"Yes. Oh, yes!"

She launched herself into his arms, sending both of them crashing to the floor. He salvaged the ring as he landed. Laughter and applause followed.

He barely heard anything else except for April's whispered words of love. He rained kisses across her face until the dogs wedged themselves in between, licking and nosing, wanting to be part of the fun.

With a chuckle full of happiness, he sat up, taking April with him. Finding the ring once more, he slipped the symbol of their feelings on her shaking finger. "You showed me kindness, goodness, compassion. Made me realize that second chances are possible and that true love is real, if you only look deep enough."

A single tear fell down her cheek. He wiped the drop away with his thumb.

"You're worth more than all the gold in Fort Knox to me." She hugged him tight. "You're the special one. Everything a woman looks for in a man and then some. I'm just thankful you chose me."

He nuzzled her neck. "How could I not? You spoiled me for anyone else. But that's okay. I don't want anyone else. I just want you. For the rest of our lives."

"Ditto." She brushed her lips over his. "A lifetime and then some."

"Does this mean April's no longer available?" Evan's voice carried across the area.

"Yes!" The entire room answered in unison.

"Well hell," Evan grouched dramatically.

Dusty laughed and nuzzled his treasure. His soul soared as joy carried him on wings. All the years of sidestepping commitment taught him a valuable lesson. When you find the right one, hang on to her with everything you have.

He'd done just that.

CHEYENNE MEADOWS

*Cowgirl Up*

When quilting isn't
an option, a girl
has to cowgirl up

# Cowgirl Up

## *Excerpt*

## Chapter One

"We've found a foal for Star."

Trinity blinked at her mother. Star, her former champion barrel racing mare and Trinity's best friend, had given birth less than twenty-four hours before to a stillborn baby. Almost immediately Lora, Trinity's mother, had signed up Star as a nurse mare in an effort to help the obviously grieving horse and give a needy foal a wonderful mama.

"Where?"

"Golden Aspirations Farm in Gentry." Her mother collected her purse. "Let's get moving. The sooner we get Star there, the sooner she can dote on another baby and be happy again."

Which was all that truly mattered. To them all.

Their world revolved around the mare, once one of the best to take on the cloverleaf pattern at regional rodeos.

Probably would have made it to the big time if Lora hadn't had a quick fling with a bull rider named Buck, ended up pregnant, then traded in her saddle for diaper duty and a job as an elementary school teacher, determined to make it as a single mother and raise her daughter right.

Trinity knew love, caring and the giving nature of her mother. What she missed was knowing her father and getting the opportunity to follow in her mother's abandoned footsteps. She wanted to surge straight to the summit of barrel racing not just by being invited to the national finals, but by winning. Her best friend, Star, might have been the springboard for her mother, but with the mare's advancing age, Lora had opted for retirement for the beloved mare and breeding her in hopes of raising the next generation of a speedy and nimble barrel racing horse. That bubble burst yesterday.

Now Trinity's dreams lay as lifeless as Star's first foal. Considering they subsisted on a teacher's salary, a kitchen garden and the fee from breaking a horse now and again, the ability to pay a hefty stud fee remained well out of their grasps.

"What happened to the mother?" Trinity glanced out of the window of the old truck, her mind whirling at this latest development.

"Complications from delivery, I'm told. Perforated bowel from what they could determine. She's already been rushed off for emergency surgery."

Being raised around horses all her life, Trinity realized how dire the situation was for the unfortunate mare. Most people wouldn't bother with the effort, but this mare obviously had an exceptional owner who strove to do right by her animal.

Maybe not all wealthy people were heartless after all.

Couldn't prove it by her. Not since her father had made a career out of his sport, raked in the prize money and still stubbornly refused to offer up financial assistance to her mother. Since his name and signature were absent from her birth certificate and he refused a paternity test, legal pursuit remained way out of reach. Oddly enough, Lora had never blamed him or held animosity for the man who'd left her pregnant and alone. Instead, she brushed the harshness of life off her sleeve and moved on.

A skill Trinity wished she could learn.

Less than an hour later, they arrived at their destination, left Star in the trailer for the moment and walked into the first barn as they'd been directed. Three people stood waiting, all with thin lips and pensive expressions. Worry emanated from each one in abundance. One of the two men flanking the lady had to be either the farm's owner or perhaps a manager, leaving the middle-aged woman with silver hair to be, presumably, the owner's representative. Trinity doubted most top-of-the-line thoroughbred breeders and owners attended the birth of their latest foal.

"Thanks for coming so soon. I'm Jerry. I spoke with you on the phone. This is Mrs. Hunter, the mare's owner, and John, the broodmare foreman." He tilted his head toward the woman next to him, then once more toward the other man.

Mrs. Hunter. The name rang a huge bell. Not only did the woman own a few racehorses, she owned some of the best, including last year's winner of the Kentucky Derby and the Preakness. Another Victory Gallop had fallen short by a nose in the Belmont Stakes to pulling out the rare and nearly impossible Triple Crown.

Totally amazed and impressed, Trinity studied the woman closer, deciding she liked the lady who stood in the middle of a stable after dark, trying to help a motherless foal even as her mare underwent surgery at the university's vet hospital.

"Yes, of course." Lora held her hand out and shook his. "I'm Lora Crocket and this is my daughter, Trinity."

The others inclined their heads toward Trinity, but her mother held their attention.

"Let's get the details ironed out so we can unite the colt

288

with his new mother," the second man said.

"Mrs. Hunter' is generously offering a nurse mare rental fee of ten thousand, including the care of your mare while here, and the farm has a handful of studs at their disposal both here and at another location, including a couple of quarter horses, to breed her back to as is traditional in this situation."

The woman pursed her lips. "Thank you, John, but I can speak for myself." She pinned Lora with her gaze. "If that amount is agreeable to you…"

Lora opened her mouth, but Trinity broke in. "We want her bred to Another Victory Gallop."

All eyes stared at her.

Jerry blinked. "Do you know what his stud fee is right now?"

"One hundred thousand as of last Wednesday." Trinity lifted her chin and met their gazes steadily. "An amount we'll never see."

Mrs. Hunter studied her for a long moment. "You realize what you ask is way overboard?"

Trinity nodded. "Yes, I do. But I know this— Star was the best barrel racer of her time just like Another Victory Gallop was in his. I know it's almost unheard of to mate a top-level thoroughbred stallion to a quarter horse mare, but it will work out. Wonderfully so. I just know it." She poured her heart out, willing the older woman to agree. Her future hung in the balance.

"What do you intend to do with the resulting foal?"

"Ride him to victory at the barrel racing national championships," Trinity answered truthfully, then held her breath.

Silence reigned.

A ghost of a smile crept up on Mrs. Hunter's face. "I believe we have a deal."

Ten years later…

Trinity plopped down in the chair directly in front of Legacy's stall. The portable tent and stanchions emulated a barn fairly well, considering only the hit-and-miss breeze broke the stifling humidity of early summer. She much preferred to be in a pasture full of shade trees, but at least the thick material offered relief from the sun and the worst of the Oklahoma heat. Not much could be done for the mugginess except a cold cloth, a bath for her horse and the fans blowing constantly at nearly every electrical outlet.

Finally, after years of hard work, she'd arrived. Well, not to her peak destination, but to the first of the large rodeos on the docket for the year. Up to this point, she'd only attended the smaller ones close by — a single night and done. Made for a lot of driving in a short span of time, but she had no choice. Money and points earned punched her ticket to the big dance at the end of the year. Luckily this one filled an entire weekend, giving her a bit more downtime from the driver's seat of her truck, but it also forced her to camp out overnight. Just par for the course.

She opened the cooler next to her and pulled out a bottle of water, resting until time to groom and saddle Legacy for the first night of events. Even now she could hear the announcer in the large building, muted, but still mostly discernible despite the walls and three hundred yards separating them.

While not the most comfortable, the lawn chair and her cot suited her for the overnight rodeos. Since she refused to leave Legacy's side, she made do with a few provisions and dreamed of her own small but cozy room at home.

Legacy. He'd grown up stout. Big for a barrel horse, brave, determined and way too smart for his own good. He made up his own mind and followed through, no matter what. Most riders wouldn't tolerate such stubbornness, but Trinity didn't mind. They'd been best buddies from day one and he'd do things for her that not even her mother had been able to make happen. Others doubted a thoroughbred could ever make for a good barrel horse, even a cross. She knew better.

After digging a peanut butter sandwich out of her

makeshift fridge, Trinity took a bite, not particularly hungry, but knowing she needed something in her stomach before sliding into the saddle for a fast and furious sprint.

A tall, dark-haired man with piercing blue eyes walked up. Recognition clicked, but for the life of her she couldn't put her finger on why. Her heart sped at the prime specimen he presented, dressed in her favorite outfit—jeans and cowboy boots. "Been a while, Trinity."

That unforgettable voice from her past did the trick. Soft, sure and low, the baritone timbre still sent shivers down her spine. He could mesmerize the most frightened animal with such a vocal gift. Probably did so on a routine basis if he'd stayed true to his roots. "Cody? I haven't seen you in ages."

Cody Winters rodeoed, just like she did. Although he was a handful of years older than she, they still crossed paths. He originated from Oklahoma and she from Kentucky, but the circuit knew no boundaries in the Midwest area of the country. Those serious about such a career drove over several states from one event to another, thus running into the same people over and over again.

If you were one of the top names in the business, you could afford to skip the smaller rodeos and focus on the largest ones held all over the continental U.S. and into Canada. There a person could rack up points and prize money in a hurry, giving them the luxury of more time off, although they balanced the reward with extra time on the road, driving all over the place from one big event to the next. Unless you were the names in the business. Some of those owned a plane and simply flew from location to location.

How they got their animals to the rodeo, Trinity didn't know, but figured it involved a hired hand performing all the hard legwork.

He stepped back, met her gaze and grinned softly. Her belly somersaulted as a small dimple popped in his cheek. The tall frame contained more muscles than she recalled and he'd been built way back when. Now he resembled a sculpted, handsome tank—tall, powerful, meaty and unmoving unless he decided to cooperate. She'd bet her saddle he carried no fat. Not with the way his clothes fit. Not tight, but cut perfectly to give plenty of tempting glimpses with each easy movement of his physique. Combined with a chiseled face, a square jaw that reminded her of a seasoned warrior and twinkling blue eyes sparkling with intelligence and something more, he presented a hot tamale package. Yeah, she enjoyed the eye candy, but drew the line there.

Over the years on the circuit, she'd seen it all. Everything from drinking and drugs to sex. Oh, man was there sex. In the chutes behind the scenes, in horse trailers, in stalls. She'd even caught a couple going at it in the bathroom. Something about attending a rodeo sent people into full-fledged heat. With the exception of her. She knew personally what happened when a woman got careless and downright stupid. She'd lived it. Still heard the mean whispers concerning her parentage and conception today.

"Yep." His attention turned to Legacy, who at that time decided to stick his head over the stall door. "That's a beaut of a horse, if I ever saw one." Cody reached out.

"I wouldn't do that if I were you," she offered in warning.

Legacy snuffled him in open curiosity for a couple of seconds before making his displeasure known. Just as Legacy showed his teeth, pinned his ears and made to bite, Cody jerked his hand back.

"Damn." He stared at the big horse with a mixture of annoyance and awe. "Just like his father, from the dappled hide and stocky build to the aggressive temperament."

Trinity cocked her head. She hadn't seen Cody in forever, yet he seemed to know lots about her and her horse. She couldn't say the same since she rarely participated in gossip and had pretty much kept to herself at each stop so far. "You know his bloodlines?"

"Who doesn't?"

She shrugged. Ever since she'd first showed up on the

huge gray stallion with the four white stockings and a blaze, they'd received more than their fair share of attention. Since she didn't care for the spotlight, it had become a prickly thorn in her side. Not to mention Legacy didn't play well with others. He bit, he kicked. Basically, he judged a person by his present mood and most of the time they came up short.

His behavior had worsened lately. The blame rested on her shoulders. Since the funeral, she'd been on a roller coaster of emotions, mostly heartache and loneliness, and Legacy picked up on each and every one. As much as she lectured herself to pull it together, she couldn't quite shake the constant companion of sadness.

*Time heals all wounds.*

How many times had she heard that particular quote? As many times as her mother said '*if only*'.

"Damn lucky to get a baby out of Another Victory Gallop. I'd still love to hear that story."

So would a lot of others who barraged her with questions, both media and fellow competitors. Too bad she didn't feel like talking.

She took another bite and chewed slowly, refusing to give in to Cody's curiosity.

The click of horseshoes caught her attention. Turning her head, Trinity spotted Lacey leading her paint mare, Candy, down the aisle before opening the door and placing her in the stall next to Legacy. The stud immediately plastered his nose to the bars separating them and nickered. Candy ignored him, turned around and started pulling hay from the net tied in the corner.

Lacey might be a couple of years younger than Trinity, but they meshed well. Both were in the business for the long haul, but not at the expense of their mounts. Their horses came first, something that most riders believed, but not all. She'd been Legacy tested and approved at the first event, which said everything in Trinity's book. Add in the fact that Lacey didn't yap all the time, knew how to keep a secret and had a good heart—Trinity counted her as one of the few close friends she possessed.

Cody chuckled and nodded. "Spoken like a true stud."

Lacey stepped out of the stall and secured the door behind her. She glanced over at them, then gave a lopsided grin. "Legacy keeps trying, but Candy isn't the least interested." She chuckled and leaned back against the row of stalls. "Haven't seen you in a while, Cody. Whatcha been up to?"

"After I burned out steer wrestling in high school, I decided it was time to get serious. Went to vet school after a stint in the military first."

Trinity blinked. She hadn't heard that juicy tidbit before. Especially the military part. She eyed him in another light. He carried himself differently than she remembered. More fluid, confident and flowing. His gaze flicked here and there as if constantly checking out his surroundings. Definitely not what she remembered of his actions way back when. Oh sure, he'd always been cocky, but this spoke of something else. More self-assurance and ability than just conceit because the women flocked to him with his link to money and good looks. Pain flashed and departed in his eyes so quickly Trinity wasn't sure she even saw it. Still, she opted to avoid the whole topic of service. From what little she knew about war, none of it made for great memories.

"Good for you. I always thought you would go in partnership with your father," Trinity said.

Cody's family owned a large ranch where his father raised both bucking bulls and horses to provide for the many rodeos around the country each year. Cody had been born into the profession, although he'd made sure to enjoy himself along the way. More than once she'd caught him flirting with a woman, then sneaking off for some alone time after the events were finished for the night. A bona fide playboy, that's for sure.

Absently she wondered if the term still stuck.

Truth be told, she'd wished she were in the lucky woman's shoes each night, absorbing all of Cody's attention, as she'd had a crush on him almost from the first time she'd laid eyes on the strapping, good-looking steer wrestler. Not surprising since every other girl appeared to feel the same way. Only she'd steadfastly refused to act on her whims whereas others jumped in with both feet. Of course, she'd been fourteen at the time, so way too young for his attentions. That hadn't stopped her from daydreaming.

"I did. Still help out around the ranch, but spend most of my time on the road treating large animals in my practice." His focus shifted back to Legacy. "Just be careful with that one, Trin. He's the last horse I want to have to work on."

"You're the vet here?" Lacey asked.

"One of a handful, yeah. I signed up to be at all the events for the circuit this year." He smiled at Lacey, wide enough to show a hint of straight white teeth. "My luck, they'd assign me to that stud and laugh as he kicked the shit out of me. All part of being the new guy on the block."

"No worries. Legacy's an angel."

Cody snorted.

"With women," Trinity added with a wry grin.

"Like that helps me. A bit short in the estrogen department lately if you haven't noticed." Cody shook his head. "Lacey's been around for a while, but I haven't seen you, Trinity. When did you come back?"

She met his gaze steadily. "This year." For the life of her she really disliked this topic of conversation, which inevitably led to the question about her mother.

"Miss the sport?" He tilted his head and met her eyes as if trying to read between the lines.

She didn't give him the chance as she gestured toward Legacy. "Finally got a horse to get me back."

"We're lucky to have her," Lacey chimed in. "She reminds the rest of us about the good old days."

Trinity rolled her eyes. *Like I'm that much older than Lacey and the other younger riders.* At twenty-five, she was hardly ready to be put out to pasture.

"Yeah, those were the good times." The corners of Cody's

lips hitched up but the smile didn't reach his eyes.

"Yeah, they were," Trinity answered on a somewhat sad note. If only she could go back.

His cell phone rang. After plucking it from his belt, he answered the call, listened for a moment then held up his hand. "Got to go, ladies. See you around." He spun on his heel and strode out of the improvised barn.

"Holy crap. Did you see that ass?" Lacey whispered, still watching where Cody disappeared out into the sunlight.

"Unfortunately." Trinity sighed. She'd always been a sucker for a man with a great rump covered in Wrangler jeans. Cody possessed one of the finest. She drew in a breath and committed the sight to memory. Because that was' all it would ever be.

\* \* \* \*

Cody couldn't shake the image of Trinity out of his head as he strode back toward the arena. She had been a gawky girl the last time he'd seen her, just entering the high school circuit. Damn if she hadn't grown up, filled out and turned out pretty. More than that. Beautiful and downright sexy.

Long, dishwater blonde hair framed an oval face with big blue eyes, the windows to her soul, where he could easily lose himself. From what he could tell from her sitting position, jeans covered a nice curve to her hips while the Western shirt, though loose, hinted at modest yet perky breasts. The top of her head might tickle his chin, but good things came in small packages. Trinity did.

Odd, he hadn't thought much about her before, when as a freshman in high school she'd attended a handful of the same events as he. He'd noticed her, seen a child, and turned his attention elsewhere. In truth, he'd spoken perhaps a dozen sentences to her in the past, a fact he now regretted.

Now, it seemed fate deemed him worthy of another chance.

He'd been surprised to see her back in competition after such a long absence. He'd thought she'd exchanged her boots for chasing men, and had long since gotten married and popped out a couple of kids like most of the girls who barrel raced as kids. Not that he put them down. No way. Everyone deserved the chance to do what they thought best, even if the phase lasted a short time. Besides, he'd essentially followed a similar path. Well, the part about leaving the rodeo and moving on to other things, anyway. The marriage and kids part, no.

A trickle of longing meandered through his system. Absently, he shoved the morose thoughts aside. He'd come to terms with everything that had happened and moved on.

*Yeah, right.*

The mocking voice in his head refused to allow him to live in a fantasy. In all honesty it was a good thing, but now and again he wished things could be different.

*If only…*

Shaking the useless phrase aside, he turned his attention back to the unforeseen yet intriguing contestant by the name of Trinity. After noticing her name on the docket and double-checking, he'd decided he had to have a peek for himself. And was glad he had.

Their short conversation ran through his mind. He recalled her facial expressions, the surprise at his approach, and when he'd called her by name. Also the spark of interest in those baby blues before they'd clouded over with sadness once more.

Curiosity piqued. He'd wager his next paycheck she grappled with emotional turmoil and discomfort instead of anything physical. After all, she appeared healthy as a horse with her trim build and slight rose hue to her cheeks. For all intents and purposes, she looked to be in tip-top shape, which pointed him back to his original assumption. Something must be bothering her.

Racking his brain, he tried to remember any hint of rumor including her, to no avail. Not surprising since he'd been out of the loop for a while, first in the SEALs, then busy in vet school before graduating a few months back and struggling to establish his practice. Now that he'd been hired by the Rodeo Association to help oversee the health and care of the livestock through the long season, he'd no doubt hear a few tidbits. Always did. After all, with pretty much the same group each weekend and ample opportunity for trysts and gossip, word would get around soon enough. He'd just have to either be patient or ask a few subtle questions here and there to appease his inquisitiveness.

On the other hand, that gray stallion of hers proved a hot topic. Understandably so. Best damn horse he'd ever laid eyes on, and he'd seen a lot over the years, both on the rodeo circuit and on his father's ranch. Despite being only half quarter horse, he had been put together just right. Muscles to his ears and a conformation judges would drool over in the halter class at shows. That horse could get the job done whatever the task, from show jumping to racing to cross-country at the Olympics. While he had yet to see Legacy in action, he didn't doubt the stud could perform. Hell, Trinity wouldn't be at this event if he ranked in the mediocre range. No, Legacy had earned Trinity's place here and, if speculation held true, would carry her all the way to the finals.

Anticipation washed over him at the thought of watching their first run tonight. Odd, since not much had captured his interest and brought excitement to his life lately. Barring a few one-night stands over the past few months, he'd been too busy working and plodding along through daily life to feel any sort of rush. Compared to active duty with the SEALs, jet-setting all over the world, battling the worst of the worst, his life had tamed to a dull beige. He enjoyed his profession, reveled in the slower pace, but still knew his life lacked something important.

Something told him Trinity and Legacy might just change that. At least for now.